THE
PROPOSAL

Tasmina Perry

THE
PROPOSAL

R
headline
review

First published in 2013 by HEADLINE REVIEW
An imprint of HEADLINE PUBLISHING GROUP

1

Cataloguing in Publication Data is available from the British Library

ISBN 978 0 7553 8354 2 (Hardback)
ISBN 978 0 7553 8355 9 (Trade paperback)

Typeset in Caslon by Avon DataSet Ltd, Bidford-on-Avon, Warwickshire

Printed and bound in Great Britain by Clays Ltd, St Ives plc

Headline's policy is to use papers that are natural, renewable and recyclable
products and made from wood grown in sustainable forests. The logging
and manufacturing processes are expected to conform to the environmental
regulations of the country of origin.

HEADLINE PUBLISHING GROUP
An Hachette UK Company
338 Euston Road
London NW1 3BH

www.headline.co.uk
www.hachette.co.uk

For John

PROLOGUE

She hesitated before she put pen to paper, her pale hand shaking as it hovered over the form.

Apparently this was the old-fashioned way of doing things – even people her age were internet savvy enough these days to submit a classifieds advertisement online. Instead she had popped into the magazine offices on impulse, having been in Covent Garden on a lunch date with some friends. Familiar people, on familiar territory, London's traditional publishing heartland. Her own former workplace was just a stone's throw away, and its restaurants – Rules, Christopher's, Joe Allen – were where she had spent many happy times, doing deals, drinking with friends. It was her life. And it had been a good one.

So was she now in her right mind doing this? Was it time to finally let go of the past rather than go running headlong into a fantasy of a life she had not even lived?

She looked up and glanced at the woman behind the desk, hoping for an encouraging gesture, or some other sign that she was doing the right thing. But the lady was on the phone and the only other thing she had to spur her on was a nagging voice in her head. The voice that had been reminding her for weeks that if she was ever going to do it, if she was ever going to go there, it was now, whilst she still could.

Today she felt every one of her seventy-two years. Recently she had noticed that society was trying to pull some sort of a con trick on millions of people just like her, that there was something good, something joyful, about getting old. She had seen the adverts around London, in magazines. Smiling white-haired women with beautiful bone structures advertised cheaper road insurance for the over-seventies. Suspiciously well-priced flats in glossy estate agent brochures were luxury retirement bolt-holes only available to the over-fifty-fives. The grey pound was apparently a potent economic force, whilst the term 'silver surfers' for those of her generation more internet savvy than herself implied an athleticism she had not felt since the eighties.

But right now there felt nothing good about being old. Her friends were beginning to die. Not many, not yet, but it was happening, and every time she heard more sad news, it was a reminder of her own mortality.

She had been thinking about it so much lately. Thinking about *him*. She wasn't entirely sure how you could have memories about things that hadn't even happened. All she had were her daydreams about a life they could have had together if it wasn't for the one night that had changed her life completely. But lately it had consumed her thoughts to the point that she just had to go to New York – the one major Western city she had never been to. The one city that represented a life unlived.

Steeling herself, she began to write. Now was not the time for regrets or doubt. Old age was about doing the things you had always wanted to do, about tying up loose ends, before time ran out.

No, she was absolutely right to be here. Absolutely right to do this. She handed her form to the classifieds woman, paid her money and, after confirming when the advert would run, picked up her bag and left the office. She glanced at her watch. It was not even four thirty in the afternoon. She had things to plan, phone calls to make, and only a few hours left in the day to do it all.

CHAPTER ONE

2012

'He's going to propose tonight, I can just feel it.'

Amy Carrell looked across the kitchen at her friend Nathan Jones.

'And what makes you so sure?' she said, picking up three plates and expertly balancing them on one arm. 'If he was whisking me off to Paris, then I might be suspicious. But we're going to an office party – not exactly what you'd call romantic.'

Nathan rolled his eyes.

'Are you kidding me? It's Christmas, darling, and the party's at the Tower of London. At night! It's what I would call the very essence of romance.'

'Nathan, they used to behead people at the Tower of London . . .'

'Correct. Anne Boleyn for one. Apparently it took several attempts because she had a very small neck.'

'As I said. Not exactly romantic,' grinned Amy, pushing

through the double doors of the kitchen and into the roar of the dining room at the Forge Bar and Grill, one of the more fashionable eating houses on Upper Street in Islington, north London. She moved with the grace of a ballerina, swaying between tables and deftly positioning the plates in front of the diners. Tonight Amy didn't need to remember who was having the squash risotto and who was having the escalope – everyone was having turkey. This was the sixth Christmas party she had done in the last week, and they weren't getting any better.

'Oi, love!'

She jumped as someone slapped her bum.

'Bring us out another bottle of the fizz, eh?' yelled a red-faced man, leering up at her. 'And what about your phone number too, eh?'

'I will send the sommelier over for you, sir,' she answered, forcing a smile.

'Ooh, a sexy American,' he laughed, pinpointing Amy's accent. 'Why don't you come and join us for a glass of champagne? Maybe after hours, eh?' he added as Amy fled back to the kitchens.

'Groper, table two,' she said to Nathan. Her friend just nodded and peered through the porthole in the kitchen door. 'Pink cheeks, white shirt?'

'You got it. Total sleazeball.'

'Don't worry, I suspect his shirt is going to be bright red when he leaves here. I feel a wine-related accident coming on.'

'Nut roasts!' screamed a voice. They turned as a dishevelled woman crashed through the door. Cheryl, the Forge's owner, had a heart of gold but swore like a trooper and was not a woman to be crossed when she had a scowl on her face like now.

'I got three arseholes giving me crap on table six; say they need their nut roasts asap or they're walking.'

'Sorry, I'll get on it,' said Amy, moving towards the serving hatch, but Nathan held up his wrist, tapping his watch meaningfully. 'I'll deal with the veggies, you better skedaddle.'

'Where are you going?' said Cheryl, frowning.

'It's Daniel's party, remember.'

'Jeez, Amy. You only just got here.'

Thanks to an audition running seriously behind time, she had been thirty minutes late for her shift and Cheryl hadn't let her forget it all day.

'I'll come in early tomorrow.'

'You'll do more than that. I need someone to take a double shift tomorrow. Think of the tips and tell me you'll do it.'

'I'll do it,' said Amy, knowing she needed the money.

'Off you go then. Go, go,' said Cheryl, shooing Amy away with both hands. 'Want to use the flat to change?'

Amy smiled gratefully as her boss pushed her hand into her jeans pocket, pulled out a jangling set of keys and threw them at her.

'He better bloody well had propose after this,' Cheryl shouted after her as Amy grabbed her bag and vanished up the stairs.

Inside the pub's top-floor flat, Amy looked at herself in the mirror and sighed. Her light blonde hair was all over the place, her cheeks flushed from the heat of the kitchen and – God, she sniffed her blouse – she stank of goose-fat potatoes. She looked longingly at the little shower cubicle, but there was no time for that. No time for anything, really.

Unzipping the bag, she emptied the contents on to the bed. Two crumpled dresses fell out, tangled up with heels, a hairbrush and her make-up. The first dress was a black knee-length shift she had found in a charity shop, the second rust-coloured and covered in sequins, bought in the summer sales for an occasion just like this one. It wasn't particularly well-made – there were sequins already floating around the bottom of her bag like little lost pennies – but there was no doubt it was a knockout look-at-me dress. Considering her options, she wondered what image she wanted to project tonight. Sexy and irresistible? Or did she want sophisticated, a woman of the world, good wife material?

Back in the kitchen, she had mocked Nathan's suggestion, and two days earlier she would have had absolute conviction that Daniel Lyons, her boyfriend of little more than one year's standing, was more likely to fly to the moon than get down on bended knee. But that was before she had gone rummaging around his sock drawer and seen a duck-egg-blue gift box tucked away among the neat balls of fabric – a Tiffany gift box. It had been too tempting to ignore it, but before she'd had further opportunity to examine the size and shape of its contents, Dan had come back into the bedroom and she'd had to slam the drawer shut.

She hadn't been alone in his bedroom since, but it had sent her giddy with excitement and she had tried to read hidden meaning into every comment, every affectionate gesture he'd made since. 'Dress up,' he'd said about tonight's party. And she was certain that he'd been a little anxious about something, which for someone as poised and confident as Daniel was very unusual indeed.

With twenty minutes to get to the Tower, she held one dress up against herself and then the other. *What do you wear for a night that just might change your life for ever?* she thought, staring at her reflection in the mirror. For a split second she allowed herself to imagine him slipping a sparkling solitaire on her ring finger in the creamy moonlight. They'd take a picture of themselves with her camera phone and she'd post it on Facebook to show to all their friends. At some later, unspecified time, it would be shown to their children and be smiled at wistfully in their old age. It would be a forever photo – an image you'd remember and talk about for many years to come and one for which you wanted to look your very best.

'Screw it,' she whispered, quickly pulling on the sequinned dress and leaning into the mirror to tie up her hair. The dress was very short and tight and she did wonder if there'd be any sequins left by midnight, but sexy had to be better than looking like someone's mum, she thought, throwing the shift dress back on the bed.

She slipped on her heels and ran out of the pub, hearing a wolf-whistle from Nathan before she exited on to the street, where a black cab pulled up almost immediately.

'Tower of London,' she breathed to the driver as she slammed the cab door. 'And don't go down City Road, it's always crazy at this time.'

Amy didn't really have any idea if City Road was mental or even if the cabbie would have gone that way, but she always tried to say something to imply she knew London inside out, otherwise the driver would hear her American accent and immediately think 'Tourist!' and add a zero to the price – a zero she definitely couldn't afford. She sank back into the seat and watched the little red numbers tick around on the meter, resisting the urge to open her bag and check the lining for stray twenty-pence pieces – after all, this was a cab ride she could barely afford.

For a brief moment, Amy allowed herself to think about what Nathan's premonition might mean. How becoming Mrs Amy Lyons would change her life for ever, because the reality was that it would change everything. No more taking double shifts at the Forge to scrape together the rent for her tiny Finsbury Park studio; no more auditions, praying that someone would finally give her a job in a chorus line; no more stumbling from date to date hoping she wasn't making a complete idiot of herself; no more rooting around sock drawers searching for validation that someone actually loved her.

'Blimey, Tower's lit up like a Christmas tree,' said the cabbie, sliding his window back as they turned on to Lower Thames Street. Ahead of them there was a queue of sleek cars and people spilling on to the street in black tie.

'Special night is it tonight, love?'

'I hope so,' she grinned, leaning forward and handing him the only twenty-pound note in her purse.

She left the cab and walked down the cobbled road towards the gatehouse. Wow, she thought, stopping and looking at the ancient building, artfully floodlit against the pitch-black sky. Her family and friends had all been surprised when she'd announced that she was leaving New York for London to take a job with Blink, a physical theatre performance group that had transferred from Broadway to the West End two years earlier.

No one close to her back home had ever left the United States – not even for a holiday. I mean, why go to see the Alps when they had amazing snowy peaks of their own? Why bother with the Loire valley when they could visit Napa for the price of an internal flight? Her dad particularly was of the mindset that if it hadn't happened in New York's Five Boroughs, it didn't happen. But Amy had always been fascinated by England, by London – its history, its culture, its majesty, the fact that kings and queens and generals and ladies in their huge skirts had walked across this very spot – so while she had been nervous about leaving her New York life behind her, now she wasn't sure if she ever wanted to go home.

She handed over her invitation and hurried inside – the wind was cutting right through the thin dress despite her coat and she didn't want any more sequins to get blown off.

'The FO, miss?' asked an old man in a dark uniform.

'I'm sorry?'

'The FO, you are here for the Foreign Office dinner?'

'Oh, yes, yes I am,' she stammered, feeling suddenly very self-conscious. Didn't she look like she should be going to the Foreign Office party? she thought, trying to pull the fabric of her dress a little further down her thighs. She glanced at the man again and could see that he was simply trying to help, make sure she didn't get lost. He gestured to her right.

The party was being held in the Pavilion in the moat area of the grounds. It was a spectacular space, the grey-white Tower walls rearing up behind it spotlit with purple neon. There were hundreds of people there already and she looked around feeling vulnerable and lost. She texted Daniel and went to look at the big table plans in front of her.

'Look at you,' said a voice as she felt a hand snake around her waist.

Turning round, she saw Daniel, handsome in a single-breasted dinner suit, standing out like a movie star in the more ordinary-looking crowd.

'You like?' she said, feeling suddenly happy and in the party spirit. Growing up, Amy had never been particularly confident of her own looks. Her hair had a tendency to frizz, especially in the humid New York summers, and a slight overbite gave her a look of Liv Tyler on a good day, but most of the time made her paranoid that she was just a bit goofy.

But standing next to Daniel Lyons made it impossible not to feel part of the beautiful crowd.

He leant in towards her ear. 'I want to put you over my shoulder and carry you home to bed, except my parents might not be too happy about it if I went missing in action.'

'Parents?' she stammered, moving a fraction away from him.

He looked at her with his bright blue eyes.

'I didn't know they were coming until today. And they're apparently on our table, but don't worry, I can do a bit of switcheroo with the place cards if we get there in time.'

'Maybe try putting us at opposite ends of the Pavilion.'

A slight frown creased the space between his brows.

'Come on, they're not that bad.'

It was her turn to feel piqued, remembering a particularly uncomfortable afternoon at the polo, in the middle of summer, when she had first met Vivienne and Stephen Lyons. Amy still wasn't sure what had upset her more. That Daniel had only introduced Amy to them as his 'friend', or the fact that Mr and Mrs Lyons hadn't thought she was sufficiently important to say more than two words to her for the rest of the day.

'How was your day?'

'Good. I had an audition.'

'Sweetheart, I'd forgotten. How did it go?'

'Well, I think. It's being choreographed by Eduardo Drummond, who is the hot new thing in modern dance, and I think it's going to go big and I got the feeling he really liked me . . .'

'Well, it certainly is a night for celebration, isn't it?' He smiled, waving across the room to a friend who had caught his attention.

Amy's heart gave a little skip.

'Celebration? I haven't got the job yet . . .'

They were interrupted by a group of thirty-something men who Daniel appeared to know well, judging by all the back-slapping. It happened a lot whenever she was out with him. He seemed to know everybody. There were friends from school, from Cambridge, work friends, football friends, female friends – she liked those sort the least . . . He introduced them to her but they all carried on talking about people in common, deals they'd made, and what they were up to over the holidays, which seemed to involve shooting and skiing and going to parties. Although she and Daniel were from two very different worlds, they never ran out of things to say when they were alone together. But she was never very comfortable in social situations like this one; she never felt funny enough or smart enough to speak up. After all, it was better to say nothing than say something stupid.

She accepted a glass of champagne from a waiter and sipped it gratefully until they were herded into the ballroom for dinner.

They threaded between the circular tables, all formally laid with crisp linens and polished silver, huge floral displays at the centre – and there on table fifteen, already standing by their seats, were Daniel's parents.

'Daniel. Amy.' They smiled tightly as their son approached. As Vivienne Lyons gave Amy a swift air kiss, she inhaled the older woman's expensive pomade and perfume, which she hoped overpowered her own eau de roast potatoes.

'How are you both? Amy, you're between Stephen and Nigel Carpenter.'

Within seconds, she found herself wedged between Daniel's father and a giant of a man dressed in full military regalia. As she sat down, the hemline of her dress shot up so that it barely covered the top of her thighs. Nigel Carpenter, 'an old friend of the family', looked down as Amy threw a napkin over her lap in case he saw her panties.

'Good evening, Amy,' said Stephen formally, touching her shoulder. 'I trust you are well?'

'Very well, thank you,' said Amy, wishing she was back at the Forge.

Everyone else on the table – three sixty-something couples and Nigel's wife Daphne – seemed to know each other.

'So what do you do, Amy?' asked Daphne. She was a sharp-featured lady with a sleek grey bob and was around half the size of her husband.

'I'm a dancer,' she said quickly.

'Anything I might have seen you in?' she replied with interest.

'Depends on where you go to the theatre,' said Amy lightly.

'We're patrons of the Royal Opera House. That's how we know Vivienne.' She smiled.

'I do more modern dance. Smaller theatres.'

'The Rambert?'

'No,' smiled Amy, fairly certain that the woman hadn't seen any of her body of work. Certainly not her most high-profile gig – an MTV video for Harlem rapper K Double Swagg.

'So what productions have you been in recently?'

'Amy's been injured most of the year,' explained Daniel, looking rather uncomfortable. To his friends, and the sort of twenty- and thirty-something revellers they had met in the foyer, he usually explained with a sense of pride that Amy was a dancer. She was not naïve – she knew that when his friends smiled and looked impressed, it was because the word 'dancer' was some sort of code for being good in bed, and as irritating as that was, at least Daniel always supported her ambitions.

'Oh dear.'

'But she had an audition today that went well, didn't you, Amy?' said Daniel, looking increasingly jumpy.

'And what was that for?' asked Vivienne Lyons.

A light was shining on the top of Amy's head and she was beginning to feel hot.

'It's a new show,' she explained, taking a sip of water. 'With original music and dance. It's about the birth of tango.'

'Tango?' said Stephen Lyons with an amused half-smile. 'That's rather racy, isn't it?'

She saw Daniel's mother flash her husband a warning look.

Amy willed herself to keep calm and not to buckle. She had to make a good impression – these people were potentially *family* – and besides, the tango was one of her favourite dances and she felt honour-bound to defend it.

'Done properly, tango is elegant, it's beautiful, passionate,' she explained.

'Tango is about sex,' said Vivienne Lyons matter-of-factly. 'It originated in the slums of Argentina, Uruguay. It was music for the bordellos. Every aspect of it is underpinned by sexuality, eroticism. Leading, following.'

She paused and smiled, although the gesture didn't reach her eyes. 'Still, at least you must be on the mend if you're auditioning.'

Amy reached for the champagne this time, her good mood completely gone. Vivienne Lyons was such a snob. It was tempting to tell her exactly how she had broken the toe that had almost put an end to her career, let alone out of action for the last six months. If anything was *about sex*, it was that mini-break she'd had with Daniel back in June. The only time they'd got out of their four-poster bed was to go for a cycle down to the river, when she had fallen off her bike and crushed her foot with the wheel. She doubted that her boyfriend would volunteer those details at the dinner table.

The thought of it made her toe throb inside the confines of her Topshop shoe, but she was distracted by the arrival of the starter, which looked like a cactus sitting on a bone-china plate.

She picked up her knife and fork, careful to choose the smaller set on the outside of the arrangement – Daniel had shown her that on their second date. 'If in doubt, always work from the outside in,' he had said.

Which was all fine, but Amy had no idea where to start. At the same time, however, she knew Vivienne was watching her, and not wanting to seem inexperienced, she clamped the artichoke between fork and knife and attempted to slice off one of the sticky-up leaves. The ball-shaped vegetable immediately flipped over, clattering against the plate and knocking the small dish of what looked like nacho cheese dip on to the tablecloth.

'Shit,' said Amy, trying to retrieve the vegetable.

'I beg your pardon?' said Vivienne, her eyes wide.

'Slipped,' said Amy quickly, 'I said I slipped.'

Daniel leant forward to his own artichoke and calmly pulled off one of the outer leaves, dipped it into the sauce, then put it between his teeth, scraping off the goop. *Damn*, thought Amy, *that's how you do it.*

Flushing red, she set about copying Daniel, her eyes fixed on the plate, not daring to look up, wishing the ground would swallow her. She sat in silence through the rest of the meal, listening as the Lyonses made bland small talk, nodding in the right places, making sure she watched which item of cutlery everyone else was using before she even attempted to begin. By the time the dessert had been cleared away, she was quite tipsy on the champagne she had drunk to occupy herself and was looking forward to going home – even if someone had to carry her out on a stretcher.

'I think it's about time for a toast,' said Stephen Lyons, clearing his throat and turning his full attention towards Daniel. 'I am extremely pleased and proud to report that our son has only scored himself a rather plum posting to Washington.'

A murmur of approval went round the table like a Mexican wave as Daniel raised his hand to object.

'Dad, please. It hasn't officially been announced yet.'

'Nonsense, a pal in Whitehall rang me this morning to congratulate me. To Daniel,' he said, raising his flute of champagne.

Amy shot a glance at her boyfriend. She knew that a promotion had been on the cards for months. She had shared his excitement, voiced her support and encouraged him, even though it had sometimes been with a heavy heart. She had always known that as a Foreign and Commonwealth Office employee on the fast track to the diplomatic corps an overseas posting wasn't just likely – it was inevitable. In fact before Daniel and Amy had met, he had just returned from a spell in Brussels, although as he had often pointed out, if he was sent back there again, it would only be like commuting from Liverpool to London.

'Washington,' laughed Amy nervously, deciding that this might be even more preferable to a European post. She reached for her coffee, but as her hand stretched across the table her fingers clipped a wine glass, knocking it over, the contents spilling across the tablecloth and into her lap.

For a moment, all was chaos, with Vivienne shouting for a waiter, Daniel jumping up to grab the glass and Stephen bending forward, dabbing at Amy with his napkin.

'Here, my dear, let me help,' he said. 'You must be soaked.'

'No, no, I'll be fine . . .' said Amy before she realised that the older man's hands were lingering. She felt his fingers brush across her bare leg and looked up in shock. Their eyes met for a split second.

'Sorry, I . . . I think I'd better go to the restroom,' she muttered.

'I think they're just about to start the speeches,' said Nigel, resting his hand on her knee for her to stay.

She nodded quickly and sat still as a middle-aged man came to the podium, eulogising for over twenty minutes about a superb year and the magic of London 2012, whilst Amy squirmed in her seat, the wine soaking the back of her thighs and dribbling towards her knickers.

As soon as he had stopped speaking and the applause faded

away, she got up and fled.

Her heart was pounding. Had Daniel's father really stroked her thigh, or had she completely misread the situation? She had no idea, because she was definitely drunk and needed to get some fresh air.

'Amy, what's going on?'

She was relieved to see Daniel come out of the main hall.

'Are you okay?'

She nodded tightly, looking down at her dress – God bless the sequins – which had covered the worst of it.

'Wow, Washington,' she said finally.

'I know,' replied Daniel. He was trying not to smile but his happiness was written all over his face. 'I wanted to tell you in private, but I happened to speak to Dad this afternoon . . . and besides, I didn't want to spoil Christmas.'

'No, really. It's great.'

'We should go and celebrate.'

'Not back in there, though. Not at that table,' she said quietly.

'You have to ignore them,' he said.

'They hate me.'

'They don't hate you. They're just a bit old-fashioned.'

'Old-fashioned? Daniel, they were just rude. Rude about what I do, rude about my ambitions . . .'

'I didn't know it was a tango.'

'Don't say *you* have a problem with it.'

'My mother went about it in the wrong way . . .'

'But you agree with her,' said Amy, trying to read between the lines.

'Come on, leave it, lighten up.'

'Lighten up! This is my career, Daniel. Perhaps you could try taking it seriously for once.'

'I do take it seriously. Very seriously. In fact you can show me your moves later,' he said, a smile pulling at his lips.

'You do agree with her,' she replied, flinching. 'You think it's slutty.'

'Amy, come on . . .'

'Admit it,' she said, feeling her hands shake.

'No, I don't think a tango show is slutty,' replied Daniel slowly. 'But you've got to admit it is pretty racy, and maybe . . .'

'Maybe what?'

He hesitated.

'Maybe you should think about whether you want to be seen performing in something like that.'

She shook her head in disbelief.

'Daniel, this is a good show. You know how long I've been out of the game. This is a great opportunity for me.'

'A great opportunity for people to look at you in a certain way,' said Daniel more sharply.

He rubbed his temples as if he had a headache.

'Look, ever since we've been together and I tell people what you do, I've got friends, family all wanting to come and see you in a production. But I'm not sure I fancy them watching you all dressed up in fishnets and some tarty leotard cut up to the wazoo, as much as I'd privately like to see you in full costume.'

'Tarty?' she said incredulously, suddenly imagining herself in black hose and lashings of red lipstick. It was a good job Daniel had never seen her in the K Double Swagg video.

'You know what I mean.'

He offered a placatory hand, but Amy felt stung.

'Well, it's a good job you're going to be in Washington then, where you don't have to see me looking tarty.'

'About that . . .'

She heard something in his voice. Apology, awkwardness, and something he'd said just moments earlier began to resonate.

'You didn't want to spoil Christmas,' she said softly, remember-ing why he hadn't wanted to tell her about his promotion. 'How long is the posting for, Daniel?'

'Eighteen months.'

It was shorter than she'd thought – many diplomatic gigs were for two or three years or more.

'Well, that's not so bad,' she said, trying to calm herself. 'In fact it could be good: I could move back to New York, get something on Broadway, and it's just a short hop on the shuttle to Washington. I was so worried it was going to be some-where like Africa or South East Asia, but at least I've got the right passport, huh?'

She gave a weak smile, willing him to speak, desperate to hear him insist that he couldn't possibly be away from her for so long, how they should get a little flat together on Capitol Hill, just the two of them, how he wouldn't even consider taking the stupid job unless she came with him. There were dance companies in Washington, weren't there? But he didn't say any of that. He just took a step away from her, looking uncom-fortable.

'Listen, I don't want you to uproot yourself because of me. Not when you've got this brilliant opportunity here.'

She looked at him, her eyes meeting his intense blue ones.

'So now it's a brilliant opportunity . . .'

'I have never led you on, never made any promises,' he said quietly. 'You know this is my job, that I was always going to get posted overseas.'

'But there's no need to write our relationship off the second a plane ticket arrives in your in-tray.'

She waited for him to say something.

'Come on, we don't want it to end like this,' he said finally.

'The end . . .' she whispered, realising what was unfolding in front of her. She thought about the Tiffany gift box in his drawer, remembering that she had come here hoping, believing, he might actually propose. She laughed out loud at her own stupidity.

'I should leave,' she said with as much dignity as she could muster.

'Amy, stop. Let's discuss this . . .'

'Leave me alone,' she roared, shrugging him violently away from her.

She began to run, the heels of her shoes wobbling as they hit the carpet.

Outside, she inhaled the cold night air and closed her eyes, glad to be out of there, glad, for once, to be alone.

Hot tears prickled in the cavity behind her eyes but she blinked them away as fiercely as she could.

Shivering, she realised that her coat was still in the cloak-room.

She turned and walked back to the Pavilion, stopping in her tracks when she saw a familiar figure standing by the exit. It was a moment before she saw that it was not Daniel, but Stephen Lyons.

'Going without saying goodbye?' he asked, lighting up a cigarette and putting the packet back in the pocket of his dinner jacket.

Arrogant bastard, she thought to herself. Stephen Lyons was in his late fifties but he clearly thought he was a character out of *Mad Men*. She didn't like to admit to herself that it wasn't too far from the truth. The lines of his jacket were sharp, his cold, hard eyes were the same icy shade of blue as his son's, his arrogance worn with the confidence of someone with millions in the bank who no longer needed to prove himself.

Behind her she could hear the voices and the laughter from the party. A band was playing now and she imagined those crusty old couples getting up to dance politely, arms held out straight so as not to touch each other too much.

'Goodbye, Mr Lyons,' she said, not even meeting his gaze.

'Stephen,' he replied casually, exhaling a line of smoke through his nostrils.

'Goodbye, Stephen,' she said, feeling goose bumps pop on her forearms.

'Do you need a car? Or money for a taxi?'

'I don't want your money,' said Amy. 'I never did,' she added more quietly as he stepped towards her.

'I know this must be hard for you,' said Stephen Lyons, his expression changing from mock concern to something more businesslike. 'But you have to be realistic. This is about Daniel's career, not your relationship.'

'Quite clearly the two are linked,' said Amy, hating the bitterness in her voice – but why hide it? They both knew that she had just been dumped in favour of a job.

Stephen tilted his head to one side – a gesture of sympathy, mixed with condescension.

'I'm sure Daniel cares for you,' he said. 'But you have to understand he is devoted to achieving his potential. Always has been, ever since he was a little boy. Always put in that little bit extra to keep ahead of the pack.'

'And I'd get in the way of all that?'

Stephen pulled a face.

'Amy, Daniel's posting to Washington is just the start of it. *Entre nous*, there's talk of an ambassadorship for him within three or four years. Do you know how unusual it is for anyone to snap up a senior diplomatic post under thirty-five?'

He crushed his cigarette stub under his shoe and continued.

'Daniel wants to go all the way. We *know* he can go all the way. HM Ambassador to France, hell, even the US ambassadorship itself. And for that to happen, for him to do the job as well as it can be done, he needs the right partner by his side.'

'And you're suggesting that I wouldn't support him?'

'Not wouldn't,' said Stephen. '*Couldn't*. The wife of a senior ambassador is a very specific role. You need to understand etiquette, procedure, small talk, how to handle delicate situations. It's not for everybody. And not everyone can do it.'

'This is about the artichoke, isn't it?'

Stephen laughed, his eyes lingering on her body just a fraction too long.

'No, it's not about the artichoke.'

He reached into his pocket, pulled out a card.

'I should go back in,' he said finally. 'But perhaps we could meet again under more pleasant circumstances. I used to like dancers myself, back in the day. Old habits die hard, as they say.' He said the word 'dancers' as though it was one step up from prostitutes.

'Screw you,' growled Amy, hot tears of humiliation threatening to fall.

'I'd say my son got off lightly. Can you imagine that sort of language at the embassy,' he said, and disappeared back into the Pavilion.

CHAPTER TWO

She got off the tube at Leicester Square and started to walk. The streets of London flashed past her like streaks of fireworks in the night sky, cars beeped as she darted between them, her brain barely processing how close they were to clipping her as she cut across Shaftesbury Avenue and into the bowels of Soho. Blinking back the tears, she reminded herself that she was tough – you didn't grow up in a blue-collar area of New York and let men get to you – but by the time she arrived at the Berwick Theatre her eyes were red-ringed and raw.

The show had long finished, and there was just a dribble of people on the pavement, drunks, and theatregoers hanging around the stage door in the hope of seeing some of the stars. Amy joined them, leaning against the wall to pull off her shoe and massage her toes. The shoes she had chosen to show Daniel how sexy and sophisticated she was. *Proposal shoes*, her mind mocked her, the ones she would never throw away, the ones that were going to have such special meaning in years to come. Well, the moment she got home – whenever that was – she was going to throw them in the trash. They were ugly and tainted, and anyway, they were too damn tight.

'Good God, woman, you look like the sky's fallen in.'

Amy sighed with relief as she saw her friend Annie Chapman bustle out of the stage door.

'Something like that,' she said, ready to cry all over again.

Annie noticed her tear-streaked cheeks and pulled her towards her.

'Sweetie pie, what's wrong? When you texted and said it was urgent, I was worried, and look at you . . . Dear me, I think we'd better get you back to the Bird's Nest, huh?'

Amy choked back a laugh, knowing that her friend had instantly sized the situation up and was taking control. As wig mistress to various shows, Annie Chapman had found a profession that suited both her flamboyant personality and her innate skills as a no-nonsense agony aunt. The wig mistress's chair seemed to function in the same way as that of a hairdresser or a shrink: actors felt they could tell Annie anything, and she was happy to dispense home-spun wisdom where she could.

'Annie, he's ended it,' whispered Amy, too angry, too shocked, too everything to even say Daniel's name.

'I can see that, sweetie,' said Annie, pulling off her leopard-skin fur coat and wrapping it around Amy's shoulders.

'No, you'll freeze,' protested Amy, nodding to the vintage fifties dress Annie was wearing.

'I think I can manage, darling – I'm much more insulated than your skinny arse. Come on. Let's go. And I think we need to stop off for Chinese on the way.'

'Honestly, I don't think I can face anything,' said Amy miserably.

'It's not for you, it's for me,' smiled Annie, slipping her arm around Amy's waist and guiding her to a small shop in

Chinatown, the front strung with soy-glazed chickens, where Annie ordered what sounded like a mountain of food. 'And make sure you put in some fortune cookies, Phil,' she said to the wizened old man behind the counter. 'I think we might need a peek into the future tonight.'

It was only five minutes' walk to Annie's Covent Garden flat, known affectionately as the Bird's Nest because of its artistic chaos. It had been left to Annie by her grandmother, a 1940s showgirl who had been the mistress of a wealthy aristocrat. Inside, you could still see the traces of what it had been like when she had entertained her lover there – the elaborate flock wallpaper, the lampshades rimmed with black lace tassels – though Annie had added her own larger-than-life personality. There was a full-sized dressmaker's mannequin standing by the door dressed in a French maid's outfit ('Makes me feel as if I have servants,' Annie had explained upon Amy's first visit), an easel with a half-finished nude in oils, swatches of garish material, piles and piles of books, not to mention virtually every available wall surface being covered in posters and photographs from the great shows. Just being in the Bird's Nest always made Amy feel like a performer, which was one of the reasons she so loved to come.

'Right, sit there,' said Annie, steering Amy to a plush velvet armchair leaking its stuffing from the seams. 'You put out the food, I'm going to fix you my pat-pending pick-me-up.'

'No, Annie, I don't want—'

But her friend silenced her by holding up a finger and pursing her lips. 'Annie knows best,' she said, crossing to the tiny galley kitchen and rummaging around in the American-style fridge. 'Besides, I always like a squirty cream daiquiri after a hard night at the wig face,' she added, 'so don't be selfish.'

Amy covered the coffee table with the little boxes of food and Annie handed her a huge glass – half cocktail, half ice-cream sundae, complete with sprinkles and a paper umbrella on the top. 'It's laced with Ukrainian brandy. After a while, you won't feel a thing,' explained Annie as Amy dutifully sipped at the concoction and found, to her surprise, that it tasted pretty good.

'Right, you tell me everything while I get stuck into this lot,' said Annie. 'Leave nothing out.'

Taking a deep breath, Amy related the events of the past few days, beginning with the discovery of the Tiffany box, going through the excitement of the dance audition and ending with her tussle with Daniel's father, pausing every now and then to blow her nose on Annie's pastel tissues and watching in awe as Annie wolfed down satay, spring rolls and dumplings.

'So to sum it up,' said Annie, dabbing at her bright red lips with a napkin, 'Daniel's family are a bunch of hideous snobs, they don't think you're good enough to be an ambassador's wife and Daniel himself has the backbone of a jellyfish.'

Amy let out a sad giggle, despite herself.

'You got it. It would have been fine if I was a ballet dancer,' she added softly. 'I bet Darcey Bussell isn't slipped business cards with a nod and a wink to come and practise the horizontal tango.'

Annie crossed the room and sat on the arm of the chair.

'Daniel's parents don't want a beautiful, talented woman by their son's side; they want a Barbie doll in Chanel who knows her place. You were never going to fit into their narrow little world, so don't start thinking things could have been any different.'

Amy nodded silently. She knew Annie was right, that she had just been a convenient distraction for Daniel while he waited for his big break.

'But I love him,' she said, her voice croaking.

Sitting in the Bird's Nest, which felt a million miles away from the formality of the Tower, all she could think of was the good times she had shared with Daniel. She had first met him at a nightclub in Chelsea – she couldn't even remember what she was doing there, but she could remember the way he had smiled at her across the dance floor and then tracked her down with a glass of champagne that had been cold and delicious, if not quite as delicious as the way it had tasted on his lips when they had finally kissed two hours later. Quite simply, life was more exciting and magical with Daniel Lyons in it. Without him, she was a struggling dancer living in a tiny apartment three thousand miles away from home, going nowhere, dreams fading. With him, she was whisked away to a world of five star mini-breaks to Paris, Rome and Prague, where he could always speak the native language and single out the hippest hotels and the hottest bars. He made her laugh. And he had the cutest Hugh Grant accent. And the bluest eyes this side of Paul Newman. And he was good, so good in bed . . .

Too good, she thought with the realisation that sometimes crept into her thoughts.

Daniel Lyons was a superstar in whatever environment you put him in. She was an ordinary girl from Queens with a thick accent, a bad toe and a tattoo of a daisy on her shoulder obtained on a night out in Harlem after the K Double Swagg video shoot. Whatever had made her think she could be a beautiful and elegant diplomat's wife?

'Listen, sweetie, why don't you go home?'

She felt Annie's hand on her knee and looked up, attempting a smile. 'I'm not sure the contents of my purse will stretch to a cab,' she said, taking a last sip of her cocktail. 'Do you mind if I pull out the sofa bed?'

'Of course not, dimbo. But I don't mean tonight, I mean for Christmas. I mean why don't you go back to New York?'

Amy looked up at her friend.

'To my mom and dad's?'

'Why not? It's the holiday season, isn't it? The perfect time to be around your family and friends and remember what's important.'

'Yes, and for that reason, I'm not going to get an air fare for less than a thousand bucks at this late notice.'

'Well, I can lend it to you.'

Amy squeezed Annie's hand.

'That's so sweet of you, but I'm a big girl. I'll deal with it. I can go home in January when the flights are cheaper.'

'In that case, you're coming to my mum and dad's,' beamed Annie. 'Can't have you moping around on your ownsome over the festive season, can we?'

Amy was touched by the sentiment, but she had stayed at Annie's parents' house before. They were, if it was possible, even more eccentric than their daughter. Thomas, her father, was a children's illustrator, but spent all his spare time working on various 'inventions', none of which ever saw the light of day, while her mother was a sculptor who made ends meet by running a pottery class at the local college. Their house was a large and rambling affair stranded in an unfashionable north London suburb. It was warm and welcoming, but Amy could only remember the scuttling noises in the roof and the smell of dog hair in every room, generously shed by Brunel, their ageing red setter.

'Yes, I know it's a madhouse, but it'll be fun!' said Annie, almost telepathically acknowledging her misgivings. 'And if not, it's certainly guaranteed to take your mind off things.'

She was right, of course, but the thought of her friend's close-knit family made Amy long for her own, and suddenly she was overwhelmed with loneliness and the tears began to roll down her cheeks again.

'Oh honey, what is it?' said Annie, gathering her up against her ample bosom.

'Maybe you're right. Maybe I do need to go home. But how? I can't take your money and I'm totally broke.'

Annie thought for a moment.

'What about those courier flights?' she said. 'You take a package on your knee – like some business documents or a donor kidney or something – and you get half-price air fare.'

'I've never heard of that.'

'They exist, I'm sure of it,' said Annie decisively. 'We'll get on the internet tomorrow. But right now, I'm putting you to bed.'

Clearing away the plates and shooing Amy into the bathroom with a pair of fleecy pyjamas, Annie set about transforming the living room into a plush boudoir, complete with a fur rug thrown over the pull-out bed.

'Ta-da!' she said dramatically when it was done. 'Now you just snuggle down and I guarantee you'll feel better in the morning.'

Nodding gratefully, Amy crawled into the bed and clicked off the light. The too-big pyjamas were soft against her skin and the brandy cocktail had done the trick of making her sleepy, but still she couldn't help going over everything in her mind.

'I can hear you,' called Annie in a sing-song voice from her bedroom next door.

'You can hear me doing what?' frowned Amy.

'I can hear your little brain going over every last conversation. Stop it. You'll drive yourself mad.'

Amy laughed out loud. Annie wasn't known as a world-class agony aunt for nothing.

'All right, all right, I'll think about something else.'

'Think about New York,' called Annie. 'Think about snow on the Empire State Building and sexy blokes skating around the Central Park ice rink in lederhosen.'

Sinking back into the pillows, Amy tried to imagine the little house on Carmichael Street, the tree trimmed with lights and baubles, the turkey on the table, her parents drinking egg nog and bickering over the bread sauce. She'd even invited Daniel to go home with her that Christmas, but there had been the usual excuses about work and family obligations, and looking back, that should have been a sign. Yes, there had been moments in their relationship that had been pure magic. A summer week in the Kefalonian village of Fiskardo, walking through the pastel-coloured harbour and drinking ouzo in the quayside bars, had been one of the best holidays of her life. She'd loved their autumn walks through Hyde Park, kicking leaves and kissing on benches, or cosying up in his Kensington mews house eating pizza and watching Netflix. Perhaps if she'd suggested nights out at the opera and afternoons at the polo then things would have been different now.

A tear trickled down her face and she wiped it away angrily and all her negative, defeatist thoughts with it. If Daniel Lyons didn't like who she was, what she did, what she enjoyed doing, then screw him. Nobody in Queens ever judged her for the way she ate stupid vegetables or what she did for a living. No one on Carmichael Street ever made her feel she wasn't good enough; on the contrary, they had always told her to get out of the old neighbourhood, to go out into the world and make something of herself, to make them proud. Back home – her real home – she was the star of the glee club, the girl-next-door made good, the little Carrell girl who had danced her way clean across to Europe. Sure, there would always be some people who would take a certain delight in her not quite having made it to the top, but screw them too. Amy allowed herself a smile; she could feel her old self creeping back, little by little. And what did she have to feel bad about anyway?

She was twenty-six and already she had danced on Broadway and in Berlin and the West End. To the goombahs back in

Queens she was a star already, and she knew that simply being with them would make her feel infinitely better about herself. But the smile on her lips faded as she remembered that she was still three thousand miles from home and that her bank balance would not cope with the strain of the flight. Before Daniel – before the broken toe – money had been tight, but she had coped. Dancers didn't exactly get paid a fortune, but when you were in a show, you danced eight performances a week and slept on your day off, so there was never time to spend what little you made. Being out of work for so long, despite the fortnightly pay packet from the Forge, had depleted her bank balance. No, depleted didn't quite cover it: her bank account was empty. If you'd thrown a dime into it, it would have echoed.

Realising she was never going to sleep now, she sat up and clicked on the little lamp next to the sofa. She could hear Annie snoring loudly next door so she knew she wasn't going to disturb her friend.

She looked around the Bird's Nest – it *did* feel as if you were inside the treetop home of some garishly plumed magpie, with all the bric-a-brac casually strewn here and there. There was a wonderland quality about Annie's flat that she loved; you never knew what you were going to find next. Reaching over to a rickety table to her right, Amy picked up a magazine from a pile and raised her eyebrows: *The Lady*. The cover featured a picture of a glamorous older woman standing next to a horse, and promised articles entitled 'Baking up a storm' and 'Dressing for the opera' and an interview with Dame Judi Dench. It seemed an unusual magazine for her friend to have in her flat, but then Annie Chapman had always walked a slightly off-kilter path.

Intrigued, Amy flicked through the magazine. It was actually strangely comforting, with features on winter perennials and recipes for jam and fruit cake. Amy felt a sort of distilled essence of Britishness coming through the pages, like an idealised version of what England was, where everyone lived in cottages with roses around the door. It was nice. As she flipped towards the back, she found herself drawn to the Appointments section, a series of advertisements unlike any she had ever seen before.

'Wanted: housekeeper and groundskeeper for stately home. Would suit a couple. Some chauffeuring required. Accommodation and uniform provided.'

Uniform? thought Amy, imagining some strapping hunk in a peaked cap and white gloves opening the door of her vintage Rolls-Royce.

'Mary Poppins required for children five and seven,' read another. 'Foreign languages and equestrian skills preferred!'

It was another world. Where were these extensive properties that required experienced groundsmen? Who could seriously require a gamekeeper or a valet in the twenty-first century? It was as if Downton Abbey had been a documentary not a drama – it was fascinating to imagine what stories lay behind each of these quirky adverts. And more than that: Amy found herself fantasising about actually applying for some of these positions. How hard could it be? 'Driver wanted for South of France second home' – she had a clean licence and she could certainly do with some sun. Or what about being a 'governess to twin girls'? The advert actually stated that qualifications were negotiable. Perhaps they'd be impressed by Amy's background in the arts – didn't all little girls want to be ballet dancers? She smiled to herself – maybe not. Besides which, she almost had a job to go to. If Eduardo Drummond called her back, of course. She was about to fold the magazine when one ad caught her eye, or rather two words: New York. Amy looked closer. The advert was small, listed under the Situations Wanted header: 'Mature lady seeks polite companion for Manhattan adventure. Must be available for travel 23–27 December. Flights and New York accommodation included.'

She paused for a moment and then reread it. *Must be available for travel 23–27 December. Flights and New York accommodation included.* Underneath the advertisement was an email address. She picked up her phone, logged into her mail and without hesitating another moment drafted her reply.

CHAPTER THREE

She had been in the shower when her phone had rung, so the message had been delivered by voicemail. Amy pulled her dressing gown tighter around her body and listened to it again, hoping she hadn't heard it right the first time.

'Darling. It's Driscilla here. I'm afraid it's a no from Eduardo about *Tango Nights*. They loved your audition, but they saw a lot of great girls, and between you and me, perhaps your toe still represents something of a problem . . .'

Amy snapped the phone shut, not wanting to hear her agent's voice any longer. *A no!* She couldn't believe it. It had been a great audition. She had danced her ass off, got on with the director; even Driscilla had said that it was in the bag, and she was an agent from the tough love school of showbiz, where nothing was a done deal until the ink was dry on the contract.

Amy sank to the sofa bed and took a sip of the glass of water that Annie had left on the table the night before. She needed it, she thought, gulping down the cool liquid and wishing she had some Nurofen to go with it. She had no idea how much she had drunk last night. There had been at least five glasses of champagne at the Tower of London dinner, and then Annie's cocktail . . . Her eyes darted to the curvaceous glass containing a green neon straw and the residue of the daiquiri – all stale and curdled, which was precisely the effect the Ukrainian brandy seemed to be having on the contents of her stomach. Urgh, she thought, feeling suddenly quite nauseous, not helped by her flashback of the night before. The artichoke, the toxic comments and sideways glances from Vivienne Lyons, and Daniel's effective dumping. She had geared herself up for a proposal and instead had got propositioned by her boyfriend's dad. As she had lain awake in bed the previous night, mulling everything over, the only thing that had kept her going was the hope that she would get the *Tango Nights* job, and now that was a busted flush.

Annie bustled into the living room and kissed the top of her head.

'How are you this morning? Sleep well?'

'No,' said Amy, rubbing her temples.

'How about we go for some breakfast?'

'Great. And then you can tell me what to do about my agent.'

'What's wrong with darling Driscilla?'

'I think she's going to get rid of me.'

Annie frowned and perched next to her on the sofa bed.

'Why do you say that?'

'She just rang to tell me I haven't got the job I auditioned for yesterday. Didn't even speak to me – just left a message.'

'I don't think that's very conclusive.'

'It's just a feeling,' replied Amy, pressing her lips together. 'I didn't even get a Christmas card this year. When I first moved to London and signed with the agency, I'd get all these little lunches in Soho, phone calls twice a week to see how I was doing. Now my toe represents something of a problem and I think I'm about to get the kiss-off. Not even Driscilla wants me, Annie,' she said, lying back and swinging her arms dramatically over her head.

'You need protein. Eggs, bacon . . . Or maybe we could go to Fortnum's for afternoon tea in the morning. I don't have to be at work till two.'

'And I gotta double shift at the Forge starting at one, which I need like a hole in the head,' said Amy, wondering if she should just keep the Bird's Nest curtains closed and not come out until the next decade.

Annie left the room to go and get dressed and Amy sat up, crossed her legs and reached for her phone, half hoping that Daniel had had a change of heart and been in touch. She was greeted by the stream of messages that usually filled her inbox each morning – Groupon and a host of other discount websites she had once subscribed to.

One address, however, she didn't recognise. Georgia Hamilton. Frowning, she clicked on the message and began to read.

Dear Miss Carrell,

Thank you for your reply to my advertisement in *The Lady* magazine. Perhaps we could meet to discuss my situation further. As I am due to travel in just three days' time, it might be better to do this sooner rather than later. Are you available today? Please call me on the number below. I look forward to meeting you.

Kind regards,

Georgia Hamilton (MA Cantab)

'What's wrong?' asked Annie, coming back into the room and handing Amy a cup of black coffee.

'I did something a bit crazy last night.'

'Do I need to call a lawyer?'

Amy explained about the advertisement in *The Lady* and her reply from Ms Hamilton.

'It's a Christmas miracle,' gasped Annie, grabbing the magazine that Amy had flung down the night before. 'It's like *Scent of a Woman*.'

'*Scent of a Woman*?'

'That movie where Chris O'Donnell takes the blind man to New York. Al Pacino. Can you imagine if you were going with someone as sexy as Al Pacino,' she said, her breath quickening in excitement.

'Well, last time I looked, Georgia was a woman's name,' said Amy, unable to share her friend's enthusiasm about this new development to the day.

'Amy, last night you said you wanted to go back to New York, and here's your opportunity.'

'Except I'm not going to be accompanying Al Pacino. Best-case scenario it's some no-friends weirdo; worst case . . . it's a psychopath who wants to kill me and bury me under her petunias.'

'It will be some little old lady who can't carry her own bags . . . Now go, give her a ring and get it sorted. Otherwise you're coming for Christmas at my parents' place and you're sharing a room with the dog.'

An hour later, Amy was getting off the tube at Chalk Farm station. She still felt terrible and looked worse. Her meeting with Georgia Hamilton had been arranged for eleven o'clock, giving her time to get over to the Forge for after lunch. It had meant there was no time to go back to her apartment in Finsbury Park to change, and not wanting to turn up to her interview in last night's now half-bald sequinned dress, she had been forced to borrow something from Annie's eclectic wardrobe: a lemon-yellow 1950s hoop-skirt dress two sizes too big and a pair of grey suede pumps one size too small had been the most conservative items she could find. What invariably looked fantastic on Annie made Amy feel like one of those crazy bag ladies she used to see shuffling around Penn Station in the nineties.

As she turned to cross the footbridge joining Chalk Farm with Primrose Hill, her phone beeped to register a text from Nathan: 'So do we have a five-carat sparkler on our finger yet? X'

Snorting, she switched off the phone and quickened her pace. It was beginning to rain, and Annie's pink parasol would provide little resistance against the December elements.

Once she had crossed the Regent's Canal bridge, it was like entering a parallel universe, she thought, noticing that the gritty minimarts and curry buffets she had spotted at the Camden end of Chalk Farm had made way for a more serene village atmosphere. Primrose Hill was quite lovely, with its Georgian architecture and leafiness, its boho bakeries, boutiques and pavement cafés, which all made Amy wonder why she didn't come up here more often.

She stopped in front of a smart Victorian town house and checked the address she'd scribbled on a piece of paper.

Georgia Hamilton. 27b Chalcot Terrace. She had spoken to Ms Hamilton on the phone, of course, but it had been a very short and rather formal conversation, all 'I'd be delighted to meet you' and 'I'd be grateful if you'd come to see me'. Amy hadn't really been able to glean much about the woman from her voice. Elderly, polite, polished: that probably described half the people living in this part of London. She had googled the name, with similar results. Georgia Hamilton could be a tapestry cleaner, a publishing executive or a minor B-movie actress who hadn't made a film since 1976. Whoever she was, she was rich. Amy could see from the two bells next to the door that the building was divided into flats, but even so, she liked to read the property sections of the newspapers on Sundays, and she was aware that a duplex apartment in Primrose Hill would cost more than a mansion with stables anywhere outside the M25.

Here goes nothing, she thought, pressing the button next to the brass plaque marked simply 'Hamilton', then jumped when the door buzzed and a disembodied voice said 'Second floor, please.'

Amy pushed into the high entrance hall. *God, it's got a chandelier in the hallway*, she thought, immediately intimidated. There was a vaguely musty smell in the air and the paintwork looked in need of a refresh, but even so, it was clearly a grand old house, with large vases containing fresh flower arrangements on each landing and expensive-looking pearlescent paper on the walls.

Ascending the wide staircase, she realised she was walking on tiptoes, trying not to make any noise in this hushed space, instinctively respectful of the history of the place. She supposed it was because it was exactly as she had imagined London to be when she had first read about it as a child: this was the sort of house that would have had servants and a nanny, the sort of place you could imagine Peter Pan visiting late at night.

'Get a grip,' she muttered to herself as she reached the top floor and knocked on the door marked with a brass '2'.

'Miss Carrell, I presume?'

Amy took a moment to examine the lady in front of her. She looked to be in her early seventies, although it was very hard to tell. Her ash-blond hair, shot through with fine silvery strands, was cut short and tucked behind her ears, and she was dressed simply in a grey blous and wide black slacks with a string of pearls around her neck and matching earrings in her lobes. Elegant, that was the word that immediately sprang to mind. The sort of high-born elegance that made Amy wonder if Georgia Hamilton knew Vivienne Lyons and all her snobby friends.

'Yes, Amy actually,' she said, shaking the outstretched hand. 'American?'

'New York,' said Amy, feeling a little awkward as the woman looked her up and down. Perhaps the sequins would have been better than Annie's yellow vintage sundress.

There was a pause, then Georgia Hamilton nodded, as if she had made a decision.

'Do come inside,' she said. 'You can leave the umbrella by the door.'

Amy followed her down a narrow corridor and out into a light, spacious living room.

'Wow!' said Amy. 'That's some view.'

The room had a wide bay window that gave an uninterrupted vista of the slopes of Primrose Hill park and the hazy city beyond.

'Yes, it is rather special, isn't it?' said the woman with a hint of amusement in her voice. 'I suppose it's human nature to become accustomed to one's surroundings, even if they are remarkable, but I confess I do often catch sight of the view and smile at my good fortune.' She gestured towards an armchair. 'Please do sit. Would you like some tea? I have just brewed a pot.'

'Yes please,' said Amy, perching on the edge of the chair and looking around nervously. She was immediately reminded of the Bird's Nest. Georgia Hamilton's home was equally eclectic and personal. But where Annie's flat was chaotic and cluttered, a mish-mash of ideas and fleeting enthusiasms, this home was understated and calm. There were abstract paintings and black and white photographs, interesting-looking pots and ethnic-style sculptures, but it all seemed to fit together like pieces of some artistic puzzle.

'You've got a lot of books.' Amy smiled, observing the bookcases stuffed with all manner of hard- and soft-backed books.

'I used to work in publishing,' said Georgia, still watching her. 'Occupational hazard, I'm afraid, though in my defence, they're not entirely for show. I have actually read most of them.'

'So you're *that* Georgia Hamilton,' said Amy, immediately regretting it. Now she would have to confess to checking up on the older woman. *I'm going to look like a stalker*, she thought.

'Google, I take it?' said Georgia to Amy's surprise as she handed her a bone-china cup and saucer. 'That's the problem with information overload. In the modern age you can know pretty much all you ever need to know about a person before you even meet them. Where is the mystery? Where is the unwrapping of a new friend, a new lover?'

'I don't really like surprises,' said Amy. 'Not where lovers are concerned, anyway.'

The old lady tilted her head thoughtfully and took a sip of her tea.

'And tell me, Amy, what do you do?'

She opened her mouth, ready to say that she was a dancer, waiting to explain about her injury and her training, but suddenly it seemed far easier just to admit that she was a waitress.

'I wait tables at the Forge in Islington. It's where I'm going after this.'

'I was a waitress myself many years ago. No better job for people-watching, observing human nature. It's probably why so many creatives are drawn to it. You think you are there to pay for your art, but actually, I rather find it helps your art.'

Amy smiled and the atmosphere relaxed.

'Down to business,' said Georgia, setting her cup aside. 'I have booked a trip to New York to leave in a few days. Incredibly, I have never been to Manhattan and I feel that at my age I should be visiting the places I . . . well, the places I have missed.'

'Sort of like a bucket list?' said Amy without thinking. *Note to self: try not to suggest that the lady interviewing you has one foot in the grave*, she thought. Luckily Georgia smiled.

'Something like that, yes. I suppose I could have gone on one of those ghastly tours for mature single travellers, but the thought of shuffling around Manhattan like a bunch of geriatric crocodiles . . .' She waved a dainty hand. 'Which is how I came to advertise for a travelling companion. There's no call for concern, I'm not likely to fall and break a hip, but I'm not quite as spry as I was in my prime.'

Amy thought it best not to reply, lest she put her foot in it again.

'So how is it that you're able to travel, Amy?'

The question took Amy by surprise, and it must have shown on her face.

'Well, it is Christmas, after all. I imagine most people your age are booked up with parties until New Year.'

'Something fell through,' said Amy awkwardly.

'Relationship entanglements?'

'Is it that obvious?' she said, glancing up.

'You have that look in your eye,' nodded Georgia. 'You don't look as if you want to leave London for the holidays, Amy; you look as though you want to flee.'

Amy could see that there was no point in denying it.

'This is my situation, Ms Hamilton—'

'Miss,' said the woman. 'But please call me Georgia.'

'I've had a really crappy week, and right now all I want to do is go back home. I figured this might be a way to see my folks, even if they have to come into Manhattan to meet me. If that's a problem say so now, because that's why I want to do this trip. But seeing my mom and dad would only take a couple of hours, and the rest of the time I'm all yours. I work hard, and I can take you to all the little places only New Yorkers know about as well as the

43

touristy things you probably want to see and do.'

Georgia didn't reply and Amy felt her heart lurch, suddenly realising how desperately she wanted to see her mum, get one of those big bear hugs from her dad. She needed to get *home*.

'At least you're honest,' said the older woman with an amused half-smile. 'That's good, because the last thing I want is some con artist who's going to run up thousands of dollars' worth of expenses on the minibar.'

'That's a lot of Hershey bars,' grinned Amy.

'Even so, I'd be grateful if you could provide a couple of references.'

'So I've got the job?'

'My dear, I'm due to leave for America in three days' time. Despite placing the advert three weeks ago, you're the only apparently sane person to apply. Can you believe I got a letter from someone at HM Prison Brixton saying he was about to go on probation and would love to accompany me, although he felt there might be issues at US customs. Besides, you don't get to my point in life without being a decent judge of character. I think this trip might work out for both of us.'

'Yes, yes, thank you,' said Amy, getting up to hug the old woman.

Georgia reeled back in surprise.

'Well, if that's settled, how about we have some more tea?'

There was a sudden buzzing sound that Amy recognised must be the intercom. She wondered if Cheryl had somehow got wind of her plans. After all, she was due to do the Boxing Day shift in the pub, and if she couldn't get Nathan or one of the others to take it on for her, then she was in big trouble.

Georgia pressed a button on a box on the wall. 'Yes?' she said.

'It's me, can I come in?' A male voice, but too crackly to tell any more.

Did Georgia have a boyfriend? Amy realised she knew nothing about this woman she had just agreed to accompany across the Atlantic. But then if she already had a companion, why advertise for one in a magazine? Either way, she'd have to wait until the old lady decided to tell her.

'I'd better be going,' she said, standing up.

'No, no, do stay. We should discuss the details before you leave.' Georgia picked up the silver teapot. 'I'll make more tea and you can tell me about this Heathrow airport I've heard so much about.'

Amy could tell the woman was toying with her. Her flat was full of books and *objets d'art* from around the world. On Google, Georgia Hamilton had been described as 'a legend' in publishing. Amy was sure this elegant, sophisticated woman had been around the globe dozens of times, even if it was the case that she had never been to New York. But wasn't the American publishing industry based in Manhattan?

She didn't have time to ask, as there was a rat-a-tat knock on the door of the flat.

That was quick, thought Amy. There was no lift, so only someone young and fit could have made it from street level to a second-floor apartment in that time.

Georgia left the room and she heard muffled voices at the end of the corridor. When the old lady returned, Amy was surprised to see that she was accompanied by a much younger man. He was obviously handsome, but week-old stubble verged on being a beard, and his dark hair trailed over his ears and was in desperate need of a cut. In a thick navy pea coat and big black lace-up boots, he looked as if he was about to go trapping.

'Amy Carrell, this is my cousin's son Will Hamilton,' said Georgia quickly.

'Hello,' said Amy, but Will merely nodded, a slight frown

on his face, and turned to Georgia, handing her a white envelope.

'I just came to drop this round,' he said.

'Thank you, Will.'

'It's from the family,' he said, glancing at Amy as if he didn't want to say more in front of strangers.

'I'm well aware of what it is, Will,' said Georgia with a rather pinched look.

'So what are your plans for Christmas?'

He was loitering awkwardly near the door. Amy noticed that Georgia had not suggested he take his coat off and join them for tea.

'I'm out of the country,' said Georgia more brightly. 'Escaping the London weather.'

'New York's going to be a damn sight colder than here,' laughed Amy, trying to defuse the tension.

'New York?' said Will, looking even more serious. He viewed Amy suspiciously with his dark, almost black eyes, the sort of eyes that made you feel guilty once they settled their gaze on you.

'We're going on a trip,' replied Amy quickly, looking to Georgia for reassurance that she had done the right thing in telling him.

'You're going to New York together?' said Will slowly. He definitely disapproved of that idea, thought Amy, watching him thrust his hand in his pocket.

'That's right, and I really have to pack,' said Georgia, making it clear that the visit was now over.

'Do you want to give me your contact details? Just in case.'

'In case of what?' replied Georgia, peering at him down her nose.

'Just in case . . .' he said, his eyes flickering towards Amy.

'Take my number,' offered Amy. She rattled it off and he punched it into his phone.

'Thanks,' he said flatly.

'And thank you again,' said Georgia. 'Please pass on . . . the season's greetings to your parents.'

The three of them stood in silence for a moment.

'Happy Christmas, Georgia,' he said finally. 'Call me if you need a lift to the airport.' And he disappeared, closing the door behind him.

Amy looked at Georgia and didn't say anything. She didn't know what had just happened there, but if her cousins came to the Carmichael Street house, her mom and dad could never get rid of them. They'd crack open a beer, put their feet up in front of the TV or shoot hoops in the yard. But perhaps the British were different.

'You should probably reassure him that I'm not some Yankee con artist,' she said finally.

'He doesn't think that,' said Georgia politely.

'I think he's wondering why a member of his family is going to New York with a stranger.'

Georgia gave her a sympathetic glance.

'William has a good heart,' she said quietly. 'But I fear the thousands of pounds spent sending him to the best schools failed to teach him the good graces of social interaction. I apologise if he made you feel uncomfortable.'

'It's fine,' said Amy, trying to imagine how she would feel if her uncle Chuck won the lottery and announced he was going on a European vacation with a twenty-something blonde.

'Now, if I show you a map of Central Park, perhaps you can point out to me where the Wollman ice rink is?' Georgia said, her whole demeanour relaxing. 'I've always wanted to see it.'

CHAPTER FOUR

22 December 2012

'The local time here in New York is 2.45 p.m.,' said the pilot. 'The weather is a bracing four degrees, but the good news is we're forecast for some sunny spells tomorrow.'

Georgia leant towards the window and peered out dubiously.

'No snow. How disappointing.'

'Believe me, you don't want to wish snow in New York,' said Amy. 'When the wind blows a blizzard up from the Battery, it can freeze you where you stand. Out in Queens, the snowploughs make drifts ten feet high.'

'Oh, I'm sure, my dear,' said the old lady. 'But I have rather been harbouring a fantasy of a light sprinkling on the pavements and in the park. I must have seen it in some Gene Kelly film, I suppose.'

She glanced out of the window again, her lined mouth turned down, looking up at the gloomy sky. Perhaps she had that seasonal thingy disorder, thought Amy – that one where people became depressed when they were deprived of sunlight. But then Georgia Hamilton seemed to have been living in north London for the past two decades – she must spend half the year under a black cloud. Either way, Amy found it hard to believe that anyone who had just sat for eight hours in the warm embrace of first-class flying could be anything but happy. She herself had only ever been on a handful of long-haul flights in her entire life, and never above cattle class, so when the uniformed waiter in the Concorde Lounge at Heathrow had stepped forward and handed her a glass of pink Bollinger, Amy had almost wanted to kiss him. The lounge itself had been like a boutique hotel; she'd had a delicious three-course meal in the restaurant and a facial in the next-door Elemis Spa. It had all been free, and when their flight was announced to board she had been tempted to stow away in one of the cute little cabanas and not go – wondering to herself if squatters' rights were in operation at airports and if so whether she should just move in and never return to her Finsbury Park apartment.

When she'd been dragged out of the lounge by Georgia, she had been amazed that the first-class cabin was just as nice. Amy had tucked in to her lobster bisque, tender fillet of beef and creamy panna cotta, accepting a glass of champagne whenever it was offered, whilst Georgia had sat quietly for most of the journey, reading a book and occasionally staring out of the window at the clouds. Amy had tried to engage her in conversation – she wasn't sure if that was part of the job of 'companion'; like a hitch-hiker, you were expected to earn the ride by distracting the driver – but while she had been unfailingly polite, as ever, Georgia had rebuffed every approach, so Amy had simply sat back and enjoyed being pampered.

They were the first down the air bridge and straight through customs with barely a glance. Amy felt a tingle of excitement and comfort as she smelt the cold, fuggy air of her home city.

'I have arranged for a taxi to pick us up kerbside, I believe the term is,' said Georgia as Amy steered a trolley with the luggage – Georgia's smart cream suitcase and matching vanity case – to the exit.

'Ms Hamilton?' said a large Hispanic man in a chauffeur's uniform, almost bowing as he said it. 'I'm Alfonse, I'll be your driver while you're here.'

Georgia smiled graciously.

'A pleasure to meet you, Alfonse. This is Miss Amy Carrell, my companion and a native of your city.'

Alfonse turned his wide smile towards Amy. 'That so? Well welcome home, Miss Amy. Back to see the folks, huh? That's real nice.'

He led them to a sleek Mercedes town car. A taxi? thought Amy as he held the door for her to climb in and she sank into the soft leather upholstery; it was a world away from the rickety estate cars of her local minicab firm in Finsbury Park. She glanced over at Georgia as they moved away. She had the relaxed look of those other passengers in the first-class cabin; an air of expectation that such a level of luxury was normal. Perhaps it was; she still really didn't know that much about Georgia Hamilton. Of course, the first thing she had done upon leaving Georgia's flat that rainy afternoon was to run another Google search on her. There wasn't a huge amount – she had worked in the pre-internet age – but what snippets she did find were fascinating. This old lady who'd had to advertise for someone to travel to New York with had once been a hugely successful businesswoman. The label 'publishing legend' barely covered it. According to the features Amy read, throughout the eighties and nineties Georgia had been one of the most formidable forces in the industry, scoring numerous literary and commercial hits, prize-winners and runaway bestsellers.

Amy realised she had even read some of the books Georgia had published. The final news piece she found, announcing Georgia's retirement, detailed the eye-watering sum one of the Big Six international publishing houses had paid for her business. No wonder she looked so comfortable in these surroundings.

'You know what I find so odd?' said Georgia, staring out of the window as they sped along the expressway. 'It's the size of the cars. I mean, the motorway could be anywhere, but the cars are so wide.'

She pointed to a truck. 'The lorries too, they are enormous compared to anything you'd see in England. But then the country is so vast. I suppose that's why everyone drives.'

'Not in New York,' said Amy. 'We're different here.'

'I heard that,' said Alfonse.

Amy gazed out the window. She could feel her heart in her throat. The irony of accompanying Georgia to Manhattan was that they had to pass through her own borough to get there; the freeway cut right through Queens. She could see buildings and street signs that brought memories rushing back: that was the hall where her cousin had tap lessons, that was the pizza place that delivered to her neighbourhood. She was almost home, but not quite.

'Heavens,' said Georgia quietly as the Manhattan skyline reared up ahead of them – a cityscape of glittering towers before a golden setting sun.

'Mm-hm,' nodded Alfonse. 'It's one hell of a sight. Never tire of that one.'

'Makes me wonder why I haven't come home sooner,' sighed Amy, knowing that although she had seen this vista many times before, it was impossible not to be moved.

Georgia nodded her head tightly, but her eyes were melancholy.

'Okay, folks, have you at the hotel in just a few minutes,' said

Alfonse as they turned into the Midtown Tunnel. Amy could feel herself holding her breath as the tunnel lights spun away past them – and then there they were, as if by magic right in the centre of the city. Coming into Manhattan via the tunnel always had that jolting effect: one moment you were on the expressway, the next you were surrounded by fifty-storey buildings and fire trucks and steam and everyone was honking and yelling.

The car turned up the wide thoroughfare of Park Avenue, where tall Christmas trees were planted all the way up the centre of the road and every business window had a holiday-themed display, and pulled up outside a building with red awnings over its ground-floor windows.

'Is this the hotel?' asked Amy as Alfonse helped them out. 'Looks more like one of those upscale apartment buildings.'

'I think that's the idea, miss,' the driver smiled. 'There are plenty of those look-at-me hotels on the island, but the Plaza Athénée is the sort of place you come for somewhere a little more discreet and elegant, shall we say? I believe Elizabeth Taylor and Princess Diana both liked to stay here and I think you're gonna like it too.'

He handed her a card. 'Here. If you or Miss Georgia need anything, day or night, you give Alfonse a call, okay?'

Amy nodded gratefully.

'Thanks.'

Alfonse's description was pretty much on the money. Georgia was in a suite which was sumptuous, but not overpoweringly so, whilst Amy was in a lovely room down the hall. Amy had been to a lot of high-end places with Daniel – he would never go anywhere that wasn't what he considered 'the best' – but she had rarely enjoyed them as they seemed to come with a sort of inbuilt snobbery, with the guests all trying to outdo each other in some sort of po-faced Olympics. But this hotel seemed to be just as Alfonse had said – more like a temporary home-from-home for the wealthy. Certainly, as the bell captain closed the door and left them alone, Georgia looked as if she was entirely at home.

'So, uh, what do you want to do now?' said Amy, looking at the suitcases sitting by the door of the suite. Was she supposed to unpack for Georgia? Iron her dresses? Massage her tired feet?

'First, I'd like you to relax,' said Georgia pointedly, as if she had read all of that from Amy's anxious expression. 'I wanted a companion for this trip, not an entertainments officer from a cruise ship. Don't feel that you have to run about picking up after me and arranging things for me to do.'

'Oh. Okay. So what is my . . .'

'Your role?'

Amy shrugged, blushing a little.

'Yes, I guess.'

'Just as the advert said: a companion, someone to accompany me wherever I go. I realise it's a little strange for you, but think of it as if we were two old friends on holiday in New York. What would you do first?'

Go and get drunk, thought Amy, but bit her lip.

'I'd probably have a shower, then get pizza.'

Georgia smiled thinly. Her demeanour had been quite prickly and severe all day, but she looked as if she was starting to thaw.

'A fine plan. I think we can do a little better than pizza, however. Why don't you settle into your room and I'll see if I can arrange somewhere to eat.'

'Somewhere to eat' was a place called Ralph, or so said the tiny gold plaque on the wall of the 68th Street building that Amy almost missed. She had never heard of it before, although the

Upper East Side had never been one of her natural habitats even when she lived in the city. It was old-money New York, where Wall Street bankers and industrialists owned multimillion-dollar townhouses, where antique shops sat cheek by jowl with apartments owned by tight-faced old ladies with Pekinese dogs, and where trophy blondes spent their days running from blow-dry appointments to lunch to Mandarin classes for their children. It was all too rich a blend, thought Amy, deciding that pizza would have been infinitely preferable.

'Ms Hamilton,' said the maître d' as they walked inside. 'Welcome to Ralph.' He pronounced it 'Rafe'. 'May I take your coats?'

Amy tried her best not to look overawed. She had been expecting gold leaf and marble, but it was more like a grand dame's elegant dining room, all crisp linens, antique furnishings and hushed atmosphere, which somehow made it even more intimidating.

They were given the wine list and looked at the menu, which was all in French.

Georgia pulled a pair of glasses from her bag and put them on. She made a gentle noise of approval, snapped the menu shut and announced that she was having the lamb.

'Where was that?' asked Amy, only recognising the words 'tarte Tatin', which was on the Forge's Specials board on Fridays.

'Would you like me to translate?' asked Georgia, peering down the end of her nose.

'I'll have the lamb too,' said Amy, not wishing to suffer any more food-related embarrassment for one week.

The sommelier approached and Amy watched quietly as Georgia spoke to the man, not just knowledgeably discussing vintages, growing regions and grapes, but asking what cut of lamb they were to be eating and how rich was its sauce, before deciding on a Napa Valley Cabernet Sauvignon. The sommelier left with a smile that said she had chosen both expensively and well.

'You know your stuff,' said Amy, sipping her water uncomfortably. 'French. Wine. The only stuff I know is from that scene in *Pretty Woman* where the manager teaches Julia Roberts to count the prongs.'

Georgia raised one thin grey brow. 'I saw that film too, and believe me, there's a lot more to it than counting the prongs. We had weeks studying at finishing school – and I do mean studying.'

'You went to finishing school?' asked Amy, wide-eyed.

'I did.'

'In the Alps?' She had read and reread *Lace*, and that bit at the beginning – where the girls were sashaying around L'Hirondelle drinking hot chocolate and fraternising with princes – was her favourite part.

'No, I went to Paris,' said Georgia. 'Madame Didiot's School for Girls. Going to Paris to finish was considered quite a smart choice. Although my mother didn't have a bean, there was a small trust fund put to one side for my education.'

'Wow,' said Amy. 'Is that where you learnt about wine?'

'A little. I didn't want to go to finishing school and I wasn't a particularly good student, as Madame Didiot would certainly have confirmed. But wine I enjoyed. I probably drank too much of it in the eighties. I think most publishers of a certain age would say that.'

Georgia had ordered for them both, and when the starters arrived, Amy picked at hers.

'So if you didn't want to be at finishing school, why did you go?'

'Because I had to. Because I was going to be a deb.'

'Deb?'

The woman raised her eyebrows. 'A debutante. The point of the finishing school was to prepare a young lady for her "coming out", when she would be presented to Her Majesty the Queen as a girl worthy of English society. And it wasn't a matter of simply turning up and curtseying properly; there was a whole *season* of events, parties and functions where the proper young lady would be expected to behave impeccably in every situation. And by that, I mean behave impeccably around young men. Because of course that was the real point of the debutante system: to produce good little wives for the next generation of upper-class men.'

'So is that what Madame Didiot taught you? How to talk to men?' asked Amy, smiling. She wished they'd had a few of those lessons at Kelsey High in Queens, where she had been so painfully shy she had broken out in a neck rash whenever certain members of the football team spoke to her.

'Amongst other things,' Georgia said as she took a sip of her wine. 'Deportment, place settings, flower arranging, grooming, musical appreciation, public speaking . . . it was endless. And I have to say, at the time I rebelled against it; I could see no point in any of it. But now? Well, maybe it's just an old woman looking at the world with jaded eyes, but now I don't think teaching young people manners is the worst thing in the world.'

'Did you find him?'

'Who?' asked Georgia, sliding her knife into her lamb.

'A husband?'

Georgia was silent for one moment.

'I did marry. But not to someone I met during the Season.'

'Are you still together?' She chose her words carefully. She had been in Georgia's almost constant company for over twelve hours, and yet she had found out very little about her.

'It was a short marriage. Philip and I divorced many years ago, although we remained friends until he passed away two years ago.'

'I'm sorry to hear that.'

'Still,' said Georgia more breezily, 'there were things I learnt in Paris and during my season which were invaluable later on, certainly when I became chief executive of my own company in the seventies. In those days it was rather unusual for a woman to attain such lofty heights. There were times when I was patronised, ignored, belittled and even threatened just for being a woman. But because of my background, I knew that I could compete at every level. I was as educated, as cultured, as well informed as even the most pompous fat cat I came up against, and looking back, finishing school was one of the things that helped me fill up my arsenal.'

Ten minutes ago, Amy would have thought that learning how to curtsey was a relic best left in the past, but Georgia didn't make it sound too bad at all.

'Do they still exist? Finishing schools?'

'Why, are you thinking of going?' replied Georgia with a tight smile.

'Course not.'

'You'll be hard pushed to find any around today. Traditional Swiss finishing schools were phased out years ago. I'm not sure it sits very well with the modern age, does it? Nowadays people believe in equality.'

'You don't?'

'I believe in a meritocracy, not quite the same thing. Whoever's best suited for a role, that's who should fill that role. Now, some women are ideally suited to being surgeons, prime ministers and judges, but some are suited to being wives and mothers. I know it sounds old-fashioned to say so, but it's the truth as I see it.'

Amy laughed.

'I know some feminists who would go purple at that idea.'

'And that is the tragic thing. Feminism was all about giving women choice – if they choose to become a brain surgeon, they should be able to. All well and good. But if a woman chooses to stay at home and raise children – or indeed, stand around at cocktail parties making riveting small talk – that should be equally acceptable, shouldn't it? In my humble opinion, feminists can sometimes be too judgemental.'

Amy looked at Georgia more closely. She had clearly underestimated this woman on almost every level. Suddenly the trip had become much more interesting, and she found that she wanted to know everything that Georgia Hamilton knew.

'And the Season. I suppose that's finished too.'

'I was the last crop, actually. Princess Margaret famously said, "Every tart in London is getting in," which was rather the death knell for the institution, I'm afraid. There are still all sorts of formal balls for girls who want that kind of thing. Or more usually, if their parents do; it's still about meeting the right sort of boy. The Crillon Ball in Paris, for example, that's quite lovely – although I believe nowadays they are attended by lots of rock stars' daughters. So yes, getting presented in front of the Queen was abolished in 1958, the year I came out. Quite a watershed year it turned out to be, in fact,' she added, sipping her Sauvignon.

'I thought the sixties was when it all changed. Miniskirts, the pill . . .'

'The sixties was the start of the sexual revolution. I believe Philip Larkin once wrote that it started between the end of the Lady Chatterley ban and the Beatles' first LP. But society was changing long before that. At the start of the fifties your average young person dressed like their parents, but by '58 there was rock and roll, Teddy boys, race riots, coffee bars – it was the birth of the teenager; certainly the first time anyone really thought of young people as being different.'

Amy started to laugh, thinking of her dad working in his garage, his old Elvis songs turned up so loud that it made the workbench shake.

'My dad says the world changed because of Elvis.'

Georgia gave a wry smile.

'Typical of you Americans, wanting to take credit for everything. But perhaps you're right. I think the truth is we were ready for change. Things were moving fast. Modern history certainly sees 1958 as a momentous year.'

'What do you think?'

Georgia nodded, her eyes taking on a distant look.

'It was certainly a summer I'll remember,' she said quietly.

CHAPTER FIVE

March 1958

'Ah, London. I smell it in the air, darling,' said Estella Hamilton, opening the window of the train carriage and pushing her long copper-coloured hair off her shoulders as if she were a great theatrical diva preparing for her encore.

'About time too,' muttered her daughter Georgia, seeing nothing but grey concrete buildings, factories and the backs of thin, tired-looking terraced houses. It had been a long, dull journey from Devon, made even more tiresome by multiple mysterious stops, and she was desperate for a cigarette. She still had a healthy supply of Gauloises, stockpiled at the Gare du Nord, in her trunk, which was not two minutes away in the luggage compartment. But liberal as her mother was, Georgia did not think she would understand her eighteen-year-old daughter's need for nerve-calming nicotine. In fact Estella didn't really seem to understand anything about her eighteen-year-old daughter any more.

'What's wrong?' she asked, looking over at her daughter with suspicion.

'I just wish I was going back to Paris,' said Georgia as a series of images popped into her mind like a technicolour montage designed to torment her. Handsome men writing poetry in streetside cafés, girls in stripy sweaters riding their bikes along the Seine, stern-looking women dressed in fur stoles buying duck and macaroons from the smart stores on the Rue Saint-Honoré, and fashion shoots at the Eiffel Tower. The City of Light was a city of constant beauty and wonder, and Georgia wished more than anything that she was still there.

'And what would you do in Paris?' asked Estella, not unkindly.

'I want to write. You know that.'

'And how will you earn money until you get something published?'

'You were in Paris at my age and you managed.'

'That was different. I went to model.'

'Maybe I could make some money that way?' It was not something she had dared voice to her mother before. Although she found the idea of posing in front of a photographer for hours on end quite boring and silly, Georgia had always loved hearing Estella's stories about her own youthful adventures in France. The daughter of two trapeze artists, Estella had never been under any pressure to conform. Too small – and some would say too interesting-looking – for the fashion world, she had been a successful model for some of the biggest artists of the time, including Rodin and Picasso, watching, observing, until she moved back to England and started painting and sculpting herself.

'You want to model?' she said with surprise.

'Everyone says we look alike.'

Georgia watched her mother's face and wondered if Estella

61

would take that comment as an insult. Although she had turned
forty three weeks earlier, there was no denying that her mother
was still beautiful – her hair fell in long russet curls down her
slim back, her face a riot of unblemished skin and angles. There
were similarities between mother and daughter – the bright,
alert green eyes, and the wide mouth with lips the colour of rose
petals – but people were being kind when they said that they
looked like twins.

'Darling, you are a beautiful girl, but you don't have the neck
to model.'

'What's my neck got to do with being a good model?'

Estella came to sit beside her and stroked her daughter's dark
blond bobbed hair.

'I know you're nervous about the Season, but there is no
need to be so uptight,' she said, her voice softening. 'The next
few months are going to be *fun*. I mean, you said you were
dreading going to finishing school, and look how much you
enjoyed that.'

'I enjoyed Paris, not wasting my time flower arranging and
learning how to eat an orange with a knife and fork.'

A blast of wind blew in from the open window, making
Georgia shiver.

'Mother, I don't know what's got into you. This whole
debutante thing is so unlike you. You were a free spirit, a
bohemian. I just don't understand why you are making me do
something you would have hated yourself at my age.'

'Darling, we've been through this.'

'And you haven't listened to a word I've got to say about it.'

'I have listened, my darling. I understand that you want to be
a writer. I understand that you want to live in some charming
little garret on the Rive Gauche. I understand it all. Because it's
me. I have felt it, I have done it.'

She shifted her position and looked her daughter directly in the eyes.

'I know you are a little embarrassed by me sometimes. I know you think I can be away with the fairies. But I am a practical woman. I don't want to live like this any more. You might not have the height or the neck to model, but you are a beautiful young girl. You can make a good marriage, and believe me, your dreams of becoming a writer are much more likely to be within your reach if you have the cushion of financial security.'

The train chugged to a halt at Paddington station with a long whistle and the ear-piercing screech of brakes against iron. Georgia knew there was no point in arguing any further. No point complaining that she felt like a fatted cow being sent off to market – or should that be a lamb sent to the slaughter? They were flat broke. Her fate was sealed: she was to go along with her mother's plan to find her a suitable husband.

Estella treated them to a taxi from the station and Georgia pressed her nose up against the glass as it weaved through the streets of London. The journey from Devon had been over six hours long. It was almost dark now, and the city was retreating into a series of lights and shadows beyond the rain-speckled window of the cab. Despite her protestations on the train, Georgia had nothing against London. She did not consider it as beautiful or romantic as Paris, which had escaped the wartime bombing, but it was hard not to feel a thrill as she saw Hyde Park, and the Dorchester Hotel twinkling in the dusk.

Their destination was the home of her aunt Sybil and uncle Peter, who lived in a handsome white mews house behind Pimlico Road. As the taxi stopped outside and their trunks were unloaded, Georgia took a moment to admire its polished stone steps and shiny front door.

Sybil and Peter's uniformed housekeeper welcomed them at

the door as Sybil swept down the staircase behind her.

Georgia had not seen her aunt since the previous summer and thought she had aged considerably since then. She did not know Sybil's precise age but she guessed it was around forty-five. Certainly in her formal dress, string of pearls around her neck and completely grey hair, she looked a decade older than Estella, who was wearing pink capri trousers, a turban hat and a long white jacket made of alpaca.

'At last,' said Sybil, kissing them both lightly on the cheek. 'Come through,' she added, spinning round so fast that the expensive-looking navy fabric of her dress made a swooshing sound.

'Peter and Clarissa should be back any time. Mrs Bryant has prepared chicken for supper, but I suspect all you want now is a pot of tea.'

Mrs Bryant, the housekeeper, hovered at the door and offered to take their coats.

'You've done the house,' said Estella.

Georgia took a minute to glance around the room. If Sybil looked older since the last time she had been in London, then her house looked decidedly more modish. The stiff furniture and fusty antiques that seemed to belong in a Victorian parlour had all gone, and the new splashes of colour around the place appeared more suited to Estella's style of decor.

'I have just painted the chicken coop back at the farm this exact shade of fuchsia,' said Estella, drifting a finger across a bright pink ottoman.

'Really, how lovely,' said Sybil, her expression at odds with her words. Georgia had often felt that her aunt and her mother had nothing in common whatsoever – Sybil's background was as establishment as Estella's was offbeat and bohemian. In fact it was Sybil's position as the youngest daughter of the Honourable

David Castlereagh that had afforded them such a comfortable home, not Uncle Peter's Civil Service job in the Home Office.

'I found a wonderful designer, David Hicks. He's doing all the best people in London right now. So how was the journey?' asked Sybil as a clock chimed five in the distance.

'I can't say I was sad to leave the farm,' replied Estella, sitting down. 'Winter has been brutal this year. Fifteen chickens died during a particularly cold snap. To avoid going the same way, I was eating dripping on toast just to get fat and insulate myself.'

'I don't know how you cope, living in the middle of nowhere,' said Sybil with a dramatic sigh. 'You should have moved back to London years ago.'

Georgia had to stop herself from nodding in agreement. She had recognised as soon as she returned home from Paris that the little pocket of Devon where she had grown up was beginning to lose its allure.

'Perhaps. But I am an artist, and I need space and light. The farm is twice the size of this place, and if we moved to London we wouldn't be able to afford a garage, let alone something with a studio and potter's wheel. Besides, James would have wanted us to stay there.'

'James would have wanted you to be comfortable, not eating goose fat to protect yourselves from hypothermia.'

Georgia felt a wave of emotion at the mention of her father. He had died when she was only four years old, a victim of the war – a solicitor by trade, dispatched to the front line and killed in his foxhole in Normandy. Although she only had very vague recollections of him, Estella made sure that his presence was all around them at the farm. His fishing rods remained untouched in the hallway, photographs were displayed around the house, his books and papers were where he had left them in the study.

Mrs Bryant came into the room and put a white china teapot in the middle of the table.

'Sybil, I just want to say again how grateful we are to you for sponsoring Georgia,' said Estella.

Georgia almost snorted out loud. When Estella had first got it into her head that her daughter should do the Season, Georgia had been relieved to discover that not everyone was allowed to do it. You had to be presented at court by someone who had herself been a debutante, and traditionally this was supposed to be your mother. But Estella had learnt that there were ways around the system, and as Aunt Sybil had been a deb in the thirties – her debutante photograph sat for all to see on the new lacquered cabinet – it was decided that she should present Georgia, which had depressed Georgia for about a fortnight.

'My pleasure,' said Sybil, not entirely convincingly. 'Although I have to say, Georgia, you are rather late arriving in London.'

'I know. The train was very slow,' she replied, sipping a glass of orange squash.

'I didn't mean that,' said Sybil more sharply. 'You do know that the debs have been here since January, and some of the mothers since before Christmas. There have been lunches, dinner parties, all sorts of little getting-to-know-one-another soirées. Invitations to the best events of the Season have been secured before you even arrived.'

'I've had things to do,' said Estella, looking unconcerned at her ticking-off. 'A very important commission to finish, for one. The Earl of Dartington wanted a life-sized portrait of his wife, and she just wouldn't stay still, so it took for ever. Besides, Georgia didn't get back from Paris until a week ago.'

'I thought Madame Didiot's school finished in February.'

'It did,' said Georgia sulkily.

'So why have you only just returned to England now?'

You're lucky I came back at all, thought Georgia, knocking back the squash in one gulp.

'Well, we can make up for lost time now,' said Estella cheerfully.

'Not if no one knows who are you. I heard that you did not submit a coming-out portrait for either *Queen* or *Tatler* magazine.'

'Mum was going to paint me,' said Georgia, sticking up for her mother.

Estella stroked her daughter's hair. 'I thought she'd look sensational in oils. But time ran away from us a bit, didn't it. Surely it's not important, though?'

'It's extremely important. The portraits mark out the girls to look out for.' Sybil had begun to shake her head. 'You are completely unprepared for this. The pair of you. The presentations at the Palace are in a week's time and you have met no one. This is no joke. If I am to present Georgia at court then we have to take it seriously.' She had a sternness that not even the most scary nuns at Georgia's old convent school had possessed.

'Actually, I have planned a fork luncheon for the day before the presentations,' replied Estella in her defence.

'Well, that's a start. Who is coming?'

Georgia rattled off the names of five girls who were attending. Four of them had been at finishing school with her. Only one of them she had actually liked. The fifth girl was someone through her mother's art world connections, the daughter of a City trader that Estella had done work for.

'I can't say I've heard of any of them,' sniffed Sybil coolly. 'How about I ask around a few friends? Drum up support? Now, I assume you've got your wardrobe ready.'

They heard a click at the front door, followed by footsteps and voices, and Aunt Sybil's face softened.

'Ah, here's Clarissa. Just in time to talk fashion.'

Georgia stood up and gave her cousin a hug.

'How are you, George? You've cut your hair. Very Paris-chic.'

'And you look fantastic.' Georgia grinned, admiring her cousin's navy pencil skirt and soft turquoise jumper.

'Well, I work at *Vogue* now. Secretary pool, but still, I have to keep up appearances.'

'Clarissa, did you ever find that checklist we used for your season?'

'Yes. I sent Estella a copy a few weeks ago.'

Georgia turned to her mother, who looked blank.

'The post is very unreliable where we are.'

'I don't think I threw it away,' said Clarissa helpfully. 'Let me go and find it.'

She returned after a few minutes and handed a sheet of pale blue paper to Sybil, who read out loud from it.

'"Cocktail dresses – four. Evening frocks – six. Three dark, two pale, one white for Queen Charlotte's Ball. Palace dress – pale blue silk. Ascot frocks – two. Shoes – seven pairs. Gloves – assorted. Nylons – two dozen. Evening wraps – two. Preferably cashmere. Suits – one. Handbags – six. Hats – four." I notice we haven't put lingerie, girdles and perfume. I know they are not going to be seen, but I always think a girl's under-dressing is so important to make her feel special.'

She looked up and glared at Georgia.

'I assume you've got all these things covered.'

Georgia smiled weakly, thinking about the contents of her trunk. It was half filled with her Paris clothes – jeans, Breton tops and black polo-neck jumpers. There was a pair of jodhpurs and a few old cashmere sweaters that had belonged to her father and which had survived the moths. She also recalled some harem pants, a peasant smock her mother had saved from her time in Provence and a couple of house dresses they had found in the Salvation Army shop in Totnes, one of which had come with a matching oven glove. But nothing as fancy-sounding as an Ascot frock or a cocktail dress.

'I think we had better go shopping,' said Estella decisively.

'We can't afford all that,' replied Georgia, aghast.

'We can improvise,' said Estella, as her eyes darted down to the smart moss-green patterned fabric that covered the table.

It was Sybil's turn to look shocked.

'Georgia can't turn up to Ascot in a tablecloth, Estella, however handy you are with a needle and thread.'

Peter Hamilton walked in smoking a pipe. He was still wearing his overcoat and had a copy of the *Racing Post* tucked under his arm. He was touching fifty but was still a very good-looking man indeed, and if Georgia squinted there was a touch of her father she knew from the photographs.

'Hello, hello. My favourite niece. How are you, pumpkin?' he said, ruffling her hair. 'What's all this about tablecloths and Ascot? Can I join in the conversation or am I excluded on account of my sex?'

'Georgia hasn't got the appropriate wardrobe for the Season,' said Sybil witheringly.

'Clarissa, don't you have anything that she could borrow?' said Peter, turning to his daughter. 'There's a closet stuffed with taffeta and all you seem to wear these days are those tight skirts.'

'Peter, those are special dresses,' protested Sybil.

'Nonsense. I spent five hundred pounds and I haven't seen her wear them once since. They can't be that special. Clarissa, take Georgia upstairs and see if she would like to borrow anything.'

'Peter . . .'

Georgia watched a look of panic pass between mother and daughter.

'It's fine,' said Clarissa with more grace than her mother. 'Come with me, George, and you can tell me all about Paris.'

Clarissa's bedroom was at the top of the house. Her brother Richard was still at Eton, so she had the entire floor to herself.

'Fancy a ciggie?' she asked, opening the window and pulling a packet of Sobranie from her bag.

'So Daddy says you're not staying with us,' she said, sitting down on the bed.

Georgia shook her head. 'No. Your dad's found us a flat in Chelsea. Apparently it belongs to some journalist friend of his who is in Cairo. I think he realised that Estella and Sybil wouldn't last a week in each other's company.'

'Chelsea. What fun,' grinned her cousin. 'There's a great coffee shop down there I should introduce you to. Lots of cute Guardsmen from the barracks, too.'

'So how is *Vogue*?'

The two girls used to be close. At Peter's insistence, Clarissa and Richard would spend every summer in Devon, but that had stopped the year before Clarissa's own season, two years earlier. Despite the odd letter, Georgia was out of the loop with her cousin's life.

'I love it. Gives me an excuse to buy lots of clothes without my dad complaining.'

'Show me what you've got, then. Your mum nearly gave me a heart attack when she read out that list. A house dress and a pair of Turkish slippers aren't going to cut it at Buckingham Palace.'

Clarissa laughed, and lit her cigarette. 'What a shame you couldn't buy anything in Paris. I'm desperate to go shopping on the Rue Saint-Honoré. Dior is a genius. I wept when he died.'

'How could I afford Dior, Issa? I could barely afford a cup of coffee while I was at Madame Didiot's.'

Clarissa nodded in the direction of the large wardrobes that occupied both alcoves of the room.

'Go on then. Have a rummage. Anything but my presentation dress.'

'Why? Saving it for your wedding day?'

'Fat chance,' she said, taking a deep inhalation of smoke.

Georgia opened the wardrobe and gasped. It was fit to burst with shoes, coats and gowns. She opened a huge hatbox and pulled out sheaves of white paper that showed the first signs of colouring with age.

'Are you sure you want these, George? They're a bit fuddy-duddy, you know. It's all about the oval silhouette these days.'

'Stuff that – these are gorgeous.' Georgia trailed her hand across the satin and tulle. 'Look at this,' she said, pulling out a deep jade dress with a full skirt. 'It's the colour of a mermaid's tail.'

'I wore it for Fiona Meadows's cocktail party at Claridge's,' said Clarissa, balancing her cigarette on an ashtray she had pulled out from under the bed.

'Put it on.'

'Don't be silly.'

With little more encouragement, Clarissa stripped to her bra and pants and slipped into the dress.

'You look lovely.'

'Fat lot of good it did me,' Clarissa said, sinking to the floor, the yards of fabric spilling across the carpet like a pool of Caribbean water.

'So how are things in the love department?' said Georgia, sitting down next to her and grabbing a cigarette from the packet on the bed.

'A very handsome Coldstream Guard asked me out the other day.'

'Are you going to go?'

'Of course I am.'

The two girls giggled.

'Are you looking forward to it? The Season, that is.'

'No. Did you enjoy it?' Georgia turned away and blew a smoke ring.

'I loved it. But don't make the same mistakes I did.'

'Which are what?'

An expression of grave wisdom clouded Clarissa's face.

'The Season isn't about having fun, George. This isn't about parties or dresses or table manners. It's a competition. Don't ever forget that.'

Georgia gave a loud snort.

'A competition? So what's the prize?'

'The best man,' Clarissa said bluntly. 'The good ones get snapped up early. Apparently the Duke of Kent has already got a girlfriend, which is rather annoying. And avoid the Cirencester lot. You've got to jostle hard for position, for status,' she continued, enjoying her role as experienced sage, even though her advice was falling on deaf ears. 'I mean, do you think girls get chosen for the Queen Charlotte's, the Berkeley Dress Show, Deb of the Year by accident? You've got to watch some of the mothers, too – they can be the worst. This isn't polite society. It's a jungle in tulle. And believe me, because the Queen is abolishing the curtseying, the competition is going to be especially tough this year. Did you see the portraits in *Tatler*? There are some very beautiful girls.'

Georgia was laughing.

'Clarissa, I don't want to be Deb of the Year – I don't even particularly want to be a deb.'

'Well, you're about to be presented in front of the Queen, so I would say it's a little late for second thoughts. Have you been to see Madame Vacani?'

'Who's she?'

'An old lady based in Kensington. Former dancer – apparently she taught the Queen and Margaret how to foxtrot, plus she is the Curtsey King. Been doing it since before the Great War, and has taught it to anyone who's anyone.'

'Well, she hasn't taught me.'

'Then how are you going to do it properly?'

'You mean there's a proper way to curtsey?' Georgia was dimly aware of a curtseying lesson at Madame Didiot's, but she clearly hadn't being paying attention.

'It's getting a little bit late in the day to be asking those sorts of questions, George.' Clarissa stubbed out her cigarette. 'I'm going to have to teach you. Stand up,' she ordered.

'There are two sorts of curtsey. One's more informal than the other. You'll need the deep court one for presentation day. One foot behind the other, weight on the right foot and down you go.'

She demonstrated the move to perfection and Georgia copied her, her cigarette still hanging out of her mouth at right angles.

'Not like that,' Clarissa muttered. 'Throw your chest out, as Madame Vacani used to say.'

'This is silly,' said Georgia, collapsing to the floor in laughter. 'I'm going to ask Aunt Sybil for a drink. Under the circumstances, perhaps she'll give me a stiff one.'

Down in the kitchen, her mother was talking to Mrs Bryant about making aspic. Interrupting them for a moment, she asked the housekeeper if she could have two glasses of lemonade. Retreating back upstairs with the drinks, she heard Aunt Sybil and Uncle Peter in the living room, her ears straining even more when she heard her own name.

'Then I will pay for a dance,' Peter was saying, struggling to keep his voice low. 'We can have it in the garden.'

'I am not having fifty, sixty youths parading through the house just because you feel sorry for your brother's child,' said Sybil, her reply disappearing into a hiss. 'No one is forcing them to do the Season and they shouldn't be doing it if they can't afford it. I mean, whatever is the world coming to? We've got Khrushchev in the Kremlin, and now Estella joining the aspirational classes.'

'I have a duty to James. A duty to his memory. I have to do this. Every girl wants to be a deb, to be a princess, and I must do everything I can to support her.'

As Georgia ran up the stairs with the lemonade, she didn't know whether to laugh or cry.

CHAPTER SIX

Georgia didn't *feel* any different now that she had come out. She hadn't expected it to be momentous, of course – not in the way the whispers at the convent had suggested losing your virginity would be. But she had at least thought she might feel a little more grown-up, more sophisticated.

Still, the day hadn't been all bad. There had been lots of waiting around, of course – waiting in the cars as they all lined up along the Mall, waiting on the spindly little chairs for their turn to curtsey. But it had been secretly quite thrilling and oh so glamorous. Despite her resistance to the entire Season, the excitement of her fellow debutantes had been infectious. She had felt quite lovely in her pale blue silk dress, the colour of a Devon summer sky, bought as a gift by Uncle Peter. Prince Philip, who had been seated next to the Queen during the ceremony, had been heart-stoppingly handsome in the flesh – thank goodness she'd had to curtsey to him *after* the Queen, otherwise she feared she might have been too distracted to pull the move off successfully. Plus she had been fascinated to snoop inside the Palace – they had seen the drawing rooms, the corridor and the stairways lined with Yeomen, then the main event, the Throne Room, before retiring for tea and chocolate cake in one of the dining areas.

But pulling up outside the large white house on the edge of Eaton Square, she felt a loss of whatever enthusiasm she had had for the Season. How could anyone live in a place like this? she thought, looking down at the white vellum invitation and back up towards the imposing house ahead.

'Never knew there was a hotel here,' said the cabbie, breaking into her thoughts.

'It's not a hotel,' she said, fishing in her small handbag for a ten-shilling note, one of a hundred crisp notes that Uncle Peter had given her in an envelope to pay for the Season's expenses.

'Who lives here – relative of the Queen?'

'They're into refrigerators,' explained Georgia; it was all Aunt Sybil had told her about the family. 'That's where the money comes from.'

The cabbie was still shaking his head in disbelief as he pulled away, his tail lights disappearing into the darkness, leaving Georgia all alone on the pavement. She took a deep breath to compose herself.

The volume of debutantes had necessitated three presentation days, the last of which had been two days earlier. But they represented not the end but the beginning of the Season, and already Georgia could feel that London was buzzing with a party atmosphere that had definitely not been so palpable the week before.

Music floated from the big house in front of her as a group of young men, all dressed in white tie, like a tiny colony of penguins, approached from the south-west corner of the square.

Georgia felt intimidated. Grand houses and beautiful gowns like the one she was wearing – Estella had customised one of

Clarissa's linen dresses with her own artwork and a yard of silk – were things she was completely unused to. They felt too big for her, even if the dress had been altered to fit perfectly.

With the exception of the infrequent trips to London to see Peter, Sybil and her cousins, Georgia was not well versed in the ways of the wealthy. Her convent school had been solid, academic – used to educating the daughters of farmers and local businessmen and solicitors; her finishing school, as Sybil had pointed out, was not considered particularly elite – nothing like the Institut Le Mesnil in Switzerland.

Of course Madame Didiot had prepared her girls for being set loose on the Season and into society. She had taught them the dos and don'ts of going into the Stewards' Enclosure at Henley or the Royal Enclosure at Ascot. And she had particularly impressed on them the art of confidence in any situation. Georgia could hear her heavily accented words now: 'Confidence can make the ordinary beautiful. Stand tall, slow down, be interested, be interesting, and if you have nothing to say, ask a question.'

But Madame's words meant very little as she approached the house. She felt wretched and lost. It hadn't been like this at her little fork luncheon – a surprising success once Mrs Bryant had stepped in and helped with the catering. But there she had been surrounded by people she knew: her mother and aunt, plus a smattering of friends from Madame Didiot's.

Taking a deep breath, she proceeded up the black and white tiled path and into the house.

After the cold outside, the heat pressed against her. It was only a quarter past seven, and already the downstairs of the house was wall-to-wall with people. It had been the cocktail party that everyone was talking about – not only because it came so soon after the presentation ceremonies, but because Emily Nightingale's family was so mind-bogglingly rich.

As her eyes searched the room, looking for someone she recognised, Georgia wished she had been a little more sociable at her fork luncheon and at the Palace. There were at least two hundred people here at Astley House, and she knew none of them.

Threading through the crowd, eavesdropping on conversations, she realised that although many of the other debutantes did not know the other young people in attendance, they all seemed to have plenty in common – boarding schools, pony clubs or family friends. Georgia, on the other hand, seriously doubted that anyone else here had gone to Sacred Hearts Convent School for Girls in South Hams.

Accepting a glass of fruit punch from a waiter, she went and stood in a corner, deciding that she would seek out the hostess, thank her for her invitation and slip out shortly afterwards. Factoring in a couple of trips to the loo and a short loiter around the canapés, she reckoned she could spin out her stay to thirty minutes without too much discomfort.

'You'll never meet your future husband in the toilet. I mean loo,' said a voice to her right, as if it were reading her thoughts.

She turned and saw a pretty blonde, her hair scooped up in a chignon, voluminous breasts spilling over her dress like party balloons.

'It is loo, isn't it?' added the girl, frowning. 'Not bathroom. I can never remember which is U and non-U.'

'Non-U?' said Georgia, grateful for someone to talk to.

'Upper class. Non-upper class,' she whispered. 'There's a long list of stuff I've got written down in my handbag. Sofa, not settee. Writing paper, not notepaper. What, not pardon – although I think that sounds frightfully rude, don't you?'

'Well, I always say loo. What does that make me?'

'Posh, of course. I love your dress, by the way. Do you mind awfully if I ask whose it is?'

'It's mine,' said Georgia, feeling herself flush. The last thing she wanted to admit in front of this highly groomed girl was that she'd had to borrow her cocktail dress.

'I mean, whose is it? The designer?'

Georgia looked down and brushed her hands modestly over the linen skirt. She had to admit that she had been delighted when Estella had unveiled it. She had taken Clarissa's pale pink dress, made a few alterations to the bust and sleeves and, recognising that the fabric made the most wonderful canvas, painted peonies all around the hem.

'It's a one-off,' she said, smiling to herself.

'Well, I love it,' replied the blonde. 'When they announced that it was going to be the last of the presentations, Mum pulled me straight out of school and took me to Paris. Dad's a wizard in business and said you have to speculate to accumulate, so we had to get the best wardrobe we possibly could for the Season.'

'You were pulled out of school to go *shopping* in Paris?' Georgia didn't know whether to be horrified or madly jealous.

'Well, my parents were desperate for me to do it. All a bit of a rush, though. Thank goodness Mum had already sorted out a sponsor for me.'

'Sponsor?'

'We paid someone to present me to court,' she said without guile. 'Some old biddy who makes a tidy living out of her aristocratic credentials.'

'I wouldn't go admitting that. You know some people around here can be complete snobs.'

'But you're not. I can tell.'

The girl thrust her hand into Georgia's.

'Sally Daly, from Birmingham. Amazing how many people are here tonight, considering.'

'Considering what?'

'Considering that not everyone who curtseys stays on and does the Season. Most don't, in fact.'

Georgia stared at her in disbelief, feeling suddenly duped by Estella and Sybil.

'I wish someone had told me that before tonight.'

'You don't want to stay around for all the parties?' said Sally; it was her turn to look astonished.

'So where are you having your dance?' she asked, more brightly.

'I don't think I am.'

'Oh,' replied her new friend with a trace of pity. 'Well, you are to come to mine and we'll have such fun, although I'm not sure how we're going to be able to compete with this. Dad will be furious when he picks me up – I'm sure he'll insist on a good nose around.'

'Competitive, is he?' giggled Georgia.

'Life is one big competition for Dad.' Sally smiled back. 'I can't complain, though – that's how I got to wear couture.'

'Wow, that dress is couture?' Georgia suddenly noticed how exquisite Sally's dress actually was – the ostrich-feather trim, the pearlescence of the stiff tailored fabric just a little more beautiful and special than everyone else's.

'I got five of them,' Sally said, guzzling down her fruit punch. 'So let's play hunt the eligible. Mum's made a list of all the top deb's delights to look out for.'

'Deb's delights?'

'The men,' she laughed. 'Are you totally clueless? Pay attention, because one of them is going to be your future husband.'

'Not likely,' huffed Georgia.

'Then why are you here?'

'Come on, Sally. You can't really look me in the eye and tell me you're enjoying this. Turning up to parties, waiting, praying to be asked to dance, hoping, dreaming that it might lead to something more serious. I mean, did you see all the parents at the presentation, shuffling around, stiff, barely saying anything to one another? They probably had personalities once but marriage got in the way and drained it out of them. You've got a life to live. You don't want to get married. You don't want your wings clipped before you've even had the chance to spread them.'

'But I want to get engaged. As quickly as possible,' said Sally with astonishment. 'You might say that you've got to live a little before you get married, but I think you only start living when you have found your other half to share the journey with.'

Georgia considered her new friend's philosophy and wondered if she had a point. She took a prawn vol-au-vent from a passing silver tray and relaxed a little. Sally clearly wanted a playmate in her man-hunt, and besides, it would while away a few minutes until she could respectably leave.

Sally pointed out three Stephens, half a dozen Davids and a Malcolm who was apparently an interesting prospect if a bit of a lech. 'Not safe in taxis' was apparently the expression for men like him.

'That's Charles Darlington-Smith,' she said, pointing to a distinguished redhead who stood head and shoulders above everyone else. 'Nice family, good-looking, but it's something like his tenth season, which does make you wonder what's wrong with him.'

'So delights are a little older than us?' asked Georgia, her eyes still scanning the room.

'Generally,' confirmed Sally. 'Which is a good thing, because I want a man not a boy.'

Through the crowd Georgia could see an upright dark-haired

young man who was standing slightly apart from everyone else in a way that suggested he was enjoying being at the party as much as she was. 'Well spotted,' said Sally, nudging her. 'That's Edward Carlyle. Very rich. Family *own* a bank. Probably why he's a bit of a snob. Nice manners, though, apparently. VSITPQ.'

'What's that?' asked Georgia, looking at Edward Carlyle with intrigue.

'More code,' giggled Sally. 'Very safe in taxis, probably queer.'

Georgia couldn't help bursting out with laughter, and at that precise moment Edward Carlyle looked across and locked glances with her. She looked away and stepped back, embarrassed by the moment, wondering if he had heard them. She might not want to be here, but the last thing she wanted to be was rude, especially to someone who was probably feeling exactly the same about this night as she was.

'Well, I'm heading back in there,' said Sally with determination. 'The husband hunt begins. Can't let good couture go to waste.'

Georgia took another canapé and watched Sally disappear into the throng, silently wishing her luck.

'Georgia Hamilton, what are you doing here?'

She glanced round to see a more familiar face coming her way. Marina Ellis had been one of her classmates at Madame Didiot's. Although Georgia was grateful for the times Marina had allowed her first-floor bedroom window to be used as an escape route for the illicit nights out the finishing school girls used to have in Paris, she had still always found her a snob and a show-off.

'Don't sound so surprised,' she said politely, not missing the insinuation that she shouldn't be at such a smart party. 'How are you anyway? Having fun?'

'We're having such a giggle, aren't we?' Marina turned to her friend, whom she introduced as Melanie Archer.

'The house is almost as distracting as the men,' smiled Melanie, her eyes darting around the room like a hungry hawk's.

'I didn't know you were friends with Sally Daly,' said Marina, squaring up for a gossip.

'I only just met her.'

Marina gave a low snort of what sounded like relief.

'Well, don't let her cling on,' she said in a dramatic whisper.

'What's wrong with her?' frowned Georgia.

'People like that, families like hers, they just make me so cross,' said Marina, as if it were perfectly obvious what was the matter with Georgia's new friend. 'She is precisely the reason why the Season is finishing. What was it that Margaret said about every tart in London buying their way in?'

Georgia had heard the famous quote uttered by the Queen's sister, but the way Marina repeated it made it sound as though the Princess was a close personal friend.

'Sally's not a tart,' she said crossly. 'And she's not even from London.'

'That's right. She's from Birmingham, isn't she? Father deals in scrap metal or something peculiar.' Marina crinkled up her button nose.

'Well, she's wearing couture,' replied Georgia, 'so Mr Daly must be doing something right.'

'Couture is something you save for your trousseau, not wear before you have even kissed a boy,' said Marina, unmoved, as Melanie nodded in agreement. 'It's typical of these nouveau riche sorts. Cart before the horse and all that. I heard they've just bought a house in Switzerland and they can't even ski.' She and Melanie set about giggling.

Georgia heard the tapping of a spoon against a glass, barely audible above the din.

'Emily's daddy wants to make a speech,' said Marina. 'She's

cringing at the very thought of it, so we should go and lend some moral support.'

Georgia let the two of them go. She hadn't realised that Marina was such friends with the wealthy Emily Nightingale, and decided that some people were here to make as many beneficial friendship alliances as they were romantic ones.

The mention of Emily's name reminded her that she had not thanked her hostess yet and it was something she must do before she left.

There was a sweep of staircase at one end of the room, and she ascended it to a mezzanine floor that overlooked the party. It was quiet up here, with a good view of Emily standing nervously beside her father. She turned and saw a set of double doors behind her. It was roped off, but that only added to its intrigue. She unhooked the rope and opened the door to see what was behind it, gasping in delight as she saw that it led on to a beautiful terrace with views of the back of Belgravia's finest houses – huge bay windows lit up and glowing like pumpkins in the dark.

Faintly she could hear that the speeches had started, and she was glad she was away from it all. She opened her bag, pulled out her cigarettes and lit a Gauloise. As she inhaled, she could taste the tar and smell the honeysuckle that was creeping up a trellis next to her.

'Could I have one?'

She turned and saw a pair of the brightest blue eyes she had ever seen.

'I've only got two,' she stuttered quickly at the handsome young man who had come out on to the balcony. He had short dark blond hair and the hint of a winter tan, and he filled out his dinner jacket better than any other deb's delight she had seen at the party.

'Perfect,' he grinned as she offered him the remnants of her pack.

He stuck his cigarette tip into the flame that Georgia offered him from her lighter and smiled languidly at her.

'Couldn't bear the speeches either?'

'He's just a proud father, I suppose.' She took another drag of her cigarette. 'No, I came out here because I hardly know anyone in there and I thought it would be better to be alone with my thoughts than alone with a bunch of strangers.'

'Well, I can introduce you to some people. This is the second year I've done it. It's not so bad if you just relax into it.'

'You're an old hand at the Season then,' she grinned.

'It's a way of getting fed and watered for six months of the year. Plus it's rather nice to spend the evening with beautiful girls on moonlit terraces.'

She glanced away, embarrassed.

He blew a smoke ring, his inherent confidence obvious without him even saying a word.

'Allow me to introduce myself. I'm Harry Bowen.'

'Georgia Hamilton. Pleased to meet you.'

'Who would you like to meet? Although I'd be happy to stand out here all night talking to you.'

'But you don't even know me.'

'I've always found people who like being alone with their thoughts more interesting than most.'

'Actually I'd rather be sitting at a pavement café with a group of friends or in a jazz club listening to music. I'm not really the painfully introspective sort,' she smiled.

'So why don't we?'

'Do what?'

'Split from this place. We could go into Soho or to the King's Road. Actually, I have an even better idea. There's another party in Richmond, starting in about an hour, that a bunch of my friends you would really like are heading over to. We could drive out there, stay up all night and head for breakfast at Heathrow.'

'Richmond? Heathrow?' she said, secretly feeling swept up in the adventure of it all.

'I love the airport. It's a good job I haven't got my passport with me or who knows where we might end up. It's one of the reasons I joined the army. Other than the fact that I was too thick for university. I love the idea that we could get deployed anywhere.'

Georgia looked at him wide-eyed.

'But surely if you were sent away, you'd be going to war? I can think of safer ways to travel.'

'You say that as if you care.' He smiled and she felt her heart do a little flip. She was blushing, too, and was glad the moonlight was dim.

'What do you say? Stay or go?'

'I've love to get out of here, but I fear the speeches might go on for some time. I get the feeling that Mr Nightingale likes the sound of his own voice.'

'So let's just slope off.'

'How? We'll be spotted and dragged back in by the waiters. They probably have lassoes in their pockets.'

He laughed, and she felt good.

'Well, let's find an escape route.'

'It's all right for you. You have training for this sort of thing.'

Harry was already peering over the balcony.

'It's only fifteen feet or so down,' he confirmed. 'And there's a drainpipe all the way to the ground. Do you reckon you can do it?'

'Are you kidding? When I lived in Paris, I used to sneak out of windows twice as high as this.'

'You get more interesting all the time.'

Harry went first, shinning down in a matter of seconds. Georgia swung one leg over the balustrade and then the other, adjusted her feet and then edged along the rim of the balcony to follow him. Her heart was thumping and the back of her neck grew clammy as she grabbed the drainpipe.

'Why didn't we just walk out of the door?' she shouted as she clung on for dear life.

As the soles of her feet hit the floor, Harry grabbed her hand and led her to a door at the end of the garden.

'Open sesame,' he said, turning the heavy knob, and then they were out on to a Belgravia back street, laughing and panting as they ran past the grand, white terraced houses as if they had escaped from jail.

'My car's just here,' he said, leading her to a little Fiat.

He opened the door for her and she got inside. As the engine revved, she watched him move the gearstick into first, showing a flash of firm tanned forearm.

'I feel naughty.'

'Feels good, doesn't it?'

He drove quickly, the car nipping through streets that became less and less recognisable, telling her about his life in the Welsh Guards – about a difficult colonel, and the regiment's recent deployment to the Suez Canal Zone.

As they took a bridge over the river, Georgia sighed in delight.

'This is wonderful,' she said, the vista making her feel giddy. 'Walking along the Seine used to be one of my favourite things.'

'So let's take a walk along the towpath,' he suggested, indicating right and stopping the car beside a small pier.

He turned off the engine and draped his arm over the back of the passenger seat.

'So do you think the speeches have finished yet?' he smiled. He had a wonderful smile, she noticed, with perfectly aligned teeth that hinted at good genes.

'They've probably sent a search party out for us. Gosh, you know I didn't even say one word of thanks to the hostess.'

'Is she a friend of yours?'

'Never met her in my life. My aunt sorted out the invitation.'

'Then she won't even notice your arrival or departure, even though I'm sure a few of the men did.'

'Why do you say that?'

'People notice when the prettiest girl at the party isn't there any more.'

She looked down at her knees and could feel him turning in his seat.

'Look at me,' he whispered.

As she turned, his fingers stroked the underneath of her chin before cupping her face.

'Can I kiss you?' he asked slowly.

She had known him barely an hour, so she felt sure that she shouldn't allow his lips to go anywhere near hers. But in this tight, intimate space, after holding hands and running around dark streets together, she felt as if it was the most natural thing in the world.

She nodded, and his mouth brushed against hers.

He made a noise as if he were tasting her, and she liked how it sounded, liked how it made her feel – beautiful and desired.

The gearstick pressing against her leg was uncomfortable, but as his tongue pushed into her mouth she could feel it less and less.

'Come closer,' he muttered, as he came up for air.

She heard a rustle of fabric and felt his hand push up under her dress, rising smoothly higher and higher up her leg as her pulse raced faster and faster.

It didn't feel so right now. She could feel a strange fluttering sensation between her legs and it frightened her a little.

His fingertips touched the strip of flesh above the top of her stockings. It was as if his skin had seared hers.

'No,' she said softly, but he didn't seem to hear. His fingers kept on probing, hot and sweaty against her skin.

'Stop,' she managed to say more forcefully. 'Get off me.' She used one hand to push him away.

'What's wrong?' he said, jerking back and frowning at her.

All of a sudden, he didn't seem so attractive. Up close in the confines of the car, she could see the open pores on his skin, flushed slightly red. His lips were cracked, and those blue eyes were cold.

'Just stop,' she panted, wiping her mouth with the back of her hand, feeling her lipstick and his saliva smear across her face.

'Why? I thought we were enjoying it.' He frowned.

She sank back into her seat and regulated her breathing.

'It's wrong. We've only just met.'

'You didn't object when I stopped the car,' he sneered sarcastically.

'I wanted to take a nice walk along the river.'

'That's what they all say,' he said, shaking his head. 'You debs are all the same. You like to keep up appearances in those pretty little dresses, but deep down you all want it.'

Without thinking, she slapped him across the face, hard.

'You bloody little bitch,' he snarled.

'Believe me, you deserve a lot worse,' she said, struggling to open the car door.

'That's right, get out.'

'What a gent!' she shouted after him as the engine gunned to life and he roared off into the night.

CHAPTER SEVEN

As she stood there on the embankment, watching the tail lights of Harry's car disappear, it started to spit with rain. Shivering, she folded her arms around her body and cursed the weather, cursed Harry and cursed the whole damn Season. She had no idea where she was and there was no one around to ask. Ahead of her she could see a tramp coming towards her. He shouted something and it frightened her. She turned to walk towards the bridge, but her shoe slipped on the wet ground and she fell on to her hands and knees, smearing the front of her dress with slime.

Picking herself up, she suddenly felt lopsided, and as she looked down, she saw that the heel of one of her shoes had broken off. She kicked off the shoe and threw it angrily into the river, then, realising that it would be easier to walk barefoot, threw the other one in as well.

She hopped off the cobblestones and on to the pavement, which was cold and grainy underfoot. Away from the river the street was busier, and when she stopped and asked a man where the nearest bus stop or tube station was, he pointed across

THE PROPOSAL

the river, where Putney Bridge station was apparently located.

She shook her head as she walked. How could she have been so stupid, getting herself into that position? She knew that she wasn't exactly experienced when it came to the opposite sex, but she wasn't completely clueless either.

When she had finished at Madame Didiot's school, she had moved into a small rented room belonging to a friend of a friend. Liberated from flower-arranging classes and shorthand tuition, she had begun slipping in to lectures at the Sorbonne – she wasn't officially enrolled at the famous Parisian university, but her French had been good enough to talk her way out of trouble on the one occasion she had been asked for her student card – and it was here, in the back row of a lecture theatre in her last week in Paris, that she had met Jacques.

Afterwards they had shared a post-lecture cigarette in the quadrangle, where he had invited her for coffee to discuss the finer points of Molière. He was twenty-one, from Nice, and liked to think of himself as a communist. A few days later he had taken her to a jazz club, and then to a dive bar on the Left Bank, where they had stayed until 3 a.m. with a group of his friends discussing freedom of the arts in the Soviet Union.

On her last night in Paris they had gone for beer and *moules* in a café on the Left Bank where Hemingway and Fitzgerald used to drink. They had wandered over the Seine, across the Pont des Arts towards the Louvre, where they had kissed quite passionately in the doorway of the museum. She had rather panicked about the kiss before it had happened. At Madame Didiot's, the girls had crept into each other's rooms after lights-out and talked about their sexual experience – or lack of it – practising their French kissing with their hands, tongues pushed through the slim hole between thumb and forefinger. But when it had happened for real, it had all been rather instinctive and very enjoyable, even when Jacques' hand had slipped under her blouse. He had invited her back to his studio apartment in the Bastille, and when she had refused, he took it like a gentleman, which was why she had been so surprised at Harry Bowen's lack of grace and manners.

It was raining harder now. She looked down and saw that she was leaving a trail of dark fuchsia paint behind her.

'I don't believe it,' she said out loud, as tears began to well.

She could hear a car slowing down behind her. For a moment she dared not look around. That was all she needed – to get picked up by the police under suspicion of being a woman of the night.

'Are you all right?'

Turning around, she saw that a dark red sports car had stopped on the bridge. The passenger-side window had been wound down and she peered through to look at the driver. He looked vaguely familiar but she couldn't instantly place him, and her pulse started to speed up in panic.

'Are you okay?' the man repeated.

'I'm fine,' she stammered, knowing that she should carry on walking.

'We were both at Emily Nightingale's party earlier. In Belgravia. My name's Edward Carlyle – we didn't officially meet, so I'm sorry, I don't know your name.'

'Georgia. Georgia Hamilton.' She hesitated, then remembered what Sally Daly had said about him – VSITPQ – and stepped closer to the car.

'Look, do you need a lift anywhere?' he asked, shouting to be heard over the rain.

'Honestly, I'm fine. I think the tube is just across the bridge.'

'If you don't contract tetanus beforehand,' he said, looking down at her bare feet.

'Then I'll watch out for any rusty nails.'

Raindrops lashed against her face and she had to wipe her eyes to see him.

'Look, I don't wish to be rude, but I don't know you from Adam. You could have been drinking. You could be a complete sex-obsessed pervert . . .'

She watched one of his heavy brows rise in the darkness.

'Or you could smell my breath, use that phone box to tell your parents that Edward Carlyle will have you home within fifteen minutes, and avoid catching pneumonia.'

She thought about his offer for a moment, then opened the car door.

She watched his gaze fall to the hem of her skirt, which was now dripping with wet paint, and she could tell from his expression that he wished he had not made his offer. On closer inspection, the car was an Aston Martin, no doubt very expensive.

'I'm sorry. I'm melting,' she winced.

He reached over to the glove compartment, removed a newspaper and spread it over the passenger seat.

'Chivalry's not dead, then,' she said gratefully.

'Interesting dress. Is it meant to self-destruct?'

'It's hand-painted.'

'Watercolours,' he smiled.

She told him her address, then sat stiffly praying that she wouldn't get any paint on the black leather seats.

'So what are you doing out here?' she asked as he revved the engine.

'I was on my way to a party in Richmond.'

'So was I,' she said, wondering if he was a friend of Harry's, wondering if she should say anything about what had just happened.

'But it's that way . . . I saw you as I was coming over the bridge. I recognised you . . .'

'And you thought I'd lost my mind.'

'Something like that,' he muttered. 'Are you sure you're okay?'

'I might have some explaining to do to my cousin. This is her dress.'

'And where are your shoes?'

'En route to the North Sea.'

She realised he must think she was a lunatic.

'So are you enjoying it so far? The Season?' he said, breaking the awkward silence.

She snorted.

'I'm off to Paris as soon as the damn thing is over with.'

'Ah, a Francophile, are we?'

'I know it well,' she sniffed. 'I used to live there. I had a life out there, a boyfriend.'

'Really?' he said with interest.

'He was a communist,' said Georgia with some pride.

'My goodness. I don't suppose you told him about becoming a debutante, then.'

She frowned, realising that he had a point. Perhaps that was why Jacques had not yet replied to any of the letters she had sent him.

'I'm going to be a writer,' she explained quickly. 'That's why I'm going back to Paris. To write a book.'

'You don't have to go to Paris to do that,' replied Edward with annoying matter-of-factness.

She turned and frowned, watching his profile – a strong nose and a set jaw gave him a look of confidence that bordered on arrogance – and decided to stand her ground.

'Several of the twentieth's century greatest novelists might disagree with you. Joyce, Hemingway, Fitzgerald, Gertrude Stein, Ezra Pound all wrote some of their best work there.'

'Not because of the nice views and decent croissants.' He

shrugged. 'They were all escaping either war or Prohibition. Paris was more bohemian and liberal; it attracted artists like a honeypot and they in turn inspired and mentored one another. But it could have happened in any number of big cities. A coffee shop in London could become the next great literary salon. It's what's here and what's there that counts,' he said, pointing to his head and his heart. 'Everything else is just geography.'

'Well I found I worked very well there,' she said, sniffing. 'I had a favourite spot right in the gardens behind Notre-Dame. By the time I left two weeks ago, I had five diaries full of thoughts and scribbles.'

'Then there's your book. A memoir. *An English Girl in Paris*. You could even finish it between parties.'

'No one is going to be interested in the memoirs of an unknown eighteen-year-old girl. I want to be a novelist like Françoise Sagan.'

She could see him smiling to himself in the dark and it irritated her.

'So what about you? What does life beyond the Season hold for you?'

'I graduate in a few months,' he said, explaining that he was at somewhere called Christ Church, apparently part of Oxford University. 'My father works at a bank. I'll go and join him there, but at some point I want to live in New York.'

'New York?'

'What's wrong with that?'

'My mum always says that New York has no culture. No history.'

'Nonsense,' smiled Edward, as if she had said something quite ridiculous. 'The Met Museum is the best in the world. Plus jazz, art, theatre, film . . . It's like Paris was in the twenties.'

'You've changed your tune,' she replied haughtily. 'You were London's biggest cheerleader a minute ago.'

'London is a great city, but it will take another decade before it is fully recovered from the war. The Empire is dead. The class system is dying. You only have to look at the end of the deb season to know that. New York is the new centre of the world. So that's what I want to do. Open a division of the bank on Wall Street. One day the City of London will be the centre of the financial world again, but until that point, the global commercial heartland is New York.'

'Well, it must be nice to have it all figured out,' she said a touch more tartly than she meant. 'Meanwhile, I've got nothing to look forward to but six more months of stupid cocktail parties and dances.'

'Get a job.'

'I'm doing the Season.'

'But your days are free, give or take the odd trip to Ascot or a pheasant shoot.'

'I don't have any experience.'

'Work in a coffee shop. Meet people, observe them, people-watch. It'll all be good for your writing. Perhaps you could even start a literary salon.'

She wasn't sure if he was teasing her. Certainly he had the innate confidence of the rich, that self-belief that made her feel slightly uncomfortable, as much as his suggestions appealed to her. They were on the King's Road now and the neon lights from a row of coffee shops spilt on to the puddles in the street. Part of her wanted to go inside one. She wanted to drink espresso and learn all about jazz in New York, suspecting that Edward Carlyle was the sort of person who knew a lot about all sorts of things.

She was going to suggest it but he was already indicating right to turn on to her street, and she felt a faint pang of disappointment.

'Which number?' he asked, slowing the car.

She could see the upstairs light on in their little flat. Estella would be waiting up for her.

He pulled in to the kerb, and for a second the two of them sat in a silence that made her feel uncomfortable.

'Are you heading back to Richmond?'

'I think I'll give it a miss,' he replied, glancing at his watch.

'I'm sorry. I'm sorry for making you miss the party.'

'I should be thanking you. I really need to be getting back to Oxford.'

'No, thank you,' she said quietly. She got out of the car and looked back at him. 'Thank you for rescuing me.'

'Have a good season, Georgia Hamilton. You know, sometimes things in life are a little easier, a little more enjoyable when you don't resist them quite so much.'

CHAPTER EIGHT

'Georgia. The taxi is here.'

'I'll be there in a minute,' she called back from the comfort of her single bed, trying her best to disguise the sleepiness in her voice. The piping-hot bath she'd taken after returning home from the Swiss Chalet coffee shop behind Peter Jones had made Georgia very drowsy indeed. She loved her waitressing job at Chelsea's grooviest café – she was allowed to take home free cake, could sit and write during the quiet periods and had even had the odd patisserie lesson from André, the pastry chef. But when she got home, she was dead beat, which was fine when she could just go home and sleep, but quite dreadful when she had a party to attend.

She heard her bedroom door creak open, and when a dramatic gasp followed it, she knew that her slumber was about to be short-lived.

'You're not even dressed,' said Estella in panic.

Georgia pulled the blanket further up her face and groaned.

'Five more minutes,' she said, feeling all warm and cosy.

'But the taxi's here. The meter will be running . . .' Her mother strode over and tore the blanket back.

'I'm sorry, I was just tired . . .'

'It's that damn job, isn't it? We're going to have to put a stop to it if all you want to do is come home and sleep. Serving cream horns all day long isn't going to—'

'Isn't going to what?' asked Georgia, sitting up, the suggestion of giving up the café angering her.

Secretly she admitted that it was proving difficult juggling the job with the demands of the Season, which now seemed to have moved up a gear. But she earned almost ten pounds a week and already had forty pounds stuffed in her knicker drawer. Her French friend Grace said she knew of a room in a house in the Bastille that could be had for only sixty francs a month, and at this rate she would have enough money to move to Paris by the autumn.

'Isn't going to what?' she repeated. 'Find me a husband?'

Estella took the white dress that Georgia was due to wear that evening and flung it on the bed. It landed on the blanket like a swan shot down from the sky. Georgia looked at Estella and shook her head. She knew that it was unfashionable to have a good relationship with your mother, but she and Estella were genuinely close. Lately, though, she hardly recognised her mother, and couldn't believe she was choosing the silly demands of the Season over her own daughter's happiness.

'I'll meet you downstairs,' she said sulkily, swinging her legs out of bed and holding up the dress.

'No, I'll wait for you,' said Estella more softly.

Georgia went into the tiny bathroom to change, slipping on the white gown. It was not one of Clarissa's. It had been a gift from Topaz, and although Georgia had no idea where the money to buy it had come from, it was quite lovely – long, with layers of net and tulle that shot out from the waist like a tutu. She tucked her hair behind her ears, securing it with two small jewelled clips, pulled on her white gloves, and glanced in the mirror. For one second it was like looking at a Degas picture.

'I should probably mention that we're being collected . . .' said Estella through the door.

Georgia stepped into the hallway.

'Are Uncle Peter and Aunt Sybil in the taxi?'

'No, we're meeting them there.' Estella's eyes darted away from her daughter.

Georgia went to the window and looked on to the street, where a taxi was parked outside the house. Even from this distance she could tell that there was someone in the back seat, that he was male, in his twenties and wearing white tie.

'Mum, tell me what's going on,' she said, twisting back and glaring at Estella.

'Aunt Sybil thought you should have a dinner date. Apparently it's the done thing,' Estella said in a low, urgent voice.

'And that's him? In the taxi?'

Estella grabbed her arm and led her firmly to the door.

'He's a nice boy, a good family.'

'I'm not going,' said Georgia, trying to twist away from her.

'You are,' instructed Estella, shutting the front door behind them and herding Georgia down the steps and out on to the street.

He had already got out of the taxi and was holding the door open for her. He was a couple of inches shorter than she was, with sandy blond hair and a pinkie ring on his little finger.

'Frederick McDonald. How do you do,' he said with an obviously anxious smile. 'It's wonderful to finally meet. I've been hearing all about you.'

Georgia couldn't bring herself to lie that the feeling was mutual.

* * *

Queen Charlotte's Ball, one of the highlights of the entire Season, was being held in the Great Room of the Grosvenor House hotel. Cocktails were to precede dinner, which was to be served at 8.30. It was supposed to be a magnificent night and tickets for the event cost four pounds and four shillings each, not that Georgia's family had had to pay for them – Donald Daly, Sally's father, had announced that he had bought an entire table of ten and insisted that the Hamiltons should join them.

'George, here you are,' squealed Sally as soon as she had deposited her wrap in the cloakroom.

Georgia was glad to see her best friend in London. The two girls had become close ever since they had met at Emily Nightingale's cocktail party. Although they hadn't traded contact details then, they had started to see one another everywhere and soon had made plans to meet up away from the Season events. Although Sally was taking the Season very seriously indeed, she was an easy-going girl with a sense of fun and generosity of spirit that Georgia had warmed to immediately.

Georgia was still in a bad mood from her confrontation with her mother but gasped in delight when she saw her friend's gown – a floor-length confection in the palest vanilla made of duchess silk and tulle.

'So, what's your date like?' asked Sally, hooking her arm through her friend's conspiratorially.

'Even *you* know I had Frederick McDonald lined up for me this evening?'

'Well, my mother was doing a table plan and needed to call Sybil, so we got all the gossip.'

'Thanks again for the tickets. It was so kind of you.'

'I could lie and tell you that Dad's splashed the cash because you're the nicest, most fun deb on the circuit,' Sally whispered dramatically. 'But it was when I told Mum that your aunt was an aristocrat's daughter that my parents insisted we should share a table tonight. Such are their frightening levels of social climbing, they've even brought my brother Keith along, and I think Mum has seated him next to Clarissa. I hope she's not frightfully cross. Look, there they are being introduced now.'

Georgia glanced across the room and saw her cousin chatting to a rotund young gentlemen with a ruddy complexion and an ill-fitting dinner suit. Sally had taken after her attractive mother in the looks department; Keith was a dead ringer for their more aesthetically challenged father. Clarissa wasn't going to be cross. She was going to be furious.

'Frederick's cute,' observed Sally as they weaved through the tables, stopping every few feet to say hello to a fellow deb. Georgia surprised herself with how many people she knew here, having served lots of them in the Swiss Chalet coffee shop, which had proved to be quite a popular place for debutantes to meet their latest paramours. Fledgling romances developed over apple strudel and hot chocolate before her very eyes, and she had even heard whispers that a couple of her acquaintances hoped to be engaged before the end of the summer. Others she knew from her own cocktail party a couple of weeks earlier, an event that had gone surprisingly well. Uncle Peter had secured a room at the Chelsea Arts Club, which they had decorated with fairy lights. It had been a meagre finger buffet – Estella's attempts at aspic had been disastrous, her hoped-for gelatinous centrepiece little more than a bowlful of cold meats floating in a pond of thin pale pink fluid after the thing had failed to set. However, their provision of cocktails had been excellent. Georgia had been in sporadic communication with Edward Carlyle – a handful of letters had bounced between them following that night in Putney, after which she had sent him an invitation to her party. He hadn't been able to attend – apparently revision for Finals was getting a little bit hairy – but instead had sent a recipe book of cocktails, which she had plundered for ideas.

She glanced around the room to see if Edward was here tonight. He hadn't mentioned in their last correspondence that he was coming, but she was hoping to see a friendly face in this sea of stiff, white-gloved formality.

They took their seats at the round table. Georgia had been placed between Frederick and Keith – clearly Mrs Daly was hedging her bets, a thought Georgia didn't like to dwell on too long.

'Save me,' whispered Clarissa into her ear, before taking her place on Keith's other side. Georgia grinned back at her supportively.

The menus were written in French, but her command of the language was good enough to translate it. Soup. Fillet of sole. Chicken and potatoes. All of which she felt sounded much more exotic and delicious left in the original French.

'I love your crown. Where did you buy it?' asked Sally's mother Shirley, eyeing Sybil's tiara with desire.

'I was given it by my uncle when I married Peter,' replied Sybil politely.

'Don, maybe we can get one next time we go to Bond Street.'

Georgia hoped her aunt wouldn't point out that it had been in the family for generations, but Sybil maintained a discreet silence.

'So tell me about business, Mr Daly,' she asked instead.

'Doing well,' he smiled, tucking his napkin into the front of his shirt and summoning the wine waiter to bring over three bottles of champagne. 'It's going through the roof, in fact. Not bad considering I started off with a couple of old bicycles on the back of a horse and cart.'

'You were a rag-and-bone man?' said Clarissa, her eyes wide.

'Not too far off, love,' grinned Don Daly. 'But there's a big future in metal recycling. You seen those aluminium cans for soda pop? The lot will be recyclable.'

'Money for old rubbish.' Sybil laughed at her own joke.

'Sally says you work for *Vogue*, Clarissa,' put in Shirley, her eyes twinkling.

'That's right.'

'Do you go on fashion shoots?'

'Not yet. I'm only in the secretary pool.'

'She plans to move out of it any time now,' said Sybil with barely disguised disapproval. 'I must phone Audrey Withers and talk about your prospects, now you've decided to become a career woman.'

Georgia glanced over towards Clarissa, who was looking down in quiet shame. It was no secret in the Hamilton family that they just wanted to get her married off.

'And Sally tells me you work in a coffee shop, Georgia,' smiled Shirley, who had perhaps picked up on the tense atmosphere at the table.

'It's great.' Georgia grinned back. 'All the cake I can eat. And I even get paid for my break time, which is brilliant because that's when I work on my book, so it feels like I'm finally getting paid for writing.'

'That reminds me,' said Peter, taking a long sip of champagne. 'I was out for dinner with an interesting chap the other day. Quite a successful author, apparently. I should introduce you. I'm sure he can give you some tips on getting published.'

Peter's offer lifted Georgia's mood, so much so that the meal passed uneventfully and was even quite pleasant. The biggest surprise of the evening was Frederick McDonald, who was exceedingly good company. Georgia hoped that, while she didn't fancy him in the slightest, they could be friends.

The ritual of the ball occurred after dinner, when over a hundred of the attendant debutantes assembled upstairs before descending the sweeping staircase to the cavernous ballroom, where a giant twinkling white cake was to be cut in front of the Dowager Duchess of Northumberland. Georgia thought it was the most ridiculous thing she had ever seen, and it was not because of any sour grapes.

'You're not going with her?' said Don Daly as Sally left to join the 'cake' debs.

'I wasn't chosen,' said Georgia in a dramatic whisper.

'That's a shame,' said Mrs Daly, not unkindly. 'Sally's having a few more sessions at Lucie Clayton. You should come along next time.'

'I think attitude rather than deportment is the problem,' said Sybil more tartly.

'Let them eat cake,' whispered Frederick McDonald, which would normally have made Georgia laugh, but she was too angry with her aunt's rudeness.

The whole thing thankfully didn't take very long, and then the Bill Savill orchestra struck up, and Uncle Peter took Georgia's hand for the traditional father-and-daughter dance. She felt a pang of sorrow that she was not here with her own father, and at that moment Peter gave her hand a squeeze, as if he had recognised her sadness.

'Allow me to take this opportunity to tell you how proud I am of you. You have grown up into an intelligent and beautiful young woman,' said her uncle, smiling gently.

'Thank you,' she grinned. 'And thanks for thinking of me when you met that author.'

'You have to ignore Sybil,' he said after a moment. 'You know she only wants the best for you and Clarissa.'

Georgia snorted. She didn't mean to be impolite after all her aunt and uncle had done for her, but Sybil's constant and obvious disappointment was beginning to grind her down.

'Why do you put up with it, Uncle?' she wondered out loud.

'Marriage is a compromise,' replied Peter matter-of-factly.

'It's not a compromise. Marriage has to be just right; you have to be perfect for each other. Otherwise what's the point?'

From the sidelines she could see Estella watching them, and she thought about her own parents' marriage.

Georgia had not been a particularly romantic child, but growing up in their old, lonely farmhouse, she had loved hearing her mother telling how she and James Hamilton had met and fallen in love, and had asked for the story again and again as if it was some sort of fairy tale.

How James had been in Paris on business and met Estella, who had been sketching on a table of a pavement café in the 14th arrondissement. They had started walking and talking, beginning in the little street in Montparnasse and ending up on the other side of the city in Montmartre, sitting on the steps of the Sacré-Coeur watching the sun rise over the Eiffel Tower. How by the time they had got to the banks of the Seine Estella had decided that she was going to marry James Hamilton, and how they had taken their honeymoon in the city just before the outbreak of war had put a stop to any further visits.

In the back of her mind Georgia had always wondered if the real reason her mother had sent her to Paris was so that she might have that same sort of heady, romantic discovery. And yet, alas, here she was being set up with the likes of Frederick McDonald, who was sweet and funny but who had as much chance of setting Georgia's heart racing as he had of setting foot on Mars. You could not force love, she decided, making a mental note to include that point in her memoirs.

Uncle Peter was tapped on the shoulder and Frederick asked if he could cut in. Georgia took his hand and they started to waltz.

'So what was all that curtseying to the cake thing about?' he asked above the sound of a soaring clarinet.

'Surely you've been to one of these things before?'

'I haven't, actually. I'm not quite sure if your aunt Sybil remembers trying to fix me up with Clarissa two years ago, but I couldn't make it.'

'You must be hot property,' teased Georgia.

'More like I'm twenty-four and my parents think it's high time I found a wife.'

Frederick danced as well as a Frenchman, which was a considerable compliment. She wasn't sure if he held his breath the whole time, but she certainly couldn't hear him panting in her ear, which was the usual hazard with her dance partners.

'How about we waltz across to the far side of the room out of eyeshot of the grown-ups and just get drunk?' said Frederick finally, and Georgia decided she liked him more by the minute.

They took two cups of fruit punch, and Frederick pulled out a hip flask and poured a stiff measure of alcohol into each.

'We're going to have to get very drunk to get through this thing.'

'I'm not that bad, am I?' laughed Georgia.

'I didn't mean it like that . . .'

'So you are going to be a diplomat?' said Georgia, remembering what he had told her at dinner.

'One day. Perhaps.'

'You don't sound very excited about it.'

'I really want to be a journalist. Can you imagine going to the theatre or to the Summer Exhibition and getting paid to write about it?'

'My mum says it's wonderful when your job is your hobby. She says you never have to retire because what you do isn't work.'

'She's an artist, isn't she? I heard she did some rather fabulous pictures of the debs at your cocktail party.'

'You heard about that?' After the disaster of the aspic, Estella had had to improvise to give the party a little kick, and had decided to do a five-minute sketch of each guest as a going-home present.

'My sister's friend went. She's quite proud of her caricature. Seemed to overlook the fact that she'd been given a nose the size and shape of a banana.'

'Mother said she was experimenting in cubist cartooning.'

'She should do a strip for the *Evening Post*.'

'That would be fun, wouldn't it?' Georgia sighed.

Glancing back at Estella, she saw that she was being asked to dance by a rather dishy-looking deb's delight. She was not wearing white so Georgia felt sure the young man could not be confused. However, she did look pretty sensational. Not dissimilar to Lola Wigan, the ethereal debutante who had modelled the bride's dress at the recent Berkeley Dress Show and who was the hot tip for winning Deb of the Year later that summer. Unlike Georgia, Estella was just impossible to resist.

She excused herself from Frederick and went to the loo to freshen up. She found an empty cubicle, flipped down the lid and took a breather. Spurred on by Uncle Peter's promise to introduce her to the author, she took out her small notebook from her silk bag and started writing some notes about her experiences of the night, including a few interesting turns of phrase that Frederick had used. She wasn't entirely sure what use it would be, except that she had decided that the sequel to *An English Girl in Paris* should be about a country girl in London documenting her experience as a debutante in 1958. How strange it was that she was writing her second book even before she had finished her first, she thought as the words came swiftly.

Her ears twitched when she heard her name.

'I see the two most curious debutantes of the season are sharing a table,' said a voice she only faintly recognised

'And who might that be?' said another.

'The Birmingham girl with the enormous bosoms, and Georgia Hamilton.'

She peered through a crack in the toilet door and saw three girls standing in front of the mirror reapplying their lipstick. It was Marina Ellis, her friend Melanie from the Eaton Square cocktail party and another debutante.

'I think she's quite pretty,' said the unknown girl.

'Pretty?'

'She wears beautiful dresses.'

'I thought you meant Georgia!' giggled Marina. 'She looks as if she has fallen out of the Salvation Army half of the time.'

'I was still surprised that Sally got to accompany the cake.'

'Her father has bought his way into everything else; why should it stop with Queen Charlotte's Ball? Probably slipped the Dowager Duchess a fistful of guineas to make it happen.'

'He's not the only one buying favours,' said Melanie, lowering her voice.

'What do you mean?' asked Marina, smelling gossip.

They huddled more closely around the basin. Georgia thought they looked like Macbeth's witches around a bubbling pot.

'I heard from a very good source that when Estella Hamilton paints a picture, it's not just the canvas she gives a bit of slap and tickle.'

Marina gasped.

'She sleeps with her clients?'

Melanie nodded.

'That's what I heard. Some friends of my mother's, the Chases, commissioned her for something or other, and apparently she got far too friendly with Mr Chase. So much so that Mrs Chase ended up throwing the painting out of the window.'

'It doesn't surprise me one bit that she's promiscuous,' said Marina with feeling. 'She looks it. All that red lipstick and hair.'

Georgia felt her hands quiver in anger. She was tempted to step out of the cubicle and confront them, but they had already changed the subject.

'How is your date?' Melanie asked Marina.

'Dull as brass,' she groaned. 'I've got my eye on Charlie Edgerton. He's already asked me to dance twice, so I need to ditch the date and take him up on his offer.'

'What are we waiting for, then? Let's go and find him . . .'

Georgia shut her notebook and took a deep breath through her nose.

'How dare they!' she whispered out loud, determined that they were not going to get away with it.

She left the Ladies' and went back into the ballroom. Estella was talking to the father of one of the debs. Melanie's words echoed in the back of her mind, but she blotted them out with force.

She could see Marina flirting with a tall, dark-haired man with saturnine eyes. Unlike Sally, Georgia had not made a mental log of all the deb's delights on the circuit; however, Charles Edgerton was a veritable jackpot of good looks and good family, too eligible not to be known – or at least recognised – by everyone.

She watched them waltz across the dance floor, his tails swinging back and forth like a raven's wing. Marina was not the most beautiful deb around, but she had certainly made an effort tonight, and even Georgia had to admit that they made a handsome couple. They danced for two songs, after which Charles excused himself. Georgia realised that this was her opportunity. She tapped him on the shoulder and he spun round.

'Excuse me,' she said, gathering herself up to her full height.

'Yes?' he replied, his eyes fleetingly looking her up and down as if he were assessing a prize filly for the Derby.

'It has come to my attention that certain debs' mothers have compiled a list about how eligible the young men on the circuit are. They have a code. NSIT. Not safe in taxis. VSITPQ. Very safe in taxis, probably queer. You rate very highly, by the way. In fact you're something of a catch.'

'Why, thank you,' he said, looking momentarily off guard.

'You should probably know that I have been compiling my own list,' continued Georgia. 'Thought it was fair to let the gentlemen know what they are letting themselves in for, considering us girls are armed with so much information.'

He smiled cautiously.

'That young lady you have been dancing with. She's on my list,' she said, pulling her notebook out of her bag and looking at her scribble. 'Ah yes, here she is. Marina Ellis. GFLPCVD.'

'And what does that mean?' he asked, frowning.

'Good fun, loose, probable carrier of venereal disease. Something about an unfortunate liaison with a sailor during her time in Paris.'

The mention of Paris made him stand up and take notice. No doubt Marina had been boasting about her time on the Continent.

'VD?' he said slowly.

'Only a rumour. I'm sure she'll deny it, but you just can't be too sure,' said Georgia, snapping her notebook shut and lowering her voice to a whisper. 'I hear these sexually transmitted diseases are dreadful to get rid of once you've been given one, so good luck. Tread carefully.'

She waited one second and watched his mouth drop open, then turned on the slim heels of her shoes and returned to her table.

'Mum, we really should be going,' she said, removing the champagne from her mother's hand.

'But it's so early,' protested Estella.

'I'm tired . . .'

'Oh Georgia, stop it. Stay and dance with Freddie.'

'Fancy another spin?' said Frederick, offering his arm.

'Go on,' urged Estella as Frederick led her off.

'Hide me,' whispered Georgia, hooking her arm through his.

'What on earth have you done? Spiked the punch? Laced the Dowager Duchess's cake with arsenic?'

'Worse.'

'Darling Georgia, you really are a feisty one.'

They went to retrieve her wrap in anticipation of a quick getaway. When they returned to collect Estella, they were met by Sybil with a face like thunder.

'We need to talk,' she told Georgia sternly.

'I was just leaving.'

'That might be appropriate,' replied her aunt, her mouth in a fixed, unsmiling line.

Georgia gulped hard.

'A debutante is in tears over there, and apparently it is all because of you.'

Georgia glanced towards the exit, wondering if she should make a run for it.

'Apparently you have been spreading wicked lies about her. Did you not think it would get back to the person concerned? Did you not think it would wound and offend her?'

'I don't care,' said Georgia defiantly. 'She deserved it.'

'Deserved it! Georgia, the organisers of the ball have got to hear about it and demand an immediate apology.'

'I'm not saying sorry. Not after what she said about my mother, and my friend.'

'The Dowager Duchess witnessed the crying!' said Sybil, not even listening to what Georgia had to say. 'You won't be able to show your face on the circuit again.'

'Good. I told you at the beginning, I don't want to be here. Stupid, snobby girls and silly tiaras and men who only want to get their hands down your knickers.'

Sybil gasped.

'If your father was alive today . . .'

'If my father was alive, he wouldn't want me to go through this ridiculous charade. Because he married my mother for *love*, and that's what makes you happy.'

Sybil's expression changed as her gaze moved beyond Georgia. She looked bemused and then frowned.

'What on earth is Mrs Bryant doing here?' she said quietly.

Georgia turned and saw the housekeeper.

'What's wrong?' asked Sybil with obvious panic.

'Mrs Hamilton, I need to speak to Miss Estella as soon as possible.'

'She was at our table a minute ago,' said Georgia, trying to locate her. 'Why do you need her?'

Mrs Bryant looked down, then back at Georgia.

'A phone call came through to the house. A phone call from Devon. Something terrible has happened, Miss Georgia. The farm, your farm in Devon. I'm afraid it's burnt down.'

CHAPTER NINE

Arthur didn't look right. As the train pulled into the station in a hiss of steam, Georgia could see the big man standing on the platform, twisting his cap between his huge hands as though he was wringing it out. He saw Estella leaning out of the open window and waved, but there was no smile to accompany it. Georgia's heart sank. Seeing Arthur Hands without a grin was like seeing roses in winter: ragged and bare. The ruddy-cheeked farmer and his wife had been running Moonraker Farm on behalf of the Hamiltons for as long as Georgia could remember, and to her Arthur was as much a part of the Devon countryside as the rocks or the oaks, and every bit as solid and strong. Yet here he was, his head bowed, his eyes red. Georgia knew in that moment that it was worse than she had imagined.

'Miss Estella, Miss Georgia,' said Arthur humbly. 'Wish I could say it's good to see you.'

Estella didn't speak; instead she threw her arms around the big man and squeezed. 'Oh Arthur, what's to become of us?' she whispered. They stood there for a long moment, then Estella broke away and took a deep breath, suddenly brisk and businesslike.

'Now tell me, how are you and Marjorie?' she said. 'Here we are sobbing away when you have lost your home too.'

'Oh, we're fine,' said Arthur, his hands working on his cap again. 'Good job Marjorie woke up in the middle of the night; all parched she was, s'pose it was the smoke. Well, she elbowed me and I smelt the burning straight off, otherwise . . .' He shook his huge head. 'It ripped through those buildings like tinder. We'd never have stood a chance.'

Georgia and her mother exchanged a glance. She knew they were both thinking the same thing: if they hadn't been away in London, they could have gone up with the farm too.

Estella squared her shoulders and looked up at Arthur.

'How bad is it?' she said.

Arthur winced.

'Bad. I ain't gonna lie, Miss Estella. It's bad.'

Georgia felt a swell of anger as she watched her mother trying not to cry. How could he have let it happen? Wasn't that why the Handses were there – to look after the bloody farm?

'Does anyone know how it happened?'

'Not sure, Miss Georgia. We might never know, the fire officer says. He's been there all morning. They think it might have started in the studio.'

'But I don't understand, Arthur,' said Georgia, unable to hide her anguish any longer. 'I mean, fires don't just magically start, do they? Was something left on? A candle, a light, a cigarette or something?'

Arthur looked at her with hurt in his eyes. He hadn't missed the accusation and Georgia immediately felt bad. After all, Estella was right, the Handses had lost their home too.

'We never go smoking in your house, Miss Georgia,' he said. 'Honest, we didn't do anything wrong. We only went in to water them plants of yours. Marjorie said some of them was looking a bit droopy.'

He looked at Estella, his face creased.

'Perhaps it was the electrics. Old wiring and that.'

'Yes, yes, of course,' said Estella, glancing at Georgia. 'No one is suggesting you did anything wrong. On the contrary, I can't imagine there'd be a stick left standing if you hadn't raised the alarm.'

'Perhaps not,' said Arthur quietly. He was looking down at the ground, but Georgia could tell that it was worse than either of them had supposed. From the farmer's expression, she doubted there *was* a stick left standing at Moonraker.

It was a twenty-five-minute drive to the village. Georgia usually loved trundling along the country roads in Arthur's bright red Morris Minor, the radio turned up loud, the windows wound right down, but not today. Every yard, every turn of the wheel was bringing her closer and closer to something she wasn't sure she could bear to see. With silent shame, she recalled the countless times over the past few months she had dismissed the farm as old, backward and unforgivably dull. She could vividly remember strolling along the Seine's Left Bank with her chic metropolitan friends, mocking the farm with its run-down hen coops and muddy streams. How they had all laughed at the ridiculously out-of-touch farmers and their tiny cottages. But now? Now Georgia would have given anything to see that tumbledown house standing proudly in its yard, the chickens pecking and scratching in the dirt. She wanted to be able to look out of the kitchen window at the distant copse, or lie on her creaky four-poster bed and listen to the sound of the pipes groaning as the old iron bath filled next door. But as they turned into the lane, she knew that she would never do any of those things again. The farm had gone. For a moment she couldn't breathe, and she covered her mouth with her hand.

The fire hadn't just charred the beams and left smoke marks up the chimney; it had completely consumed the house. The brick walls were still standing, but where the shuttered windows and the cheery yellow door had been were gaping holes, like pulled teeth, while the roof was nothing but blackened rafters twisted and cracked by the heat, poking up into the sky like a witch's fingers.

They climbed out of the car in a trance. 'It's gone,' whispered Estella. 'It's all gone.'

'We can save some of it,' said Arthur. 'Them walls is still . . .' He trailed off.

'No, Arthur,' said Estella, shaking her head. 'Look at it. Everything's gone.'

A squat woman with a tear-stained face ran over and embraced Arthur. Marjorie Hands looked terrible, white and exhausted, and she seemed to disappear as Arthur put his arms around her.

'Marjorie,' said Estella sternly. 'Have you slept at all?'

The woman shook her head.

'Then we must find you a bed as a matter of urgency.'

Georgia looked at her mother with surprise. This was a woman who could have a meltdown if she couldn't find her favourite painting smock, but now, in the midst of all this chaos, she seemed to be rising to the challenge.

'We were going to go and stay with my sister,' said Arthur.

'The sister who lives in Minehead? Heavens, Arthur, that's two hours' drive from here. No, you must stay at the Feathers.'

Arthur looked awkward.

'Actually, I've already spoken to Phil at the bar, arranged for you and Miss Georgia to stay there.'

117

'Nonsense,' said Estella firmly. 'There is only one room at the Feathers; you must take it.'

'Mum . . .' said Georgia.

'No, darling, Marjorie's need is greater than ours. I'm sure we can make do here. Please, Arthur, be so good as to take her there straight away.'

Georgia watched longingly as the couple silently got into the car and turned back on to the road. There was still a fire engine parked some distance away from the main building, and a cluster of firemen standing by the barn. She pulled her mother to one side, out of earshot of the men.

'Mum, how are we supposed to "make do" here?' she said urgently. 'Look at it, there's nothing left.'

'There's the potting shed, that's still standing,' said Estella. 'And I believe it's well stocked with horse blankets.'

'We can't sleep in the potting shed,' said Georgia, wide-eyed. Was her mother serious?

'Well, we're going to have to start lowering our expectations now, Georgia,' said Estella.

'The Feathers is hardly the Ritz.'

'Now don't be uncharitable. We are responsible for the Handses, don't forget. Besides, we are younger and more robust than them. We will be fine.'

She might have been younger than Arthur Hands, but you would be hard pressed to find anyone more delicate or highly strung than Estella Hamilton. The fact that she was seriously contemplating sleeping under horse blankets made Georgia look more closely at her mother. Perhaps the shock had been too much for her. She was about to say something more when a tall man in uniform approached. 'Mrs Hamilton? I'm Geoffrey Marks, the chief fire officer. I'm sorry to meet under these circumstances.'

Estella offered a dainty hand.

'Not at all, Mr Marks, it's kind of you to be here. What can you tell us?'

'The buildings are too precarious to examine at the moment,' he said, looking across at the still-smoking ruins. 'So I could only hazard a guess as to the cause. But I can say the fire seemed to begin over there.' He pointed towards the studio – or rather, what little was left of it: a chimney breast and a pile of black timber. 'It then spread to the main farmhouse and across to the annexe where I believe Mr and Mrs Hands live. They were very lucky, I have to say. By the time they woke up, the heat must have been fierce.'

He took them around the farm, taking care not to get too close, and it was only then that Georgia could see the true extent of the destruction. There was literally nothing left. Paintings, carpets, curtains, even that creaky four-poster bed, all reduced to ashes.

'When I go back to the station, I'll make a few calls,' said Mr Marks. 'I'm sure we can find you temporary digs. You can stay with me and my family if needs be.'

Georgia almost smiled at that. She was sure that no one she knew in London, even with their huge houses, would have offered to personally put them up. *And to think I was mocking the country,* she thought, her face flushing.

They stood there alone and watched as the fire engine turned back into the lane and disappeared.

'Oh Georgia,' whispered Estella.

Georgia held her mother as she sobbed into her shoulder. It was as if she had been holding herself together while other people were there – that British stiff upper lip – but now that they were alone, all her anguish, all her heartbreak was pouring out.

'Come on, it's not that bad,' said Georgia uncertainly. 'Look, there are still walls. We can rebuild it.'

'What with?' asked her mother. 'How will we pay for it? There was no insurance. And everything we owned was inside those buildings.'

Her voice was trembling now, her earlier stoicism replaced by open distress, her body shaking.

'Then we will do it ourselves.'

'How? I don't even possess a paintbrush any more.'

'I have my savings from the coffee shop,' said Georgia. 'Almost forty pounds.'

'That's sweet, darling. But how far do you think that is going to get us? Will it pay to rebuild the farm? Will it pay for a new apartment when Peter's friend returns from Cairo in the autumn and wants his place back? The war widow's pension isn't very much, believe me. I just don't see how we're going to get by.'

'We will,' said Georgia firmly, squeezing her mother's slim shoulders. 'And remember, we've got each other, that's the most important thing.'

'I suppose,' said Estella, but she didn't sound convinced.

'Besides,' said Georgia, determined to look on the bright side, 'we didn't lose everything in the fire. We have all our things in London. And you still have those paintings you did for the exhibition last Christmas.'

'You mean the paintings that didn't sell.'

Estella looked towards the black pile of the farm.

'There's nothing left of him,' she said in a whisper.

Georgia knew what she was talking about. Him: her father. Everything they had owned of James Hamilton had been stored in three large trunks and scattered around the house here and there: photographs, mementoes, letters, clothes, all the things that could not be replaced even if they had bucketloads of money.

Every last scrap of paper, every last hint of him had gone in the fire. It was as if he had been wiped from history.

Georgia hugged her mother again. There was nothing else she could say. Finally she stepped back and took a deep breath.

'Right, I'm going for a walk.'

'Where to?' frowned Estella.

'There are three pubs and a guest house between here and Dartmouth. One of them is bound to have vacancies. I'm not convinced the potting shed will be very comfortable.'

'Darling, it's almost four o'clock. It will be getting dark by the time you've walked to Dartmouth and back.'

'I'll be fine,' she said, swinging her bag over her hip. 'Why don't you stroll down to the Feathers and check on the Handses? Perhaps Arthur has some ideas about rebuilding the farm.'

Georgia felt better as she tramped across the meadow. She felt less helpless now she had a purpose, plus she needed to get away from that horrible burnt-out shell and everything it represented. In front of her were fields and a glimmer of the sea. Behind her was a life she couldn't go back to even if she wanted to.

She breathed in the warm air, smelling the cut grass and the meadow flowers, the constant buzz of bees everywhere.

If only we could just build a cosy nest out of nothing, like the bees do, she thought.

As she walked, her mind drifted to her friend Flip, the only girl from school she had invited home during the holidays. Flip was a quiet girl, but she had a big heart, unlike many of the catty pupils at Sacred Hearts Convent School. Georgia had been aware that Flip was rather nervy at school – so obsessed with cleanliness she had to wipe down the loo seats with surgical spirit. She had worried that her friend would despair at the tip they lived in – Estella had never been particularly concerned with tidiness or indeed any sort of order. But Flip had thrived during her week with the Hamiltons. The girls had gone walking in the Dart Valley, shrimping along the beaches of Blackpool Sands, getting scrapes on their knees, sand in their shoes and dirt under their fingernails. Estella had declared that they looked like little wild girls, with twigs in their hair, and Flip had told Georgia that Moonraker Farm was her idea of paradise. Perhaps she was right. The South Hams looked particularly glorious today. The fields were a patchwork of colours – from the palest yellow to the deepest and most luscious green. To her left was a field of corn with tall yellow flowers punctuated by a rash of scarlet poppies, and every now and then she would get a flash of the distant sea, glinting in the sun.

The first pub she came across – the Swan – did not have rooms, and the guest house at the crossroads was full. But Georgia found a Vacancies sign outside a little Bed and Breakfast just a mile outside Dartmouth. Seeking out the wizened old owner – she had to be at least eighty, Georgia guessed – she managed to bargain her down to a pound a night. Having secured accommodation for two nights at least, she pressed on down the hill into Dartmouth, the tang of salt in the air getting stronger as she drew closer to the harbour. The tiny post office on the winding high street was still open, the postmistress just beginning to cash up, although she grudgingly allowed Georgia to buy a pad of paper, a thick black crayon and a packet of drawing pins. Georgia winced at the cost – suddenly every last penny seemed vital – but she knew that helping Mr and Mrs Hands was the right thing. She felt awful about accusing Arthur earlier – there was no way he would ever have done anything to endanger Estella or her family. Besides, without Moonraker Farm, the elderly couple were in exactly the same situation as Georgia and her mother, and she couldn't let Estella shoulder the additional burden of looking after them. She walked down to the quayside and sat on the wall, dangling her feet over the edge, her eyes drifting across the River Dart to the boats bobbing on the silvery-green water. She tapped the crayon against her lips thoughtfully, then began to write.

LOST HOME IN FIRE

Hard-working mature couple available for work.
Lodging preferred. Contact Arthur Hands at the Feathers, Capton.

She nodded with satisfaction – short but to the point, and once she had posted them all around town it would certainly have an impact. She used all fifty sheets of paper, nailing her posters to noticeboards, trees and telegraph poles, using one of her stout walking shoes to bang in the drawing pins: wouldn't do to have them blow away now that she'd gone to all this effort.

Happy with her handiwork, Georgia set off back up the hill towards the farm, snaking back through copses and overgrown country lanes as the sun slowly sank behind her, leaving a chill in the air. It wasn't until she got close to the farm and caught the scent of charred wood on the breeze that she remembered with a jolt what was waiting for her at the end of that little lane.

She found Estella picking through the debris in her studio, her back bent like a coat hanger. From this distance she looked like an old woman, her face as pale as the ash settled on the fence posts.

'Darling, you've been ages,' she said, straightening up with some effort. 'I was worried.'

Georgia bit her lip as she saw the pathetic collection of items her mother had dragged from the dirt: an oil lamp, a charred picture frame, a blackened teapot. She couldn't cry now; today had been all about being positive, about doing things, not looking backwards. She had to be strong for Estella's sake.

'The fire officer told you not to go in there,' she said.

'Nonsense!' said Estella, rubbing her hands on her already filthy skirt. 'As if there's anything else to collapse. Anyway, I thought I might find . . .' She shook her head. 'Silly really. I'm going to have to get used to the idea that it's all gone, aren't I?'

'Well, I've found us somewhere to stay – that black and white B and B outside Dartmouth. Apparently their bookings don't pick up until midsummer, so we have plenty of time to sort things out.'

Her mother's eyes opened wide.

'Oh no. We can't stay in Devon,' she with astonishment. 'No, no. It's out of the question.'

'But Mother,' said Georgia, gesturing towards the ruined farm, 'there's so much to do. We can't go back to Chelsea and behave as if nothing has happened.'

'Well, we can't do anything here,' said Estella. 'Not until we get some money anyway. No, we shall go back to London and I'll begin straight away.'

'Begin what?'

'Finding a man, of course,' said Estella.

'A . . . man?'

'Oh, don't worry. I don't have to love him,' said Estella airily. 'No one will ever replace your father. This is simply a practical step, a career move really. I will wear neutral clothes, a touch of make-up and cut my hair – I am too old for long hair now.'

'But Mother, you don't need to change.'

'Oh, but I do. All this,' she indicated her unkempt appearance, 'all this is scaring men away. I'm too *unusual.*'

Too eccentric, too highly strung, too artistic. That was what she meant. Bohemian. Fast. All the words Georgia had heard whispered behind her back by so-called society women jealous of Estella's beauty. But she supposed they might have a point when it came to securing a husband. After all, her mother had hardly been snowed under with offers since the war. There had been interest, of course, but there had been gossip too. Marina and her friends laughing at the artistic Estella Hamilton, insinuating things, giggling and whispering.

'Can I ask you a question?' said Georgia.

'Of course, we have no secrets, darling.'

'Did you sleep with those men?'

'Which men?' said Estella, her face going even paler.

'The men who asked you to paint their wives' pictures.'

Estella looked away.

'That's not the sort of question you should be asking your mother.'

'But did you?'

Estella shook her head, but Georgia wasn't sure if she was answering or thinking about the depths to which she had sunk.

'Why do you think I wanted you to do the Season?' she said finally. 'Because I tried to marry well – and I failed. I failed because no man was interested in me. No one, not really.'

'But you're beautiful,' said Georgia softly.

Estella gave a small, hard laugh.

'Oh, it would have been easy to find someone who was willing to keep me in some small apartment in Marylebone, just visiting at the weekends. I'd have had furs and jewels and plenty of time to do my nails. But anything more? No.'

Georgia frowned. She knew about the stigma attached to divorced women in polite society, but Estella was a widow – a war widow, in fact. There was no shame in that. There could only be one reason why men would not be interested in someone as attractive as her mother. Georgia herself. The inconvenient daughter.

'Is it because of me?' she asked. 'Did the fact that you had a child put them off?'

Estella laughed.

'Don't be silly. It's not because of you, it's because of me. I mean, look at me. What do you see?'

Georgia took in the clothes: dirty, but stylish in their own way; the smudged face, lovely even behind the soot; and her elegant frame. She thought her mother looked a little like an ageing fairy. A touch past her prime, perhaps, a little worn, but still sparkling with magic.

'I see a unique, wonderful woman with so much to offer,' she said honestly.

Estella snorted.

'Well, let me tell you, that isn't what men see. Yes, they find me attractive – for an evening or two. But there are plenty of pretty women in London.'

'Not as pretty as you.'

'Perhaps, but those women are happy to be . . . simple, I suppose. To sit there and simper and nod and give the occasional little laugh. Those are the sort of women rich men want to marry: the easy ones. They want a wife, not a challenge. And they certainly don't want someone whose heart belongs to another – and always will do.'

Georgia glanced towards the farm, as if her father might be sitting there in the kitchen window watching them. But of course he couldn't be. He was dead, however much she might wish otherwise. And anyway, there was no more kitchen, no more farm. They needed a plan – and quick.

'Well, I have another idea for you,' said Georgia. 'Actually it was my friend Frederick's idea. You're an artist, aren't you? You paint, of course, but that's not all you can do.'

'Georgia, you don't need to be kind. I love what I do and I think I am quite good at it, but I'm not deluded. I realise the big, famous artist's career isn't going to happen.'

'I was thinking you could just diversify. Those cartoons you did at my cocktail party were fantastic. Why don't you think about doing that for a living?'

'Cartoons?'

'A funny for one of the papers. There're lots of different types of art and lots of different ways to make a living as an artist. In the meantime, I'll go back and do the Season. And this time I'll do it as it's supposed to be done – to land a decent rich boy.'

Estella's face clouded.

'Don't be so silly; *you* must marry for love. It's one thing me looking at marriage as a career move; I've had my love match.'

'Yes, but you and Dad were special.'

Estella shook her head.

'Darling, you'll be nineteen soon. Every girl of your age must aspire to one great romance in their life. What about that French boy, Jacques?'

Georgia shook her head.

'Jacques who has never responded to any of my letters? Hardly the grand passion.'

In that moment, it all became clear to her. All those emotions she had poured into her letters, the longing and the dreaming; it had just been a fantasy. A silly schoolgirl fantasy. Yes, she had loved Jacques, even if he had never returned the feelings. But what was the point? Why pine after a man who just saw you as a plaything? If men were so very fickle, so unreliable, she might as well direct her affections towards someone who could bring something to the table. Like money. Like security. Like a house with an actual roof and windows, not charred timbers and gaping holes.

'No,' she said. 'I'm not going to throw myself in front of some eligible bachelor just on the strength of his huge mansion in Gloucestershire, but there's no harm in finding a man who can give us a little more than this.'

They both turned at a rumbling sound coming up the lane and saw the Handses' red Morris Minor trundle into the yard.

'Come on, Mother,' said Georgia, stepping towards the car with purpose. 'Let's check you in to the B and B and a nice hot bath. Things will look much clearer in the morning, I promise.'

'Miss Georgia, Miss Georgia,' beamed Arthur Hands as he got out of the car. 'You'll never believe what has happened. A hotel in Dartmouth has just called and offered us room and board in return for doing their gardening!'

Georgia grinned at him, then allowed herself one last glance back at the farmhouse.

It's only a house, she said to herself. *It's only bricks and mortar.* It was time to leave it behind. It was time to move on. Things could only get better.

CHAPTER TEN

23 December 2012

Amy poured two black coffees from the urn in the lobby of the Plaza Athénée and took a welcome sip of one of them. She smiled as the hot liquid slid down her throat. Not only did she need an injection of caffeine to chase away the jet lag, but the thick black liquid reminded her how good coffee always was in New York. It was one of the many things she missed about her home city. She was very glad to be back, even though the winds were bitter and she still hadn't got any Christmas presents for her folks, with the exception of a tin of cookies her mom loved from Fortnum and Mason that had cost her three days' worth of tips.

Through the hotel doors she could see Georgia standing on the sidewalk, pulling up the collar of her cashmere overcoat to protect herself from the cold.

'Here. Coffee. That will warm you up,' she said, going out to join her.

Georgia eyed the Styrofoam cup and shook her head politely. 'That's kind, but no thank you.'

'Are you sure? A cup of coffee is like the world's best hand-warmer.'

Amy caught Georgia's expression and looked down at the cup.

'Is this one of those finishing school things?' she said, remembering Georgia's stories from the previous night.

Georgia smiled.

'I'm sure it seems horribly old-fashioned to a generation brought up on Starbucks, but we were taught that food and drink should be consumed inside. Unless it's a picnic, of course.'

Amy stood there holding the cups, not knowing what to do. 'Ma'am?'

The doorman stepped across and took them from her.

'I'll take care of them,' he said with a wink.

'Thanks,' she said, blushing.

When she turned back to Georgia, she saw Alfonse pulling up at the kerb.

'Where are we going?' she asked.

'I thought the Frick this morning,' said Georgia as Alfonse trotted around to open the door for her. 'I would rather like to see Van Gogh's *Portrait of a Peasant*. Apparently it's just around the corner, but at my age it might as well be the other side of the city.'

It wasn't far – six blocks or so – but Amy wasn't going to complain about being driven in luxury. Besides, she had never been into the Frick Collection, though she had passed the grand building on many occasions, and it seemed fitting somehow to pull up in a town car. The entrance was impressive, with grey stone pillars and wide polished oak doors.

'Say, you know this used to be one guy's house?' said Alfonse, as he opened the car door for Georgia.

'Henry Clay Frick. He was chairman of Carnegie Steel,' said Georgia briskly.

'That's the guy. S'all right for some, huh?'

Inside, the Frick was sumptuous. Beautiful wooden floors, long drapes with stiff pelmets and floor-to-ceiling panelling, all created specifically to house Frick's collection of art. Amy tried to imagine it as a private house, with maids and butlers buzzing around tending to their master.

'It must have been magical to live here,' she said.

'I'm sure it was. Considering.'

'What do you mean?'

'Considering Frick claimed that he only built it to make Carnegie's house look like a miner's shack.'

'Rich people are competitive, aren't they?' said Amy, struggling to imagine what it would be like to be so rich.

Georgia nodded.

'I suppose that's why they are rich.'

Amy wandered over to pick up a headset for a commentary on the collection, but Georgia held up a hand, taking a guide-book instead. Once again Amy felt she had made a mistake; the feeling obviously showed on her face, because Georgia touched her arm.

'Force of habit,' she said. 'I've spent a lifetime around books, so I always go there first.'

Amy nodded, put on her headphones, and began to listen to the commentary about the museum. As she took in the history of the great house, she realised how little she knew not just about art but about New York's heritage. She'd passed the enormous buildings along Museum Mile a million times but she'd had little idea that most of them had once been the private houses of the city's greatest industrialists. Her lack of knowledge embarrassed her but did not surprise her. Dancing had always been the priority in her life. From the age of four when her mom had first taken her to Miss Josephine's dance academy, nothing more than a room above a laundromat, Amy had chanelled any spare time she had into dancing, training and dancing some more. It wasn't that she was stupid – in fact she had graduated from Kelsey High with a 2.1 grade point average. Not terrible considering that she had spent most of her school life in ballet shoes. But she was self-aware enough to know that there were holes in her learning. Holes that had been particularly exposed when she had been out for dinner with Daniel and his Oxbridge friends and they had started talking about politics, literature or world events.

She pulled off her earphones and walked over to Georgia, who was standing in front of a portrait of a man in a spotty fur coat.

'Quite a collection of Old Masters, isn't it?' said Georgia, glancing at Amy before returning her gaze to the picture.

Amy eyed it dubiously. To her, it looked just like a rather dark painting of a gay nobleman long dead, but she wasn't about to say so. She looked at the label. 'Titian, *c.*1488–1576.' *Should I have heard of him?* she wondered.

'So when does a New Master become an Old Master?' she asked, deciding that she needed to enter into the spirit of things.

Georgia smiled.

'Officially, an Old Master is a European painter who worked before 1800 – Vermeer, Fragonard, Albrecht Dürer. After that, it's considered the modern era. Henry Frick was by all accounts a difficult individual, but at least he should be congratulated on his taste and his vision. This collection is quite splendid.'

She looked at Amy, who had fallen quiet.

'You don't agree?'

'It's not really my taste,' she said diplomatically. 'It's a bit old-fashioned.'

Georgia nodded and touched her arm.

'Come this way,' she said, walking across to another painting, this time of a rather grumpy-looking man with a big chain around his neck.

'Hans Holbein's portrait of Sir Thomas More. Now ignore all the velvet for a moment,' she said. 'Just look at the face and the hands.'

Amy peered closer. She couldn't deny that it was an amazing bit of painting. The skin seemed to glow with life; the man even seemed to have stubble.

'Now imagine he's wearing a suit and tie. Or a baseball cap if you prefer. Can you picture him as an actor or a folk singer, someone you might see on TV?'

'Yes, I mean, it's like a photograph really,' said Amy. 'Only more real, somehow.'

'This painting is almost five hundred years old, but even so, you somehow get the feel of the man.'

'Yeah, he looks really ticked off,' laughed Amy.

'Funny that you should say that: he was executed by Henry VIII shortly afterwards.'

'Executed?'

'Beheaded at the Tower of London, I'm afraid to say.'

'I know the place.' Amy grimaced.

Her eyes searched the painting once again, and instead of dwelling on that last night with Daniel, she found herself transported back in time, back to the days of Thomas More and Henry VIII, and although she knew very little about that period of history, it suddenly came alive in front of her.

They walked slowly through the rooms, Amy looking at the art in a wholly different light, wondering who all these people were, frozen in time, what their stories were and how they came to be immortalised on the walls of this amazing house built on greed and spite.

'This is pretty amazing,' she said, wandering around, wanting to reach out and touch it. 'It must be worth a fortune.'

'The money of the Gilded Age.'

'Georgia, can I ask you something?'

'Of course.'

'How do you know so much about art? Well, not just art, but all sorts of things.'

Georgia stopped and looked at the slim gold watch on her wrist.

'Well, I think that's a question best answered over lunch.'

Amy looked at her own watch. Damn, was that the time? They'd been in the Frick for hours.

'Actually, I have a confession to make. I booked us in somewhere.'

Georgia looked surprised.

'Yeah, I know it's your trip and all, so feel free to say no, but I thought that as I'm kind of your guide to the city, I could show you a little slice of my New York. It's not far away.'

She bit her lip. When she had made the booking, she had imagined it being a wonderful surprise where she could impress the naïve old lady with her insider knowledge, but now she just felt presumptuous.

'Sorry, I really shouldn't have . . .'

'No, no,' said Georgia, taking her arm and turning towards the exit. 'I'd love to see a little of the real New York while I'm here.'

Amy pulled a face.

'I'm not sure it quite counts as the real New York, but it means a lot to me.'

'Then that's good enough reason,' smiled the old lady.

* * *

Amy's misgivings increased as Alfonse pulled up outside the restaurant. There was an enormous queue snaking from the entrance down the street.

'Serendipity 3?' said Georgia, reading the sign on the black shop frontage as they stepped out of the car. 'Is this the place?'

'Don't worry, we have reservations, we don't have to queue,' said Amy as she led the way through the narrow entrance, past racks of aprons, New York paraphernalia, cookbooks and brightly coloured confectionery that looked as if it came straight out of Willy Wonka's chocolate factory. No wonder Serendipity was a New York institution, the dining equivalent of Disneyland, the sort of place kids pestered their parents about for a birthday treat. Or at least that was how it had been for Amy. Growing up in Queens, a trip to Serendipity with her mom was like a visit to the circus and the fairground all rolled into one, sitting under the giant stained-glass lampshades and eating banana splits until she thought she would burst, or coming here for ice cream before the annual trip to see Santa Claus at Macy's. As they walked up the stairs, all those happy memories came flooding back, and she couldn't help smiling, despite the noise – inevitably, most tables were crowded with eight-year-old kids out of their minds with excitement and sugar. Georgia looked absolutely bewildered.

The waitress showed them to a table for two and handed them the enormous black and white menus. Georgia put on her reading glasses and seemed to be examining hers in forensic detail.

'Foot-long hot dogs,' she read, and then looked at Amy over the top of her half-moon lenses. 'Now tell me, what exactly is a chilli dog? One hears of these things in movies and so forth, but I have always wondered.'

Amy giggled.

'It's a hot dog with chilli on the top.'

'Together? I mean, spooned on top of the bun thing?'

'Exactly.'

Georgia turned back to the menu.

'My goodness!' she exclaimed. 'There's a pudding here for a thousand dollars.'

'The Golden Opulence,' said Amy. 'I never tried it, but I think you get gold leaf sprinkles and flavoured caviar and a golden spoon to eat it with.'

'Hmm, my mother used to have a phrase: "more money than sense",' said Georgia.

'Well, my mom used to bring me here on my birthday and she had a saying too: "you don't come here for a salad". You've gotta splurge. Seeing as it's a special occasion.'

'Speaking of which, when are you planning on seeing your parents?'

'That's up to you . . .'

'You should go tomorrow night, of course. Christmas Eve. You should certainly wake up in your own bed on Christmas morning.'

What Georgia was suggesting was far more generous than Amy had been expecting.

'But what about you?'

Georgia waved one thin, crepey hand.

'Don't worry about me. I intend to have a quiet night with a good glass of wine. Now, let's order. How about a pot-pie and this thing called frozen hot chocolate?'

Amy giggled.

'You've read my mind.'

They ordered from the waitress and Amy smiled at the sight of a table of noisy kids laughing and making a glorious mess. As she slurped her frozen hot chocolate, she glanced up and saw Georgia looking at her.

'You didn't feel very comfortable in the restaurant last night, did you?'

Amy shrugged.

'The food and the wine were great, but it just reminded me of a night I had in London a couple of weeks ago. The night when me and my boyfriend kind of finished.'

Georgia prodded gently, and Amy found herself unburdening the story of the Foreign Office dinner.

'I never thought it mattered which glass or knife you used, not really. But apparently it does to some people.'

'It sounds as if your boyfriend's parents set you up to fail, deliberately. I find unkindness more of a cardinal sin than any lapse in table manners.'

'I think Daniel was just too influenced by his family, by his background.'

'Are you making excuses for him?'

'No,' she said. 'I'm just sad. Sad that there are still people out there who want to make you feel bad about yourself just because of where you come from.'

'I believe it was Eleanor Roosevelt who said that no one can make you feel inferior without your consent.'

'So now it's my fault?' she queried.

'Not at all. I just think you should stop thinking you're not good enough and remind yourself precisely how wonderful you are.'

'Easier said than done,' Amy said, twisting her spoon around her empty glass. 'I live in a tiny studio apartment, I have some great friend at the Forge, but we all know it's just paying the rent. My career is going nowhere. My life is going nowhere . . .'

'Then make it go somewhere.'

'It's easy for you to say.'

'Because I have money?'

Amy nodded.

'I never used to.'

'I'm sure you had a classical education; that can take you places.'

Georgia looked thoughtful.

'Indeed, education can be the key that opens many doors. But in my day, university wasn't considered a serious option for well-brought-up young ladies.'

'So did you go?'

'I went to Cambridge.'

'There you are.'

Georgia laughed softly.

'I worked very hard to get there, with very little encouragement. Well, with the exception of someone . . . someone I met at the Season. Someone I cared for very deeply. He encouraged me to value education, curiosity, wherever it could be found. So when it came to it, I thought I should try and get into the best place I could, seeing as everyone was rooting for me to fail.'

'Why the hell didn't people want you to succeed?'

'Certain people.' The old woman's face was inscrutable. 'So I worked very hard to show them what I was made of,' she continued as if she did not want to dwell too much on the details. 'I graduated, joined a publishing house. I always had rather lofty ideas about being a writer, but as it turned out, I was better at shaping other people's words and ideas. I got married to someone I met in the industry, got divorced, had a little money and decided to start my own company.'

'Make money for yourself rather than for other people,' smiled Amy.

'I was certainly focused. But it was more about the love of books and being able to publish those books my way that drove me.'

'You make it sound so easy,' said Amy, putting her elbows on the table and resting her chin in her palms.

'It was easier building up a company without a family and children to distract me.'

'Exactly. Who needs men?' said Amy defiantly as Georgia asked for the bill. She had felt wretched at Annie's, when all her dreams of a future with Daniel had seemed to be in tatters. But talking to Georgia made her realise that there were new dreams out there to chase and catch hold of, like running after dandelion clocks in a summer field.

'Will you help me?' she said softly.

'Help you with what, dear?' asked Georgia, tapping her pin number into the credit card machine the cheerful waitress had brought over.

'Help me make a fresh start, change my life, improve it . . .'

'I'm not sure how I can help . . . I could certainly point you in the direction of some interesting authors, give you some books . . .'

'Teach me to stop being such a klutz. Teach me to be elegant. Teach me to be a lady.'

Georgia was chuckling softly. Not unkindly.

'I thought we were talking about being a modern woman, not some old-school deb whose life revolves around a man.'

'Please,' said Amy, remembering how stupid and uneducated she had felt at Daniel's dinner parties. 'Please teach me stuff.'

'Amy darling, much of what I learnt at finishing school is outdated now. I'm sure your ballet training means you can do a better curtsey than I can. Things change, move on. Besides, you shouldn't be motivated by the way Daniel and his family treated you. They don't matter.'

'You said yourself that all that stuff you do without thinking was part of your arsenal. Learning all those things you know wouldn't be about pleasing Daniel or his parents; it's about never again feeling like I did at the Tower of London. It's about never feeling so freaking awkward because I don't know how to behave, about never feeling stupid even though people probably haven't noticed I've got nothing to offer to their intelligent conversations. It's about never wanting to feel not good enough again.'

Amy felt her shoulders sink, her whole body consumed by the force of her emotions.

'Now that, that I can understand,' said Georgia quietly.

She looked at Amy for a long time.

'All right,' she said, wiping her lips with her napkin and placing it at the side of her plate. 'First lesson: leave the napkin where you found it.' She stood up.

'Where are we going?'

'If you're going to play the part of a lady, then we need to start where every good actor starts.'

'Where's that?'

Georgia's eyes twinkled.

'With the shoes.'

CHAPTER ELEVEN

Alfonse dropped them on Madison Avenue. Amy pulled her thin coat around herself. The wind was tugging at her skirt – she hadn't been exaggerating when she had told Georgia that New York could be one of the coldest places on earth. When the wind blew past Liberty Island, across the Hudson Bay and up through the concrete canyons of downtown, it only seemed to get colder on the way.

'Brrrr!' she said, stamping her feet. 'Are we going far?'

Georgia smiled. 'Far? But my dear, we're already there.'

Amy looked up at the building in front of them, a huge limestone pile almost grand enough to rival the Frick. She glanced at the small type either side of the arched doorway.

'Ralph Lauren?'

'My New York friends assure me that this is the most elegant store in the world.'

'But I can't go in there,' said Amy.

'Why ever not?'

'Well, for one thing, I can't afford anything they sell.'

'You're a woman, Amy,' said Georgia. 'I'm sure that's never stopped you before.'

'That's exactly what I'm worried about,' she replied, immediately picturing some snooty sales assistant railroading her into buying a pair of five-hundred-dollar shoes she'd spend the next two years paying off. But what was really stopping her was the fact that she had often yearned to go inside shops like this but had always kept on walking, feeling too insecure, thinking that someone would spot her and shout, 'Impostor!'

Georgia linked her arm through Amy's. 'Come on, before we both freeze,' she said.

Still Amy resisted.

Georgia held up one finger.

'You've been on the stage; think of this as the same thing, all right? You're playing a role. Remember that no one in any shop knows who you are, they have no idea of your background and they can't magically see inside your bank account. Look as if you were born to be there, that you can afford to buy the whole store, and they will treat you accordingly. I promise.'

Amy nodded and stepped inside.

Even remembering Georgia's words, she found it hard not to let her mouth drop open. This wasn't like any old shop; it was like walking on to a movie set. A sweep of elegant staircase dominated the lobby. Crystals dripped from giant chandeliers. An upstairs room decorated like a billionaire's wife's boudoir with thick oyster-coloured carpets and pastel-hued silk camisoles hanging off rails was in fact the lingerie department. Another room was decorated like a de luxe drawing room, panelled on all walls by racks of beautiful clothes.

'Look at the price of these,' whispered Amy from the side of her mouth, holding up the label on a pair of knickers. Georgia put her hand over it.

'Never look at the price,' she said.

'You're kidding, right?'

'No, my dear. First look at the garment, feel the quality, assess whether it will last for years. Finally ask yourself – and answer honestly – "Is it right?"'

'Is it right?'

'Is it right *for you*? Will it flatter you? Ignore what the magazines have told you is all the rage this season, ignore what you feel comfortable in, and certainly never, ever buy anything you think will fit if you lose five pounds. If you can follow all those rules, you will only ever buy clothes that show you off to your best.'

'But Georgia, they cost—'

The old woman held up a finger.

'Price is irrelevant. If you buy only classic, quality pieces you will have a much smaller wardrobe, but it will be a wardrobe of clothes you wear. Expensive they may be, but they will be clothes you look forward to wearing. And – this is the most important thing to remember – just by getting dressed in the right clothes each morning, you will not only look like a million dollars, you will feel it too.'

Amy was about to argue that it was hard to look like a millionaire on her meagre clothes budget when she noticed that Georgia was already moving back downstairs to the shoes. Her stomach gave a jolt. *Oh God, she doesn't expect me to choose a pair without looking at the price, does she? I'll be working double shifts at the Forge until next Thanksgiving.*

'Size seven?' asked Georgia absently.

'Six,' replied Amy, picking up a hot-pink strappy heels and sighing. She had a soft spot for anything high and strappy. Her greatest ever bargain was a pair of sparkly Gina heels she had found in a charity shop in Chelsea, which she had worn and worn until the straps had literally fallen apart in her hands, because they made her feel as sexy as Beyoncé even if she was only doing the ironing.

But as she looked up, she saw Georgia shaking her head. One look told her to put the pink shoe back down. Instead she held aloft a black, mid-heel suede pump scooped low, with a pointed toe.

Amy couldn't help wrinkling her nose.

'Try these,' ordered Georgia.

'I'm not sure they're me,' said Amy diplomatically.

'Why ever not?' asked Georgia with surprise.

'Well, I don't work in an office.'

'A shoe like this shouldn't be hidden under a desk,' gasped her friend. 'They are special-occasion shoes.'

Amy smiled weakly, remembering her last big night out. The time before the Tower of London party. She'd gone clubbing in King's Cross with some guys from the Forge – their unofficial works night out. The floor had been sticky, beer had been flying everywhere, but at least she'd been wearing trainers. Special-occasion shoes like the ones Georgia was holding wouldn't have made it through the night in one piece, and if she turned up to the Forge in them, Cheryl would think she was on her way to a job interview. No, without Daniel in her life, shoes like this didn't have any place in her closet.

'Just try them,' said Georgia more kindly as the assistant brought over the other shoe.

As Amy slipped them on, she overheard a customer asking for three pairs of the same suede moccasin in size eight, telling the assistant to send one pair to her New York apartment, one to the house in Houston and the other to the ski lodge in Aspen.

'I know what you're thinking,' said Georgia as the customer moved to the cash desk. 'It's easy to look that elegant when you have an unlimited budget. Well, here's a secret. Stylish women don't have to spend a fortune. They just have to take the time to find their own style.'

Amy was only half listening. She couldn't believe how great her whole leg looked in the plain black shoe, a shoe that on any other occasion she would have overlooked, even if it was half the price.

'I thought they would suit you,' said Georgia firmly, motioning to the assistant to put them in the box.

Amy resisted smiling. She couldn't believe she was getting fashion advice from a seventy-something.

'Now back upstairs.'

Amy did as she was told and followed Georgia into a room where there were mannequins adorned in sumptuous gowns. She walked around, trailing her fingers across the fabric, imagining herself dressed for a ball. She was beginning to relax and enjoy herself.

'Oh wow, look at the feathers sewn into the skirt! It's like Tallulah Bankhead meets *Swan Lake*.'

'I didn't realise that young people were aware of Tallulah Bankhead,' smiled Georgia.

'My nona – my grandma – was a big fan, had all her videos. She always told a story about how she had met her once, uptown in some speakeasy in Harlem, but I'm not sure Nona was really old enough. It was a nice story, though.'

Georgia sat down on a long sofa and Amy joined her.

'I think I could set up home in this place,' said Amy.

Georgia smiled.

'It's not a shop. It's a house full of clothes. It doesn't get more perfect than that.'

Amy looked at the older woman with interest.

'You're a dark horse,' she said. 'You, fashion . . .'

'I can't like clothes because I'm old? Is that what you're saying?'

'No, no,' said Amy quickly, still finding it difficult to picture Georgia leafing through *Vogue*. 'You've got great style.'

'There are some women who can just throw together a little something and make it look fabulous. I'm not one of those women. But one can look and learn from the women who do dress well. When I was at finishing school in Paris, I had a French friend who worked in a café across the road from where we lived. She was as poor as a church mouse, but she was still as stylish as a Dior house model. She had such style, but I soon noticed that she didn't have very many clothes. It was like a uniform: black cigarette pants, white shirts, those little stripy tops that everyone seems to wear these days, every-thing in the most flattering cut for her shape. Of course, true style is knowing who you are and not giving a damn. My old friend Gore Vidal said that, and it's as true now as the day he said it.'

'Nice clothes help, though, you gotta agree.'

'Clothes can give you power, I'll admit that,' said Georgia. 'Choosing the right outfit, a flattering outfit that makes you feel good, can change your whole personality.' She smiled and patted Amy's hand. 'Next time you go to the Tower of London, you'll need your armour.'

She gestured for Amy to stand.

'You have excellent deportment,' she said with a pleased nod. 'A dancer's posture, I noticed that immediately. You have a won-derful figure, of course, but your stance is much more important. An erect head will make any woman look taller, more elegant and more confident.'

She stepped over to a rack of dresses and began flicking through. 'Hmm . . . possible . . . no, no, too short . . .' she mused as she went. 'None of these are right.'

'I wonder if you could help?' she said, turning to a sales assistant. 'My friend would like a little black dress. Simple, classic, not too revealing.'

'Size four?' said the assistant, looking Amy up and down, then nodded and disappeared, emerging with three black dresses draped over her arm. Georgia held them up one by one, squinting at Amy like an artist regarding a life model.

'This one, I think,' she said, handing it to her.

'Georgia . . .' said Amy, widening her eyes meaningfully, but the other woman simply gave a quick shake of the head. 'Try it on, come on, chop chop.'

Amy could tell the moment she stepped into the dress that it was going to look fabulous. Georgia had been modest; she clearly had a very good eye for clothes. It clung to her curves in all the right places, but without being in any way revealing. It was sophisticated; it made her poor sequin-shedding dress look like something from a little girl's dressing-up box. She turned and stepped out of the changing room.

'Ah,' sighed Georgia when she saw her. 'I believe it was Wallis Simpson who said that when a little black dress is right, there is nothing else to wear in its place.'

She stood up and pinched the back of the dress.

'This is almost perfect,' she mused. 'I can recommend a tailor in London to take it in slightly. All the smartest women have even the finest clothes altered to exactly fit their shape. Couture clothes for off-the-peg prices.'

'It is lovely,' smiled Amy shyly. 'It makes me want to go and hang outside Tiffany's with a doughnut. Shame I can't afford it.'

'Did you look at the price tag?'

'No, but . . .'

'Then don't. We'll take this,' said Georgia quickly to the sales assistant.

'Georgia, I'm serious. I don't have any money,' hissed Amy urgently.

'But I'm paying for it,' said Georgia matter-of-factly. 'And the shoes.'

Amy looked at her wide-eyed.

'I can't accept that.'

Georgia tilted her head.

'Whether it is a gift or a compliment, a lady should accept it graciously.'

Amy looked at Georgia, then back down at the dress.

'This isn't a joke?'

'It's no joke,' she said, shaking her head. 'Now come along, we have to be somewhere else by six. And a lady – or at least these two ladies – is never late.'

It was dark outside, and New York looked even more magical. Alfonse collected them, and as they drove down Fifth Avenue, skirting Central Park, Amy drank it all in. The streets were crammed with New Yorkers wrapped up warm and doing last-minute Christmas shopping, laden down with bags – the distinctive brown and white stripes belonging to Henri Bendel, the crisp black and white of Saks. Best of all, she loved looking in the shop windows. New York stores always did wonderful holiday windows, she thought, catching sight of the art-deco-inspired displays in Bergdorf Goodman.

'Look at that,' said Georgia gleefully, pointing at the mannequins. 'They look like beauties on their way to one of Gatsby's Great Egg parties.'

The car continued downtown all the way to 24th Street and back on to the lower reaches of Madison Avenue.

'Here we are,' said Georgia briskly, getting out of the car.

'Eleven Madison Park. I don't know this place. What is it? A hotel?'

'Further education,' smiled Georgia.

They went inside, off the cold street, where Georgia asked to speak to Clive.

Amy's eyes were fixed on the glamorous and powerful clientele. Growing up in New York, she had often walked past these fancy places – restaurants with French names, or names carved in tiny letters, as if you were simply expected to know what they were; famous restaurants, bistros that you read about in Page Six, restaurants that appeared on magazine hot lists and Michelin lists – but she had never been inside one. She wished she was wearing the Ralph Lauren little black dress that was in the stiff cardboard bag in her hand, but she realised that she had an even better accessory by her side – Georgia, whose presence gave her a quiet reassurance that she had never felt when she went to these sort of places in London with Daniel.

'Who's Clive?' she whispered.

'An old friend who worked in Claridge's for many years. Ah – here he is now.'

A fifty-something gentleman in a beautifully cut suit extended his hand towards Georgia, who seemed to soften in his presence.

'It's so good to see you again,' she said warmly as they shook hands.

'It has been far too long, Miss Hamilton.'

'Well, I finally made it. I suppose asking you to call me Georgia after so long would be futile?'

They all laughed, and Georgia introduced Clive to Amy before they were led upstairs away from the main dining area.

Amy had assumed they were here to eat, but perhaps not.

'Here we go. The South Room,' said Clive, ushering them into a small, elegant dining space on a mezzanine floor over the restaurant.

'Look at this place,' said Amy, gazing out through the long windows on to Madison Square Park. 'Are we the only people here?'

'This is one of our private dining rooms,' explained Clive, handing her a menu.

'I thought we could kill two birds with one stone. We get to sample some exceptional cuisine, and I can help you with this.'

'With what?'

'This,' said Georgia, gesturing towards the table, formally set as if for a banquet for two.

Amy's eyes opened wide. 'Now? We're going to talk about bread rolls and stuff now?'

'Why not?'

'Well, it's just that I'm not sure I'll be able to remember it all. I haven't got a notebook or anything. I mean, I'd write it all on the back of a napkin if they weren't made out of linen.'

Georgia patted her hand.

'Relax, my dear. The point of this exercise is not to make you an expert, rather to make you comfortable being in this environment. And to learn that not everything is important.'

'Okay. I'll try.'

'So, food is served from the left,' said Clive, bending to place a small plate in front of her. He stepped around her and picked it up from the other side. 'And cleared from the right.'

'The idea was to prevent the servants crashing into each other,' said Georgia. 'And that's why drinks are always served from the right.'

150

'I'll remember that for the pub,' grinned Amy, but Georgia gave her a stern look.

'Do you want to take this seriously?'

'Sorry,' she said, holding up a hand. 'I'm just a bit nervous. And confused. I mean, I've been a waitress for a while now, and no one at the Forge ever told me there was a right way to serve.'

'What do you know about wine glasses?' asked Georgia, already moving on.

'Without them, we'd be swigging out of the bottle like a hobo?' Another stern look.

'Okay, okay, I know the answer to this one,' said Amy quickly, not wanting another reprimand. 'Red wine goes in the big one. White wine in the smaller one, although if it was down to me, I'd take the big one every time and fill it up all the way.'

'And don't forget the biggest glass is for your water,' said Georgia, pointing to the herd of glasses that Clive had arranged on the table.

'You're our advanced glassware class, Clive. What can you tell us?' said Georgia with the hint of a smile.

Clive placed two glasses of champagne in front of Georgia and Amy, each receptacle a different shape. He explained that one was a flute, the other a saucer – the shape of the latter apparently modelled on Marie Antoinette's right breast.

'But which one is better for champagne?' asked Amy,

'Well, the saucer looks prettier,' smiled Georgia. 'But the flute has less surface area, so the champagne retains the bubbles longer. Personally I never like to leave it in the glass that long.'

Next she was introduced to a magnum glass, apparently reserved for particularly aromatic Burgundy and usually only filled halfway to allow the bouquet to collect inside the glass.

'So how is a Burgundy different from other sorts of wine?' she asked. It was the sort of question she'd never have asked Daniel even in the privacy of her own home, let alone at one of the smart dinner parties he occasionally took her to. But even after this short time she felt comfortable asking Georgia and Clive anything; the fact that she barely knew the pair of them somehow made it easier.

'Burgundy is simply the region of France the wine comes from,' explained Clive. 'It's a highly respected wine-growing area – you've probably heard of Chablis – and produces many of the top wines in the world. But it's most famous for its reds – like this one. Full-bodied, smooth, aromatic . . .' He poured a little of the wine and asked her what she could smell.

Tentatively Amy picked up the big glass and pushed her nose inside, inhaling. It was wonderful: sweet, fruity and rich, like a basket of freshly picked berries. She looked up at Clive, wondering what she should say.

'Cherries,' she said hesitantly, unsure whether this was the right answer.

'Very good,' he said, his eyes twinkling. 'I can smell cherries, and chocolate too.'

'Sounds good to me,' grinned Amy, taking a long, delicious sip.

Clive walked away to get their starters, their little wine appreciation session over.

'Wow – my folks at home aren't going to recognise me when they bring out the cheap stuff and I stick my nose in it.'

'Price isn't always an indicator of quality. I've taken a great ten-pound bottle of wine to many dinner parties. Because it's good and I like it and I want to share it with my friends. Have faith in what you like. Have courage in who you are and your opinions. It doesn't matter if you can smell cherries or chocolate or chalk dust so long as you believe what you say and you are respectful of what other people believe.'

'Even if it's wrong?'

'And how do you define wrong? Why should your opinion be any less valid than the next person just because they have more money in the bank or have studied at all the right places?'

Clive brought over three successively delicious courses, during which Georgia explained the intricacies of modern table manners. Apparently bread rolls were always broken, never cut with a knife; soup bowls were gently tipped away from you. Napkins were placed on laps, salt and pepper added after food had been tasted. Plates were never pushed to one side, elbows were kept off the table no matter how strange this might at first feel, although a light lean was allowed if there was no food present. Fidgeting was not elegant. Smiling apparently was.

'Will you come?' said Amy quietly.

'Come where?'

She looked into Georgia's tired grey eyes and thought of her ordering room service and a bottle of good Burgundy at the hotel the following evening. No one deserved to be alone at Christmas, even if they believed that was what they wanted.

'To my house. In Queens.'

'Don't be silly. It's your family time.'

'I want you to come and I think you'd enjoy it. No one there knows a Beaujolais from a Budweiser, but my mom does these great butterscotch carrots that have just got your name on them.'

'In which case, we had better brief Alfonse.' And Amy swore she could see Georgia's eyes sparkle.

CHAPTER TWELVE

May 1958

'I'm so glad you agreed to come,' grinned Sally Daly as they passed through the gates of Giles House on the outskirts of a picturesque village near Wytham Woods in Oxfordshire.

The debutante parties and dances had moved into the country-side, and Georgia clutched the little cream suitcase on her lap tightly as the two girls arrived at their destination.

'We'll have a great time,' she said, smiling as brightly as possible, though her heart was sinking at the thought of spending the next twelve hours in the house ahead of her. But she had made a promise to herself and to her mother that she would throw herself wholeheartedly into the Season. After all, what was it someone had said to her recently? That if she resisted life less, she might enjoy it more.

So she'd had a makeover at the cosmetics counter at Debenham & Freebody and had her hair trimmed into a neat and stylish crop, which somehow made it look more blond. She had been to the polo at Cowdray Park, the horse trials at Badminton, throwing herself into the Season with such aplomb that she even had Sybil smiling.

Tonight's festivities were being hosted by one Mr and Mrs Charles Fortescue for their daughter Judy, a tall, red-haired debutante who was part of a rather cliquey and competitive set who loved horses. According to Sally, who seemed to know every deb on the circuit and was plugged into all the gossip, tonight was not a dance, but a house party, with almost sixty guests staying at the property overnight. Deb's delights were apparently being shipped in from the university, and from the agricultural college at Cirencester, and hopes were high for meaningful encounters, even though the men would apparently all be leaving at midnight.

Georgia had painted her toenails, waxed her legs, and cleared up a blemish with a face mask. Perhaps if she found her husband-to-be sooner rather than later, she would save herself from having to go to more parties like this one.

As the taxi made its way up the long drive, she took a moment to observe the Fortescue property, which was large if a little faded around the edges. The past few weeks had been quite wet ones, but tonight was a clear and warm evening, and as the sun dipped behind the line of trees, it sent streamers of golden light across the grounds.

At the front door, the girls were met by a stern-looking housekeeper dressed in black.

'You're late,' she said, not even bothering to look at them directly.

'We caught a different train from the one we were supposed to.'

'They are all outside playing croquet. Drinks are being served any minute on the terrace. You should go to your rooms and unpack, but you had better be quick.'

Outside, Georgia glimpsed at least seventy people in the garden. Tables groaned under the weight of jugs of Pimm's and silver bowls of strawberries.

'I assume you are Georgia Hamilton and Sally Daly,' said the housekeeper, running her finger down a clipboard. 'You're the only ones not accounted for.'

They both nodded.

'Follow me. I'll show you to your rooms.'

The girls trailed behind her through the house, past a boot room where two enormous elephant's feet now stored umbrellas, and up a flight of stairs.

Sally was in a single room that overlooked the back garden.

'Goody, a room to myself,' she cheered.

'You are upstairs,' said the housekeeper to Georgia as they headed towards the attics, the house getting progressively more dark. Many of the bedroom doors were open, and she peered inside at camp beds and mattresses covering every floor. It looked more like an army barracks than a family home.

Finally she was led into a small room in the eaves. There was a single bed and two camp beds squashed in, which left barely enough room to swing a cat.

Despite the snobbish whispers she still heard about Sally – that her mother was on her third nose job, and how the Rolls-Royce that dropped her off at parties was definitely *de trop* – it was no surprise that she had been allocated the good room, whilst Georgia was banished to Siberia. Sally spent her days inviting impoverished aristos to the Dalys' house in Biarritz; Georgia had to dodge questions about why she wasn't having her own dance.

Shimmering into a pale green silk dress, she pinned a white gardenia she had picked from the grounds on the lapel, which disguised the smell of cigarette smoke she had picked up from the train. On her way downstairs she dropped into Sally's room but her friend had already gone, and even before she reached the ground floor she could hear the arrival of the first of the buses that were shipping the Cirencester boys from the village pub where they were staying.

'Come along, come along,' said a man with a magnificent moustache. She assumed this must be Judy's father. 'Grab a bevvy and then into the barn.'

'I knew this was going to be a great party,' giggled Sally, clutching a glass of orange squash. 'Have you seen how dishy those Cirencester boys are? Thighs on them like sycamores.'

'I was rather distracted by the waiters.'

'Judy says her mum hand-picked the most handsome boys from the village and paid them three shillings each to tend to us all night long.'

'Go easy, Sal. It's a marathon, not a sprint,' said Georgia, watching her friend tip brandy from a hip flask into her glass.

'Dutch courage,' she grinned. 'See the tall guy over there? Broad shoulders? He winked at me as soon as he got off the bus.'

'It could have been a twitch rather than an invitation.'

'That's a shame,' said Sally, adjusting her cleavage.

Georgia watched her friend introduce herself to the strapping Cirencester student, remembering that her cousin Clarissa had warned her to avoid them. As Sally giggled and flirted, Georgia wanted to go over and tell her to stop. On the train she had confided that she had cut the neckline of her colbalt-blue couture gown into a daring scoop with a pair of scissors, and now her breasts were barely contained in her dress. There were several girls on the circuit who were getting a reputation for being a little 'fast', and Georgia did not want her friend to be one of them.

Before she could take action, she was shunted into the timber-framed barn, which smelt of hay and a lingering scent of horse manure, and introduced to Judy's aunt Betty, who had come all the way from Cumberland for the party. For the next hour she was stuck with Aunt Betty, discussing the merits of John Donne over William Wordsworth until the finger buffet was served.

In London, the dances didn't usually start until 8 p.m., but people here appeared to have been drinking punch or Pimm's since late afternoon, and most of the guests seemed intoxicated. Judy's parents and the more elderly guests had long since retired to the drawing room to drink gin, whilst several couples had left the barn, no doubt to go snogging in the bushes.

'Fancy it?' asked one of the heavy-thighed Cirencester students, sidling up to her with a canapé.

'Fancy what?' she replied, guessing that he was not referring to his cheese and pineapple nibble. Her best withering expression was enough to drive him away, and she decided that she definitely needed a cigarette.

She'd tried, she really had tried this evening. The problem was that other than Sally, she had no real friends at the party. Besides which, everyone had already paired off, and even if there were some single men still available, she knew she couldn't flirt to save her life.

Feeling like a complete gooseberry, she went outside to have a smoke. In the bushes she saw a familiar flash of cobalt blue, and for a moment she wondered if she should go and fish out Sally from her al fresco assignation.

She looked up at the house, which was lit up and glowing in the dark. It seemed to be laughing at her.

Bugger this, she thought, stamping out her cigarette. She was so tired, even the thought of her attic camp bed had considerable appeal. She kicked off her shoes and ran across the lawn, enjoying the feel of the cool grass under her feet, then upstairs to the attic, slipping past a couple who were kissing on the staircase on the way. The door was closed. She pushed it open and saw a deb lying on one of the camp beds with her skirt hoicked up above her waist, her white panties on full show. A young man dressed in black tie turned round and growled that the room was taken.

'But this is my bedroom,' argued Georgia before being told to clear off.

She grabbed her suitcase, which she had thankfully not properly unpacked, and slammed the door behind her.

It was the same story in the room next door and the one next to that. She had no idea what the adults downstairs were doing, but they were clearly not paying any attention to the 'socialising' going on upstairs.

'No wonder it's called the Season,' she muttered to herself as she found another bedroom occupied. 'Everyone's on bloody heat.'

She sat down on the threadbare carpet on the staircase until she was moved along by the housekeeper, who told her to hurry back outside. The sober realisation that she had no desire to go back into the barn and nowhere to go in the house made her feel excluded and miserable.

Then it struck her that she did not have to stay here.

She was invisible, but there was an upside to that.

If she was invisible, then no one would know she was gone. She glanced at her watch. It was only a few miles into Oxford, and it was just past nine o'clock. She could get the train back to London and be home before midnight. And even if the trains had finished for the night, she could check into a hotel. Certainly if her mother had moved to Provence at seventeen, then Georgia could find her way home from a miserable party in Oxfordshire.

Her mind was made up. At finishing school, good manners and etiquette had been drilled into them, but Georgia no longer cared what people like the Fortescues thought of her. And whilst she felt a pang of guilt for leaving Sally, her friend was otherwise occupied by Cirencester farmers and alcohol, and wouldn't notice she was gone until breakfast.

She crept into Sally's room, where there was a carafe of water and three sheets of crested writing paper and a pencil on the bedside table. She scribbled a few words of goodbye and apology, asking Sally to cover for her absence and suggesting that she have a banana and a glass of still ginger beer – Estella's recommended hangover cure for the morning after. She left the note on Sally's pillow and picked up her suitcase.

She heard footsteps in the distance – the quick, efficient steps of the housekeeper against the house's stone floors – but they were going in the opposite direction, so she took her chance.

The front door was closed but unlocked and she slipped outside. As she ran down the gravel path, the sound of the jazz band playing 'I've Got You Under My Skin' soared up into the evening air. She loved that song, but it was not enough to keep her there.

The journey from Oxford train station to the Fortescues' house hadn't seemed very long in the taxi – just a few minutes, although as she and Sally had been gossiping the whole way, it was hard to tell. It was certainly too far to walk, so when a bus came that apparently stopped in the city centre, she flagged it down. 'Night's drawing in, young lady,' said the conductor with a note of disapproval.

'Can you let me know when it's the stop for Oxford station?' she asked as politely as she could.

She took a seat and leant her head against the window, enjoying the cool sensation of the glass against her cheek, glad that she had escaped the party. She was lost in her thoughts when she realised that the conductor was shouting at her that it was her stop. She jumped out of her seat with a start, grabbed her suitcase and leapt off the bus.

The train station was almost deserted. It seemed to be colder than the rest of town, and smelt of smoke and soot.

'Has the last train to London left yet?' she asked the attendant anxiously.

He shook his head. 'It goes in a couple of minutes.'

'A single to Paddington then.' She smiled with relief.

He told her the price and she reached to get her purse.

'My purse, my handbag . . .' she whispered with dawning horror. She felt sick as she realised that she had left her little black handbag on the bus.

'That's two shillings and sixpence,' repeated the attendant.

'I haven't got any money,' she croaked with panic.

The man shrugged apologetically.

Georgia ran into the street, but there was no sign of the bus. Sinking to the floor, her case wedged between her legs, she put her head in her hands as she heard a whistle blow and the last train leave for London.

She was stuck, stranded, she thought, feeling the cheese and pineapple nibbles curdle in her stomach.

Forcing herself to think, she realised that she had two options. There was a shilling in her pocket, left over from the taxi fare earlier, and she could use it either to get the bus back to the Fortescues' or to make a phone call to Uncle Peter asking him to come and collect her. Neither option was appealing. Or was there a third way? she wondered, suddenly thinking about Edward Carlyle, who often popped into her head unbidden.

He lived in Oxford. Surely he wouldn't be hard to find. Edward Carlyle. He would have to save her once again.

CHAPTER THIRTEEN

She found a small tobacconist's shop that was still open and pleaded with the owner to show her a map that was for sale on the counter.

Remembering that Edward was at Christ Church, she located where she was now, and tried to find where the college was in relation to that. Then she left the shop and began to walk in the direction of Christ Church Meadow, down alleyways, past honey-coloured buildings and gated entrances through which she could glimpse quadrangles and gardens. It was almost dark and her suitcase was heavy, but although she wanted to get to Edward's college as quickly as possible, there was something so bewitching about Oxford that she wanted to pause every few minutes to drink it in.

She took a left on to St Aldates, looking for the entrance to the college, realising with further panic that as it was Saturday night, he might not even be at home. Her heart pounding, she spotted a gateway marked Tom Tower, which from the map had looked as if it constituted part of the college.

'Can I help you?'

An old man in a bowler hat by a porter's lodge indicated that she should go no further.

'I'm looking for Edward Carlyle,' she said, putting down her suitcase. 'He lives here.'

'And you are?'

'His cousin,' she offered, not entirely convincingly. 'I've been stranded in Oxford. I lost my bag in a taxi on my way to a debs' ball . . .'

'A debs' ball?' he said suspiciously.

She nodded more confidently, her little fiction gaining truth in her own head as she spoke it.

'I need to speak to Cousin Edward and ask him to lend me some money to get to the venue. Otherwise I'll be stranded and the host will be furious and the debutante whose party it is will be just devastated that I haven't made it to probably the most important event of her life . . .'

She felt a little spike of guilt, remembering her escape from the festivities. She wondered if Sally had found the note and alerted anyone to her disappearance.

'Stranded, you say?' said the old man. 'In which case, I had better enquire as to his whereabouts . . . Wait here, please, Miss . . .'

'Hamilton. Georgia Hamilton. Related on my mother's side,' she added quickly.

The porter frowned and disappeared down a stone path across a quadrangle with a beautiful stone fountain in the centre sending feathers of water into the night sky.

It was a further five minutes before he came slowly back across the quad towards her, although it felt like a lot longer.

'Sorry. Mr Carlyle is not in his room or in the JCR.'

'Then what am I supposed to do?' asked Georgia with a flood of panic.

The man didn't seem to understand the urgency of the situation.

'I'm afraid we can't let young ladies into the college at this time,' he said in his slow, measured voice. 'But perhaps you would like to use my telephone?'

And phone who? she wondered, knowing how worried – no, how *furious* everyone back in London would be.

'The Eagle and Child and The Bear are both popular with the students. Perhaps you'll find your cousin there,' offered the porter. 'But really, it is rather late, young lady.'

'I'll try there,' she said quickly, picking up the suitcase.

She felt a chill on the breeze and shivered.

'Pubs, pubs . . .' she muttered as she walked, wondering if she should just use her shilling to buy a pint of beer.

She popped into one pub and then another, all crammed with confident, clever-looking students. Several times she thought she saw Edward, although the truth was, it was hard to even remember what he looked like.

She stood at the bus stop, letting fate decide her next turn. If a bus came headed in the direction of the Fortescues' within the next ten minutes, she would take it. Otherwise . . .

Looking up, she saw a figure walking towards her, his hands stuffed in his pockets and a newspaper in the crook of his arm.

'Edward!' she shouted joyfully, running towards him.

She threw down her case and embraced him, and he stepped back in surprise.

'Georgia. What on earth are you doing here? Running away?' he asked, glancing down at her bag.

'Yes! How did you know?' she said. 'I've run away from a party. I felt a complete gooseberry, and even though I tried really hard to enjoy it, it was quite ghastly.'

'Was it in Oxford?'

'Somewhere countrysidey,' she said, waving her hand. 'I thought I'd get the train back to London, but I left my purse on the bus and now I'm stranded and I didn't know anyone and I went to your college and said I was your cousin and—'

'Slow down a minute . . . So you've got no way of getting home?'

She shook her head and looked embarrassed.

'Looks like you've got to rescue me again.'

'I didn't think you'd be the type to need a white knight once, let alone twice.'

'It's an emergency. I need to borrow some money, though I've missed the last train now.'

'It's a good job you saw me,' he said cynically.

'I did have a plan B,' she said, trying to muster some dignity. The last thing she wanted was to look desperate in front of Edward. 'I quite liked the sound of Christ Church Meadow, so I thought I might just anaesthetise myself with beer and sleep under a tree. I have the contents of my suitcase, so I wouldn't freeze.'

'I think, under the circumstances, you might prefer the Randolph,' he said with a note of amusement in his voice.

'What's that?'

'A hotel, just by the Ashmolean. We can walk there now and sort it out. You can get the train back to London in the morning.'

'You'd do that?'

He smiled slowly.

'What are cousins for?'

He took hold of her case and started walking, snaking through the back streets, pointing out various places as they passed: New College, Brasenose, Queen's. He told her about all the famous people who had studied here: J. R. R. Tolkien, who had first read *The Lord of the Rings* to a group of like-minded scholars, 'the

Inklings', in the Eagle and Child pub; and Lewis Carroll, who'd based his character Alice on the Dean of Christ Church's daughter.

'It's all so beautiful, so magical,' she sighed, thinking that she could listen to him all night. 'And it's so lucky it wasn't bombed.'

'That's because Hitler wanted to make Oxford the new capital city if he conquered England. So he gave orders not to bomb it. In fact, rumour has it he wanted to live in Blenheim Palace, down the road.'

'You know a lot.'

'I've read a lot. The advantage of four years' university study. You get to read a lot, learn a lot and never feel guilty about it, because that's what we're here to do.'

'It sounds wonderful.'

'Didn't you apply?'

'To university? No,' she said, shaking her head quickly. 'We couldn't really afford it.'

'There're grants available. From the board of education, from charities.'

'I don't want to be anyone's charity case, thank you.'

'Did you do A levels?'

She nodded.

'Then you could try and get a last-minute place to start next term. Were your grades decent?'

'Two As and a B,' she replied, almost apologetically.

'Georgia, you could, you *should* apply to Oxford.' He said it mischievously. As if he was goading her. 'There are women's colleges – St Hilda's, LMH, Somerville. Personally I think you'd be more suited to one of the more spirited ones, like St Anne's. I can see you on your bicycle, pedalling down to the Eagle and Child, reviving the Inklings . . .'

For a moment he made it sound almost tempting. To live in

this beautiful city that had spawned so many great people and moments in history. But then she reminded herself of her situation.

'Edward, how on earth can I go to Oxford?'

'There's an exam in November.'

'I've done enough exams. I've been to finishing school. I just don't think university is on the cards for me.'

'So what is?'

'A good marriage,' she said softly.

He looked at her with surprise.

'You've changed your tune.'

'Well, things are different now.'

He frowned, urging her to speak.

'Our farm burnt down two weeks ago. No one was hurt, but it took everything we had with it, including most of my mum's paintings. She's an artist, so it was a bit of a blow. All she's got left are a few canvases in a lock-up unit in Hammersmith. The only options open to us are the streets or a good marriage.'

'Not the only two, surely?' said Edward, frowning.

'Marriage is just a contract,' she said dismissively. 'Look, the Randolph,' she pointed out, wanting to change the subject. 'Is this the hotel you were talking about? It looks expensive . . .'

'Don't worry about that,' he said touching her on the shoulder and leading her inside. She stood back as he booked a room and a bellboy disappeared upstairs with her case.

'Edward, this is so kind of you. I have a job now, like you suggested. I have savings. I can repay you as soon as I get back to London.'

'Why don't you just buy me a drink?'

'I've only got a shilling.'

'Then I'll sub you the difference.' He smiled. 'Come on. We might just catch last orders.'

Usually he had quite a serious face, but when he smiled, the corners of his dark grey eyes creased and a small dimple appeared in his lower right cheek. She wanted to tell him that it suited him, but was disturbed by the concierge, who handed over two room keys.

'Have a pleasant stay at the Randolph, Mr and Mrs Carlyle.'

Georgia stifled a laugh and they both rushed back outside.

'I'm your wife now?' she giggled. 'That's a promotion from cousin.'

'It was easier than explaining why a single young woman was coming in off the streets,' he smiled. 'The Randolph is frightfully respectable. By the way, here's some money for your train fare tomorrow.'

They started to walk, and passed three or four pubs without going inside. Georgia stopped seeing the beauty of Oxford and started to listen to Edward, whose own life seemed to contain as much magic and wonder as the buildings around her. She couldn't believe that in the last year alone he had packed in as much as she had done in a lifetime. He was twenty-two and in the fourth year of a classics degree, which had meant lots of long holidays filled with adventures. He had skied in Switzerland, safaried in Kenya and spent the previous summer driving from London to Constantinople. In return she told him all about Paris – the secret little places that she loved: the beehives in the Jardin du Luxembourg, the canals that fed into the Seine, the Forney library with its Rapunzel turrets and La Pagode Japanese-style movie house. And as they walked and talked, laughing and listening to each other, she felt for once as if she had something interesting to say, although occasionally she did lose her train of thought. When he laughed and that dimple appeared in his cheek; when he looked at her directly with his dark grey eyes; when she noticed that he really was very good-looking indeed.

'Well, I wasn't expecting this,' he said as they walked over a bridge and past a beautiful college called Magdalen.

'Expecting what?'

'A good night coming from nowhere. I only slipped out for a packet of cigarettes.'

'And two hours ago I was trapped at some terrible party.'

Edward nodded.

'That's what's so scary and exciting about life. It can turn on a coin toss.'

'Or a drunken decision.'

'Or a person you meet on the street.'

She felt his hand brush against hers and it almost made her jump out of her skin. She had no idea if it was deliberate or accidental, whether he had just bumped into her or whether he had wanted to take hold of her hand. Whatever it was, it had set her heart racing and the air between them had turned thick with an energy that she had only noticed a few minutes earlier.

A car horn beeped behind them and made her jump.

'Carlyle! Is that you?'

A large convertible slowed down and stopped in front of them. It seemed to be full of people – six or seven at least, all dressed in black tie, with the exception of two girls wearing layers and layers of tulle.

'All right, boys. Where are you off to?' He seemed to know them well, although there was a hesitancy in his voice that suggested he wasn't exactly overjoyed to see them.

'Tried to gatecrash the Pembroke Ball. No bloody luck, though,' said a floppy-haired blond boy almost hanging out of the back seat. 'Security is tighter than a Scotsman's wallet. We're heading over to Mark Headingly's party instead. Only on Circus Street. Do you fancy it?'

'Not tonight, Bradders,' replied Edward, as Georgia breathed a silent sigh of relief.

'Come on. It's Saturday night and it's literally just there. You can almost see it. In fact, bugger it, I'll walk with you. Darling Julia's been sitting on my leg.'

'Oh blast, is that what it was?' said another voice, to a chorus of guffaws.

There was the creak of a car door and three boys tumbled on to the pavement, spilling a bottle of champagne one of them was holding.

'Seriously, it's fine,' protested Edward. 'I was just about to turn in.'

'Nonsense,' said Bradders, taking a drag of his cigarette. 'The night is young and we have a bootful of champagne. Who needs Pembroke?' he roared.

Two of the young men scooped Edward into a chair lift, and as they started running down the street with him, Georgia felt a wave of disappointment so strong it made her lose her breath.

'Ride with us,' shouted the girl called Julia, and Georgia felt she had no option but to hop in the car for the thirty-second journey to Circus Street. They beeped Edward and Bradders as they zoomed past them, Georgia giving them a half-hearted thumbs-up sign.

By the time they had parked the car, Edward had caught up with them.

'Hijacked. I'm sorry.'

'It's fine,' she said, pasting on her widest smile.

'We can stay for five minutes and then leave.'

'We can stay as long as you like,' she replied, not knowing if he was just being polite and really wanted to be with his friends.

They stepped inside the house, which was heaving with people, some wearing ball gowns and black tie, others in more casual attire. Loud jazz was playing in the background, smoke obscured couples kissing in dark corners.

'Who are these people?' whispered Georgia.

'Boys I knew from school. They're all right usually. I just think everyone is determined to go out with one last blast before we graduate and settle down to responsibility.'

'I think I owe you a drink,' said Georgia, feeling nervous.

'I'm sure there's a supply of something horrible and home-brewed in the kitchen. Let's go and find it.'

And then he took her hand. This time she knew it was for real, as his fingers knitted between hers, and she felt a heady blend of nerves and excitement course around her.

There was indeed home brew in the kitchen, and it was not good. Edward wondered if it was potato liquor, and they both decided they were not going to risk drinking it. Edward went to ask Bradders about the stash of champagne in the car boot whilst Georgia nipped to the loo. She looked in the tiny mirror in the bathroom under the stairs and tried to rearrange her hair. Her rouge and lipstick were still in her handbag on the bus, so she pinched her cheeks to try and give them some colour.

When she emerged, it felt as if she was stepping out of the house on a date. Yes, she had preferred it when it was just the two of them. Walking around the streets of Oxford had been extra-ordinary and magical, and yet it had been warm and familiar, as if she were playing out her own version of Estella's night-in-Paris story she had heard so many times before.

But the party fizzed with another, intimate sort of promise, and the thought of retreating to a dark corner with Edward was one that thrilled her.

'How on earth did you get Edward out on a Saturday night two weeks before Finals?'

Georgia turned and saw Julia inches away from her holding a cigarette.

'Why? Where should he be?'

'He's been locked away for the last month revising, although I've no idea why. He's going to walk a first and it's not as if it matters. They're keeping the top seat at the family bank warm for him even if he gets a gentleman's degree.'

She laughed, her lips, stained purple by red wine, making her teeth look bright white and slightly frightening in the dark.

'I haven't seen you before. Which college are you at?'

'I'm not.'

'The secretarial college?' she asked with faint disapproval.

'I live in London.'

'So what are you doing in Oxford?'

'A long story.' Georgia grinned. 'I'm en route somewhere and Edward's helping me get there.'

'He's adorable, isn't he?' replied Julia, blowing a smoke ring. 'Oxford's top catch. We all think that Annabel is the luckiest girl in the world.'

'Annabel?'

'His girlfriend, of course. Every boy at Oxford is a little bit in love with her too, so I suppose you could call them Oxford's beautiful couple. No one is going to want to be photographed next to them at the Magdalen Commem ball, that's for certain. I've already seen the dress she's picked out for it, and she's going to look divine.'

Georgia felt as if she had been punched in the stomach. He was handsome and smart and rich – of course he had a girl-friend. It certainly explained why he hadn't been seen at any more debutante parties – the catch of Oxford had been caught. As Julia made her excuses and left, Georgia could see Edward threading through the crowd towards her. His eyes locked with hers, and as he smiled, the disappointment almost crushed her.

'Champagne,' he said triumphantly, raising the bottle.

'I should go,' said Georgia quickly. 'It's late. I don't want the hotel to lock its doors.'

'Then we could stay up all night.'

'I don't think that's a good idea. I have to get an early train.'

'How about breakfast?'

She shook her head, determined that her expression shouldn't betray her emotions.

'I think the first train is very early.'

'But you don't have to catch that one. There'll be plenty of others.'

'I need to get back.'

'Of course.' He nodded. 'I'll walk you back to the hotel.'

'Really, there's no need.'

'It's time I went back too.'

They took the short route back. Down the High Street and right at Cornmarket Street. She babbled about the many debutante parties that were coming up, and even threw Jacques – by now almost a forgotten name – into the conversation for good measure.

'Good night, Mrs Carlyle,' said Edward as they stood on the steps of the hotel.

'Thanks again, Edward. You're a real pal.'

They stood in silence for a second. He stretched out and touched her fingers, but she flinched away.

'Good night,' she said quickly, and ran inside the hotel, and when she turned back to see where he was, he had gone.

CHAPTER FOURTEEN

June 1958

'Someone looks nice. Are you going on a date?' André, the pastry chef at the Swiss Chalet café, gave a wolf whistle as Georgia emerged from the staff loos in a dark green pencil skirt and a white shirt knotted at the waist.

'Not a date. An appointment,' she grinned, pulling her manuscript out of her bag to show him. 'It's almost finished, André, my Paris memoirs, and I'm going to meet a writer, a really successful one, to find out how to get published.'

The door of the café opened with the tinkling sound of a cow bell that André had brought over from his most recent visit to Innsbruck.

'Sorry, we're closed,' shouted Georgia, glancing at her watch and noticing that she was running twenty minutes late.

'Can you not even spare any leftover *Sachertorte?*' said a familiar voice. Georgia looked up and started laughing.

'Sally, what on earth are you doing here?'

'I was in the area and just telling Gianni here how absolutely delicious your cakes are.'

Sally was holding hands with a tall, swarthy young man dressed in cream trousers, a white shirt with the collar turned up and dark sunglasses. All he needed was a Ferrari or a yacht and he would have looked like Gianni Agnelli, the Fiat heir who often graced the pages of *Paris Match* – which Georgia suspected was exactly the look that this Gianni was after.

'Gianni, meet my dear friend Georgia Hamilton. This is my Italian friend Gianni.'

'Come this way, my friend,' shouted André. 'You won't find a finer *Sachertorte* this side of Salzburg.'

'Who is he?' mouthed Georgia as she led Sally to a corner table.

'I met him last week at Penny Pringle's dance at the Dorchester. He's utterly dreamy, isn't he?'

'He's an absolute dish,' Georgia agreed.

'And he's a count,' gushed Sally, unable to hide her glee. 'He's got a title, and a castle in Perugia, not that it matters, because he is so lovely and I am head over heels . . . Stop me. I'm gushing.'

Georgia didn't like to point out that it had been only a month ago that Sally had announced she was in love with Andrew from Cirencester. She hadn't minded in the slightest that Georgia had left the Fortescues' party, because that night she had found 'the one' – until Andrew had refused to take her phone calls, finally getting his room-mate to come to the phone and request that Sally stop bothering him.

'You see, there are some decent men out there,' Sally said sagely. 'You just have to find yours. Don't think that just because you've had your fingers burnt with Edward, it doesn't mean that your Mr Right isn't still out there.'

'I'm off men.'

'I know. I've introduced you to so many, and you've not given any of them a chance. You're not still thinking about him, are you?'

'Who?'

'Edward Carlyle, of course.'

'I haven't thought about him in weeks,' said Georgia scornfully, wishing she had never told Sally about her adventures in Oxford. 'He has a girlfriend. End of story. And now I'm concentrating on my career. Speaking of which, I have to scoot. You can stay here until André leaves, though.'

On the tube, Georgia reminded herself that she hadn't lied to Sally deliberately. She had tried her very best to forget about Edward Carlyle since that night in Oxford. She had packed her days and nights with work and writing and as many invitations as she could manage – Ascot, dances and Eton's Fourth of June celebrations by the Thames, where her cousin Richard had looked ever so smart in his cream flannels and boater hat. She'd been introduced to many attractive and polite young men, a couple of whom had even taken her for coffee or to the picture house, but it had been impossible not to compare them all to Edward, and they had all suffered badly in that comparison. She veered from feeling duped that Edward had held her hand and made a connection with her that seemed so real and palpable she could still feel it when she lay awake at night, to feeling simply sad and unlucky. After all, he had not kissed her, or made any false promises. He had been nothing but kind and generous and had even returned the money she had sent him for her hotel and train fare with a note saying that it had been his pleasure.

She got out at Piccadilly Circus and walked briskly into Soho, checking the address in her diary and finding Wheelers Restaurant on Old Compton Street. She was informed that her dining companion had already arrived, and was led through the restaurant, her eyes peeled for a likely-looking author.

Ian Dashwood was not what she was expecting. He was in his mid thirties, rather than the fifty- or sixty-something she had assumed. He had heavy brows and a light tan, and the pale grey suit with a blue triangle of silk sticking out of the top breast pocket was both smart and sharp.

He stood up and shook her hand.

'A pleasure to meet you,' he said after brief introductions. 'I've heard a lot about you. To know everything you need to know about me, here's my latest book.' He pushed a hardback across the white tablecloth.

'Is it an autobiography?'

'No. Just read the author blurb,' he laughed. 'All my interesting bits are there in three hundred words.'

He poured her a glass of wine and glanced up at her.

'So you want to be a writer.'

'I am a writer,' she smiled. 'I just haven't had anything published yet.'

'Confidence. I like that in a young novelist. You're going to get rejected at some point. We all have been. But you've got to have a thick skin, and a determination to keep writing, keep telling stories, even when there's no money coming in, even when people keep telling you that there are too many hoops to jump through to make it. I hope you don't mind oysters,' he added, glancing through the menu.

'I've never tried them.'

'Best place to have them in London. Bacon loves it in here. Apparently he's just left, which is a shame. He usually buys the whole place champagne when he's in.'

'Bacon?'

'Francis Bacon.'

'The artist,' said Georgia, wide-eyed. 'Do you know him?'
Ian nodded.

'One of the many benefits of living in Soho. You get to meet and see all sorts of interesting people and places. There's a coffee shop on Meard Street where I go and listen to jazz. It has coffin-shaped tables and ashtrays made from skulls.'

'Real skulls?' asked Georgia, spellbound by this man.

'I've no idea. It's a great place to go and write, though.'

The oysters arrived and Ian ordered another bottle of wine. He explained how he knew Uncle Peter, described the plot lines of his ten best-sellers and told her all about his morning with a Hollywood producer who was interested in turning his latest novel into a movie. He hadn't always been a novelist – he had trained as an actor, and was quietly optimistic about his ambition to write screenplays and ultimately direct films. He told her about his working day: getting up at noon, playing chess with eccentrics in Soho coffee shops like the 2i's, the White Monkey and the Grande, evenings spent either writing or meeting fellow creatives in drinking dens like the Colony Room. He made it sound a little bit too louche and glamorous, but left Georgia in no doubt that there could be no more enjoyable way to earn a living, and whilst he was not lacking in confidence when it came to listing his many achievements, he was generous with his advice and information, promising to introduce her to his agent and read anything she had written.

'Actually, I've brought something with me,' she said, pulling her manuscript out of her bag. 'It's just a first draft, but hopefully you can get an idea of whether it's any good or not.'

'Confidence, young lady,' he said, wagging a finger.

'All right. I think it's pretty good. I think I can be the English Françoise Sagan,' she said, suddenly feeling emboldened by drink.

'Have you seen the film?'

'*Bonjour Tristesse*?' She grinned at the mention of her favourite book. 'I loved it. Not quite as good as the novel, but I thought Jean Seberg was brilliant.'

'You look like her,' he said softly. 'The hair. The smile.'

She took it as an enormous compliment and one that was definitely overly generous. But the way he said it, looked at her, made her feel special. She liked feeling like this. Beautiful and sophisticated. She liked sitting with a famous author in a fashionable place where interesting creatives came to eat and drink. She felt one of them.

She blushed and took another long slug of wine. It was hot in the restaurant and she was starting to feel dizzy.

'I should get you back home.'

She nodded and waited whilst he paid the bill.

'Parking is a devil for Soho residents. Blast, I haven't got my keys. I'll just pop up and fetch them.'

'Don't worry. I'll get the tube.'

'It's dark,' he insisted. 'I won't be a minute. Come up and see the flat. I have to just make a quick call to New York and then we can set off. I need to catch my US agent whilst he is still in the office. In fact, I can mention you to him.'

Georgia beamed with excitement and followed him down Dean Street.

There was a doorway on a side street and he beckoned her inside. The flat was smaller and darker than she had expected, with just a view from the window of an alleyway and some bins. He went over to a small drinks cabinet and poured some vermouth and vodka into a shaker, then emptied it into two glasses.

She winced at the taste of it but tried to disguise her reaction.

'It's good, isn't it? I knew you'd be a martini girl.'

He excused himself and went into the bedroom to make his

call, whilst she flipped through her manuscript, wondering if she had been too hasty in letting him read it.

After a few minutes he came back into the room.

'I know what you're thinking,' he said, pointing at the manuscript. 'It tough, isn't it, letting other people read your stuff.'

'No one else has seen it,' she admitted, feeling a sense of complicity between them.

He walked right up to her and stood only inches away.

'*An English Girl in Paris*,' he said, taking the manuscript out of her hand and reading the front page. 'Is that you, then?'

She blushed and nodded.

'*Très chic*. You should be my muse.'

'Muse. What's that?'

'From ancient Greece. An inspiration to the literature and arts.'

'Me?' She laughed gently, not knowing where to look.

'Yes, you,' he said, stroking the soft skin underneath her jaw.

He looked at her, his gaze probing deeply into hers, and she didn't know whether the headiness she felt was the martini and wine or something more carnal.

'Take off your blouse.'

At first she wasn't sure if she had heard him correctly.

'I want to see you. I want to be inspired by you.'

Her throat tightened and her heart started hammering.

'My muse,' he whispered as she closed her eyes and felt him undoing her buttons.

She felt the fabric slip off her shoulders and cool air blow against her skin. His fingertips stroked the length of her arm.

'You're so beautiful. I want to write about you. I want to fix you forever in history.'

She stood there, her eyes still closed, as he asked her to turn around. He unclipped her bra and it fell to the floor.

'What do you feel?' he asked, his lips so close to her ear.

She shivered and felt her nipples harden. She blushed furiously and was glad that he was standing behind her. She heard him take a step towards her. She could feel the cotton of his shirt against her bare back.

'I'm going to make you a woman,' he said softly, the metal zip of her skirt offering no resistance to his fingers.

Her breath started quickening and she felt a sensation, an excitement between her legs.

'No,' she said, spinning round and clutching at her waist to hold up her skirt.

'No?'

'No,' she said more forcefully, scooping up her bra and blouse from the floor and putting them back on. Her cheeks were burning and she was too ashamed to look at him.

'This isn't what you think,' said Ian quickly.

'What is it then?' she asked, tears burning behind her eyeballs.

'You've got the wrong idea,' he spluttered back. 'I need inspiration for my new book. The lead character is a young woman. About your age. Innocent, beautiful, just like you. She is seduced by an older man, a wealthy white landowner in Rhodesia. You are my inspiration. My research.'

'Is that so?' she replied, taking deep breaths to force the air back into her lungs. She grabbed her bag and her manuscript and made for the door.

'Don't tell your uncle.'

'I'm sure he'd understand if it was just inspiration.'

She clattered down the stairs and ran out on to the street, tears of shame streaming down her cheeks as she leapt on to the number 22 bus.

It was almost midnight by the time she got home. Even from the road she could see the light on in the living room of their flat and knew that Estella had been waiting up for her. She wiped her face and rubbed her cheeks, hoping there was no telltale redness around her eyes.

She went inside and found Estella in her best dress holding a glass of champagne.

'My darling, you shall go to the ball,' she said, smiling and swaying gently on her heels.

'What are you talking about?' muttered Georgia, wanting to head straight into her bedroom.

'My exhibition. *Ribbons* . . . It's sold out. Colin called me this afternoon and said that a wealthy collector had seen the brochure from my exhibition and loved it and bought the lot. He's retrieving it all from storage and delivering it at the weekend. We have money, my love. You can have a dance.'

She tottered up to Georgia and put both hands on her shoulders.

'Darling, what's wrong? I thought you wanted a dance.'

A tear slipped down Georgia's cheek. She couldn't help it.

'You know, just because we've had a little windfall doesn't mean to say we should spend it all.'

'But we deserve it,' Estella said, clasping her daughter's face between her hands. 'Don't cry, my love. This is a good day. I thought we could have it next month on your birthday. I've mentally designed the invitations already. I'm thinking the moon and stars and calligraphy on dark blue vellum. And we should invite everyone. Everyone we know.'

Georgia nodded softly.

'And how was your night?' Estella asked breezily. 'How was the author? Tell me all. Was he interesting? Was he helpful?'

'He was fine,' said Georgia, heading for her bedroom and locking the door.

CHAPTER FIFTEEN

July 1958

Planning her ball distracted Georgia from dwelling on her night out with Ian Dashwood. She had told no one about it and didn't even intend to channel the experience into one of her books. Some things were best forgotten, although every time she saw Uncle Peter, it was difficult not to tell him to choose his friends and acquaintances more wisely. Certainly Dashwood was not on the guest list for her dance, although it seemed that almost anyone that Georgia and Estella had ever met had been invited.

'So who's coming?' asked Clarissa, sitting in Estella and Georgia's flat sipping a cup of coffee as they prepared to go and decorate the venue.

'Guest list's on the table,' said Georgia, trying to find the fourth box of fairy lights they had bought from Peter Jones the day before.

Clarissa picked it up and examined the list.

'Edward Carlyle plus one?' she said, her eyes wide.

Georgia stood up holding the fairy-light box, which had somehow wiggled its way under the sofa in the past twenty-four hours.

'He's helped me out a couple of a times so I owe him a night on the tiles,' she said casually, thinking about the hours she had spent debating whether to invite him.

'Helped you out?' Clarissa raised an elegantly arched brow.

'Nothing like that,' said Georgia quickly. 'Besides, he has a girlfriend. Hence the plus one.'

Estella appeared at the door.

'Time to go,' she said. 'All hands on deck.'

Although she was not known for her organisational ability, for the past week she had been behaving like a sergeant major, even commandeering Mr and Mrs Hands to come up from Devon, where they were enjoying their work at the Bigbury Sands Hotel. Nothing, apparently, was being left to chance.

'Clarissa, are you going dressed like that?' she said, eyeing her niece's pretty lemon sundress. 'We have walls to paint, floors to sweep, magic to make. Just because it's Georgia's birthday doesn't mean we don't have to put in a bit of work today.'

Clarissa rolled her eyes, whilst Georgia laughed. It had been good of Clarissa to borrow her father's car to transport all the stuff to the party venue – yards of white net and cheap satin, hundreds of long, furry willow twigs, cans of silver paint, hurricane lanterns that had been used in bomb shelters, plus food and drink.

The venue itself was a disused boathouse on a quiet stretch of the Thames between Putney and Barnes. It had been the home of a London rowing club many years earlier, but had fallen out of fashion and was subsequently abandoned. It belonged to a friend of Colin Granger, her mother's art dealer, who had never been off the phone to Estella since the sale of her *Ribbons* series.

As they set off from their Chelsea flat, she scooped up the pile of post from the doormat. She glanced at them quickly, guessing that they would be an assortment of birthday cards and RSVPs. When she didn't recognise Edward Carlyle's handwriting among them, she stuffed them into her bag for later.

'Look at this place,' gasped Clarissa, as they arrived at the boathouse. The path to the entrance was covered in brambles, and even from this distance they could see that it was in considerable disrepair. 'Have you not visited it before today?'

'I came for a quick look,' said Estella, waving her hand dismissively. 'It's nothing we can't handle. Isn't that right, Arthur?'

Arthur Hands opened the boot and took out a hacksaw.

'We'll have this spick and span in a jiffy,' he said. Georgia thought he was going to need more than a rusty farm tool to get the place ready by September, let alone seven o'clock.

For the next five hours they painted and swept and cleaned, and by late afternoon the boathouse looked unrecognisable.

'Clarissa, can you take Georgia home to change?' said Estella, wiping her brow with the back of her hand.

'Thank you,' said Georgia gratefully, appreciating how much graft and thought had gone into the ball.

'You might even enjoy it tonight,' said Clarissa, glancing across from the wheel as they drove back along New King's Road.

'Do you think people will come?' Georgia said, feeling suddenly nervous.

'Of course people will come. Everyone gets anxious before their own party. Besides, it's your birthday. People will definitely make more of an effort.'

Georgia nodded, although she knew her cousin was just being kind – Barnes wasn't exactly central, and Georgia was certainly not one of the first-division debs with party pulling power.

By six thirty, the two girls were back at the boathouse. This was not a traditional debutante dance, most of which were preceded by a dinner party at the home of the hosts. You couldn't swing a cat in their Chelsea flat, especially with Mr and Mrs Hands staying, let alone invite thirty people for a sit-down meal. Besides, if Georgia had to do the Season, she wanted to do it in her own offbeat way.

This time Clarissa gasped in delight when they arrived. The fairy lights, wound around tree trunks and balustrade, twinkled like diamond dust in the darkening sky. She could hear nightingales in the distance and the sound of bats fluttering overhead, and soft jazz was floating out of the window.

Sometime in the past hour Estella had changed out of her paint-splattered smock into a long gown that swept all the way to the floor.

'Here she is, here she is,' she said, her arms out wide. 'The birthday girl. The belle of the ball. Come inside. You have an early visitor.'

Georgia held her breath, half hoping it would be Edward, and stepped inside, admiring the white and silver walls, and the willow that had been sprayed silver and artfully arranged in terrocotta pots.

André from the Swiss Chalet was standing by the window overlooking the Thames.

'André! You came!' She suddenly felt a little less anxious about people turning up.

'My darling, I have something special for you tonight.'

'Promises, promises,' she grinned.

'Come this way,' he said, leading her to the far end of the room, where a five-tiered coconut cake was perched on a table.

'It's like Queen Charlotte's Ball all over again.'

'I made this once for a society wedding. The recipe is good.'

'You made this? For me? How the hell did you get it here?'

'Freddie McDonald brought it over in his car. I can't believe I kept this a surprise.'

'I know! I was in the café yesterday – how did I never notice a four-foot confection!'

'I work late. I am used to it.'

She threw her arms around him.

'I have some wonderful friends,' she whispered gleefully.

'Darling, your guests are beginning to arrive,' said Estella, looking serious.

Sybil, Peter and cousin Richard were among the first. Georgia watched Sybil's eyes scan the room and wondered what she could possibly criticise.

'Your mother has gone to a lot of effort. It looks lovely. And so do you.'

She breathed a sigh of relief and touched her aunt's arm in gratitude.

'If I disapprove, it's because I want the best for you,' said Sybil, turning to look at her. 'I see Clarissa and I wonder if she hasn't left it too late to find the right man. I don't want you to make the same mistake.'

'Clarissa is only twenty-one,' said Georgia, wanting to defend her cousin.

'Perhaps for your children twenty-one will be nothing at all. It will be an age of irresponsibility, of freedom. But not now. I do not want my daughter to miss the boat, to miss out on a good marriage. Because life alone is hard. I admire Estella, I really do.'

'Georgia, how are you?'

She looked up and saw Frederick McDonald. Aunt Sybil squeezed her arm encouragingly and walked away.

'Happy birthday, darling,' he said, kissing her on the cheek. 'Bloody good bash. What do you think of the cake?'

'I love it,' laughed Georgia, glad to see her friend. 'I can't believe you've all been in cahoots over it. Who else knew? Sally?'

'I don't think so.' He smiled, looking around the party. 'Say, is she here? She promised to liberate some Krug from her father's wine cellar for this evening.'

'Our Pomagne not good enough for you?' she chided. 'Actually, I haven't seen Sally. She said she'd come and help decorate the place this afternoon with Clarissa. But she didn't show up.'

'She's probably debating which couture gown to wear,' said Freddie, and they both laughed, knowing that their friend wouldn't mind the good-natured banter. Since Queen Charlotte's Ball, Sally and Freddie had spent many afternoons at the Swiss Chalet waiting for Georgia to finish her shift, and the three of them had become firm friends.

The boathouse had filled up considerably now. Uncle Peter had turned up the music and Mr and Mrs Hands, who had insisted on dressing up, were dispensing the canapés that Mrs Hands had spent all morning making.

Freddie asked Georgia to dance and they waltzed by the open window, the breeze blowing in off the river. She relaxed into his body and felt contented. When she thought of Freddie, it was of someone who was comfortable and safe. And whilst they might not be the magical, heady emotions she experienced when she was with Edward Carlyle – the thrill of feeling drunk just from the way someone looked at you, or the charge you felt when they touched your hand – it was infinitely preferable to what she had experienced with Ian Dashwood.

That night had taught her a lesson. It had made her feel dirty and used, and she never wanted to feel like that again. If finding a husband meant getting out there, meeting semi-strangers in London's bars and clubs and restaurants, making yourself as vulnerable as she had been in Ian Dashwood's Soho flat, then she wanted no part of it.

She rested her head on Freddie's shoulder and swayed with the music, wondering if this was enough. Wondering if a happy marriage could be had with a loving friend, if not a heart-stopping lover.

'You know, when I was younger, my mother never used to let me have a pet,' said Freddie quietly, as if he were reading her thoughts. 'She said it wasn't worth it. Pets die, and I'd be so distraught and feel so much pain that it wasn't worth having one in the first place.'

Georgia lifted her head and looked at him.

'She was wrong,' continued Freddie after a moment. 'You are nineteen years old, George. You need to get out there and open your heart and fall in love, and maybe even get that heart broken. But it's worth it to feel alive, to feel love and be true to yourself. A friend isn't enough, and you certainly don't want to settle for me.'

'You don't fancy me either, do you?' she said sadly.

'I adore you, George. But do I think we should announce our engagement because it's what will make our parents happy?' He shook his head.

'So is there anyone here you do like?' she asked playfully.

'I should probably consider it over a drink. Pomagne, you say . . .'

Georgia turned round, and stopped as she bumped into the solid shape of a man in a crisp black dinner jacket.

'Happy birthday, Georgia.'

She gasped as she looked up.

'Edward. You came,' she said as Freddie discreetly walked away.

'You invited me.'

She noticed he had gone a little red in the face. He accepted a glass of Pomagne from Mr Hands, who was enjoying his role as Jeeves.

'How are you?'

'Great. It's my birthday,' she stammered. 'I've been drinking, dancing . . .'

'You should introduce me to your boyfriend.'

She didn't know what he was talking about, but she found herself nodding. It might not be a bad idea to pretend she was popular and eligible and taken, she thought, expecting to see the beautiful Annabel appear at any moment.

'Anyway. Your present.'

'You shouldn't have . . .' she smiled, tearing off the red tissue paper to find a navy box. She gasped as she opened the lid and saw the snow globe inside. Its base was painted in gold and lapis, and inside the dome was a night-time street scene of Paris.

'You should have,' she beamed, lifting it off its tissue paper bed.

'I'm sure you'll be back there soon. But in the meantime . . . just turn the little key and dream of "La Vie en Rose".'

She did as he said, and the famous French melody floated out of the box. She looked into his eyes, desperate to know what he was thinking and why he had bought her this little treasure.

'Thank you, Edward. I love it,' she said, feeling a thickness in her throat.

'Look at you. The place is packed.'

'My mum had a windfall. I think she may have used our life savings to bribe people to come.'

'Well, I didn't need a bribe.'

He gave her a soft smile and she was sure that he was flirting with her. She wanted to tell him to stop, that it wasn't fair, but the last thing she wanted to do was reveal her feelings to him. She had spent the last month steeling herself and she wasn't going to let herself down now.

'Well, here's someone you didn't invite. Not officially. Georgia

Hamilton, meet my brother Christopher.'

A thinner, younger version of Edward came over and shook her hand.

'He's my plus one, for my sins.'

'Your brother is your plus one?' she asked, her pulse racing.

'This is a seriously good party, Georgia,' said Christopher, smiling. 'I've met a famous pastry chef, an artist and an Italian count from Perugia, and I've only been here ten minutes.'

'A famous pastry chef?' laughed Georgia, feeling giddy. 'Is that how André is describing himself now?'

'Pardon the interruption, but could I have a word?' Estella looked serious as she led Georgia to one side.

'What's wrong?' asked Georgia, out of earshot of her guests.

'Don Daly has just arrived. They haven't seen Sally since last night. They called us at the house this morning to see if she was with you, but we must have left for the boathouse. They know that your party is this evening and wondered if she'd turned up.'

'You know, I don't think she has,' said Georgia, looking around. 'I thought it was strange I hadn't heard from her all day, considering it's my birthday and she promised to help us decorate this afternoon.'

'Do you have any idea where she might be? Mr and Mrs Daly are pretty frantic.'

'Wait. Wait a moment,' she said, remembering the bundle of letters she had received earlier that day. At the time she had been on the lookout for Edward's handwriting, but thinking about it, there had been one unfranked envelope covered in Sally's girlish scrawl.

She went over to the canvas sack she had brought with her that morning. She fished out the purple envelope and ripped it open. There was a single sheet of paper inside.

Happy birthday, darling Georgia.

Wishing you the merriest of days. I'd love to be celebrating with you tonight but something strange and wonderful and exciting has happened and I'm afraid I won't be able to make it. I am moving to Italy with Gianni, you see, and we are leaving today. I know some people won't understand this decision. Some people might even try to stop us. That's why I haven't told my parents yet, but I hope you will show them this note after you have read it.

Rest assured that I am happy. I always said that my life would begin when I found the person I wanted to spend it with. And here I am – ready to start my adventure.

Don't spend your special night worrying about me. Gianni is capable and strong. I will contact you all when we have settled in Italy, which I expect will be in just a few short days.

Your friend Sally

'I don't believe it.'

Estella grabbed the letter out of her hand and scanned it.

'Who on earth is Gianni?'

'An Italian count.'

Estella looked momentarily impressed.

'My goodness, Don is going to be furious,' she muttered. 'I'm going to have to tell him.'

Georgia watched her mother speak to Don, who was turning more and more purple. After a few minutes he stormed over and demanded that Georgia tell him everything she knew about Gianni.

'Honestly, Mr Daly, I don't know a thing. I met him once for just a few seconds.'

'You don't even know his surname? How can the police help us if we haven't got his surname? A port alert. That's what we need. A port alert,' and he was gone, flying out of the boathouse into his waiting Rolls-Royce.

Georgia stood on the path in a glow of a thousand fairy lights and felt a wave of concern for her friend.

She supposed Sally would be all right, but really, they didn't know Gianni from Adam, and just because he had the right breeding didn't mean to say he was the right sort. After all, Sally's previous track record with men proved she was not a particularly decent judge of character.

She frowned, thinking about something Christopher Carlyle had said when they had first met, and went back into the boat-house.

She tapped Edward on the shoulder, and he spun round, looking pleased to see her.

'Where's your brother?'

'Talking to whichever pretty girl will listen to him,' he smiled, his grey eyes twinkling.

They found him at the makeshift bar, chatting to Clarissa.

'Christopher. You said you'd met an Italian count here tonight. Which one is he?'

Christopher rubbed his chin and looked around.

'Dark hair. Dinner jacket.'

'That could describe anyone here,' said Edward.

'He had a red carnation in his buttonhole. There can't be many of those,' Christopher said weakly.

'Help me look,' said Georgia, quickly explaining about Sally's letter.

'She's run off with her boyfriend?' said Edward, incredulous.

'It looks like it.'

'Okay. You go that way, I'll take the other side.'

There was no sign of the count inside the boathouse, so she went outside, praying that he had not yet left. A few couples were holding hands and watching the Thames shimmer like Indian ink, but none of the men had a red carnation in his lapel. She moved to the side of the building – a tangle of trees and bushes. She knew from the party in Oxfordshire that this was the perfect clandestine spot for young lovers. If he was not here, then her only lead to Sally's Gianni was gone.

She heard a rustle, and then a soft sound like a moan.

She pushed back the undergrowth and saw two people ahead of her, close together, almost touching. Her eyes searched for a red carnation, and then a beam of moonlight caught them and she realised that it was André and Frederick.

They both turned and saw Georgia, but she sprang back and ran towards the boathouse.

Edward was standing on the balcony with a dark-haired man with the identifying flower.

'You'd better explain yourself,' he said gruffly as Georgia approached.

The dark-haired boy looked sheepish.

'What's going on?' said Georgia, still shocked from what she had seen in the bushes.

'Georgia, this is Pietro. He is a count from Perugia. Or so he's been telling all the debs and their mothers when he gatecrashes their parties.'

'You're not a count?' said Georgia, her mouth dropping open.

'Tell her what you just told me,' ordered Edward. Georgia felt quite excited by the way he had taken charge of the situation.

'I work in the Rubens Hotel,' he said, not looking at her.

'Doing what?'

'I am a bus boy in the restaurant,' he said awkwardly. 'It started out as a joke. A mistake. One day we were walking home from work in our dinner suits. We saw a party, people, beautiful ladies spilling out on to the street. We went to the door, and we walked straight inside. Someone asked who we were and we couldn't say we were two Italian bus boys from the Rubens, so we pretended to be Perugian aristocracy. It seemed a good way to meet girls.'

'Who's we?' asked Georgia.

'Myself and Gianni.'

'Sally's Gianni?'

'Where are they?' asked Edward firmly.

Pietro hesitated.

'If you don't tell us, I am going to call the police and they will have you deported back to Italy quicker than you can say con artist,' growled Edward.

'They are going to Italy.'

'We know that from Sally's letter. Where? When?'

'First they are going to Scotland. They are going to get married.'

'Married!' gasped Georgia.

'He loves her!' insisted Pietro.

'He loves her? He's a fortune-hunter who wants to get his hands on her money.'

'When did they leave?' asked Edward more calmly.

'They were catching the afternoon train to Carlisle.'

'Do you know where they are staying?'

Pietro shook his head.

'How old is Sally?' asked Edward quickly.

'Seventeen.'

'They'll be in Gretna Green,' said Edward bleakly.

'Gretna Green?'

'You have to be eighteen or over to marry without your parents' consent. In Scotland you only have to be sixteen. Gretna is the first Scottish town over the border – maybe ten miles from Carlisle. It's geared up for runaway weddings.'

'We should tell Sally's parents, and then the police.'

'The poor family,' Edward said drily. 'If the police know, it will leak out to the press. A deb eloping to Gretna . . . That's going to be one hell of a scandal.'

Georgia imagined the shame of her friend in the newspapers. She knew how brutal high society could be, and she thought of all Mr and Mrs Daly's good intentions being thrown away thanks to the charm and cunning of a hotel waiter.

'Then let's stop them.'

'Stop them?'

'Stop them getting married. Edward, I have to.'

'We'd better get going, then,' said Edward decisively.

'You'll come with me? To Gretna Green?'

'If you can think of a way to leave your party and get in the car before I change my mind.'

CHAPTER SIXTEEN

They waited another hour, until the crowds drifted off and Peter, Sybil, Clarissa and Estella were ready to go home. Georgia told her mother she was going on to Soho with some friends, which was not a particularly unusual occurrence. Many debs floated from dance to nightclub to house party, and parents turned a blind eye to their daughters returning home at dawn.

It was not possible to catch the train to Scotland. Edward's family had a shooting lodge north of the border and he knew the timetables up there off pat. There was the Royal Scot morning train, an afternoon departure and the evening Caledonian, but if they left it until the next day, they ran the risk of Sally already being married. There was nothing for it but to drive. The road map of Great Britain was changing – motorways were being built which would apparently cut the travel time north by hours. But for now they had to take the A1 up to Birmingham and then Manchester. Edward's Aston Martin was fast, but the journey was long and tedious. Georgia chatted as much as she could to keep him awake, although she found herself nodding off at intervals.

She wound down the window to let some fresh air into the car.

'I think it's a bit sad that Sally wants to get married alone,' she sighed, sucking on one of the sherbert lemons they had bought from a tobacco shop.

'I do believe she'll have Gianni at her side,' smiled Edward, his eyes fixed on the road.

'She's always been in love with the idea of love and was almost certainly seduced by the idea of *la dolce vita* and being a countess in Italy. It's just so sad that she's been duped. It's going to turn her hard and cynical . . .'

'A bit like you?'

'How am I hard and cynical?' she said, sitting up in her seat.

'"Marriage is just a contract" . . . Does your boyfriend know that?'

'Boyfriend?' she said.

'At the party. You were dancing with him. Head on shoulder. You looked quite in love with the idea of love yourself.'

'Ah, Frederick,' she said quietly. 'I'm not entirely sure I'm his type,' she said diplomatically. 'The truth is – we're just friends.'

They sat in silence for a few more minutes. Edward looked thoughtful, concentrating hard at the wheel. Watching him, she felt a wave of emotion so strong it almost took her breath away. She told herself she was just tired, and prayed that all the Season's silliness hadn't turned her into the sort of girl who loved the idea of being in love. But sitting inside the close confines of the car, she wanted to stay like this for ever. She liked the way she could tell him everything about her day. She liked the anticipation of what he would reveal about himself next. She liked the way her tummy felt – all fluttery and light – when she glanced over at him and saw his profile: straight nose, long dark lashes and those eyes that seemed to look right inside her and know what she was about to say before she had even said it. She liked the way everything just felt right when she was with him. Even if she had lost her handbag or been unwelcomely groped by a Welsh Guard or thrown her broken shoes into the river. Just being with him mended it all.

It was dawn now, and the soft sun rising over the rolling hills of the Lake District was quite beautiful. Another ninety minutes and they had passed the Welcome to Scotland sign and followed the road into Gretna, past the marriage rooms, which apparently had seen more than a thousand marriages performed since 1830. She hoped Sally and Gianni's hadn't been one of them.

The village was still quiet and Edward switched off the ignition of the car.

'They could be anywhere,' said Georgia, listening to the engine slowly die down.

'That's if they are even in Gretna.'

'Now you tell me,' she said, realising that their long, long drive could have been a total waste of time.

'It's a small place. There can't be too many guest houses and hotels.'

'And Sally definitely likes her luxury. She's not going to put up with some poky cottage even if she is deliriously happy at the prospect of being a countess.'

'Good thinking,' said Edward.

He got out of the car and started walking, his eyes scanning the street. Finally they saw a black and white manor house, approached by a long drive.

'What about here?' he asked as Georgia read the sign – Gretna Hall.

'I bet this is the grandest place in the village,' she agreed.

They went inside and peered into the dining room, where

couples were beginning to collect for breakfast. But there was no sign of Sally and Gianni.

Edward approached the receptionist and asked if Sally Daly was staying with them.

The man at the desk looked hesitant.

'We do value the privacy of our guests here,' he said diplomatically in a gentle Scots accent.

'In which case, can I have two rooms?' Edward requested, getting out his wallet.

'Are we going to stake out the hotel?' asked Georgia, with a slight nagging disappointment that he had requested two rooms.

'We need to find Sally, and then I don't know about you, but I need to sleep.'

She looked at his handsome face, dark shadows forming moon-shaped circles beneath his eyes, and felt a spike of affection that he had done this for her. For Sally, she reminded herself.

'We should sit in the breakfast room and see if they come down,' he said.

'That's if they're here.'

They took a table by the window and ordered some smoked mackerel.

Georgia's eyes drifted outside and she saw a couple strolling hand in hand across the lawns.

'I don't believe it. It's them,' she said, jumping out of her seat. 'Are you coming?'

'I think this is a conversation you need to have with Sally alone.'

Georgia ran out of the hotel towards her friend, who looked startled as she approached.

'Georgia. What the hell are you doing here?'

'Looking for you,' she gasped. 'Your family are frantic. You can't do this. Have you done it?'

She looked at Gianni sternly.

'Could I talk to my friend alone for a minute?'

Gianni glanced at Sally, who nodded. He squeezed her hand and walked back towards the hotel.

Georgia could barely get her words out quickly enough.

'Don't marry him,' she pleaded. 'Don't step anywhere near the anvil with this man. That's what happens, isn't it? A blacksmith can marry you right here, right now. Well, don't do it, because I have something to say.'

'We can't get married today,' said Sally quietly. 'We thought we could, but the rules have changed and we have to wait over two weeks. That's fine, though, because this is what I want to do, George.'

'No you don't,' Georgia said, not even having time to register the relief that Sally was not yet married. 'There's something you should know. Gianni is not a count. He's a bus boy at a London hotel and he's been gatecrashing parties with his friend to hook up with pretty, wealthy girls. Don't marry him. He's after your money, and even though you probably think you're happy, this is all just going to make you horribly miserable.'

'I know he's not a count,' Sally replied simply.

That response floored Georgia.

'You know?'

'I know he's a waiter from Padua. His name is Gianni Adami. He came to London to work because he lost his father in Mussolini's war, and he sends money back to his family. I knew from our second date,' she said quite cheerfully. 'He told me over hot chocolate and Chelsea buns at the café in Victoria round the corner from the hotel where he works.'

'You know he's a bus boy? You don't think he's a con man . . .'

Sally laughed.

'Darling Georgia, you always think the worst of people. So

Gianni and his friends lied a little to get into the deb dances and parties. They were young men having fun.'

'Do you love him?'

'With all my heart. He is handsome and kind and good and I know he adores me. If that's not what a girl is looking for in a husband, then I don't know what is.'

'I understand that you like him,' said Georgia, shaking her head. 'You might even think you love him. But Sally, you don't have to marry him. Take your time,' she implored.

'But I'm pregnant,' replied her friend simply.

Georgia couldn't help gasping.

'Oh Sally . . . But Gianni . . . How can you be?'

'The baby's not Gianni's. We haven't . . . we haven't, you know, done that yet.'

'Then whose is it?'

She grew suddenly sheepish.

'You remember the house party in Oxfordshire?'

'Andrew from Cirencester,' said Georgia, feeling wretched. If only she hadn't abandoned her friend. If only she had rescued her from the bushes.

'Sally, I'm so sorry, I shouldn't have left you.'

'It was entirely my own fault. We had sex in an airing cupboard before I'd even discovered that you'd gone. It was over in minutes . . . However, the consequences might last a little longer.' Her voice was clear and matter-of-fact but her eyes had started to water, and Georgia rested her arm gently across her friend's shoulders.

'Sally, there's things we can do . . .'

'What?' she replied flatly. 'Some dirty back-street room where they'd kill my baby with carbolic soap and a knitting needle and possibly kill me too? I've read the newspapers.'

Georgia had read the same stories. In Paris, a newspaper

clipping, possibly planted by Madame Didiot, had been passed around the dorm like some warning to wayward students who let their morals get too loose.

'Does Gianni know this?' she asked carefully.

'Georgia, can't you see? That is why I think he is so wonderful. I mean, look, I am beginning to get a tiny belly so I knew I couldn't hide it for much longer. I was desperate to tell someone, so I confided in Gianni, thinking he would finish with me on the spot, but he was so gentle and loving. Together we made a plan.'

'To marry,' said Georgia softly.

'We were going to pretend that the baby was his. But we thought people might accept it more if we ran away and got married. I knew it would still be a terrible scandal, so Gianni thought we could go and live in Venice. He has an auntie there and it sounds so wonderful, Georgia. You can buy oranges the size of footballs and go to work by gondola. Isn't that the most romantic thing you've ever heard?'

'But what now?'

'Now we have to think again. It's around two weeks before we can marry and I can't leave my parents in the dark for that long.'

'They're frantic,' said Georgia softly.

'Thank you for coming, George. Thank you for caring.'

'I was worried about you. We drove through the night to get here before the day's weddings started.'

Sally looked anxious.

'*We?* My family aren't with you, are they?'

'No. Edward Carlyle. He drove me up here. All through the night.'

Sally nodded thoughtfully.

'Then he's handsome and kind and good and I know he adores you.'

'I wish it were true,' said Georgia, shrugging her shoulders.

'But he has a girlfriend and I think he sees me as this silly little debutante he has to keep saving. Maybe he has some psychological condition . . .'

'But are you in love with him?'

She looked up and nodded.

'Then go and tell him. Right now. Don't stop and think about it. Just tell him.'

'What about you?' asked Georgia, her heart thumping out of her chest.

'I've found love. Now it's your turn, and what better place to be true to your heart than here. GO!' she ordered.

Georgia went back into the dining room, but Edward had left.

'Your husband asked me to tell you he has gone upstairs,' said the waitress, clearing away the plates of mackerel.

'Remind me of our room numbers,' Georgia said. The waitress checked her list of diners.

'Sixteen and seventeen,' she replied.

Georgia followed the signs and knocked on the door of number sixteen on the first floor. It was a few moments before it creaked open. Edward stood there with slightly ruffled hair and sleepy eyes.

'Can I come in?' she asked.

'Sorry. Your room key,' he said, rubbing his face.

Her eyes skirted over the rumpled bed and she felt a flood of excitement and nerves.

'So how is she?' asked Edward anxiously. 'She's not married yet, is she?'

'She's fine. Sally is fine. They can't marry for at least two weeks and she knows all about Gianni. Always has done, but she loves him. It's that simple.'

'Is it?' said Edward, rubbing his cheek.

'We always hope love is simple, but sometimes it's not, is it?'

'No, it's not,' he replied softly.

'Why are you here?' she whispered, closing the bedroom door behind her, willing herself to stay strong. 'Everything we have done together suggests that . . . suggests that you like me. I know you have a girlfriend, and I know she is probably very smart and rich and beautiful, but sometimes that's not everything. Sometimes it's about two people who just feel happy being together, and when that happens, those two people should *be* together.'

He didn't reply immediately, and the silence spun embarrassingly around the room.

'Georgia, I don't like you,' he said finally.

'Oh,' she said, feeling her courage desert her and her heart shatter.

'I think I have fallen in love with you.'

'With me?' she whispered.

'I don't have a girlfriend. Not any more. There was Annabel, and I went to the ball with her and then we left university and it's over. Because I can't stop thinking about someone else. I can't stop comparing every single woman I know with someone who has come into my life and lit it up like a Catherine wheel.'

He stepped forward and took her hand.

'There's a place just outside called the Kissing Gate.'

'Do we need to go that far?' she whispered.

He took her face between his hands and kissed her softly on the lips. And somewhere deep down, she felt her own fireworks go off in her heart.

CHAPTER SEVENTEEN

24 December 2012

It had been a busy day. The busiest Christmas Eve Amy could remember. Much of it had been spent eating: breakfast pancakes with strawberry butter and maple syrup at Good Enough to Eat, hot chocolate and pumpkin muffins at Sarabeth's Bakery in Chelsea Market, and cupcakes from Sprinkles on Lexington. She had shopped for Christmas presents for the family in Bloomingdale's, popped into the Plaza Hotel to see their giant *Great Gatsby*-themed Christmas tree, watched the ice skaters on the rink in Central Park, and even queued up to get inside the iconic toy shop FAO Schwarz – which Georgia agreed was all part of the Christmas experience.

But pulling up outside Carmichael Street, Amy reconsidered the wisdom of inviting Georgia round to her house, which looked so much smaller and more shabby than she remembered. Her dad had said 'the more the merrier' when she had rung to check, but then he had once invited a hobo to dinner when he'd spotted him panhandling outside Dempsey's: any excuse to break out his Old Navy Rum was a good one to her dad. She knew her mom would be fretting about the food and the seating and the dishes, probably furiously polishing the 'good' silver – that was the cutlery set from Macy's rather than Kmart – at this very moment. Amy was more worried about the rest of the family. Would her brother Billy embarrass her with tales from their childhood? Would Uncle Chuck get drunk and insist on singing? More to the point, would it all be a little, well, lower class for such a sophisticated lady as Georgia Hamilton?

'A charming house,' said Georgia, as if she was reading Amy's mind. 'I am very much looking forward to meeting your family.'

'Well, don't expect too much,' said Amy.

'On the contrary, Amy,' said Georgia, taking her arm as they walked up the path, 'I am a great believer in nurture over nature and I do not think people appear from nowhere fully formed. You are a product of your family, Amy Carrell, and on that basis, I expect them to be perfectly charming.'

Amy was about to say that she could expect all she liked but that wouldn't stop Uncle Chuck from groping her ass, when the door flew open and Amy felt herself sucked into a huge hug.

'Merry Christmas, Aunt Amy!' cried the two children clinging to her waist.

'Hey, hey,' she laughed. 'Careful or you'll crush all these presents I brought.'

The children started clamouring for the gifts, but Amy held them out of their reach until she was inside the house. 'Here, go and put them under the tree.'

She looked around and was immediately hit by a rush of affection and nostalgia. The tree was where it always was in the hallway, sagging under far too many trimmings, the battered and threadbare angel she'd so loved as a girl still clinging gamely to the top. There were old-fashioned paper chains strung along the beams of every room and crêpe paper reindeers and snowmen tacked to the windows, just as there always had been. But most of all it was the smell that made Amy go weak with longing: that mixture of pine needles and cooking and punch and candles, each smell laid over that indefinable scent of 'home'.

'Hey, honey,' said a gruff voice. 'Welcome home.'

Amy fell into her father's arms, loving the feel of him: his strength and warmth. He felt safe and right. In his embrace she was five years old again and doing cartwheels of excitement waiting for Santa.

'Dad,' she said. 'This is my friend, Georgia Hamilton.'

'Hey, how ya doin'?' he said, stepping forward to offer his ham-hock hand. 'Nick Carrell. Ya takin' care of my little girl for me, I hear.'

'Dad . . .' said Amy, blushing.

'Oh no, Amy has been taking care of me, Mr Carrell,' smiled Georgia, meeting his gaze. 'And she's been doing a wonderful job.'

'Amy! Honey,' screamed Connie Carrell, running out of the kitchen.

Her mother had literally wept tears of delight when Amy had called her a week earlier to say that she was coming home, and her excitement still hadn't subsided.

'This is just the best Christmas present I could ask for. My little girl home. Nick, get Georgia a drink.'

'You like whiskey?'

'Nick!' said Connie, slapping his arm. 'You can't offer this nice lady whiskey.'

'Actually, Amy has been telling me about your egg nog on the way over here. I confess I've never had egg nog before.'

'Comin' right up,' said Nick, smiling.

Amy gave Georgia a sideways smile. The older woman certainly knew which of her dad's buttons to press.

'Come through and meet everyone,' said Connie. In short succession Georgia was introduced to Amy's brother Billy, his wife Helen and their three children Candice, Billy Jr and baby Gretel, as well as Uncle Chuck, who seemed to be reasonably sober and immediately took a shine to Georgia, hovering over her, passing her nibbles and refilling her glass as soon as she took a sip. Amy sat back and watched, so happy to see her family again, but also happy to see them welcome her friend so warmly. She had only been away for a little over two years, but it had felt like decades. Too long.

Finally Connie clapped her hands to summon them all through to the tiny dining room.

'Family tradition, Georgia. We have a big ham on Christmas Eve. It leaves us too stuffed for turkey the next day, but hey, you got to start Christmas as soon as possible, then keep it going for as long as you can. Those have always been the rules in this house.'

'So long as we're not having goose tomorrow,' grumbled Uncle Chuck. 'Should have seen the size of the thing. It was like a goddam pigeon.'

Everyone sat down, arguing over the merits of turkey versus goose, ten of them crammed around a table that could really only comfortably seat six, but their elbow-to-elbow proximity only added to the feeling of togetherness.

'So why hasn't Dan the Man come?' asked Billy, leaning back in his chair and rubbing his stomach, his blue shirt straining at the buttons. 'I want to meet your fancy English guy finally.'

'We both wanted to be with our families over the holidays,' Amy replied, wondering what Daniel was doing at this moment. She imagined him in the family home, a honey-stone manor house straight out of a Jane Austen novel. She had been there only once and had felt on edge all the time, not wanting to ruin the perfect picture by actually sitting down anywhere. She pictured him sitting at the formal dining table, cutting into his quail or whatever fancy British families ate at Christmas, making strained conversation with Vivienne, planning with his father to conquer the world. Well, he had made his choice – made his bed, as her friend Annie liked to say. Now he had to lie in it.

'Say, Candice. How's the ballet coming along?' she asked her seven-year-old niece, wanting to change the subject.

'I love it,' she grinned with a gap-toothed smile.

Billy's wife Helen bounced baby Gretel up and down on her lap.

'She wanted to see some real ballet, so I took her to the Lincoln Center, saved up for months for those tickets, and she got so damn bored we had to leave after twenty minutes.'

Candice made a face and pushed some potatoes into her mouth.

'Still, she wants to be a ballet dancer when she grows up. I told her she gotta keep practising, keep it up if she wants to be like her auntie Amy.'

Amy smiled hard, deciding this was not the right time to tell Candice about the pain and the constant rejection and the fact there was a good chance your boyfriend's parents might think you were a slut. Best to let a little girl have her dreams. After all, she had been the same as a student at Miss Josephine's dance academy on Quebec Street, the school that Candice now went to. She still kept in touch with Miss Josephine, who had been like a second mom to her growing up. When she'd moved to England they had swapped regular letters and emails, but these had dwindled as Amy grew more and more embarrassed about the state of her career. She wanted Miss Josephine to think she had produced at least one star.

Nick Carrell topped up Georgia's glass.

'So, Amy tells me you have a great apartment. It's like worth a million bucks or somethin'?'

'I did not!' gasped Amy.

'You told your mom it looked like a duchess's house in some swanky part of town,' said her father, looking offended.

'I suppose Primrose Hill is rather lovely,' smiled Georgia. 'I bought at the right time. The nearest thing London has to a village, and yet when you climb to the top of the hill it's all there before you. The BT Tower, the London Eye, St Paul's.'

'Have you got family, Georgia?' asked Connie politely. Amy noticed her friend stiffen.

'Yes, but I don't see them very often. They live out in the countryside.'

'What are they up to back home in England?'

'Uncle Chuck . . .' said Amy with a warning tone.

'No, it's fine,' said Georgia. 'I suppose they'll be doing much the same as here. Having a party, eating and drinking too much. Won't be anywhere near as much fun as here, though. And this food's much better.'

Amy saw her mother's proud smile.

'You gotta watch the British,' said Chuck, waving a finger. 'Poor teeth, poor food. To think you're going to marry into that!'

Amy blushed furiously.

'I haven't got any plans to get married, Uncle Chuck.'

'Really?' said Connie with interest. 'I thought it was serious with Dan.'

'I wanna be a bridesmaid,' shouted Candice with her mouth full.

'Stop it, all of you!'

'Hey, don't knock it until you've tried it, sis,' said Billy, squeezing Helen's hand. 'It ain't so bad, huh?'

'So come on, Ames. Tell us. Can I expect a visit from this Daniel asking for my daughter's hand in marriage? Guess he's going to do things the proper way, huh?'

She was glad when Uncle Chuck changed the subject to talk about the upcoming Jets game and the clean-up operation in Queens after Hurricane Sandy.

Mrs Carrell served two puddings – a home-made pumpkin pie the colour of autumn leaves and a plum pudding complete with thick cream. When every last spoonful had been scraped from their bowls and the detritus had been taken to the kitchen, Amy and Georgia were shooed through to the sitting room. 'You're the guests today,' said Connie. 'Everyone else can help with the dishes.'

Amy flopped into an armchair.

'Overload,' she groaned, patting her flat stomach. 'I need to go and lie down.'

'Sounds like a good idea,' said Georgia. 'In fact, I think that's my cue to leave.'

'Don't go,' said Amy, sitting up. 'You're welcome to stay. In fact Mom and Dad will be offended if you leave.'

'I should go,' she said with such finality that Amy didn't challenge her further.

'I got you a present,' said Amy, looking around for the bag of gifts she had brought with her. 'It's not as extravagant as that amazing dress and shoes you got me, but I think you'll like it.'

She rooted around in the bag until she found Georgia's present.

'Open it now,' she said.

'But it's not Christmas yet,' smiled Georgia.

'Please,' said Amy.

Georgia's thin fingers unwrapped the paper. Inside was a snow globe of New York.

'Shake it and all the snowflakes – fake, of course – will sprinkle over the city. I know how much you wanted it to snow, and I can't fix the weather, but when I saw this, I knew you'd love it.'

She looked up and saw that Georgia was crying. Just two single tears slipping down her cheeks, but still her reaction surprised her.

'Don't you like it?'

'I love it,' whispered Georgia. 'Someone gave me something similar once. A snow globe of Paris. It's one of my treasures.'

'Now you have two,' grinned Amy.

Georgia held the globe in both hands and looked at her.

'Do you know what really constitutes being a lady?' she said softly. 'Kindness. Kindness is at the heart of it all, and you have that quality in spades, Amy Carrell.'

She cleared her throat and straightened her back, the more aloof Georgia returning.

'I think Alfonse has just arrived,' she said, seeing two beams of light outside. 'I should go. Have fun tomorrow with your family.'

'Thank you so much, Georgia. Thanks for making this happen,' Amy said, leaning forward and hugging her. She was surprised how slight and fragile the older woman felt in her arms. Georgia seemed to flinch at her gesture, but then gave her a small squeeze.

'No rush to get back to the hotel. Have a very merry Christmas, Amy.'

The whole family stood on the stoop and waved her off. Amy watched the tail lights disappear around the corner, until her dad put his arm around her shoulders and led her back into the kitchen, which was already clean and tidy.

'It's good to have you back, honey,' he said, switching on the coffee machine. 'Are you okay? You're okay for money?'

'Dad, everything is fine.'

He gave her that cocked-head quizzical look he'd given her as a kid when she'd been keeping something from him, that 'Dad knows everything' look. He'd always trusted her to do the right thing then, and he didn't say anything now.

'I can't believe you asked Georgia how much her apartment was worth,' said Amy, sitting down at the kitchen table and giving him an embarrassed half-smile.

'I did not.'

'You did.'

'So I'm interested.'

'It's not the done thing. It's rude.'

'What's rude?'

'To ask personal questions. Questions about money and how much you earn.'

'Says who? The Queen of England?'

He handed her a cup of coffee and sat opposite her.

'She's a nice lady,' he said, taking a sip.

'You sound surprised.'

He shrugged.

'Didn't know what to expect. Y'gotta admit, it's kinda a strange set-up. I mean, why's she not with her own family at Christmas?'

'Yeah, well, you shouldn't have kept bringing her family up, either. She doesn't seem to like talking about them.'

'I thought there might be a story there. You know, something we could have helped with?'

Amy fixed her hands around her coffee cup.

'What do you mean?'

'It's just a bit odd. Why isn't she with her family? Or friends? Why does she have to come to New York with a stranger? It doesn't make sense. Not a nice fancy lady like that with money.'

Amy shrugged.

'I met her cousin's son in London, but I could tell there was some history going on.'

'See? You should ask her. Might do her some good to talk about it.'

'Georgia's not like that. The English aren't like that. It's rude to ask.'

'What is it with this *rude* thing? Maybe the lady's got a problem. Maybe she *wants* to talk about it to someone.'

He snorted again, shook his head.

'Each to their own, I guess. Anyway, how's London treating you? You still working at the bar?'

Amy sipped her coffee.

'You sound disappointed.'

'In you? You kidding me? Never.'

'Seriously? I haven't exactly got my name in lights.'

'Amy, nobody worked harder than you to get outta Queens and make something of themselves. You've been all over the world doing what you love – you know how rare that is? Sure, I'd rather you were closer, but that's just a dad being selfish. Truth? Every time any of the guys at Dempsey's asks after my little girl, I feel ten feet tall.'

Amy wasn't sure she was going to get away without crying.

'You just say the word and you can come home. I can paint your old room, you can stay there until you find someplace new. We can help you with money. Your old dad hasn't done too bad. Just say the word.'

Amy looked at him, sorely tempted. After all, what was there for her in London? Daniel was gone, she'd had one audition in six months and she was barely managing to eat on her wages from the Forge. But she couldn't let her family down. She remembered them waving her off at Newark – even Uncle Chuck had been crying, but they had all told her a dozen times that it was worth it if she could build a better life for herself outside of Queens. They'd had such faith in her, such cast-iron belief that she was going to dance her way to stardom and find herself a handsome British prince at the same time – her mom had seriously suggested she get a job in the Buckingham Palace gift shop, so convinced was she that Prince Harry would fall in love with her if only their paths would cross – that she couldn't come crawling back now, no job, no boyfriend, nothing to show for her two years in exotic Europe. What would her dad say to the guys in Dempsey's then? What would Candice tell her friends at Miss Josephine's?

'I miss you guys like crazy. But I have a life in London. I like it. I've got friends and I can't come running home just because I'm not dancing,' she said, determined not to let the cracks show.

'It's Daniel, isn't it?' He smiled. 'Home is where the heart is, I guess.' A look of such pride settled on his face that she knew it was not the right time to tell him her relationship had ended. Not on Christmas Eve.

Billy walked in rubbing his hands.

'Fenies is open. What say we all go down and toast Santa?'

Amy shook her head.

'I've had enough to drink and I've got a long flight on Wednesday.'

'Which is two whole days away,' he said, throwing over her coat. 'Come on. All the old gang will be down there.'

Fenies was an Irish pub, but it was a world away from the ones you could find in Finsbury Park. There were none of the grand Victorian mouldings and high ceilings of the British tradition, just a long low room with a wooden bar at one side and beer served in bottles. Even so, it was heaving. *Christmas Eve, I guess*, thought Amy, glad she had changed into a pair of her mom's trainers; she had been wearing her new shoes and it would have been heartbreaking to have them ruined by spilt Miller and trampling toes.

'It's busy,' she said, as Billy elbowed his way towards the bar, a twenty held up between three fingers like a shark's fin.

'Two Bud,' said her brother and handed one to Amy. Behind the bar there were hundreds of photos from parties held here over the years. She scanned them, wondering if she was in any of them. Fenies was like a youth club to her high-school year; no one was ever carded here.

As she sipped her cold beer, listening to the good-natured rabble around her, she felt a pang of affection for her home town. The little part of Queens she had grown up in – just a mile from the Atlantic seaboard – was not really the New York you saw in the movies. It lacked the glamour of Manhattan, the beatnik cool of certain pockets of Brooklyn, and for a place with such a stately name, it was pretty unremarkable. But this was where people lived, real people: the local high street was still full of delis and bagel shops, funeral parlours and hardware stores, all the things you really needed.

'No way! Amy goddam Carrell!'

Amy turned, her mouth open.

'Suzie?' she gasped. 'It *is* you!'

She threw her arms around her friend and squeezed.

'I don't believe it! I haven't seen you in – what is it? Two years?'

'Well, a lot's changed since then,' said Suzie, holding up her hand to show off a diamond ring.

'You're engaged?'

Suzie darted into the crowd and grabbed a burly man with dark close-cropped hair.

'Brian, meet Amy Carrell,' she said, planting a kiss on his neck. 'Amy is my oldest, best friend from kindergarten. She's a dancer in London.'

Amy saw the same pride in Suzie's face as had been in her dad's expression. Maybe she hadn't been such a failure after all.

'Good to meet ya, Amy,' said Brian, grinning.

'Yeah, put your tongue away, Romeo,' said Suzie, slapping his arm. 'Remember who you proposed to.'

Brian threw a possessive arm around her. 'Yeah, like I'd ever forget that. So what you dancing in now, Amy?'

'A new production about tango. In the West End in London. Rehearsals start in the new year,' said Amy, stretching the truth a little.

'London, huh? Maybe I'll take Suze along if you ever make it to Broadway.'

'Contemporary dance, honey,' smiled Suzie. 'Not your thing.'

'Hey, I like modern dance,' protested Brian. 'Half-naked girls in hose.'

'You like Hooters,' said Suzie, pushing him back into the crowd. 'That's what you like. Now go get us two drinks so we can catch up, huh?'

Brian winked and disappeared into the throng.

'He's cute,' said Amy.

'He's a firefighter over in Brooklyn. Looks very cute in his uniform. Even cuter without it.'

'Same old Suze, huh?'

'I know what I like, is all. Besides, we don't all have your legs.'

Amy raised her eyebrows. She had always been jealous of Suzie's curves and easy sex appeal. 'I think you made out okay.'

'So your mom told my mom that you got a rich boyfriend?' She clinked her beer against Amy's. 'I'm so happy for you, Ames. It all worked out for you, didn't it?' she said wistfully.

'You remember all those times when we were ten and you tried to persuade me to come to dance class? What was that teacher called? Miss Jo-Jo?'

Amy nodded.

'There's times I wish I'd kept it up like you, or at least held out for a job I loved, instead of dealing with sick pooches over at the Blue Cross.'

'You always loved animals, Suze.'

'Yeah, but the sort in tight pants.'

They giggled.

'Well, it looks like you did okay too,' said Amy.

'Yeah, Brian's a keeper. What about you? Mom said your boyfriend's some British millionaire.'

She opened her mouth to tell Suzie that it was all over – she was desperate to tell someone – but Suzie was motioning towards the back of the bar.

'Shame, 'cos your old high-school hottie is over there.'

'Chris Carvey?' Amy said, feeling suddenly nervous.

'Go and say hi. In fact let's both go and say hi. He always did brighten my day,' Suzie said with a wink.'

'Suze, no. It's fine. I'm only staying for one drink.'

But she had already been marched out towards a covered backyard area. Since her last visit, someone with green thumbs had turned what had been the delivery yard into a beer garden, with trees and big shrubs in pots, and little seating areas. It was cold outside, but even Amy had to admit that the fairy lights added a bit of Christmas magic. She stopped in her tracks as a man turned to face her.

'Chris,' she said.

'Hey, Amy,' he replied casually, as if they'd just bumped into one another in the corridor at high school. The years seemed to melt away at the sound of his voice, and suddenly she was back in twelfth grade. Chris had been her first love, her high-school sweetheart, and everyone had expected them to get engaged on prom night, like Billy and Helen had done, and settle down in his grandmother's house soon afterwards. But it hadn't quite happened that way.

219

'You look great,' she said, and it was true. He'd always had that cute boy-next-door look about him, but now he seemed to have grown into it. A few laughter lines and a day's worth of stubble had taken the prettiness from his features and made him a proper heartbreaker. Only it had been Amy who had done the heartbreaking, leaving the city in the autumn after graduation to go to dance school upstate.

'So you're back for the holidays?'

'Sure am,' she said. 'Thought I might bump into some old friends.'

'I had the same thought. I haven't been here for years.'

'You used to love Fenies,' she grinned.

She was surprised by the instant crackle of chemistry between them. Perhaps that never went away between first loves, she thought, a little embarrassed that she had felt it.

'I did, but I don't live around here any more,' replied Chris quickly. 'I'm just back for Christmas, visiting the folks.'

She nodded to hide her surprise. She never thought Chris would ever leave Queens. It was one of the reasons why their relationship had ended. She'd wanted to be a dancer and travel the world. When Chris left high school, his destiny was to go and work at his dad's tyre shop at the end of Carmichael Street, and one day to take it over.

'We moved to Westchester a couple of years ago,' he explained. 'Schools are good up there.'

Schools? She looked at his ring finger, but it was bare.

'You're married?' She cringed as she heard her voice squeak. She didn't know why she was feeling so territorial; after all, their relationship had finished eight years ago. *She* had ended it.

'Not yet. Still with Amber, though. We've been engaged for ever. We always said we'd get round to it when the kids were big enough. Jack's five next summer, so I guess we're running out of excuses.'

'That's great. I'm so happy for you,' she said honestly.

'Guess we've just been too busy. We're got ten tyre shops now. Business is going great. Five in Queens, one in Staten Island, four in Westchester. Just say the word when you ever need a discount.'

'Wow, that's great. And so generous, Chris, it really is.'

'What about you? Married? Engaged? Living happily in sin with some lucky Brit?'

She took a breath, ready to tell him how great life was with Daniel, but then stopped herself.

'I won't tell you that version of events,' she said quietly.

'What?'

'You always did know when I was lying.' She smiled, remembering who she was with and how well he knew her.

'That little spot under your left eye, it always used to tic.'

He touched the top of her cheek, and for a moment she was back in high school, her whole life ahead of her and true love living at the end of the street in the two-storey house next to the tyre shop.

'I was dating someone for a while in London, but it finished a couple of weeks ago. It's fine, though.' She smiled, taking a sip of her beer.

'So tell me about Amber. I'm sure she's terrific.'

Chris nodded.

'She is. You know, you were always my yardstick and I never thought anyone would ever match you. But she's up there. Amber's a great girl.'

The space around them seemed to contract so that it was just them. Her heart was pounding and she had to look away from his dark brown eyes. She felt a wash of nostalgia so strong she sighed audibly.

'Our timing was off, wasn't it?' she said finally. He always knew what she was thinking, so she figured she might as well say it out loud. They had never really discussed the end of the relationship beyond the argument that had finished it.

'Is that what it was?' he said in a tone that said he didn't believe her.

'It was always going to be hard when one of us went away to college,' she said, looking back up at him.

'Do you ever wonder what would have happened if you'd got into Juilliard?' His voice had softened. It was more wistful now, rather than the hurt pride that had been evident before.

She closed her eyes and remembered that day. It had been no surprise she hadn't got into New York's most prestigious arts college. Her audition had been awful. She'd felt unwell and out of sorts and for years she had blamed her rejection on the bad luck of an off day. Now she realised that perhaps – probably – the competition had been too fierce. She was good, but not good enough. On the day the rejection letter had arrived, she had gone to Manhattan with Chris and they had sat on a bench in Battery Park watching the Staten Island ferries sail back and forth and just held each other. She remembered how she felt as though her world had fallen apart. The pain of not accomplishing her dream, the fear of leaving her boyfriend to go upstate to her second-choice college, which had offered her a full scholarship.

What would have happened if she'd got into Juilliard? she asked herself, seeing a sudden flash of an alternative life. She felt sure she would be dancing now, not waitressing. She would be in demand in all the repertories around the world. And perhaps she would still be with Chris, who had always been one of the good ones. Instead he had come up to Albany for the weekend a week before the end of the first semester at college and she had told him it just wasn't working. It had been as simple as that.

Because it hadn't felt as if it was working. Not when she had got sucked into college life and rehearsals.

'I didn't fight for you,' he said quietly.

'It wasn't your fault,' she replied softly, not wanting to reopen old wounds.

'Maybe I should have done what I came up to do that weekend.'

She looked at him and felt her head spin a little with all the beer.

'Do what?'

He rubbed his chin awkwardly and didn't look at her.

'Do what, Chris?' she asked, her interest piqued.

'Hell, look . . .' He hesitated, looking for his escape route out of the conversation. Realising he had none, he jumped straight in. 'I came up to Albany that weekend to propose to you. I had the ring in my bag, a little cabin booked for the Saturday night . . .'

'Propose to me?' she said in disbelief.

'I know we were only kids, but I guess it just felt right. For me, anyway. Back then,' he added with a self-preservative disclaimer.

She felt frozen to the spot as she heard a holler from across the courtyard: 'Hey, Amy. Want another beer? Bri's buying.'

She shook her head and wiped her mouth.

'I should go,' she said, feeling too emotional to stay.

'You don't have to,' said Chris, putting his hand on her forearm. 'Have another drink. For old times' sake.'

'Happy Christmas, Chris,' she said absently as she forced her way through the courtyard crowd.

By the time she reached the street, she wasn't sure if any air was reaching her lungs. She puffed out her cheeks, and a spout of white air escaped into the night sky to confirm that she was still breathing.

She hadn't been prepared for what had just gone on back there. Chris Carvey had wanted to propose to her. That weekend she had finished with him. She remembered he had come up on a snowy Friday night and left on the Saturday afternoon when a long walk through Tivoli Park had turned into an argument fraught with her frustrations of the semester. She remembered watching him walk away; the back of his beaten-up leather jacket, his favourite army rucksack thrown over his shoulder. A ring had been in that bag. A ring meant for her. A ring that meant he loved her, would love her, always and for ever.

Our timing was off. I didn't fight for you. Well, it didn't matter now, because he had moved on and had a family and another girl now.

I didn't fight for you.

She kept hearing those words over and over again. She thought of Daniel and his feebleness in the face of his family's expectations and desires. He hadn't fought for her. Had she wanted him to?

Looking out on to the cold and lonely street, she knew with absolute certainty that she had. She could still feel the heart-racing excitement of seeing that Tiffany box in his sock drawer. So he'd behaved like a jackass, but she had loved him, from that first moment she had seen him on the nightclub dance floor. The most handsome man in the room, the smartest, most successful person she had ever met, who had singled her out and made her feel like his queen. Well, until his job offer in Washington and his ambition and his parents' snobbery had forced him to make a choice. Love or career. And he had chosen his career.

I didn't fight for you.

Well, she was a better person than he was.

Perhaps it was the egg nog and the punch and the Bud talking, but suddenly she wanted to talk to him. She wanted to fight for him. Pulling her mobile out of her pocket, she dialled his number.

Her heart was thumping as it rang.

Ring ring.
Pick up, pick up.
Ring ring.
No, don't pick up.
Ring ring.
Where are you?
Ring ring.
Are you out with another girl?
Ring ring.
What the hell am I doing?
Ring – click.

There was a moment of relief as Daniel's phone finally went to voice message. She snapped her own phone shut and closed her eyes tightly.

Idiot.

'Who you been calling?'

She looked up. Billy was standing there, a bottle of beer aloft.

'Just a friend.'

'A friend in England by any chance?' He winked. 'Someone who doesn't mind getting woken up at five in the morning by his girl, huh?'

Amy gasped in horror. Her brother was right. It was the middle of the night in England. He would be at his parents' house and the call might have woken people up. Another goof . . .'

'Come on. Suze's fella has just got a round of tequila shots in.'

'Sure. That sounds like exactly what I need right now.'

And she walked back inside. Back to the life she had left behind.

CHAPTER EIGHTEEN

Amy wanted to lay her head on the plate and go to sleep. The scrambled eggs looked so fluffy and soft, she could just shut her eyes and then maybe when she woke up this horrific headache would have gone and . . .

'Amy?'

She sat up straight, the sudden movement sending a shower of sparks across her vision.

'Yes, yes, I'm fine.'

'I didn't ask if you were fine, I asked if you'd heard what I was saying.'

Amy squinted. Georgia's voice had adopted the distinctive tone of a sergeant major.

'Of course. Totally. You asked if I was packed.'

Georgia raised a quizzical eyebrow, and Amy realised she was supposed to answer.

'Almost,' she said.

That was 'almost' as in 'not at all'. She hadn't got back until eight o'clock the previous evening – the whole day lost to eating, drinking and vegging out with her family. Throw in the Christmas Eve visit to Fenies, after which she had finally got home at 2 a.m. and still had the remnants of the resulting tequila hangover, and she was fit for nothing, let alone packing.

'Well, we leave the hotel at noon,' said Georgia, summoning the waiter.

'Ungh,' said Amy.

The waiter bent his head and listened as the old woman whispered something, then nodded and moved away.

'What did you say to him?'

'That my friend needed a little pick-me-up,' smiled Georgia. 'A bloody Mary with a couple of my secret ingredients might make the packing a little easier to bear. And then some fresh air. How about a brisk walk before we check out? Well, not too brisk.'

The hotel was just a few blocks from Central Park. They entered at the East 65th gate and walked past the zoo, hearing the occasional screech and squawk, then down towards the picturesque Gapstow Bridge, where the skyline reared up ahead of them once more. Amy had always loved the park for that very reason – one minute you could feel as though you were in the great outdoors, the next you were very much in the centre of a huge, beating metropolis.

There was a vendor in the park selling coffee, and Amy put her hand in her pocket for a five-dollar bill to buy one.

'Are you sure?' she asked Georgia, confident that the old woman would refuse.

'A black coffee would be marvellous.'

'What would Madame Didiot say?' grinned Amy.

'Sometimes you have to shake things up a little.'

They walked a stretch in silence, soaking up the view and the gentle buzz of the park – the joggers, and the hum of noise from the Wollman rink – then stopped off at the Dairy Visitor Center, where Amy bought Annie a Central Park charm bracelet she knew she'd love.

'So a new year is around the corner. What do you hope it holds for you?' asked Georgia as she sipped her coffee.

'Hopefully a little less rejection,' Amy said quietly.

'That sounds a bit defeatist. Seems to me like *you* need to shake things up a bit. Remember sometimes that that involves changing course.'

'Like what? Give up dance for good?'

'My mother was an artist. Not a very successful one, unfortunately. But she had the courage to give up the oils and fine art and become an illustrator. Quite a famous one, in fact. I was involved in publishing some of her work. You might have heard of the Shellies.'

'I used to love those books,' cried Amy, remembering the adventures of a dancing tortoise.

'Use your skills to their best advantage,' said Georgia sagely.

'You know, I did have one idea.' It was something she had thought about during the subway journey back to the city – an idea that she couldn't shake out of her mind once it had popped into it.

Georgia tilted her head with interest, and it encouraged Amy to talk.

'It was something my niece said. About ballet being boring. I mean, it is sometimes. Too long, too serious. Sometimes I just think it was created for art snobs and dinner party bores who can pay hundreds of pounds for tickets. But why shouldn't it be aimed more at the people who can see the most wonder in it – kids. Can you imagine junior versions of *Swan Lake*, *Sleeping Beauty* or *Cinderella* full of pink and glitter and fun music? It would be a sell-out. Especially at Christmas.'

'It's a good idea,' said Georgia, giving it some thought. 'I've been to the Royal Opera House dozens of times, and there are always little girls there in their sparkly tutus, dying to see the ballerinas, but by the first interval they're tugging at their mothers' hands and asking to go. So you'd be the producer and choreographer? Start your own dance company? There's certainly no shortage of talent going to waste in London that would love to get involved.'

Amy nodded to herself, feeling both reassured by Georgia's words and quite overwhelmed at the idea of tackling something so big, so expensive, so overambitiously *ridiculous* as starting her own dance company. She remembered Nathan telling her that he'd had to pull his one-man show from its mooted run at the Edinburgh Fringe when he discovered it would cost £5,000 – and that was only for two nights. How on earth could she afford anything close to the proposition she was suggesting?

'I think you Brits would describe my idea as pie in the sky.' She smiled sadly.

'Why would that be?'

'Money. Lack of it.'

'Forget about cost for a moment,' said Georgia sagely. 'Remember what I said when we were shopping: ask yourself, "Is it right?" If your ideas are good enough, there will always be a market, and where there's a market, there are always ways to raise money.'

She felt her mobile vibrate in her pocket and realised she had not checked it since the night before. She had three unread messages, and as Georgia walked ahead, she stopped to read them. One was from Annie asking about her Christmas, another from her American phone provider, the third from a number she did not recognise. 'Just checking everything is okay Stateside. Will H.'

She frowned, unable to place the name and number, and was about to bury the phone back in her pocket when it started to ring. Looking at the caller ID, she almost gasped in surprise.

'Daniel,' she said out loud as Georgia turned around to see what was going on.

Ever since she had made the drunken call on Christmas Eve, she had been cringing about her weakness in the face of egg nog, condemning herself for being sentimental, maudlin and definitely not cool. She carried on walking towards Georgia, letting the phone vibrate in her hand.

'Perhaps you should take it,' said Georgia, who went and sat discreetly on the nearest bench.

Amy hesitated and then pressed accept, giving herself no time to think how to play it.

'Hello?'

'Happy Christmas,' he said.

Amy felt her heart flip over at the sound of his voice. *Don't freak out*, she scolded herself, angry that his call was making her feel like this.

'Is that you, Daniel?'

'Forgotten my voice already?' he replied, joking but with an undercurrent of hurt.

'No, I'm just surprised to hear from you.'

'Well, you did call . . . Where are you? There was a strange ringtone when I dialled.'

'Long story.'

And not one I'm about to tell you – like answering an advert in the back of The Lady *doesn't smack of desperation.*

'Have you gone home?' he asked.

'Yes and no.'

There was a pause, and a surge of cold wind cooled her angry cheeks.

'Why are you being so cagey?' asked Daniel. He sounded funny: not his usual confident master-of-the-universe self. She wondered where he was. What he was doing on a Boxing Day afternoon in England. Probably something involving tweed and guns and shooting poor little birds out of the sky, she thought, remembering his conversation with his friends at the Tower party.

'I'm not being cagey,' she said defensively.

Another pause.

'I want to see you. I was glad that you rang.'

It was on the tip of her tongue to tell him that she'd been drunk, that she wished she had been stronger and not called, but she knew that would be the wrong move. Besides, *he wanted to see her*. Her heart was beating faster just listening to his voice.

Don't screw it up now.

'I'm flying back tonight. Ring me tomorrow,' she said, as casually as she could.

'So you *are* in New York.'

She longed to tell him she had been staying at the Plaza Athénée and had bought clothes on Madison Avenue and had learnt about wine and food from Clive at Eleven Madison Park, but she sensed that it was the mystery that was making him suddenly interested. Why hadn't she tried this before?

'What time do you land? I can pick you up,' he added. He sounded eager now.

'It's fine. We have a driver.'

'Who's we?' he asked, his voice lifting in pitch. 'Who's got a driver?'

'As I said, it's a long story,' she replied. She could feel herself smiling now. She was enjoying this power switch, this feeling that she was in control and calling the shots.

'How about you tell me about it tomorrow night? I can book somewhere nice.'

She looked over at Georgia, who glanced away quickly when

she realised Amy had caught her watching her.

'I really have to go, Daniel.'

'How about Claridge's? You like it there,' he said, now sounding desperate.

She let him dangle for a moment. She did love it in Claridge's. They had gone there for their third date. In the days when he had pulled out all the stops to impress her, the days before she had actually slept with him.

'Okay. I'll see you there at eight. If you can't get a table, let me know and I can make a few calls.'

'Of course I can get a table,' he said as Amy pressed the end call button.

Georgia stood up from the bench and smiled.

'It looks as if your luck is about to change, Amy Carrell,' she said, and Amy knew that she had played that phone call perfectly.

CHAPTER NINETEEN

'It seems weird saying goodbye.'

Amy was sitting in the idling taxi, peering up at Georgia's Primrose Hill apartment building, not really wanting to get out, not wanting the adventure to end. It had only been a matter of days since she had first stood there debating whether to go up and meet the crazy old lady from the advert, but so much had happened in that time, it felt like weeks – years even. *The weather hasn't improved*, she thought, eyeing the grey clouds, but it was warmer than New York. And at least it wasn't raining. You always had that to cling to in London: it could be worse, it could be raining.

Georgia smiled.

'You know, as soon as I handed that advert over to the magazine, I thought it was a mistake. But I was wrong. And I am glad it was you who answered, Amy Carrell.'

Amy hovered for a moment, unsure what to say. It was clearly time to say goodbye: should she hug the old lady? An air kiss? Or just a handshake? She considered Georgia a friend, felt they had shared a great deal over the past few days, but she really had no idea if Georgia felt the same way or if she simply thought of Amy as the hired help.

'Thanks, Georgia. Thanks for everything,' she said simply. 'I hope, you know, it was as good as you wanted it to be.'

Georgia touched her hand.

'It was certainly more fun than I expected,' she said, her eyes twinkling. 'We should do lunch in the new year. Or maybe go to the Courtauld – you'll love it there, it's just as inspiring as the Frick.'

'Does this mean we're friends?' said Amy with a grin. ''Cos you can't shake me off that quickly. And I want you down at the Forge next weekend. I'm going to whip my friends there into shape – serving from the left and all that fancy stuff – and I want you to come and see if we've got it nailed.'

'I'd like that very much.'

'You should bring Will. Your cousin's son. That was his name, right? We'll probably still be serving Christmas dinners . . . I feel guilty you've spent Christmas with me rather than your family.'

'I think Will is very busy over the holidays. I will probably come alone to the Forge,' Georgia said more tersely.

Amy looked at her pointedly.

'Some families don't get along quite as well as yours, Amy,' said Georgia after a moment.

'Maybe you all need to try a bit harder.' Amy wasn't sure whether she had overstepped the mark. 'Take my uncle Chuck. He can be tricky. My mom still hasn't forgotten the time he pinched the principal's ass on my high-school graduation day. But he's still there every Christmas, every big family occasion.'

'Was your principal female?' asked Georgia quizzically.

Amy laughed.

'You know what I'm saying. Forgive. Even if you don't quite forget.'

'So it's your date tonight,' said Georgia, noticeably changing tack.

'Claridge's, apparently.'

'How do you feel about it?'

Amy laughed awkwardly.

'You mean after Dan's awful behaviour am I going to sock him one in the face with one of Claridge's famous desserts?'

'I mean do you want him back,' said Georgia simply.

Amy looked at the older woman's face, trying to work out if she disapproved of her plans. She wouldn't blame her after what she had said in New York about Daniel and his snobby family.

'I don't know. My head is telling me to not even bother turning up tonight. But my heart . . . We had some pretty good times, you know.'

'So you're prepared to give him a second chance?' Georgia asked sceptically.

'Everyone deserves a second chance.'

She saw the older woman's expression soften.

'Come with me, Amy. I have something to show you.'

Georgia got out of the car and had a word with the driver. Amy followed her up the path with a sense of anxiety. What did she want to show her? A bill, perhaps, she thought with sudden panic. The *Lady* advertisement had said flight and accommodation provided, but Georgia had paid for countless extras and Amy hadn't even thought that she might have to settle up at the end of the trip.

They walked slowly up to Georgia's second-floor apartment.

'Come through,' she said, leading Amy inside. 'I know you have your little black dress, and it will carry you through many occasions in your life, but tonight is special. And sometimes a special night demands something out of the ordinary.'

At the far end of the flat was a set of polished double doors. The old lady pulled them open and Amy gasped.

It was a huge dressing room, but no ordinary dressing room, she could see, stepping closer. There were built-in cupboards down either side, crammed with gowns and dresses of every type.

'One thing the Season gave me was a love of beautiful dresses,' said Georgia. 'But I didn't really have any myself. In my twenties I could never afford them, but then when I had some success in business, it gave me the opportunity.' She beckoned to Amy. 'Don't be shy, come and see.'

The walk-in closet was brightly lit. Dresses, blouses, cashmere jumpers, all colour-coded on little wooden shelves. She had always imagined Georgia as a bookish, academic woman. Stylish, yes. But here there were flamboyant prints, lace, feathers, floor-length gowns fit for a Hollywood princess. *You think you know people*, thought Amy, *but they still find ways to surprise you.*

'These clothes,' she said, shaking her head in wonder as she touched the fabric, 'they're wonderful.'

They were, in Amy's eyes, even more fabulous than the clothes they had seen in Ralph Lauren, because these clothes had been lived in. Every garment spoke of a lover, a chance meeting, a triumph or a loss. Every one told a story.

'None of it is couture, I'm afraid,' said Georgia. 'I could never bring myself to pay those prices. Most of it is ready-to-wear from the sixties, seventies and eighties.'

Amy nodded, dumbstruck, as she pulled out various items. There were Ossie Clark evening gowns, a low-cut Halston that looked like it had been to Studio 54, an eighties Calvin Klein, a beautiful beaded Dior dress, an Yves Saint Laurent with moa feathers around the collar.

'They're just . . . amazing,' she said. Georgia nodded appreciatively.

'I always think that people who rubbish fashion, those who think it's frivolous, have never worn a truly spectacular dress. There's nothing like a wonderful gown to make you feel like you can conquer the world. Pick one,' she said finally. 'Wear it tonight.'

'Really? You really mean it?'

'Absolutely. They're just going to waste sitting here.'

Amy blew out her cheeks and looked around.

'Georgia, I am completely spoilt for choice. I genuinely don't know where to start.'

'Well, how about here,' she said, unhooking a dress from the rail and pulling it out with a flourish.

'Wow,' said Amy. It was Grecian in style, with intricate folds of silk jersey. The colour was sumptuous – like the soft blush of a sunset.

'A dinner was thrown for me a few years ago,' said Georgia, holding it up against Amy. 'I'm not really comfortable with things like that, so I wanted something that would make me feel bullet-proof. Anyway, I had a friend who worked in fashion. She found this vintage Madame Grès for me.'

'Madame Grès?'

'I hadn't heard of her either,' confided Georgia. 'But she was considered one of the greats. You would never believe this dress was over forty years old, would you? It looks quite modern, don't you think?'

'It's amazing.'

'It was the dress I always wanted for my coming-out.'

She took it over to an Oriental concertina screen.

'You can try it on behind here.'

The fabric slipped over Amy's body; it felt perfect, just as

TASMINA PERRY

Georgia had said. Sexy, powerful, but just formal enough to make her feel in control. Plus, as she admired it in the mirror, she could see that it accentuated her curves. She had no make-up on – had not even put a brush through her hair since the day before – but even so, she knew she looked a million dollars.

'I love it.'

'Then go and show Daniel what he's missing.'

'I'll try. And I promise I'll bring it straight back.'

'No rush,' said Georgia, closing the doors of the closet. 'It's not like I was planning on wearing it on a date myself.'

Amy looked at her.

'Do you miss it?'

Georgia raised a brow.

'Love? Sex?'

'Well, it's complicated, isn't it,' said Amy, blushing at the old woman's blunt reference.

'Love can indeed complicate everything,' replied Georgia softly. 'Love is a glorious emotion, but it's the negative ones it inspires that are the problem. Envy. Insecurity. You know, someone once told me that throwing oneself into one's career is just selfish. I believe it was self-preservation.'

'Can I ask you something?'

'We've spent Christmas together. I think that qualifies you to ask anything.'

'What happened to the man you met in the Season? The one who encouraged you to go to university? It's just that whenever you've mentioned him, you get a little smile on your face, like . . . well, like you were very much in love. And yet you split up.'

'Oh Amy. As you say, it was complicated. But you're right. Edward and I were very much in love. My marriage didn't survive because of it. There was simply too much to live up to. Philip could never, ever compete.'

238

Her eyes clouded with tears, and Amy could tell she didn't want to talk about it any further.

'Go, Amy. Go home and get ready for this evening.'

'No, I'll stay. We can go to a café and get some tea. If you want to talk about any of this, I'm here . . .'

'It was all a very long time ago, dear,' she replied with a snort. 'Now off you go. If Daniel is what your heart desires, then go and get your happy ending. Remember what I said about wine, but if Daniel should get stuck, nudge him in the direction of the rosé. There is a wonderful Chardonnay that goes perfectly with the veal.'

CHAPTER TWENTY

Amy was fairly sure she had never looked or felt as lovely as she was tonight. All the way to Claridge's she had been catching glimpses of herself reflected in windows, car doors, even on the security cameras on the tube as she passed through Bond Street station. It was partly Georgia's dress, of course. Its intricate folds felt different against her skin, soft and light, and yet the tailoring of the bodice made it feel as if it had been welded to her body – like a protective layer of delicate jersey. Georgia had been right, it also felt like armour, supporting her body and making her feel bulletproof. She knew that men were looking at her, and for once, she was enjoying it, soaking up their glances and smiling to herself.

She turned off Brook Street and into the side entrance of the hotel. Ahead of her, waiting to go into the dining room, was a party of thirty-something media types. The men were in expensive-looking suits, but the women were wearing variations on classic lo-fi London chic: tailored trousers, spiked heels and chiffon blouses poking out from under trendy leather jackets.

For a moment it threw Amy. She felt overdressed and out of time, old-fashioned even in her simple dress.

'Madam?' She looked up to see the maître d' staring at her. 'May I help?'

Amy closed her eyes and took a breath. *You look beautiful*, she reminded herself. *You look the best you've ever looked.*

And when she opened her eyes, the anxiety was gone. *That was the old Amy*, she thought to herself as she gave her name to the maître d' and stepped into the restaurant. *Right now, I can do anything I want.*

Daniel was already there. That was a surprise; Amy had lost count of the times she had sat alone waiting for him to arrive, sweeping in citing some huge meeting with the Americans or terrible traffic on some bridge. He stood up as she approached, and she was gratified to see his eyes widen.

'Wow,' he said, bending for an awkward peck on the cheek. 'You look amazing.'

I know, thought Amy. And for once, she felt it too.

'This was a good choice,' she said, as the waiter pushed her chair in. 'I really love it here. Always reminds me of an ocean liner, all the art deco glamour. Wouldn't it have been amazing to travel that way?'

Daniel nodded.

'Yes, I suppose you're right, now I think about it.'

Daniel agreeing with her? That had to be another first. She wanted to giggle. Poor man really was on the back foot tonight.

'So, did you have a good Christmas?' he asked casually.

Perfectly nice, considering my boyfriend dumped me a week before, thought Amy, then pushed it from her head. *Give him a chance*, she told herself. And at the very least he was here now, trying to make amends.

'Yes, I went to New York.'

'So I gather. How are your parents?'

'They're fine, but I only saw them a couple of times. I was staying with a friend in Manhattan, actually.'

Daniel cocked his head. She could tell his interest was piqued.

'Oh really? Whereabouts?'

'The Plaza Athénée,' she said as casually as she could, loving the fractional lift of his eyebrow in surprise.

'Which friend was this? The friend with the driver?'

'Daniel, stop. You're beginning to sound jealous.'

'Maybe I am,' he said with a slight huff. 'When my girlfriend disappears out of the city for Christmas and starts talking about rich friends with drivers, of course I'm going to get a bit jealous.'

'I went with Georgia Hamilton.'

'Who the hell is he?' he spluttered back, his cheeks turning a little bit flushed.

Amy had to pinch herself under the table to stop herself from laughing. His jealousy was so obvious, for a moment she actually considered carrying on with the story of 'George' just to teach him a lesson. But while that would afford her satisfaction for a short while, it wasn't really in the spirit of giving him a chance.

'Georgia, Daniel. A woman. She is over seventy. She's a rather celebrated publisher, if you must know.'

'Oh.'

Now that Daniel was reassured he wasn't in direct competition, he quickly recovered his composure. Even so, Amy could tell he couldn't take his eyes off her, and she felt a surge of power.

'Besides, I'm not your girlfriend any more, Daniel. I can do as I please.'

Daniel had the decency to look shamefaced.

'About that,' he said finally. 'What happened the other night. It blew up out of all proportion. In fact it's what I wanted to talk to you about tonight.'

She stopped herself from saying anything.

'It was wrong. Letting you go like that. Letting my parents make you feel as if you weren't wanted in my life. They were wrong. I've missed you like mad over Christmas, and when you rang, I just realised . . . I realised that I love you.'

It wasn't the first time he'd said it. He'd murmured it a few times after sex, many more times in circumstances that had concluded in bed. She looked deep into his clear blue eyes, trying to work out his sincerity now.

'You could have called me,' she replied, gently testing him.

'I knew how pissed off you were, and frankly, I don't blame you. But that's in the past. We're here now, together, and let's enjoy it.'

Her nerves returning, Amy picked up the menu and began to scan it.

'Shall we start with a drink?' she suggested, her voice still cool. 'How about the Shiraz? This South African red,' she said without thinking.

Daniel's face betrayed his surprise. She had never even expressed a preference for red or white before.

'Okay,' he said. 'Why not?'

They ordered the wine and their food and Daniel pushed his hand across the table so that their fingers touched.

'Tell me about New York.'

And over their delicious dinner, she did. She told him all about the Holbein in the Frick, and Serendipity, and Christmas Day with her family. In return, Daniel told her about his promotion, and the holiday period in Oxfordshire, which seemed to involve Cotswolds pubs and horse racing with his father.

'I couldn't wait to escape,' he confided. 'I couldn't wait to get back to you.'

Whether it was true or not, Amy was happy to hear him say it at least. Daniel was certainly back to his affable, charming self. The Daniel she had fallen in love with almost twelve months earlier. The Daniel she could spend hours with just walking around a park or by a river, holding hands and swapping stories. The Daniel who was attentive, exciting and clever, the Daniel who had been chosen for the fast-track diplomatic service because he could make you feel so interesting and smart just by the way he listened to you. She had always thought that he could sort out various international hostilities just by taking all parties concerned to the pub for the night – no wonder he had smoothed over their argument at the Tower by the time the starters had arrived.

'Come on,' he said finally as he polished off his beef Wellington. 'I can't be bothered with pudding – can you? Let's just get out of here.'

And as they stood and walked out of the restaurant, suddenly the question of whether they were back together didn't need to be answered. Amy could tell they were together again, she could feel it in his touch, the protective way he led her through the hotel, the feeling when his fingertips found hers.

'Daniel . . .' she said, turning. 'I—'

'Dan Man! Is that you?' A booming voice interrupted what she was about to say and an overweight man lurched towards them. 'It *is* you, you old bugger!'

'Gidster, how the bloody hell are you, old man?' replied Daniel, gripping the man's arm like they were long-lost brothers. He broke away and turned to Amy.

'Amy Carrell, meet Gideon Maybar. We were at school together.'

'Hell-o, Amy,' said Gideon lasciviously, shamelessly looking her up and down. His tongue might as well have been hanging out. 'You've fallen on your feet, eh, Dan-Dan?' he added, nudging Daniel in the ribs.

'So what brings you here, Gid?' asked Daniel. 'Christmas drinks?'

'No, nothing so fun. We're at a wedding in the ballroom. I've just come for a time out, quick puff on the old Cohiba.'

'A wedding?' laughed Daniel. 'Not yours, I hope?'

Gideon laughed and shook his head.

'No, Alex Dyer – you remember, in the year above us? Hey, why don't you come and have a drink?'

'Do you think he'll mind?'

'Course not – anything to distract him from the trouble and strife, eh?'

'Should we pop in for one?' asked Daniel, turning to Amy. Amy couldn't think of anything she'd like less than walking into a room full of his drunken school friends, but she forced a smile. She could cope with this. In this dress, she could cope with anything.

'That sounds great,' she said, squeezing his warm hand in hers.

They followed Gideon into the ballroom, where Amy was surprised to find the dance floor full of couples dancing to a six-piece band. The whole place was done like a winter wonderland, and the bride, dressed in a long cream gown with a white fur shrug over her shoulders, looked like a Siberian queen.

'Shall we dance?' said Daniel.

'You?' laughed Amy.

'I think I can dredge up a few moves, if you don't mind me stepping on your toes every now and then.'

'Then I accept, kind sir,' said Amy, doing a mock-curtsey and grinning as he led her to the floor. He turned to face her and pulled her in close, one hand laid over hers, the other in the small of her back.

'Not bad,' she smiled. 'You learnt some decent moves at that fancy school of yours.'

'And I've learnt a few more tricks since I left,' he said, pulling her tighter and beginning to guide her around the floor. He was rusty, but he had a natural kind of sway, and Amy resisted the urge to correct his mistakes – the man was supposed to lead, after all. A lady knew that, even if she was secretly calling the shots.

As the song finished, he deliberately brushed his lips against her neck. 'You're absolutely beautiful,' he said softly.

'You're not too bad yourself,' she replied with what she hoped was a sexy smile.

'I don't ever want to let you go.'

'Then try a bit harder to keep me.'

'I'm sorry about what happened. I was an idiot. You're right. It's about trying harder, and you know, Washington isn't far. I was thinking, if we both do a transatlantic flight each month, then we can see each other every other fortnight. I know bankers who see their wives less than that.' He gave a low, soft laugh, but she could tell he was anxious.

'Do you mean that?'

'Let me make it up to you. Let me start right now.'

'Right now?' she smiled pulling away from him.

'I've checked us into the hotel,' he said, searching her eyes. 'If that's what you'd like.'

'I'd like that very much,' she said, taking his hand and leading him from the dance floor, feeling sexy at being in charge.

They went up in the little lift to the second floor. One hand still holding hers, Daniel pushed open the door and then pulled her into the darkness of the room, not bothering to turn on the lights.

He pushed up the silk jersey and pressed her against the wall, cupping her buttocks, his hands searing through the soft fabric, his mouth lowering to kiss her bare shoulder.

'That's a lot of dress you've got on there. Is this some sort of designer chastity belt?' he said as he struggled through the acres of fabric.

'Let's just get it off, shall we,' she laughed softly as they stumbled towards the bed.

She pushed her hands down his boxer shorts, feeling the firm contours of his body, then brushed her palm over his prickle of pubic hair, over the entire length of him until he grew hard in her hand.

He unclipped her bra and peeled off her thong, and when they were both naked, they fell back on to the mattress. He straddled her and swooped down to suck her tight brown nipples, one, then the other, then down to her belly, kissing and stroking it with his breath, his lips, as if she were the sweetest thing he had ever tasted. He licked his fingers and pushed two of them inside her, finding such a hot, delicious spot that she groaned and arched her back, enjoying the sensation of feeling so desired. And as she spread her legs, she felt him push inside her, slowly at first, until she was full of him and they were moving in rhythm, the sweet energy building and building to such a white-hot climax that she did not want it to stop but at the same time she wasn't sure if she could bear it to continue.

When Amy opened her eyes, the thin winter sun was leaking through a small gap in the blinds. Daniel, she thought with a smile, her hand sliding across to check he was still there, warm and solid. It wasn't a dream after all. She looked across the room and saw Georgia's dress lying on the floor like a pile of melted silk jersey.

'Oh crap,' she hissed, leaping out of bed to scoop it up, smoothing down the fine fabric. *Please don't be damaged*, she thought. Georgia had been so kind to lend it to her, she couldn't take it back screwed up in a ball.

'Nice view.'

She jumped and straightened up, quickly holding the dress in front of her naked body. There was a pause, then she burst out laughing.

'No point in hiding it all now,' said Daniel with a lazy grin. He held out a hand to her and she carefully laid the dress on a chair and walked back to the bed.

'You're awake,' she said, smoothing his hair back.

'Sleep is a waste when I've got you next to me.' He hooked his hand around her waist and tried to pull her back under the covers. 'Come back to bed,' he smiled.

'Honey, I can't. I'm due at the Forge later and I've got to go up to Primrose Hill, see Georgia, return some stuff.'

'That won't take long.'

'I have to go home and change first,' she said, standing up and pulling on her knickers.

'You're still pissed off, aren't you?'

'Dan, I have things to do today.'

He swung his legs out of bed and came up behind her, wrapping his arms around her.

'When can I see you again?' he said, nuzzling his lightly stubbled chin against her shoulder. 'If it makes you happy, we'll take it slow, but right now, I want to spend every night until I leave for Washington just like last night.'

'That might be an expensive undertaking,' she smiled, realising immediately that he could actually afford a room at Claridge's from now until next Christmas just from the interest on his trust fund.

'What are you doing on New Year's Eve?' he said, planting light kisses on a strip of her neck.

'I think Cheryl wants me to work.'

'Take the evening off. Tell Cheryl I'll pay her staff wages for the night if I can get to spend it with you.'

She turned around to face him.

'You're kidding, right?'

'Gideon mentioned he's having a house party,' he said, playing absently with his cock. 'He has this great place in Docklands. We could go to that, then go to my mum and dad's for this lunch thing they always have on New Year's Day.'

'No, no, no. I think I need to be kept away from your parents for a while.'

He stepped towards her and held her face in his hands.

'Amy, I love you. I want to be with you and my family have to understand that. They're not all bad, but if they make you uncomfortable, then say the word and we'll just go to the party and spend the first day of the new year in bed at my place. We can call in pizza and watch crappy movies all day long. How about it?' he said, stroking her nipple.

'That sounds like a plan,' she smiled, as they turned around and fell back on the bed.

CHAPTER TWENTY-ONE

The sunshine had pushed its way through the clouds by the time Amy emerged from Chalk Farm tube. It was still cold, her breath puffed in front of her and the frost on the pavement sparkled, but she had a spring in her step. In fact, it could have been pouring with rain and she would have felt like doing a Gene Kelly-style whirl around a lamp post. After leaving the hotel, she had been back to her flat to change and had a suit bag containing Georgia's magic dress draped over her arm. She was back with Daniel, she had friends who cared – she felt on top of the world.

She stopped at the florist in the village and bought a nice bunch of tulips and rose verbena. As an afterthought, she popped into the newsagent's to buy a Kit Kat. Usually she would have denied herself chocolate – in fact she had been denying herself pretty much everything since she was eleven, since her seriousness about ballet demanded that she stay flyweight and slim – but since her trip to Manhattan, things had changed. Not only did she feel lighter, more confident in her skin; she felt that there was a future ahead of her, a future with Daniel and maybe, just maybe, a future that didn't involve dancing. Or at least one that might not involve Amy obsessively logging and justifying every calorie going into her body.

She was just turning into Georgia's street and savouring the illicit joy of the chocolate when she spotted someone familiar. Early thirties, wearing jeans, a thick fisherman's sweater and a stripy college scarf, he had the sort of brooding good looks of a Heathcliff or a Mr Rochester. For a moment she couldn't remember where she had seen him before – some BBC period drama? she wondered to herself – before she realised it was Georgia's relative Will.

He had obviously recognised her too. She watched him hesitate in his tracks, then, as he realised that a confrontation was unavoidable, slow his pace.

'Hello,' she said awkwardly when they were a few feet apart.

He stopped and nodded.

'All right?'

'Amy, Georgia's friend,' she said, feeling a little embarrassed.

'I remember,' he said tersely.

'Happy Christmas,' she said brightly. 'Or should we be saying happy new year by now?'

'I thought it was all happy holidays in the States,' he replied in a tone that suggested that Americans were colonial heathens.

Hmm, and a merry Christmas to you, grumpy, thought Amy.

They stood in clumsy silence for a second.

'So did you have a good trip?'

'It was great.'

'You didn't text me back.'

His dark eyes made her feel guilty again.

'Will Hamilton,' she replied as the penny dropped. 'That was you.' She tried not to squirm as she remembered the mystery text that she had read just a minute before Daniel's call had distracted her from everything else.

'We were on our way to the airport, then I turned my phone off,' she said, flushing at the lie.

'For twenty-four hours?' he replied, his black eyebrows knitting together to suggest his disapproval.

Her arm was aching and being in Will Hamilton's presence was unsettling. She had known from the second she had met him that he was suspicious of her, and ignoring his text, his concern about his relative, had undoubtedly done little to make him trust her any more.

'I'd better go,' she said, nodding to the suit bag that contained Georgia's dress. 'Heavy.'

'Santa suit?' he said wryly.

'A dress. One of Georgia's actually; she lent it to me for a special night out. Hence the flowers.'

'Result dress, was it?'

She wondered what a result dress was and then blushed at the thought of it lying in a heap in the Claridge's bedroom and knew exactly what he was talking about.

'Well, this isn't just a dress, it's a work of art. It deserves to be carefully looked after.'

Will smiled for the first time and his whole face lightened.

'I can see that you've been spending too much time with Georgia; you're starting to talk like her.'

'No bad thing, surely?'

Will shrugged and looked down at his watch, indicating that their conversation was over.

'Are you okay there, bag, flowers? Or do you need a hand?'

'I don't need a hand,' she said as a thought occurred to her. 'But I wouldn't mind a word . . .'

He glanced down at his watch again as if her request was an inconvenience.

'Please, Will, it's about Georgia. I'll only keep you five minutes. Girl scout's honour,' she said, raising three fingers.

'You were a girl scout?' he said, taking the dress bag out of her hand.

'Buy me a coffee and I'll tell you all about it,' she said, leading him into the nearest coffee shop.

The café they had entered was bristling with boho shabby-chic trinkets – of course it was: this was Primrose Hill, where everything had to be elegantly distressed. Immediately she could see that it was Will's local coffee place, because of the reaction of the girl behind the counter as he walked in.

'Hello, Will,' she smiled, batting her eyelids shyly behind her fringe.

Amy suppressed a smile: the girl was practically handing him her phone number. She gave Will a sideways glance as he ordered two lattes. She could certainly see why the pretty blonde barista would notice him. He was a good-looking guy with a crooked smile, clever eyes and the sort of aristocratic bone structure that came with generations of good breeding and which not even his messy dark hair could disguise. In his college-boy jeans and sweater he looked a lot like the handsome young men from the drama department at college, the particularly good-looking ones who always thought they were destined for movie stardom. In another life, her life pre-London, pre-Daniel, she might even had had a crush on him.

She took a seat by the window, put down the flowers, and allowed her gaze to drift out on to the street. She smiled as she thought back to the night before. The dinner, the sex, the promise that Daniel would skip his parents' New Year's Day lunch to spend the day with her.

'Latte,' said a voice as a lightly foaming mug was put in front of her and she returned to the present.

'Thanks.' She smiled back at Will, who pulled off his scarf and took a seat opposite her.

'So I take it you're a regular here,' said Amy.

'I spend more time and money here than I probably should, yes,' said Will, blowing on his coffee. 'In fact I could probably hang-glide in here.'

'Hang-glide?'

'See that shop across the road?' he said, pointing through the window. 'Above it – that's my flat.'

'The one with the socks hanging off the balcony?'

He nodded.

'It's not exactly drying weather, is it?'

'I think they've been there since the summer.'

'And I think you've just put me off my latte.' She laughed, and the tension between them softened.

'I'm sorry I didn't reply to your text.'

'I was probably being a little overprotective,' he said, looking up at her from over his coffee cup.

'I think Georgia is definitely capable of looking after herself.' She smiled back. 'But I'd have been suspicious too – the mystery American taking a member of your family on a Manhattan magical mystery tour.'

'I wasn't suspicious,' said Will, looking at her directly.

'Yes, you were,' laughed Amy. 'I could tell you were wondering if it was part of an elaborate plan to liberate Georgia from some of her money.'

'Occupational hazard,' he said, not denying it. 'Overactive imagination.'

She took a sip of her own drink.

'So what do you do? For a living, I mean.'

'Is this the pressing thing you wanted to discuss?'

'No, I've just realised I don't know what kind of man would have his underwear out on display.'

'Take a guess,' he challenged her.

'Lawyer? No, not neat enough.'

'Cheers.'

'That also puts accountant and banker out. Doctor, maybe? Not with all that hair. PR. Possible, but I always thought they had a sort of insincere charm.'

'So I'm charmless. That's what you're saying.'

'No, I didn't say that . . .'

'I'll put you out of your misery. I'm a writer.'

'As in books?'

'Nothing so grand. Plays. The clichéd deluded artist starving in his garret, I'm afraid. You wanted to talk about Georgia?'

She watched his face, wondering how much to tell him. The last thing she wanted to do was betray the confidence of a friend, but it was precisely because she considered Georgia her friend that she had to speak to Will.

'I don't know Georgia very well. Not before New York, anyway.'

'So why did you go with her?'

'Because she asked me to. It was a job,' she said, struggling to find the right words.

'A job?' he said with a note of surprise.

'I was a companion. A professional companion. For her trip. She didn't want to go alone, and anyone can understand that.'

He was looking at her intently, and she could tell he was trying to assess the nature of their friendship.

'Look, I know it's none of my business,' she said, taking a deep breath. 'But I don't think it's right that Georgia should be spending Christmas alone. Or at least with someone she doesn't know very well. She has a family, doesn't she? So why isn't she spending this most important time of year with them?'

'Our family is complicated,' said Will. His tone was brisk, but it was slightly undermined by the little froth moustache sitting on his top lip.

'Complicated,' repeated Amy, remembering that Georgia had used the same word about an old boyfriend. 'But what is it that's so complicated, Will? It seems to be pretty straightforward to me. Your family has abandoned her at a time when she needs the most support.'

Will narrowed his eyes. His look was so intense that she had to glance away from him.

'Why? What's wrong with her?'

'She's old!' said Amy, exasperated. 'I mean, she can walk and talk and look after herself, but she shouldn't be living on her own at the top of all those stairs with no one to support her, or advertising for strangers to come and accompany her on holiday.'

'I try,' said Will, his own frustrations becoming obvious. 'I go round, I offer to help, I even bloody moved down the road so I could keep an eye on her, but seriously, Amy, she doesn't want to know. She's cut herself off from the family. Barely tolerates me, and that's the way she wants it.'

'But why? Why did the family fall out?'

Will put down his cup.

'It's not for me to discuss.'

'Why not? It seems as if you're the only one who cares about her. Please, Will. She's been very kind to me and I want to help, but unless I know what she's dealing with, I can't do anything.'

Will glanced at her and hesitated.

'It was something that happened when she was a girl, a teenager really. There was a party and . . . something happened, something bad. People took sides – you know how families can get. Let's just say it didn't end well.'

'Come on, Will, you've got to give me more than that.'

'Everything I know is hearsay – family gossip and whispers,' he said, pushing a sheet of hair away from his face. 'No one ever sat me down and said, "Okay, Will, this is why Georgia never comes for Christmas." And I suspect that even if they had, it wouldn't be the truth anyway. The only person who really knows what it's about is Georgia.'

'Maybe I'll ask her, then.'

'With respect, I doubt she'll want to talk to you about it either.'

Amy had to admit that she agreed with him. After all, she barely knew Georgia, and this was the sort of conversation that would be difficult even for someone's closest friend. For a moment Amy thought about her own family, all of them squashed around a tiny table. Would they ever ostracise her? Could something that happened when she was a girl have driven such a wedge into her family? She really didn't think so. Her family was separated by distance, but the ties that held them together were strong – bound by blood and love and memories.

'Jeez, what's wrong with you Brits?' she said, feeling suddenly angry. 'Is it just this stiff upper lip, or is it emotional constipation?'

'Nice image for first thing in the morning,' said Will tartly as she threw her filthiest look back at him.

'It's not funny, Will.'

'You're right, it's not funny,' he said, pushing his coffee cup angrily to one side. 'A family torn apart isn't funny. But here's the truth: Georgia hates us. She doesn't want anything to do with us. And if you really were a good friend of hers, then you'd step back and respect that.'

Amy shook her head, disappointed and disgusted.

'Well, I'd better go and return the dress – and check up on *your family* while I'm at it.'

'So now *I'm* the bad guy,' he said, throwing his hands up in exasperation.

'That's for your conscience to decide,' she snapped back, reaching into her purse, taking out two pound coins and putting them on the table. 'For the latte,' she said as she picked up her things and stood up and brushed past him.

'Amy, wait.' He touched her arm and caught the bare strip of wrist. She flinched and felt her cheeks burn hot.

'Happy new year, Will,' she said, pulling away from him, and left the café without even looking back.

Something bad happened, repeated Amy to herself as she walked towards Georgia's building. Typical British understatement, she thought as she mulled over what Will Hamilton had said. Something that was difficult to discuss, so they made light of it, swept it under the carpet. And what happened then? A kind old lady ended up locked up in her flat with only gowns and memories for company. What kind of way was that to live out your life? *Something bad happened?* What on earth could it be? What could split a family for over fifty years?

She pressed the intercom and ran up the stairs. Georgia had left the apartment door ajar and she could hear the sound of the kettle boiling in the kitchen.

'Oh, flowers, there was no need,' said Georgia, appearing from the living room.

'Yes there was, it was so kind of you to lend me such a beautiful gown.'

'Well, they're lovely,' said Georgia, busying herself with a pair of secateurs, snipping the ends from the stems and arranging them in a cream enamel jug.

'So how was it? How was Claridge's?'

Amy blushed slightly as her mind leapt back to the moment they had stumbled into the hotel suite and the wonderful dress had finally come off. *You're not with Nathan now*, she reminded herself. If she had been, Amy was sure she would have told her friend every detail – they had that sort of relationship – but Georgia was from a class and era that didn't believe in sex before marriage. Amy was coming to believe that being a lady involved mastering the art of holding back.

'Well, Daniel wants us to spend New Year together,' she said finally.

'That's got to be a good sign if it happens,' said Georgia.

If it happens? thought Amy with mild irritation, even though she knew Georgia was only looking out for her.

'How did the dress go down?'

'It worked like magic,' she grinned.

'It's not the dress, Amy. It's you. You are a beautiful young woman and men can't help falling in love with you. The dress just gave you the confidence to believe that you can be that woman.'

Georgia gave a wry smile.

'Shall we have tea?'

Amy nodded dumbly as Georgia moved into the kitchen. She looked over at the garment bag, wondering if the older woman was right. The dress had certainly seemed to have some sort of special qualities.

'I just saw Will,' she said, remembering that she wasn't just here to return the dress.

'Ah, now there is someone we need to find a lovely girlfriend for,' said Georgia. 'He's very serious. Too serious. I've read some of his work. He's a very talented young man but he has a tendency to be a little ponderous. I think he needs to get out of that flat of his. Have fun.'

Amy paused for a moment, not sure if she should say any more. *Come on, don't be a wuss*, she scolded herself.

'I asked him why you don't talk to your family,' she said, and bit her lip, steeling herself.

Georgia was silent for a few moments, then stepped into the living room. Amy had expected her to be annoyed, but she was unprepared for the look of fury on Georgia's face.

'I would have thought you might try to respect my privacy a little more than that,' she said evenly, cold anger in every word. For a moment Amy could see her for the powerful CEO she once was.

'That's what Will said,' she replied quietly.

'Then you should have listened to him.'

'Look, I didn't mean to upset you,' said Amy, trying to catch her gaze. 'But where I come from, friends and family care what happens to each other, and yet you spent Christmas alone. Well, with me, but I don't count. I am worried about you.'

'Amy, we have spent a sum total of four days together. That's all. Really, you don't know anything about me. Please do not get involved in my business.'

But Amy knew she had gone too far to stop now.

'Will said that something happened when you were a girl. Something that has driven your family apart.'

Georgia looked away.

'And I thought better of Will, too.'

'Is that the reason you've never been to New York?'

Georgia flashed her a look of anger.

'Perhaps you'd have better luck as a psychic than a choreographer.'

'Come on, Georgia. Whatever it is, you shouldn't hold it inside you. You told me that yourself. It's not too late to change things.'

Georgia shook her head and sat down on the edge of a sofa.

She looked suddenly very tired. As she sat there, Amy could see that the old woman's eyes had welled with tears.

'I'm sorry,' she said, her voice thick with emotion. 'I shouldn't have snapped at you. It's just . . .' She trailed off, and Amy jumped up to pass her a box of tissues.

Georgia nodded, her head bowed, her whole body defeated. Amy could see her pale, veined hands trembling on her knees, twisting the tissue around her fingers.

'Should I make the tea?' she asked.

'You better had,' said Georgia. 'It's a long story.'

'I'm not in a rush,' said Amy quietly.

'Make the tea and I'll tell you. I'll tell you about the night that changed my life.'

CHAPTER TWENTY-TWO

September 1958

Peter Hamilton pressed his nose against the glass of the car window and whistled.

'Now that's what I call a house,' he said. Their taxi was slowly approaching Stapleford, caught in a queue of grand cars snaking around in a loop, each stopping before the steps to the front door, where uniformed staff were helping the passengers out.

'Peter, stop leering out of the window like that,' scolded Sybil, pulling her husband back. 'People will see and think you've never seen a house before.'

Georgia was fairly sure *she* never had. Not like this, anyway. Oh, she had been to the Palace, of course, and she had strolled around Kensington Gardens – and obviously, many of the balls and parties during the Season had been held in amazing buildings with painted ceilings and minstrels' galleries and fountains in the courtyard. But this? Stapleford was on another scale entirely, with wings that seemed to stretch off into the night either side of the blazing entrance. There had to be two hundred windows that Georgia could see, every one of them spilling warm yellow light out into the grounds. She had expected the Carlyle family to push the boat out for Christopher's twenty-first birthday party, but clearly at Stapleford, pushing the boat out was more like launching a transatlantic steamer.

'Isn't it marvellous? The house, I mean,' said Clarissa, her eyes wide. 'Edward said it was big, but . . . Gosh, wouldn't it be wonderful to live here?'

'You never know, Georgia might be lady of this particular manor one day,' said Peter with pride.

'I think that might be a little previous,' said Sybil, adjusting her stole around her shoulders. 'They've only been friends two minutes.'

'Well, it was jolly nice of him to invite us all here today,' said Clarissa as the car pulled to a stop.

'Very generous,' whispered Estella as the footman opened the door and they were ushered up the stone steps and into the house.

Once inside, Georgia thought that Uncle Peter's initial response to Stapleford was only natural: the entrance hall was exactly the sort of place that should make you gape. It was huge, as tall as the building itself, and seemed to have been carved from a single block of white marble. Directly in front of them a wide staircase that split into two and curved around the hall. There were oil paintings and sculptures and Oriental ceramics; everything inside the hall seemed expensive and exotic and delicate. Georgia could no more imagine herself living somewhere like this than she could imagine going over Niagara Falls in a barrel.

They followed the flow of partygoers to the left of the staircase.

'There are supposed to be eight hundred guests here tonight,' whispered Clarissa. 'Can you imagine knowing that many people?'

Georgia thought there must have been two hundred in the

ballroom alone, all standing in groups, talking and laughing, as a chamber orchestra played pretty music from a stage at one end. They walked the length of the room, nodding and waving to family friends and acquaintances from the Season, then out through tall French windows into the grounds, where the wide ornamental gardens were full of people. It was like Hyde Park on a warm summer evening: groups strolling along the paths, others standing next to the large white marquees or listening to the jazz band set up on a stage next to the lake at the rear, polite laughter and conversation filling the fragrant air.

'This has to be the party of the year,' said Sybil, looking over at Georgia appreciatively. *Well done*, she might as well have added, *you've finally got us into high society.* Although within the Hamilton family Aunt Sybil was considered top drawer – and an inheritance had paid for their house in Pimlico – she was far from the sort of status and wealth that the Carlyle family possessed. Far from it.

'Do you mind if I go and speak to my friends over there?' said Georgia.

'Not at all, darling,' said Estella. 'You girls must mingle. Go and have a wonderful time.'

Georgia watched as Clarissa joined a group of older girls, who immediately began giggling. She moved in the opposite direction. It had been a tiny white lie to her mother: she had seen a group of fellow debs, but she had no intention of talking to them. If she had to discuss how dreamy James Kirkpatrick looked in white tie one more time, she thought she might scream. Besides, the Season was drawing to a close. A few Highland balls in Scotland and Ireland for the more intrepid, but the coveted Deb of the Year award had been announced – a Home Counties beauty named Sally Croker Poole had nabbed the title – which meant that Christopher's party would be the last big social event for those lucky enough to swing an invitation.

Georgia walked back inside the house, keeping to the edge of the ballroom and skirting around any groups of debs she spotted. Her plan – such as it was – was to avoid contact with anyone while she tried to track down the only person she wanted to see at this party: Edward.

Two months after their first kiss, and even the very thought of him made her shiver with excitement. They had had a wonderful summer together; although Edward had started working at the bank and she was still doing shifts at the Swiss Chalet, they had spent every possible moment in each other's company. There had been nights out at Soho jazz clubs, picnics in the park, and drives to the coast, where they would park the Aston Martin and take long walks along the cliff paths, kissing and holding hands, sharing their secrets and dreams. Sometimes she would lie in bed at night and worry that it would all come crashing down around her ears, that Edward Carlyle would one day wake up and realise that she was actually nothing special, and when he had taken her out for lunch one day and said he had something to discuss, she had wondered if the axe was about to fall. Instead he had invited her and her family to Christopher's twenty-first.

She looked around the party, wondering where he was, then realised that, this being a formal party, the elder son would be a social focus. She imagined him having to nod and look interested as his many relatives told him at length how things had been better before the war.

'Georgia!'

She turned, thinking she had been ambushed by a debutante but she was confronted by Christopher's cheerful face. He was wearing full white tie and a pink face, which suggested he was suffering underneath that stiff collar.

'Happy birthday,' grinned Georgia. 'I'm surprised to see you unaccompanied.'

'Rare moment,' he said, rolling his eyes. 'Mummy has been forcing a parade of dull girls in front of me all night. Managed to slip away for a quick nip.' He reached into his inside pocket and pulled out a silver flask. 'Fancy a belt?'

Georgia shook her head.

'No thank you. It's hard enough keeping tabs on my mother when completely sober.'

'Know what you mean,' nodded Christopher. 'I have to go the other way – I can't get through it otherwise. You know I'd much rather celebrate my twenty-first with a night on the town with the fellows from the bank. At least they don't expect you to waltz with some distant cousin with a face like rice pudding.'

Georgia giggled.

'There must be a few nice girls here?'

Christopher raised his eyebrows.

'Don't you start . . .'

Just as she was turning away, Georgia felt someone grab her hand. She snapped it away, then turned to face her assailant.

'It's you!'

'Who did you think it would be?' said a grinning Edward.

'That randy butler everyone keeps talking about.'

'I'd better whisk you away then. I don't want your head to be turned.'

'Shouldn't you be socialising?'

'I've done my bit,' he said, grabbing her hand again and leading her away from the party, first down a corridor, then into another passageway and up a flight of stairs.

'Where are you taking me?' she whispered, laughing despite herself.

'You'll see,' he said, glancing back as he opened a door on to a landing. 'Only a few more steps. Keep up!'

By the time they had reached the top of a winding set of stairs and pushed through a door into a small bedroom, Georgia was out of breath.

'Right. Next bit's a little tricky.'

He jumped up on to the narrow bed and yanked at the window, sliding it up and getting one foot up on to the sill.

'Here,' he said, extending a hand towards Georgia.

'You want me to climb up there?'

'Yes. Just don't look down.'

'Very well,' said Georgia, gathering up her long skirt and hoisting herself up after him. 'But if I split a seam, you can buy me a new dress.'

Edward caught her around the waist.

'Georgia Hamilton, I will buy you all the dresses in Selfridges if that's what you want. Now come on.'

He lifted her on to a small platform, and as Georgia straightened, she could see where they were.

'We're on the roof,' she gasped.

'The only place for the queen of all she surveys,' grinned Edward. He disappeared back into the room and came back with a bottle of champagne and a blanket, which he spread out on the sloping tiles. Nervously Georgia sat down next to him in the little nest he had created; they could see most of the garden, with all the people milling around, yet they were hidden from view, even if anyone had thought to crane their necks upwards.

'As you can see, I have come completely prepared,' said Edward, pulling two champagne glasses from his jacket pockets and pouring them each a drink. He chinked his glass against hers.

'To adventure,' he said.

'To us,' she replied, smiling.

They sat in silence, sipping the wine and enjoying the simple pleasure of being somewhere they shouldn't, peeking down on the party unobserved.

'This is a really amazing place,' she said, wishing she could stay up here for ever.

'Best bit of the house,' he grinned.

'I'm sure this house has lots of great bits.'

He nodded.

'And as kids, Christopher and I probably found every single one. You know it's got dozens of hidden passages and stairways, all put in so the servants could creep about without disturbing the lords and ladies. We'd use them to pretend to be explorers or ghost-hunters. This little hidey-hole was our lookout in case pirates decided to sail across the lake to steal Daddy's silver.'

Georgia laughed, imagining the two boys playing their games, just as she had, building dens and climbing trees in Devon. The Carlyle boys both seemed so grown up and formal, but she supposed they had once wanted to play just like everyone else. The tragedy was that no one was allowed to carry on playing once they grew up.

'I still don't understand why you started work at the bank so soon after you left Oxford,' she said, staring out into the darkness. 'We should never stop having adventures. That was one of the things I liked about you when we first met. You'd done so many interesting things, and I don't think we should stop just because people think that we should all become responsible once we graduate.'

'Well, I was supposed to go to Borneo to see the jungle and the orang-utans, but something cropped up.'

'What?'

'You,' he said simply.

She turned to look at him.

'You never told me. We could have gone together.'

'Plus there're plans afoot for something I suggested a while ago. My father took it seriously and the wheels are in motion.'

'What's that?' she asked, hearing the hesitancy in his voice and feeling nervous.

'My father wants to open a New York branch of the bank.'

'Great, that was always the plan, wasn't it?' said Georgia with more enthusiasm than she felt.

'They want me to go over there with my father's number two and set it up.'

'When?' she asked with increasing panic.

'Before Christmas.'

'So you're moving to New York in three months' time,' she said slowly.

'New York is wonderful at Christmas. There's the skating rink and the giant tree outside the Rockefeller Center. There's the Rockettes at the Radio City Music Hall and the snow . . .'

'You make it sound good.'

'I know. I'm trying to tempt you.'

'Tempt me?' *Torment me*, she thought to herself. It just didn't seem fair – now that she had found him and they were happy, he was going to leave again. New York wasn't Manchester or Leeds – it was a whole different country. Four days away by boat.

'Georgia, I want you to come with me.'

Her heart was pounding so fast she could almost hear it in the still night air.

'To New York?' she gasped.

He nodded.

'I can't do that. It would be . . . improper,' she said, searching for the right word.

'I want you to come as my wife.'

'Wife?' she said, hardly able to breathe.

'Marry me,' he said simply.

Georgia felt her heart stop, then begin to hammer.

'W-what? Really?'

Edward grinned.

'I think the correct response is "yes". Perhaps I didn't do it right, but I fear that if I get down on one knee, one or both of us might come careering off the roof.'

'Don't worry, we've got hold of each other,' she whispered as he took her hand and squeezed it.

'Let's get off this thing,' he said, and they inched off the terrace back into the small bedroom.

Inside, they stood motionless for a minute in the dark. He pushed a stray strand of hair away from her face and then took it between his hands and kissed her as if she were the softest, sweetest fruit.

'I don't think you've officially given me your answer yet,' he said, pulling away from her slightly.

'Perhaps if you stopped kissing me I'd be able to say yes.'

'Yes?' he said, his innate confidence suddenly disappearing for one moment.

'Yes, you idiot, I will marry you,' she said, kissing him on his lips, his cheeks, his eyelids. 'I don't care if we go and live in York or New York. All I know is that I want to be with you. I want to spend the rest of my life with you.'

'That's good then,' smiled Edward, and reached into his inside pocket, bringing out a ring. The stone was plump and clear, surrounded by a circle of smaller diamonds. It was beautiful, perfect, but all Georgia could think was: *A ring! He has a ring!* That meant he'd planned this: he really, really meant it.

He slipped it on to her finger.

'Oh, it's a little loose,' he said, disappointed.

'I don't care,' said Georgia, kissing him again, harder this time, her longing, her desire washing over her like a wave.

His kisses trailed down her neck and his hand pushed her dress off one shoulder so his lips could brush the soft strip of skin. She tipped her head away from him and groaned. One of his hands curled around her waist to pull her closer, and she could feel her own heart thumping against his chest.

Her breathing was getting ragged and she could see the longing in his expression too.

'I want you,' he said softly. 'I want to make love to you.'

She just nodded and turned away from him, leaning back against him and then closing her eyes as she felt him unzip her dress and unclip her bra, which both fell to the floor.

Still standing behind her, he slipped his hand into the front of her cotton pants as he kissed her neck. She shivered, partly with desire, partly with the thrill and spike of fear of the unknown. She had never been touched there, and the sensation of his skin against hers made her hot. But she pressed her palm on top of his hand, urging it deeper, until his fingertips touched the dark triangle between her thighs.

They moved to the bed and Edward took off his own clothes. For a split second it seemed strange to look at his strong, naked body, so alien and exotic.

He lay down next to her and started to kiss her breasts. She flushed with embarrassment as her nipples hardened. She touched one, and it felt so big and hard against her fingertip.

'Is this okay?' he asked softly.

'It's very okay,' she whispered as he positioned himself on top of her, moving her thighs gently apart and pushing himself inside her.

She gasped a little, and froze. She really wasn't sure what to do next, but within moments they were moving together, slowly at first. Her hands pressed down the curve of his back and she thought perhaps that they were locked together. Lifting her knees a little, she felt him even deeper inside her.

Faintly she registered a cool breeze coming in through the

window and it seemed to lift her into a dream-like state. And then she felt nothing except a sweet pulse that seemed to build inside her, stronger and wilder, until a wave crashed over and Edward moaned and seemed to collapse on top of her.

After a few seconds, he moved and she could hear his breath regulate.

'You're alive,' she managed with a small laugh.

'What did you think had happened?' He smiled and stroked her hip.

They lay like that, entangled on the blanket, for a long time, just gently kissing and listening to the revelry that floated into the room from the party below. Georgia felt beautiful. She felt like a woman. *An engaged woman,* she thought, twisting the ring around her finger. It was a little large, but they could get it adjusted. They could fix anything. Anything at all.

'Married,' she said finally.

He smiled at her.

'Now we've just got to decide when, where.'

'You know I've never even thought about it before.'

'I thought all girls spent years dreaming of their wedding.'

'Not this girl,' she grinned.

'So think about it now.'

'Well, I can picture us on honeymoon,' she said, closing her eyes dreamily.

'Where are we?' he asked, stroking her nipple.

'Somewhere like Capri? We're stuffing ourselves on delicious food, swimming in the clear waters, riding around on those little motorbikes. Although I'm not sure about having all those sultry Italian beauties competing for my husband's attention.'

'This man will have eyes only for his new bride,' said Edward. 'Now and for ever.'

'Maybe we need to plan the wedding around the honeymoon,'

said Georgia thoughtfully. 'I'm sure Capri and Ravello aren't quite as wonderful in January.'

'So you want a summer wedding.'

'But what about New York?'

'I suppose we don't have to be married to move out to New York together. Being engaged will save our blushes.'

'We could get married in America,' she said, her eyes wide.

'What would your mother say about that? I thought she thinks America has no culture or soul.'

'I don't suppose your parents will be too happy either. I expect they always hoped for a grand wedding at the house. I mean, I bet you even have a chapel in the grounds.'

'We do,' he laughed.

'The sooner we tell people, the sooner we can get planning.'

'We should probably hold off from that until tomorrow. I guess it's Christopher's day today. I don't want to distract attention from him. Not on his birthday.'

'Absolutely,' nodded Georgia in agreement.

'We can tell them over breakfast,' he said in a tone that indicated it was all decided.

Georgia was nervous as they went back into the party. From a distance she could see Lord and Lady Carlyle, who suddenly seemed more intimidating than they had an hour earlier. She wondered how they would react to the news that their darling son – the heir to all she could see around them – was marrying penniless, homeless Georgia Hamilton from South Hams, Devon. In bed, Edward had confided that the reason he had invited Georgia's family to the party was so that the Hamiltons and the Carlyles could meet. Georgia hoped that his plan would not backfire, and was particularly concerned that Estella was not being inappropriately bohemian with someone important.

She felt the engagement ring she had tucked into her bra press against her heart and she smiled, not sure she was going to be able to keep the news secret until morning.

'What are you grinning about?'

She turned to find Estella standing behind her.

I'm smiling because I'm going to marry the most wonderful man in the world, she thought, but she held her tongue.

'I was just thinking what a brilliant party this is.'

'Rather smart, isn't it? Where's Edward?'

'Back on host duty. Apparently it's a three-line whip that he talks to everybody.'

Estella looked at her daughter quizzically.

'I suppose you're glad you did the Season now.'

'Because of Edward?'

'He's a very impressive young man.'

'Because he has money?' said Georgia, more sharply than she meant.

'Because of the way he looks at you. Because I know he can see all the wonderful, special qualities in my daughter.'

Georgia's mind jumped back to the blanket nest on the tiles, her own dress unzipped, Edward's lips on her skin . . . She quickly turned away from her mother, sure that she would see it all in her face.

'I love him,' she said simply.

'I know. How about we go and listen to the jazz band in the garden? I can't see Peter, Sybil or Clarissa anywhere. And I'm not sure I can bear to talk to anyone else about their racehorses or how their darling daughter is coming along with her pianoforte.'

They moved outdoors to the ornamental pond, where a handsome man of around forty struck up a conversation with Estella about Chet Baker.

In the past, Georgia had not wanted to consider the possibility of her mother finding a new husband. Occasionally the thought crossed her mind. She remembered thinking during her dinner with the author Ian Dashwood that she should introduce him to Estella, although she did not want to dwell on that night too long. But tonight, as the air seemed to fill with romance and magic, she looked across at her mother and hoped that this man was interesting and that he was interested in Estella, who looked quite beautiful in a scarlet tea dress that skimmed the lawn.

Discreetly she moved away from them. She could see Clarissa now, talking to two boys by the champagne fountain. Her cousin waved and Georgia went over. They had a short conversation with the young men – who were both at Edinburgh University – over a glass of champagne, which was deliciously cold and fizzy.

'Do you know, they've even got a swimming pool in the walled garden,' said Clarissa, taking a peach cocktail from a waiter. 'It's beautiful. Do you want to come and see it? I might even take a dip.'

'Edward was telling me all about it,' Georgia said, smiling. 'The place seems incredible. It's got a grotto and a summer house, where he and Christopher used to play, and there's even a bird's nest on the roof where you can see all the way to Gloucestershire.'

'Been given the guided tour already?' asked Clarissa, raising one plucked brow.

Georgia knew she couldn't keep it to herself any longer.

'All right, let's walk. I have something to tell you.'

'What is it?' asked Clarissa, hooking her arm through her cousin's.

'Not here,' said Georgia, looking around. 'I don't want anyone to overhear.'

They ran across the lawn towards the walled garden and she pushed open the heavy oak door. In front of them the pool shimmered like a sheet of turquoise satin.

'Tell me!' said Clarissa, who also looked as if she was ready to burst.

Georgia took a deep breath.

'Edward proposed.'

She watched as Clarissa's eyes opened wide in astonishment. She looked shell-shocked, her reaction suggesting she had never really thought Georgia's romance with Edward was serious. Just like everybody else.

'Do Lord and Lady Carlyle know?' she said finally.

'No, we're keeping it quiet for the moment. We didn't think it was fair to announce it on Christopher's birthday. Today is about him.'

'Fair enough. I suppose it will give you a bit of time to win her over.'

'Win who over?' she asked in alarm.

'Lady Carlyle. I met her earlier and she seems a frightful snob. I mean, Edward is the heir to a dynasty that goes back twenty-five generations. His mother is not just going to wave a hand and say "How lovely, Edward, I'm so pleased for you." They don't want him to get married; they want him to have a union with some equally rich and aristocratic young lady. How else do you think these families get to have such wealth and class?'

'I don't think Edward cares what his parents think,' Georgia said with dignity.

'Is that what he said? They all say that before Mummy and Daddy have the chat about family responsibility and lineage. Believe me, his parents will cause problems if they don't think you cut the mustard.'

'But Clarissa, it was so romantic,' she said, trying to put these negative thoughts out of her head. 'He proposed up there, on the roof, and it was as if we were on top of the world. You know, we're going to move to New York. Maybe we'll get one of those glorious apartments you see in the movies that overlook the park.'

'Have you got a ring?' asked Clarissa, peering at her hand.

Georgia reached into her bra and pulled out the diamond sparkler.

Clarissa gasped. Georgia handed it to her for a look, and its reflection twinkled in her pupils like stars.

'Gosh, Georgia. This is real.'

'Isn't it just,' she grinned.

'Okay. Put it away and keep it hidden,' said Clarissa, giving her back the ring. 'I won't breathe a word of this to anyone. In the meantime, find Lord and Lady Carlyle and impress them. Impress them tonight and next weekend and the weekend after that. You'll win them round. And then you can tell them about your engagement. You want them on side, not against you. And no corridor-creeping tonight.'

'Corridor-creeping?'

'Slipping into Edward's bedroom, of course. Now he's proposed, he probably thinks he can get into your knickers.'

Georgia felt herself blush.

'You've done it already, haven't you!' gasped her cousin.

'Clarissa. It was beautiful, incredible. I never thought my body could feel like that.'

'You did it here? Tonight?'

'In a tiny bedroom up in the eaves. I felt as if I had gone to heaven.'

'Will you get off cloud nine and come back down to earth,' Clarissa said sternly. 'Did you use a condom?'

Georgia shook her head.

'Well, you'd better hope to hell there's no patter of tiny feet coming along in nine months.'

'Wouldn't that be good?'

'Are you completely naïve?' snapped Clarissa. 'Do you really think Lady Carlyle is going to let her son and heir marry *any* woman – and I would even include Princess Margaret in this – who is with child before the wedding? These people will do anything to avoid scandal, Georgie, *anything*.'

'How do you know if you're pregnant?' asked Georgia after a moment.

'You won't know now, that's for sure. Perhaps you'll be lucky, and in the meantime I suggest you keep your knickers on.'

The girls stood in silence for a minute.

'I should get back to the party,' said Georgia finally. 'Are you coming, or are you staying here for your dip?'

'It looks pretty inviting, doesn't it?' said Clarissa as the water shimmered in front of them.

'I dare you,' grinned Georgia, the tension of their earlier conversation dispersing.

'Do you think there are towels in the hut?' asked Clarissa, pointing at a pale green summer house.

'I don't think the Carlyles want for anything,' smiled Georgia as her cousin slipped off her dress and dived into the pool with a clean splash.

She came up for air and wiped her hair back off her face.

'Go on then,' she said, waving her hand at Georgia. 'What are you still here for? Get back to the party!'

Georgia was still smiling as she walked across the quiet lawns. The party hadn't sprawled out this far and the music and laughter were still a quiet hum in the background. She considered what Clarissa had said and knew that she had a point. Rich people didn't get that way by accident; they got there because they were ambitious. Because they always wanted more. And now that the Carlyles had a son of marrying age, it was a chance for the family to become more, to merge with another great family perhaps or to gain a proper royal title. Georgia knew she didn't add anything to the pot, except perhaps the prospect of children.

She touched her stomach and hoped she wasn't pregnant. It felt selfish to even think it, but she wanted at least five years of married life with Edward before they settled down to having a family. She wasn't even twenty, for goodness' sake – there were so many things she wanted to do as a woman before she became a mother.

Glancing at her watch, she was amazed that it was past midnight and the party was slowly beginning to wind down. There were still at least two hundred people here, but the dancing in front of the band had definitely thinned.

Georgia found Uncle Peter leaning against a wall in the ballroom, his head nodding down to his chest. *Great*, she thought. *Just when I'm trying to keep the family out of trouble, my uncle chooses this night to go on a bender.*

'Uncle Peter?' she said gently, and he jerked awake. 'Wurr? Whassup?' he slurred.

'It's Georgia.'

'I can see that, old thing. I might be old, but I'm not senile just yet.'

'I was just wondering if you'd like to have a seat for a moment?'

She took his arm and led him to a chair, propping him against a pillar.

'Thanks, old girl, think I've overdone it a bit. I'll be right as rain in a minute.' And he promptly began to snore. Well, it was better than falling flat on his face, thought Georgia.

She turned as she heard her mother's tinkling laugh coming from the library she had passed earlier. She quickly walked over – and stopped dead in the doorway.

Estella was sitting in a high-backed wing chair holding a glass of wine, directly across from none other than Lady Carlyle. *Oh God.*

'Darling!' she called, lifting her glass as she spotted Georgia. 'I've been searching for you everywhere. Come and join us.'

Her heart sinking, Georgia walked slowly across and perched on the edge of a sofa, feeling Lady Carlyle's eyes on her all the way.

'So this is the girl who appears to have won Edward's heart,' said the grand dame. 'Well, I can see why; you are a pretty little thing, aren't you?'

Georgia forced herself to look into the woman's eyes.

'But have you inherited anything else from your mother?'

'I – I hope so,' said Georgia, completely thrown.

'Well said,' smiled Lady Carlyle. 'We could do with a few more children who wish to follow their parents' example, who understand the importance of family.'

Georgia looked over at Estella, hoping for some sort of sign to explain this insane turn of events, but her mother just looked away and took a sip of her drink.

'Your mother was just telling us about the tragedy at your house in Devon. Terribly shocking, I imagine.'

'Yes, yes it was,' said Georgia.

'And I understand it began in your art studio, Mrs Hamilton? Most distressing. You must let us know if we can do anything to help. Tell me more about your work. Perhaps we have a friend who could loan you some studio space.'

Her mother's eyes started to sparkle.

Oh no, thought Georgia. *Don't tell her about the abstracts, please don't tell her about the abstracts.*

'It's fine art, portraiture mostly. Some landscapes, but I feel my forte is in the human form.'

Perhaps sensing some sort of impropriety at the mention of the human body, Lady Carlyle pursed her lips.

'Portraiture? Might I have seen anything?'

'I have recently completed a commission for the Earl of Dartington.'

Lady Carlyle's face broke into a smile.

'Indeed? Oh, I know Hugo very well. Was it a family portrait?'

'No, just Lady Linley actually. She sat in the Long Gallery, do you know it?'

'Oh, very well. I have spent many a pleasant hour gazing out towards the Lizard. How is dear Abigail?'

Georgia watched in amazed silence as her mother and Edward's began to bond, discussing the various country houses and London retreats of England's gentry. Estella's hitherto scandalous career being at the beck and call of wealthy men was instantly recast. Instead of a subversive bohemian, she was simply a well-connected and seemingly much-in-demand artist to the upper echelons of society, her familiarity with the bedrooms of various earls and lords no longer suspect or grubby. And Estella played her part brilliantly: self-deprecating, knowledgeable, witty, she was the perfect balance of well bred and interesting, the sort of artist it was safe to invite to dinner. Georgia sat quietly, offering up a prayer of thanks to whatever deity had seen fit to turn Estella Hamilton into Thomas Gainsborough for the night. Perhaps they might pull this off after all.

'Well, I'm flabbergasted that Edward never informed me of your family's artistic side, Georgia,' said Lady Carlyle. 'I had no idea your mother was so accomplished. Perhaps we could call upon your talents sometime soon, Mrs Hamilton? I have been meaning to commit my two boys to oil before they run off and start families of their own.' She smiled over at Georgia. 'I wonder if we might . . .'

Slowly the smile slipped from Lady Carlyle's face, to be replaced by a look of disbelief, then horror.

'Oh my word,' she whispered, her hand flying to her throat.

Georgia turned and gasped. Standing in the doorway of the French windows that led to the gardens was Clarissa, her dress torn from one shoulder. There was a cut over her eye and scratches and dirt along one side of her face.

'I'm sorry,' she said, then slid to the floor.

Suddenly the room exploded into pandemonium. Estella ran across to Clarissa's side, crying for help, Lady Carlyle jumped to her feet and began calling for footmen and butlers, and Peter, Sybil and Lord Carlyle appeared from the other room demanding to know what had happened.

'Will everyone please stop shouting?' said Estella, her voice cutting through the hubbub. With Peter's help she carried Clarissa to a sofa and a maid brought a blanket to drape over her bare legs.

'What happened, darling?' said Estella, kneeling down next to the girl.

Clarissa's face was pale and she distractedly pushed a shaking hand through her hair. Georgia could see that her knuckles were scraped and her nails torn.

'I – I don't want to cause a fuss,' she stuttered. 'I'll be all right in a moment.'

'Tell your aunt, Clarissa,' said Lady Carlyle with authority in her voice. 'This is clearly a serious matter and we need to get to the bottom of it quickly.'

Clarissa looked up at her like a frightened rabbit, her eyes darting back and forth. The confident, unflappable girl from the walled garden had gone – she looked terrified.

'Answer us!' shouted Sybil. 'Who did this to you?'

Estella silenced her with a glare, then turned back to the girl, gently touching her hand.

'Who was it, darling? You can tell us.'

Georgia was shocked to see that Clarissa was looking directly at her.

'I'm sorry,' she whispered. 'But it was Edward. He came to the swimming pool and started touching me. I tried to push him away, but he forced me into the hut . . .' She started to sob.

The room erupted again, and Georgia found she had added her own voice to the noise.

'How dare you say such a wicked thing about him,' she shouted. 'Edward would never do any such thing.' She stepped over to Clarissa, grabbing her wrist. 'Take it back!' she yelled. 'Take it back!'

'He raped me,' roared Clarissa. 'How can you stick up for him when he did that to me?'

Sybil looked as though she was about to faint.

'We had better call the police,' said Peter, his voice a low, menacing growl. Georgia had never seen him look more angry.

'I think we should find out what's gone on first,' said Lord Carlyle. He was a commanding presence in the room, but as Georgia looked at him, she could tell that he was sick with worry.

'Let's call the doctor first,' said Lady Carlyle, her voice barely audible.

Everyone agreed that that was the first thing to do.

Georgia could barely remember what had happened next. Everything was sucked up into a hole of accusation and disbelief. The rest of the party guests were quickly and discreetly escorted off the property in such a way that it was impossible for any of them to know anything of the true drama that was going on. Georgia ran around the grounds looking for Edward, but before she could find him, she spotted him being bundled into a distant wing of the house by some officious-looking gentlemen. Her mother relayed to her the version of events that Clarissa had told her parents and the Carlyles, and Georgia had sobbed all the way through it.

Apparently Clarissa had been in the walled garden, drying off from her swim, when Edward had come in looking for Georgia. Clarissa had been wrapped in a towel and he had come over to talk. He'd stroked her chin and told her she was beautiful. He'd asked her to drop the towel, and when she had refused, he had turned rough.

Georgia had screamed that it was all a lie. She had raced to find Clarissa, to plead with her to tell the truth, but she was being examined by two doctors – one who had been called by the Carlyles, the other by Peter Hamilton.

The final thing she remembered of the evening was hearing a car draw up to the front of the house and a familiar voice pierce the still night air.

'Georgia, I did nothing,' roared Edward as she ran to the window and watched him being pushed into a waiting car.

It was the last time she ever saw him.

CHAPTER TWENTY-THREE

28 December 2012

Amy's cup of tea had gone cold. She gazed at Georgia in amazement as the old woman finished her tale.

'What do you mean, it was the last time you ever saw him? Did he get put in jail?'

'He was sent to Singapore almost immediately afterwards, like some hideous upper-crust version of transportation.'

Amy could see the old woman's lip trembling as she told her what had happened next.

'He contracted typhoid out there – I have no idea how, or why he didn't respond to treatment. But he died within nine months of the party. They flew his body back to England. I only found out about his death after the funeral.'

She looked down at her hands.

'I was nineteen years old and I had lost the love of my life.'

The simplicity of her words made Amy catch her breath. She

stood up and went to sit beside Georgia, putting her hand gently over hers.

'He was buried in the grounds of the village church close to Stapleford, their family home,' said Georgia, looking up, her eyes glistening. 'I go to see him every year. Not on his birthday or Christmas – I've always worried I might run into one of them, although I doubt they ever go.'

'Who? I mean, who are you worried about running into?' asked Amy.

'Oh, Clarissa or Christopher. The Happy Couple.' She smiled, but her face was stiff.

'The Happy Couple?' frowned Amy.

'Oh, they were married, didn't I say? My cousin and Edward's brother. In fact, you could say that Clarissa got everything she wanted.'

Amy didn't know what to think. It had been a horrible story, a terrible way to treat someone in your family – and she could certainly see why Georgia hadn't wanted anything to do with the Hamilton or Carlyle clan after that. All the same, she wondered if her bitterness – and the passage of the years – had begun to cloud everything.

'I know it's difficult to accept what happened, but . . .'

Georgia looked at Amy, her chin raised defiantly.

'But what?'

'Well, isn't it about time you let it go?'

'Let it go?' said Georgia in disbelief. 'But she was evil. Clarissa was evil.'

'Evil?'

'She lied, don't you see that?' said Georgia. 'She lied about everything. Edward didn't rape her.'

'So you still don't believe her story? None of it?' asked Amy carefully. She didn't want to upset her friend any more than she had to, but at the same time, it wouldn't do Georgia any good to see out the rest of her days being so angry, lonely and estranged.

'I know what you're thinking,' Georgia said quietly. 'Which is easier to believe: that a young man gets drunk and sexually assaults a woman at a party, or that a woman is prepared to destroy a man's life by claiming that he did?'

Amy didn't know the answer to that one. Both crimes were heinous.

'Well, I never accepted Clarissa's story for one minute, and I never will,' said Georgia, her voice fraught with emotion. 'I never believed that Edward did what she said – no, it's more than that. I always knew deep in my heart that he would never have done that. And he swore to me in his letters that nothing had ever happened with Clarissa. He said that yes, he had come into the walled garden looking for me, but he had gone straight out again when I wasn't there.'

'Then why did she do it? Even if she was that wicked, why do it? The scandal would have had an impact on her life, her prospects of marriage.'

'You are absolutely right.' Georgia looked at Amy with a new respect. 'Clarissa didn't mean for Edward to die. I think her plan spiralled out of control,' she said, her mouth fixing like concrete.

She settled her hands back in her lap and took a deep breath.

'Like you, I couldn't fit the pieces together at first. And remember, this was the fifties; rape was much more difficult to prove – and to disprove. There was certainly no DNA testing. It really did come down to one person's word against another's.'

'So no one was ever sure if Clarissa was raped?'

'Exactly. This wasn't about whether she consented to sex with Edward; it was whether she had sex with him all.'

'Wasn't she examined?'

'By a doctor, yes. But again, back then, they simply confirmed that she'd had sex. Even that was hard to prove because she had been swimming. The doctor examined Edward too, and confirmed that he had recently ejaculated, but Edward confessed that he'd recently had sex with me.'

'But if she hadn't had sex – of any kind – with Edward, who *had* she had sex with?' asked Amy.

Georgia sighed.

'About a year after Edward's death, I heard that Clarissa was dating Christopher Carlyle. I immediately thought that was strange. I mean, her story was that she had been horribly traumatised by Christopher's brother – would you want a daily reminder of what had happened? Would you want someone who looked like him to come anywhere near you?'

There was a definite logic to that, thought Amy. If it was her, she certainly wouldn't, but again, it wasn't proof.

'Maybe they just fell in love,' she said.

'Maybe,' replied Georgia without conviction. 'Either way, within another six months they had announced their engagement. I had just gone up to Cambridge, and one day in the quad I met an old friend of Christopher's. He told me that he'd seen Clarissa and Christopher together in the summer of '58. They definitely knew each other then. I remember seeing them together at my birthday dance.'

'What does that prove? Surely they would have bumped into each other – they were on the same social circuit, weren't they?'

Georgia shook her head.

'Christopher had confided in him – he and Clarissa were an item. So I think the person Clarissa had sex with that night was Christopher, not Edward.'

'But why on earth would she accuse Edward of something so awful?'

'Envy? Greed? Spite?' she said softly. 'I've been asking myself that question for the past fifty years.'

She fell silent for a moment, seeming to gather her thoughts.

'Whatever the reason, Clarissa got what she wanted: a good marriage. A great one, in fact. The Carlyles were one of the most prominent families in England at the time. When I found out about Clarissa and Christopher, I did a bit of digging around. I spoke to a few debs who had done the Season the same year as Clarissa. It turns out she'd been after Edward Carlyle – "set her cap" at him, as we used to say. I mean, to be honest, Edward was the catch of the Season – rich, titled, handsome and clever, he was the one all the girls were after. But according to her friends, Clarissa was obsessed.'

Amy shook her head.

'But she didn't get Edward, did she?'

'No, but Christopher was the next best thing. With Edward out of the way, Christopher moved up the pecking order to elder son. And as Christopher's wife, she became chatelaine of that great house: a real lady. Although only in name, of course, not in the ways that count.'

Amy tried to take it all in. It was a big accusation that Georgia was making; no wonder it had caused such a bitter rift in the family, and no wonder Will had said they didn't want any whisper of the scandal getting out.

'Did you tell them what you thought had happened?'

Georgia nodded.

'Of course, how could I keep that to myself? My family thought I was wicked for even thinking such a thing. I was an outcast. Even my mother thought I was deluded. She knew how much I wanted Edward to be innocent, but like everyone else, she believed Clarissa. Why wouldn't she? So my relationship with Estella never really recovered either.'

'What happened to you? What did you do?'

The old woman shrugged.

'What could I do? I left home, got a job. At night I studied. I lost myself in a world of books and kept thinking about university and how Edward said I'd be happy there, how I would flourish. I took the Cambridge exam and got in. I didn't apply to Oxford. It would have been too painful for me. I went up to Newnham College and I made a new life for myself.'

She spread her hands.

'And here we are.'

Amy looked around the apartment. When she had first come here, it had looked so impressive, all the art, all the books, the wonderful view. Now she could see it as Georgia must have done from time to time down the years: big and lonely, a consolation prize at best, a pale substitute for the grand house and the happy life she should have had – the life she should have shared with the man she adored.

'Have you seen Clarissa since?' she asked.

Georgia shook her head.

'There was one occasion when I saw her on Regent Street. I know she saw me too, but she looked the other way. She knows what she's guilty of, so it suits her to have *deluded* cousin Georgia wiped from her life. She doesn't want a reminder of what she did. A reminder of the guilt, the shame, the fear.'

'Fear?'

Georgia gave a low snort.

'The fear of getting found out, fear of scandal.'

She was crying now, tears running down her pale, elegant face.

'Edward proposed to me that night, he put a ring on my finger. We talked about our wedding day, about our honeymoon, the life we were going to have in New York. Does that sound like a man about to commit a terrible crime?'

Amy shook her head slowly.

Georgia beat her frail hand against her chest.

'He did not lie, Amy, he just didn't. He wouldn't have done that. Not then, not any night. And if you don't believe that, then you don't believe in love.'

She bowed her head, her shoulders heaving as she sobbed. Amy moved closer to her on the sofa and put an arm around her.

'So now you know,' sniffed Georgia. 'That's why I am reduced to advertising for a companion in a magazine. That's why I have no desire to spend Christmas with my family.'

'And it's why you've never been to New York.'

'I think I was the only senior person in the publishing industry who had never been,' she said with a sorry laugh. 'But I could never go to the one place I could have been truly happy.'

'Oh Georgia, I'm so sorry.'

The old woman took a deep breath and pushed herself up.

'Well, let's not spoil the day. It's all water under the bridge anyway. Nothing's going to bring Edward back, however many tears are shed.'

She bent to pick up the jug of flowers.

'These are beautiful, you know,' she said. 'I am going to put them by the window.'

She took two steps, then seemed to stagger and pitch forward, one hand reaching for the window ledge.

'Georgia!' cried Amy as the vase tumbled in a slow-motion arc, clattering to the floor and spilling the flowers. She scrambled across and hooked her arms under the old woman's shoulders, half lifting, half pulling her into an armchair.

'I'm fine. I'm fine,' said Georgia.

'No you are not fine,' said Amy, hands on hips. 'I am going to call a doctor.'

'Please, Amy, no.'

'Georgia, I think something is wrong. I really think we should get someone to look at you.'

'No,' she said fiercely.

Amy was already at the phone.

'Tell me the name of your doctors. I'm phoning them.'

'There's no point.'

'No point?' said Amy, her concern making her snap. 'This is your health we're talking about.'

'There's no point because I know what's wrong with me. My doctors know what's wrong with me.'

Amy felt the temperature in the room drop.

'What is it?' she said, her voice almost a whisper.

Georgia waved a pale hand, as if it was nothing of concern.

'I was having headaches, the odd fall, so I had all the tests. In the end, they found something. It's being managed.'

'What's being managed?' Amy hardly dared to breathe.

Georgia fell silent, as if she didn't want to say the words.

'You're going to be okay, aren't you?' asked Amy, rooted to the floor.

'Well, they can't operate, too far gone apparently.'

'What does that mean?' asked Amy, her voice shaking in panic.

'I means I'm going to die,' said Georgia, quite simply. 'It happens to us all, doesn't it? For me it will just be sooner rather than later. That's why I had to go to New York.'

'Your bucket list,' said Amy in a voice so soft she could barely hear it herself.

'It was the only thing left in my life I had to do.'

CHAPTER TWENTY-FOUR

At least it wasn't raining. Amy squinted up at the grey sky, searching the building across the road. *There.* The socks were still hanging on the balcony. Counting the windows across and the floors down, she worked out the number of Will's flat and walked to the entrance. *Ah,* she thought. The names were on the buzzers anyway.

She pressed the button next to 'Hamilton, W.' and was rewarded by a familiar baritone.

'It's Amy,' she said. 'From the coffee shop.'

'If this is about the socks, I was just about to bring them in.'

'Just let me in, okay?' she said crisply.

Compared to the grand chandelier and staircase of Georgia's entrance hall, the communal area for Will's building was small and gloomy. She took the two flights of stairs to where Will was waiting on the landing and handed him a fistful of envelopes she'd grabbed down in the hallway.

'Your post,' she said, making for the open door of his apartment.

'Come in,' said Will sarcastically under his breath.

Inside, a narrow corridor led to a small, crowded living room. It was untidy, of course – this was a man who left his washing out for a whole season – but the few pieces of furniture in the room – a sofa, coffee table covered with heavyweight magazines, and a heaving bookcase – were smart and tasteful. There were framed film posters on the walls: bold technicolour prints of Billy Wilder classics – *Some Like It Hot*, *The Apartment* and *Sunset Boulevard*. It was not a room that was ever going to appear in an interiors magazine, but it was a space that hummed with the personality of its owner.

'I like those movies too,' said Amy, suddenly feeling nervous. After all, she had barged into his inner sanctum without an invitation – very unladylike behaviour, she recognised, by any standard – and now she wasn't entirely sure she wanted to deal with all the issues her morning at Georgia's place had thrown up.

'I was just over at Georgia's, Will,' she said, realising that now she was here, she could hardly back out again. 'She's not well. She had a fall when I was there, and it meant I found out a whole heap of stuff I'm not even sure you know about.'

'What?' he said, looking alarmed. 'What kind of fall? Is she all right?'

'She's dying, Will,' she said, feeling her hands begin to shake.

Will looked at her incredulously as Amy told him what had happened at the apartment. When she had finished, he sank into a chair and ran his fingers through his dark hair.

'Shit,' he repeated again and again, then looked up at Amy. 'How long has she got?'

'I don't know.'

'Are we talking months? Years?' he said impatiently.

'Will, I don't know.' She felt overwhelmed with emotion. 'She doesn't want to talk about it, but it's not good. And it's all the more reason to do something about your family. She might not be around for too much longer.'

Will exhaled deeply.

'Amy, listen. There's something you should know . . .'

'I know all about it!' snapped Amy. 'The rape allegation, Edward and Christopher – Georgia told me everything.'

Will sucked in air through his nose and puffed out his cheeks.

'Is it too early to have a beer?' he said, getting up.

'Definitely not, if you've got any.'

She perched on the edge of the sofa as Will went into the small galley kitchen and she heard the distinctive 'hiss-clunk, hiss-clunk' of two bottletops dropping into a sink. He walked back and handed Amy a cold bottle and sat down opposite her.

'I think "assault" was the term they used when I first began asking questions about why the family had nothing to do with Georgia,' he said. 'I kind of filled the gaps in myself. As you can imagine, we don't exactly discuss it over the Christmas dinner table.'

'Do you believe the story?'

'Which bit?'

'The rape. Do you think Clarissa told the truth about what happened that night?'

Will took a long swig of Stella.

'You think she *wanted* to have sex with Edward?' he said.

'Georgia is adamant that Edward didn't have sex with Clarissa at all that night. Neither rape nor consensual sex.'

He gave her a sideways look.

'How is she so sure?'

'Did you know that he proposed to Georgia that night?'

Will looked surprised and shook his head.

'As I said this morning, no one's ever given me a blow-by-blow account. I've had to piece things together.'

'Well, I've been thinking it over,' said Amy. 'And I just don't believe it makes sense that Edward would rape Clarissa that night, not after he'd been planning a new life with Georgia.'

'With respect,' said Will, 'having spent a few days with Georgia doesn't make you an expert on our family.'

'Of course not,' said Amy, irritated. 'And I was as sceptical as you when Georgia was telling me all this. But you should listen to her side of things. She's very compelling. She just doesn't believe that Edward raped Clarissa, never has, not even after all this time.'

Will shrugged.

'You believe what you want to believe, don't you?'

'But have you ever asked your Aunt Clarissa?'

'No, of course not! Have you ever asked *your* family about their sex lives?'

Amy pouted. It was a good point.

'But Will, you're a writer, you understand how stories work. You know how versions of events can get twisted over time.'

He took another long drink, seeming to mull it over.

'Let's just say Georgia has it right and Clarissa wasn't raped. Why would Clarissa lie about it? Imagine the shame that must have been attached to rape back then. Why bring all that down on yourself?'

Amy shrugged.

'And to destroy Edward's life like that? Clarissa would have to be cold as ice. Even if he hadn't died in the Far East, it was a sick allegation to make.'

Amy had thought all the same things herself and she didn't know the answers.

'People in love, rejected people, jealous people, angry people, they've done a lot worse. You only have to read the papers,' she said finally.

Will drained his beer and looked at her.

'But these people are my family, Amy. They're respectable people.'

She appreciated how difficult this must be for him to take on board.

'Maybe they are in many ways,' she said as gently as she could. 'But Clarissa was young, buzzing with hormones, feeling snubbed – young people can do some crazy, impulsive things. They think about the rewards, not the consequences. And with Edward discredited, Clarissa married Christopher and got everything she ever wanted. The stately home, the title, the admiration of her family. That's the sort of prize that could make you do some pretty mad stuff.'

Will stood up, pacing up and down. Amy could see he was struggling with it.

'We need to do something,' she said.

'Do what?' he asked, shrugging in exasperation. 'Even it's true – and how will we ever know for sure? – Clarissa and Christopher, if he knows what really went on, aren't exactly motivated to tell us the truth, are they?'

'So you think it's best to let sleeping dogs lie?' said Amy sarcastically.

'Tell me the options, Amy. Confront Aunt Clarissa and call her a liar?'

'Perhaps that's exactly what we should do,' she said, feeling her cheeks turn pink with fury. 'Then maybe Georgia will get to hear the truth. Maybe she'll get some closure finally. Don't you want justice? For Georgia? For Edward? For everything that was taken away from them?'

Will stared out of the window, as if he was thinking. When he turned and looked back at her, she could see the conflict on his face and she could sympathise. Here she was, a virtual stranger, turning up in his tidy little life, begging him to chuck an emotional grenade into his family. It was crazy, wasn't it? If their positions had been reversed, Amy was pretty sure she would have thrown him out on to the street long before now.

'There's a party,' he said finally. 'It's at their house.'

'You'll help me to do something?' said Amy, running up to him and throwing her arms around him. He smelt nice. Like Christmas trees and soap.

'All right, all right,' he said gruffly, stepping away from her. 'So what's the plan?'

He walked over to the mantelpiece and handed her a stiff white card.

> *You are invited to a New Year's Eve celebration*
> *Stapleford*
> *31 December*
> *8 p.m.*
> *Black tie*

'This is pretty much the only time we are guaranteed to get Clarissa and Christopher on the spot before Easter. They have a house in Antigua they usually disappear to in January, and stay there for three or four months. And if Georgia's . . . well, maybe we can't wait that long to do something.'

'And what *are* we doing?' asked Amy, looking up at him.

'Probably wasting our time,' said Will cynically. 'Clarissa's almost certainly not going to admit anything.'

'We can only try,' said Amy, putting a grateful hand on Will's shoulder. 'We definitely owe Georgia that much.'

'See you on New Year's Eve then,' he said finally. 'Dress up.'

'It's a date,' she said as she pulled up her coat collar and went back into the cold.

CHAPTER TWENTY-FIVE

Amy huddled in the doorway of Daniel's house, her shoulders hunched against the rain, which came down in hissing silver ribbons, backlit by the street lights. She had run all the way from High Street Kensington tube, but her speed hadn't seemed to make any difference: her jeans were sticking to her legs, her thin trench coat – never the best choice for a torrential downpour – was sodden and heavy with dripping water. She felt like she'd been dunked in a swimming pool.

'Surprise!' she said in a monotone, as Daniel opened the door.

'Amy! Good God, what have you been doing? You look like a drowned rat.'

'Thanks,' she said. 'Just what I needed to hear.'

'Sorry, come on, get inside before someone calls the coast-guard.'

She caught a glimpse of herself as she walked past the mirror in Daniel's hallway. *Oh no*, she thought. Her hair was plastered against her forehead in a kind of weird Hitler fringe and her mascara had run, making her look like a refugee from an eighties goth band. *Great.*

Daniel ran upstairs, taking two steps at a time, and came down with a towel, which he started rubbing over her head.

'I didn't even know you were coming.'

She had been playing phone tag with Daniel all day, but he wasn't picking up, and she'd figured it was best just to come straight over. The bijou mews house just off the High Street had been a present from Daniel's parents for his thirtieth birthday, and the bathroom still had that just-finished sheen. In fact, so did the whole house – Daniel was something of a neat freak – and Amy couldn't help but notice how it was the polar opposite of Will's flat: sleek and shiny, with designer furniture and stark black and white prints on the walls. Even the glossy magazines next to the toilet were arranged in a dentist's-waiting-room-style fan.

'I'm sorry, Dan, I couldn't get in touch and I needed to see you.'

'Is everything okay?'

She puffed out her cheeks and felt the emotion of the day start to get the better of her.

'Hey, hey,' he said, stepping forward to kiss her. 'Come on, what's wrong?'

'Long story.'

'How about I order Chinese and you can tell me?'

She nodded weakly and looked around the room as he went to the phone. There was a computer games console sitting on the coffee table, next to a copy of the *Telegraph*. She felt her nerves calm a little as she surveyed the picture of bachelor bliss. Arriving on his doorstep unannounced had unsettled her. She wasn't even sure why – did she expect him to be entertaining a beautiful blonde on the quiet? – but still, she had been reassured to see nothing out of the ordinary.

She peeled off her wet jeans and put them on the radiator just as Daniel walked back into the living room with a bottle of wine and two glasses.

'What's this? Naked takeaway?'

'I will if you will,' she flirted back.

He smacked her bottom playfully and handed her a wine glass, which he topped up with red. Then they both sat back on the sofa and she spun around so that she could rest her feet on his lap. He stroked her bare legs and she felt the stress drain out of her.

'I've told Gid we'll be there about eight on Monday night.'

'Monday night?'

'New Year's Eve. The party.'

'Shit,' she muttered. 'About that . . .'

He sipped his wine and frowned.

'What's up? Got something better to do?' he said playfully.

'I don't know about better. I have to be somewhere else.'

He looked confused.

'But Gid's parties are apparently epic.'

'There's a party in Oxfordshire. Georgia's cousin, actually.'

'Who's she?'

'Clarissa Carlyle, some place called Stapleford.'

Daniel's jaw dropped open, his annoyance suddenly replaced with interest.

'We've been invited to Stapleford? Bloody hell, Amy. How did you wangle that?'

'You've heard of it?'

'Heard of it? It's one of the best houses in the entire country. Great shooting. My parents have been desperate to go for years. An invitation always seems just out of reach, however.'

'Well, it's not something I'm looking forward to,' she said quietly.

'Why not? It'll be a blast. Hey, we could even pop into my parents' on the way home. That will keep them quiet, telling them we've been to Stapleford.'

'It's not a plus one, Dan.'

'What do you mean, it's not a plus one?'

'You can't come.'

'I can't come?' he frowned.

'Someone's invited me.'

'Who?' he asked, looking completely miffed.

'Georgia's cousin's son.'

Daniel was shaking his head angrily.

'What's going on, Amy? Is this some sort of revenge for what happened at the Tower?'

'Revenge?'

'Or are you having an affair?'

'Of course I'm not having an affair. He's gay, Daniel. I'm going to meet the family because some things need to be said about Georgia.'

Daniel fell silent, but at least he looked partly mollified. Amy had no idea about Will's sexual orientation. From his banter with the pretty Primrose Hill barista, he was almost certainly straight, but it would keep Daniel quiet.

'We'll make a little networker out of you yet, Miss Carrell,' he said finally, smiling.

Amy wanted to tell him she wasn't doing it for that reason, that she didn't care about social climbing, that she was only doing it for her friend. She wanted to ask his opinion about what to say to Clarissa and Christopher Carlyle, but just then she heard the gentle 'put-put-put' of the delivery bike arriving.

'Chinese is here,' Daniel said, standing up.

'Well, I'll go and put some PJs on while you sort it out, okay?'

He hooked his arm around her waist and pulled her closer.

'PJs? Killjoy,' he purred. 'I wasn't joking about naked Chinese.'

If the delivery man hadn't been ringing the bell so insistently, Amy felt quite sure they would have slid down on to the floor right then and there. Instead, she turned Daniel around and swatted at his behind to send him on his way, then ran up the stairs to the bedroom.

'PJs, PJs,' she mumbled, opening cupboards. Working at the Forge three or four nights a week meant that she had never spent more than a night at a time at Daniel's, so she had only ever got around to leaving a toothbrush. Generally she didn't wear anything to bed, but after the rain, her legs were cold. Where would he have put his pyjamas? All of his clothes were impeccably cleaned, pressed and stacked in neat little piles, his shirts on hangers and lined up in descending order of blueness. It was all so pristine, Amy didn't want to disturb anything.

'Ah, here we go.' She found some cotton pyjama bottoms and pulled them on. No matching top, though – not a bad thing, she didn't want to look entirely sexless. Maybe she'd left a vest top here. Amy was nowhere near as organised as Daniel; she was pretty sure there were a few odd things of hers around somewhere. As she searched, a flicker of something caught her eye in the darkness of the wardrobe. She reached out and pulled it down. A sequinned cardigan.

What the hell?

Her heart began to pound as she examined it. It was heavy, expensive; Giorgio Armani Black Label. *Definitely* not hers. Definitely.

'Amy? Are you coming?'

She looked up as Daniel called from the bottom of the stairs, then back to the cardigan. Her throat was dry; she wanted to swallow but couldn't. Perhaps there was a logical explanation for a strange cardigan being in her boyfriend's wardrobe. Perhaps.

But her mind was leaping to one conclusion: it was another woman's. A chic, rich woman, a woman who had been here – in his bedroom.

'Amy?'

Ignoring Daniel's calls, she strode over to the chest of drawers and yanked the top one open, pulling the neatly paired socks out in handfuls, dropping them on to the floor.

Where is it? Where is it? Three weeks ago, there had been a Tiffany box hidden there. A ring, a necklace, some exciting gift certainly. But . . . Her hands ran along the back of the drawer. Nothing. Nothing there except socks. So where was it? Where was the box?

She looked up suddenly. Daniel was standing in the doorway, holding a bag of prawn crackers.

'What's going on?' he said. 'It's getting cold.'

Amy couldn't speak. Instead she held up the sequinned cardigan, now screwed up into a tight ball.

'What's that? A cardigan?' he said innocently.

'Yes,' said Amy, glaring at him. 'It's a cardigan. Not *my* cardigan.'

And there it was: the flicker of recognition, quickly followed by a look of dismay. If Amy had blinked, she would have missed it. But she didn't.

'Oh. It must be my mum's,' said Daniel, recovering himself. 'She was here over Christmas. I must have put it away thinking it was yours.'

It was plausible, if unlikely; a decent actor might have been able to pull it off. But Daniel was not a good actor and he was a terrible liar. Why would he ever have had to develop the skill? He'd always had everything handed to him on a plate.

'Your mother?' said Amy, her voice dripping with contempt.

'She was shopping on the High Street, dropped in for lunch.'

'Really?' she said quietly. 'Is that the best you can do?'

'Amy, what's got into you?' he said, taking a step towards her. 'You're behaving like a crazy lady.'

'Where's the Tiffany box?' she said.

'What Tiffany box?'

'The Tiffany box hidden in your sock drawer before Christmas,' she said slowly, deliberately, watching his face. Another flicker. Her heart sank – so it was true. Right then, she knew it was all true.

'What were you doing going through my sock drawer?' said Daniel.

Yeah, good move, thought Amy. *Go on the attack.*

'Answer the question,' she said, feeling suddenly weary. 'Where is the box?'

'It was a present. A key ring.'

'For your mother, I suppose.'

'No, not for my mother,' he said with a touch of sarcasm. 'For my secretary.'

'And you hid it in your sock drawer.'

'Look, are you going to tell me what's going on here? What are you trying to imply, because I don't appreciate—'

'Who is she?' said Amy, holding up the cardigan.

'I've already told you, that belongs to my mother.'

'Don't lie to me, Daniel.'

He threw his hands in the air.

'Amy, you are being absolutely ridiculous. If we are going to get things back on track, you are really going to have to start trusting me.'

She nodded slowly.

'Okay,' she said.

She untangled the cardigan and slipped one arm into a sleeve, then the other. It fitted perfectly. Amy was a size eight, a long, lean dancer's physique. Daniel's mother was in her sixties, a size fourteen at least.

'It fits,' she said quietly.

'Well, maybe Mother bought something too small at the shops—'

'WHO IS SHE?' screamed Amy, making Daniel jerk back at the sudden ferocity.

'Amy, stop it.'

'You're going to make a terrible diplomat, Daniel,' she sneered. 'Your mother? Was that an example of you thinking on your feet? Christ. At the very least you should have pretended it was my Christmas present. Seeing as the Tiffany *key ring* has gone missing.'

He blinked at her, then looked away. The smooth-talking rich boy finally lost for words.

Amy pulled off the cardigan and dropped it at his feet.

'Who is she, Daniel? You owe me that at least.'

He let out a long breath.

'You don't know her,' he said, still not meeting her gaze. 'She works in finance. We met at a function.'

'How long has it been going on?' She knew she should just walk out, try to scrape up whatever tiny crumbs of dignity were left, but she had to know, *needed* to know every last detail.

'It wasn't like that . . .'

'How long?'

He lifted his chin, a little of the old arrogance back.

'We were on a break, Amy.'

'A week,' she hissed. 'And in that time, she's been here. Been to your house, left her belongings . . .'

Her voice faltered as she realised what all that meant. If Daniel had broken down and confessed, said it was just a one-night stand, that he'd been drunk, that it meant nothing, she knew she might actually have forgiven him. But it wasn't like that, she could see that now. This girl was serious.

'Two months,' he said. 'I've been seeing her a couple of months.'

Amy nodded. She had expected the tears to come, but instead she just felt a crushing inevitability, a hollowness.

'Let me guess, it's someone "appropriate", right?'

'Amy, don't . . .'

'No, seriously, Daniel,' she said. 'I bet she's not a waitress at the Forge Bar and Grill. I bet she's not a showgirl in some tacky West End production no one has ever heard of.'

'Amy, stop it. Listen to yourself.'

'Who. Is. She?' said Amy.

Daniel could see he was cornered.

'She's a friend from university – well, a couple of years younger. She's an analyst at Goldman's now. We just bumped into each other, I really didn't mean for anything to happen.'

'Well, I'm sure you've got lots in common,' she said tartly.

'Seriously, Amy, nothing happened until we split up.'

'Bullshit.'

'Oh what does it matter anyway?' said Daniel, suddenly angry. 'You're right, we do have things in common, she does fit into my world. What's so bloody wrong with that?'

'What's wrong with that?' snapped Amy. 'Me, that's what's wrong. Your *girlfriend*, remember? The one you screwed last night, the one you wanted to show off at new year.'

'Amy, you are beautiful, and fun and . . .' He trailed off. 'But this is different. Harriet can get a transfer to the Washington office, our lives are compatible.'

'Yes, Harriet does sound suitable.'

'Don't be like that.'

'But I am like this, Daniel,' she said. 'This is who I am. And it seems that's not good enough.'

She pushed roughly past him and down the stairs, grabbing her still-wet jeans and coat and pulling them back on.

'I'll leave my toothbrush in the bathroom,' she said as Daniel followed her down. 'Perhaps Harriet might like to use that too.'

He stopped her just as she was opening the front door. The rain was still pounding down, sending up little flowers of spray from the surface of the road. He put his arm across the door frame, blocking her exit.

'Amy, don't go off like this, please. I do care about you . . .'

She turned to face him.

'The last few days have been an education for me, Daniel. I know which knives and forks to use, I know which wine glasses to drink from. I even know how to eat a goddam artichoke properly. But none of that matters any more. Because the one thing I know, the one thing I've always known, is that I am too good for you. I really am.'

And she pushed his arm away and walked out into the rain.

CHAPTER TWENTY-SIX

Amy stared out of the window of the moving car, her eyes focused on the darkness. Now and then she would see a farmhouse, its lights glowing, or an isolated home, the Christmas tree still illuminated in a window, but otherwise Will's silver Jeep seemed to be floating alone in the blackness, headlights on full beam as they twisted and turned along the narrow country lanes.

'Are you sure you know where you're going?' said Amy. 'I think we left the main road about twenty minutes ago. I keep expecting to see werewolves.'

Will smiled, his teeth white in the gloom.

'Country houses,' he said. 'The clue's in the name – they tend to be in the middle of nowhere. But don't worry, I've been coming to Stapleford since I was a kid. I think I could find it blindfolded.'

'I'd prefer you kept your eyes on the road.'

They fell back into silence. Amy had to admit she wasn't exactly sparkling company tonight – but then who would be when you'd been dumped twice in the space of a couple of weeks? She was still struggling to come to terms with it; that moment when she had found the cardigan was etched into her mind. How could she have been so stupid? How?

'So what were you supposed to be doing tonight?' asked Will.

'Going to a party hosted by someone called Gideon.'

She could see Will suppressing a smile.

'What's wrong with the name Gideon?'

'Nothing,' said Will. 'Nothing at all. It's just . . . I can picture him, just from the name.'

Amy snorted.

'The stereotype actually fits in this case. But then most of Daniel's friends were like that: public school, protected, very pleased with themselves.'

'Daniel? Is he your boyfriend?'

'Ex-boyfriend.'

Will glanced across.

'Ex? But the other day. Your big night out. Georgia's dress. The result dress.'

'Well, things change,' she said briskly. 'Turns out he was sleeping with a tall, thin banker called Harriet. He gave her something from Tiffany for Christmas.'

Will's eyes widened.

'He *told* you this?'

'No, I found the "something from Tiffany" in his sock drawer before Christmas. I thought it was my engagement ring,' she said. 'Can you believe that?'

'I'm sorry.'

'So am I. So, would you have been going to this party if it wasn't for me forcing you into going?' asked Amy.

'Probably not. No date, you see. Turn up without a girlfriend and the family start asking all sorts of awkward questions.'

'You don't have a girlfriend?'

'Hard to imagine, I know,' he said with the hint of a smile.

He paused, turning back to the road.

'Actually, I did. Until last summer. Then I found out she was sleeping with a tall, thin lawyer called Jonathan. No Tiffany box, but they had been on a mini-break together under my nose.'

Amy looked at him.

'That sucks.'

'I haven't really had time to dwell on it. Work has been busy.'

'The plays? Well, it's good you're getting work.'

He laughed.

'Not you too. Seems the standard reaction to telling anyone you're a playwright is "Oh, you can make a living out of that?"'

'Sorry, I should know better,' said Amy. 'When I tell people I'm a dancer, they automatically assume I'm unemployed.'

'So what might I have seen you in?' He looked over, his dark eyes flashing.

'An apron at the Forge Bar and Grill,' she said grimly.

'You just need a lucky break,' he said with confidence.

'What about you? What was your last play?'

'It was called *About Face*. It had a short run. You probably won't have seen it,' he said, shrugging his shoulders modestly.

Amy was about to ask more when suddenly her attention was elsewhere.

'Jeez, is that it?' she said, looking at what lay ahead of them.

'Uh-huh,' said Will. 'Impressive, isn't it?'

'Wow.'

'Impressive' didn't really do Stapleford justice. Lit from the outside by spotlights, it looked to Amy like a palace from a story book. She had occasionally been to visit Daniel's friends at their country places, but compared to Stapleford, they looked like twee cottages.

'How big is it?' she said as Will pulled up on the drive, parking his Jeep between a Bentley and a silver Maserati.

'Two-hundred-odd rooms, I think,' said Will. 'Actually, maybe more than that now they've converted the stables. They don't live in all of it, of course. The main house is open to the public these days. Taxes, you see.'

'Must be tough,' said Amy, gazing up at the tall windows, twinkling from the inside. 'Light bulbs alone must cripple them,' she added sarcastically.

Will got out of the car and came round to open the passenger door for her.

'We're guests here,' he whispered. 'Let's try to be nice.'

She stepped out of the car, her Ralph Lauren heels crunching on the gravel drive.

'Ready?' asked Will, looking at her.

She was momentarily distracted by how great he looked. He had picked her up from her apartment, waiting in the car until she had come down to the street. On the two-hour journey to Oxfordshire, she had tried not to notice how handsome he was – how his hair had been cut, his face cleanly shaved – but standing in the shadow of Stapleford, he looked tall and strong and manly, like someone straight out of an aftershave advert.

She looked away from him, and rubbed her hands up and down her little black dress nervously.

He touched the small of her back and led her past the uniformed valets and into the house.

Amy took a second to compose herself. The outside of Stapleford was intimidating enough, but stepping into the crowded entrance hall – God, that was the tallest Christmas tree she'd ever seen – did nothing to ease her anxiety. *What am I going to do exactly?* she thought. *Go up to the lady of the manor and say, 'Hi, you don't know me, but you're a liar'?*

'Don't worry, it's just a party,' said Will in a low voice that no one else could hear.

'Just a party.' She laughed nervously. 'Just a party where I'm completely out of my depth,' she said, playing with a cocktail ring she'd bought at Walthamstow market.

'You know, if you accepted that you are the most beautiful woman in this place, you might relax and stop fidgeting,' said Will, accepting two glasses of champagne and handing her one. 'Here, try that. It might help,' he said, leading her through the entrance hall.

She was still blushing at his compliment as they threaded through the many well-dressed revellers and into what Amy had to assume was the ballroom. There was a raised platform at one end with a seated jazz band playing gentle swing tunes, but there was no dancing; rather the floor was filled with people standing in groups laughing and talking.

'Hey, there's my dad,' said Will. 'Let's go and say hello.'

Amy stopped him and pulled him to one side where they wouldn't be overheard.

'You know, I think I should do this. Talk to Clarissa.'

Will opened his mouth to object, but she stopped him.

'It's better coming from a stranger. But before we do, remind me of the set-up so I don't balls it up. Your dad is Clarissa's brother, right?'

Will nodded.

'And what does Clarissa do these days?'

'Do?' he smiled.

'Like a job.'

'She doesn't do jobs. She is big on the charity circuit. Formidable, in fact. I think there are various wings of museums and libraries named after her.'

'That's why she'll do anything to avoid scandal,' Amy muttered under her breath. 'Who'd want to endanger all this?'

A tall man with grey hair approached them. He was in his sixties, Amy guessed, but you would still classify him as handsome. He gave Will a chummy slap on the back.

'Amy Carrell,' said Will. 'Meet my father, Richard Hamilton.'

'Pleased to meet you, Amy,' said Richard, with a genuine smile. Perhaps it was his obvious resemblance to Will, but Amy instantly warmed to him.

'Amazing house,' she said.

'Yes, I have to keep reminding my sister of that; she's constantly moaning about the roof. I suppose when you're here all the time, it becomes commonplace. Anyway, you'll get a chance to have a look around. I think they've put you two in the Trafalgar Suite.'

Will glanced at Amy.

'Oh, we're not . . .' he stuttered. 'Amy's a friend, not a . . .'

His father started to laugh.

'It's the twenty-first century, Will. We're not that old-fashioned, you know.'

'Well, we were going to drive back tonight.'

'To London? Tonight?' said his father, shaking his head. 'What on earth for? Your aunt Clarissa will be so disappointed. Come on, drink up,' he said.

After a while, Amy excused herself, leaving the two men talking. It was nice to see the warmth between Will and his father. She had rather imagined the Hamiltons as a wholly dysfunctional family, clawing at each other for advantage, money and power, but now she could see that she had judged them only on Clarissa's actions. Yes, it had been wicked and it had had terrible consequences, but it had happened decades ago. Perhaps throughout the intervening years they had enjoyed a normal life, just like Amy's family: the occasional spat and argument, but nothing they couldn't overcome. Somehow, though, Amy didn't think so. It was possible that someone could do what Clarissa had done and learn from it, a shock to the system that would cure you of your selfish ways. But more likely it would only confirm whatever self-image you already had. After all, Clarissa's deceit had given her all this: the chandeliers, the polished woodwork, the gilt-framed oils and the marble fireplaces. The human mind had a way of justifying its actions to itself. Amy was fairly sure that Clarissa would have taken the success of her scheme to mean that she deserved this life. She somehow doubted whether she had lost many nights' sleep over it.

She walked slowly around the ground floor of Stapleford, taking in the grandeur – the red drawing room with its crimson velvet drapes and painted ceiling, the library stacked floor to ceiling with leather-bound books – and watching the party guests mingling: the ladies in their fine gowns and the flashing jewels that probably only came out of their safe deposit box one night a year; the gentlemen in their dark suits and their red cheeks; all of them laughing, smiling, seemingly comfortable in this world. Had any of them done things like Clarissa had? Had their fathers or mothers? Was all this smug, easy wealth founded on self-interest and evil? After all, unlike Daniel's family – one generation of public school and they thought they were the House of Windsor – this was real old money, proper wealth, founded on exploitation and quite possibly corruption. Maybe Clarissa wasn't alone; perhaps that was what it took to live this way.

Amy was just passing through the vast entrance hall when she saw her, and her heart jumped. She had demonised Clarissa Carlyle over the last few days, imagined her as some sinister Disney version of a wicked queen; even in the society-pages snaps she'd pulled up on the internet, Clarissa seemed to have a slightly evil gleam in her eye. But in the flesh she was nothing like that. She was just an ordinary woman. Or rather, an ordinary woman who had lived her life in extraordinary luxury. She certainly had that poise, that regal air as she walked towards Amy, helped by her long taffeta dress and the diamonds around her neck. Her bone structure was less fine than Georgia's, but the family resemblance was clear.

Oh God, do I really want to do this? thought Amy, wondering for a moment whether she should just walk past, perhaps leave it until the next day. Or the day after that.

'Hello. You're Will's new friend, I hear,' said Clarissa, stopping in front of her.

Oh hell.

'Yes,' stammered Amy. 'I suppose I am.'

The old woman held out a hand and Amy took a moment to study her. Georgia had revealed that Clarissa had been a secretary at *Vogue* in her younger days, and that love of fashion certainly shone through now. Looking at the exquisite beadwork and tailoring of her gown, Amy was certain it must be couture.

'Clarissa Carlyle. I'm Will's aunt.'

'Amy Carrell.'

'Oh, you're American?' said Clarissa. 'How delightful. I was so glad to hear he had a new – what do you call it these days? – partner, is it? He's such a lovely boy.'

Amy didn't think she would achieve much by correcting the old woman, so she just smiled.

'What are you doing wandering around on your own like this?' Clarissa asked in her cut-glass accent.

'I think Will's seen this house a million times before. I didn't want to bore him asking for a guided tour.'

'Our family never tires of showing off the house. It's quite special. Will tells me you're a dancer. Did you meet through the theatre? What was Will's latest project? The one at the Royal Court?'

The Royal Court? thought Amy. *Who's been hiding his light under a bushel?*

'No, we met through a mutual acquaintance,' she said, knowing that this was her moment. 'A member of your family. Georgia Hamilton.'

Clarissa's face did not move; there was no change in her expression at all – and to Amy, that was more telling than a sneer.

'Georgia?' she said evenly. 'How is she?'

Did she really care? Was she genuinely curious about the cousin she hadn't seen, barring that glance on Regent Street, in fifty years? She must have thought of Georgia from time to time – how could she not, given the traumatic circumstances of their rift? Or had she really learnt to live with it, to put people and inconvenient events from her mind?

'She's not too well actually,' said Amy. 'In fact she doesn't think she has very long to live.'

Now *that* got a reaction. Clarissa looked as if she had been slapped; her face drained of colour apart from two pink dots in the centre of her cheeks.

'Can't they do anything?'

Amy shook her head.

'Apparently not – although she's not in any pain, and she's still able to walk and look after herself.'

'That's something at least,' Clarissa said, looking down at the floor.

'In fact, we have just been to New York together,' said Amy.

'New York?'

'Yes, it was something Georgia was desperate to do. I finally found out that she wanted to go there because New York was where she had planned to go on her honeymoon with her fiancé.'

Clarissa frowned.

'Yes, I heard she had been married.'

'Not that fiancé,' said Amy. She looked straight at Clarissa. 'I mean Edward.'

The old woman shook her head.

'I'm sorry, I haven't seen Georgia in many years. Do I know Edward?'

'Yes, Clarissa, Edward Carlyle. Your husband's brother. You might remember him. He's the one you accused of rape.'

Amy had heard the expression 'her face hardened', but she had never understood it properly until that moment. Clarissa's features looked as if they had been carved from stone.

'I believe you have confused me with someone else,' she said in clipped, even tones. If she had been disconcerted, wrong-footed by Amy's unexpected mention of Georgia, it disappeared in an instant and she was once again the lady of the house, the formidable grande dame.

Come on, Amy, don't give in now, she said to herself. She thought of Georgia falling in her flat, the flowers scattering across the carpet; she thought of the story she had told and the look of unhealed pain on her face when she had spoken of Edward, her love, and the fate that had befallen him.

'No, Clarissa,' she said, meeting the older woman's gaze, 'I don't think I have confused you with anyone else. You do remember Edward, I take it? The man whose life you destroyed? The man who – because of your accusations – was banished to Singapore and his death?'

'I am well aware of the tragedy, young lady. This is my family. I am simply denying your very unpleasant insinuations.'

'Oh, they're more than insinuations,' said Amy. 'They are facts.'

'Facts?' Clarissa barked harshly. 'Says who? Georgia? There are no facts here, only slanderous lies, lies that I will vigorously contest if need be. Do not underestimate me, Miss Carrell.'

Amy shook her head.

'I don't want you to take me to court, Lady Carlyle. I just want you to tell me the truth. Finally admit what happened that night in 1958. Nothing will change. Not after all these years. You won't lose your house, your precious title. Even if you don't want to do it for Georgia or for Edward, do it for yourself. That's what you're good at. Looking after number one. Do it now, while you still can. Clear your conscience before it's too late.'

'How dare you come here, into my house, with these accusations. Georgia's accusations.'

'Oh no, Georgia has no idea I'm here. She has more dignity than to accuse you of anything. I am here because I saw what your scheme did to her. It broke her in *half*,' said Amy, her anger rising. 'She wasn't interested in all this. She didn't care about the house or the title or the money. She only wanted Edward. She loved Edward.'

'So did *I*,' snapped Clarissa, then stopped, a look of shock on her face, as if she had been tricked into saying something she hadn't even admitted to herself.

'You? You loved Edward?'

Clarissa's lips formed a thin line.

'This conversation is over.'

Amy stepped forward.

'No, no it's not. If you loved Edward, then why did you . . .?'

Amy was aware that someone was standing behind her before she heard the cough. She turned to see a tall, thin elderly gentleman standing there. His face was pale and he looked shocked. She could tell that he had heard everything.

'Clarissa, m'dear?' he said. 'Is everything all right?'

'Everything is fine, Christopher,' she said crisply. 'I believe this young lady was just leaving.'

Amy felt the older couple's eyes meet.

'Do we need security?' he asked, his voice even and firm.

'No, that won't be necessary,' said Amy, holding Clarissa's gaze. 'Lady Carlyle is correct. I was about to leave. Thank you very much for a wonderful evening.'

She looked at Clarissa's husband.

'And I'll be sure to give your regards to Georgia Hamilton,' she added, then turned and walked out of the front door.

CHAPTER TWENTY-SEVEN

She texted Will as soon as she got outside: 'Just met Clarissa, been ejected. Out front. Help!' His Jeep was gone, and with a sinking feeling she wondered if he had been kicked out as well and had simply bolted and left her there.

She shivered and wrapped her arms around her Ralph Lauren dress, wondering if she was going to have to sleep out here and would be found dead from hypothermia in the morning. Her dress was lovely, but it wasn't doing much to keep the cold out, that was for sure.

'Hey.'

Amy almost jumped in the air and whirled around.

'Don't worry, it's me,' laughed Will, approaching from the opposite direction. He was holding up a set of keys. 'My dad sorted out the keys for the gardener's cottage. Apparently it's empty; he said we can have it. I've already moved the car.'

'Should we not just drive home before they send the bloodhounds out to get me?'

'I've had a couple of glasses of champagne. I'd better not drive for at least another few hours. Don't worry, I don't bite.'

'I trust you,' she said, her teeth chattering. 'But hurry up and sober up, for Chrissake. I don't want to be hanging around here any longer than I have to.'

It was just a few minutes' walk to the gardener's cottage. Will opened the door, turned on a small lamp and went to light a fire whilst Amy made coffee.

'Black. No milk, sorry,' she said, handing him a mug.

'So are you going to tell me what happened? Warts and all?'

'I knew I should have gone in there with a plan. I just started accusing her, and needless to say it didn't go down too well.'

'What did she say?'

'Not much. Admitted that she loved Edward, though. I caught her right off guard. Christopher was standing behind me too. I've probably caused a whole heap more trouble.'

'Or maybe you've just set the wheels in motion.'

Will took off his dinner jacket and put it on a chair.

'Just because things don't happen immediately doesn't mean to say they won't happen. I've told my dad about Georgia's story, and I can tell he believes it. At least believes it *might* be true. We're going to speak to them both tomorrow. Clarissa and Christopher.'

'No, don't,' said Amy softly. 'It's out there now. You don't want more family fighting.'

He took a sip of coffee and looked at her.

'Thank you,' he said, taking a step towards her. 'Thanks for everything you've done.'

As she nodded, noise exploded around them – the sound of a thousand firecrackers – and bright red and white light flooded into the room.

'The fireworks.'

'Let's go and look.'

The cottage was on a small hill looking down over the grounds. They went outside and as Amy watched the sparks of light explode in the sky above the house, she nudged Will.

'I have an idea.'

'Oh yeah?'

'You know Edward's buried around here somewhere. In the graveyard of the local church. We should find out when the gruesome twosome are off to Antigua and bring Georgia here.'

'That's a good idea. Maybe we can go and see her tomorrow and put it to her. We can pick a day and I can drive us over here.'

'Speaking of which, how are you feeling?'

'You know, I think I'll be all right to drive home in twenty minutes,' he said as the fireworks faded.

'Let's stay out here. Just for a little while.'

'Okay.' He sank to the grass and crossed his legs in front of him. 'So,' he said, 'what would you do if this was your last year on earth?'

'That's a bit of a depressing thought,' she said, turning to look at him.

'In a way. Or you could look at it as though you were putting your life into sharp focus. What do you want to do? What's important to you? How do you really want to spend your days?'

'Big questions.'

'Big night,' he replied.

'I want to set up a children's ballet company this year.'

'Oh yeah?' he said with interest. 'What does that involve?'

'Ballets for kids. Fun ones. Happy ones.'

'How far have you got with it?'

'Oh, not very. It's just an idea. It was something Georgia was encouraging me with.'

'Need any help with a script? I've directed a few things too.'

'You'd help me?' she frowned.

'I'd like to.'

'Payback for Georgia?' she asked.

'I want to help you,' he said simply.

She started to laugh softly.

'What's so funny?'

'I thought you hated me.'

'Well, I don't make these offers to every girl,' he smiled and stood up. 'Do you want some more coffee?'

'If it's the night of big questions, we'd better stock up.'

He brushed some grass off his trousers, and as he looked at her, she could see a sudden crack in his relaxed confidence.

'Tomorrow. After we go and see Georgia, do you want to go for some dinner?'

He smiled shyly in the darkness and she felt something pop and fizz inside her.

'I'd like that very much.' She nodded, trying hard not to beam.

'Keep my seat warm,' he grinned as he went back inside the cottage.

She put her hand on the spot where he had just been and smiled. A new year, a new start.

'I will.'

CHAPTER TWENTY-EIGHT

Georgia poured herself a cognac, wondering what she should do for the rest of the afternoon. She usually went to her good friends Sally and Gianni Adami's for their rumbustious annual New Year's Day lunch. Since Frederick McDonald and André Bauer had retired to Salzburg five years earlier, Sally and Gianni were the only people she regularly saw from the debutante scene, a scene she had deliberately tried to distance herself from after everything that had happened. Although they were bound together by so many old and emotional memories, some of which she didn't want to remember, Sally and Gianni were enormous fun and it was impossible to stay away from them. Besides, Georgia was godmother to their eldest son, Lucas, who, quite terrifyingly, was in his fifties now – a lawyer by trade and a father himself to four beautiful children. She remembered him as such a tiny little thing, born in Venice, where Sally and Gianni had lived for many years before they returned to London. Just that morning she had dug out an old photo album and looked at some faded old pictures of them all together at the Lido, in St Mark's Square, on the Bridge of Sighs. Georgia had spent many happy holidays in Venice. Her old friend had been right when she said the oranges were like footballs, and travelling around by gondola – the handsome gondoliers, the candy-striped poles sticking out of the water, the canals that shimmered green in the sunshine – was pure magic.

She glanced at her watch, wondering if it was too late to make the lunch after all. Gianni had promised it would be a particularly lavish affair this year, and had threatened to make his famous limoncello cocktails to celebrate the recent sale of his nationwide chain of Italian restaurants to a private equity firm. Sally hadn't understood why Georgia had declined this year's invitation. Then again, her old friend didn't know quite how ill Georgia was. And the New York trip had certainly taken it out of her.

But at least her Manhattan adventure had been everything she had hoped it would be. As good as it could be, anyway, going with someone she had never met before, someone who was not the person she was supposed to have experienced the delights of New York with for the first time.

Young Amy Carrell had been delightful company, but it had been hard on the trip not to think about what it would have been like with Edward at her side. On Christmas Day morning, whilst Amy had still been at her parents', Georgia had enjoyed taking a long walk on her own around Central Park, imagining them together.

Of course, she could remember exactly what Edward looked like. She only had a few photographs of him, but she had looked at them so many times she could never forget. What was harder was remembering the less tangible things about him. His smell, the way he walked, the way he tossed a quip into the air, the way he smiled at her and made her feel as if she were ten feet tall. Fifty years did that to you – it rubbed away the edges until the memories were so faint, it was hard to believe they even existed.

She had been thinking a lot about death lately. It was hard not to when your body was surrendering to it. She had been furious that she had allowed herself to become emotional in front of Amy. She was a sweet girl and it wasn't fair to burden her with problems that certainly weren't her own. But returning from New York – her trip of a lifetime – had reminded Georgia that she was ready for the end of her life.

Her death was an inevitability that she knew would come sooner rather than later. Her doctor had told her two weeks ago that she might survive another twelve months. That was the real reason why she had refused the invitation to the Adamis' lunch. This was probably her last New Year's Day, and she wanted to spend it quietly with her memories and her thoughts.

The one thing she did know about death was that she didn't fear it. Perhaps that was one of the main benefits of being alone. There were no children to despair about leaving behind. Not even a cat to worry about when she had gone.

She had already decided that she would leave some money to Lucas, although he was wealthy and successful enough not to really need it. Some would go to charity, and she would give some to Will too. She was glad that she had bought Amy Carrell the Ralph Lauren dress, and would speak to her solicitor about finding a discreet way to bankroll her children's ballet company. She had worked hard for her money and she didn't want it to be frittered away, but she had a feeling that young Amy would do something special with her windfall – and even if her business wasn't a success, she would have a great deal of fun trying.

She made a note to find out a little more about Amy's plans this evening. She had been surprised to receive a phone call from Will asking if the two of them could drop by for coffee. He'd sounded dreadful – apparently it had been a very late night, but she supposed that was the way things were with young people: staying up all night to bring in the New Year. The thought of Will and Amy arriving together even gave her a little thrill. She knew Amy had a boyfriend – who she hadn't liked the sound of – but perhaps she could encourage a friendship between her cousin's son and her new friend. She thought they would be good for each other. She'd lived long enough to know a good love match when she saw one.

The buzzing of her intercom disturbed her from her thoughts.

Other than Will and Amy, who'd said they would come round at about six o'clock, she wasn't expecting any visitors. She peered through the fine voile curtains at Primrose Hill's rare, ghostly calm.

'Georgia Hamilton?'

'Yes,' she said hesitantly, not instantly recognising the voice. It was elderly, well-spoken, with a touch of familiarity . . .

'It's Christopher. Christopher Carlyle.'

The name took her so much by surprise that she had to lean against the wall. She inhaled slowly and closed her eyes for one moment.

'Christopher,' she said, steeling herself. 'What do you want?' She hadn't meant it to come out so curtly.

'May I come up?'

She could almost hear her own heartbeat as she waited for him to climb the stairs. Of course he took his time. He was older than she was and the flat was a long way from the ground floor. She left the door open and went back into the living room, standing by the window and looking out as she waited for him.

It was a shock to see him. It had been fifty-four years, but for a moment those years vanished in a heartbeat. He was still tall and thin – advancing years had not given him a stoop or shrunk his frame. His blazer and cream chinos were smart – in fact he looked as if he were on the way to a cricket match, and if it wasn't for the fact that it was January, she would imagine that he was.

'Don't you have better things to do on New Year's Day?' she said quietly, sipping at the cognac she had left on the drinks cabinet.

'We always have a quiet New Year's Day.'

'Of course – the annual Stapleford party was last night.'

'How are you, Georgia?' he said quietly.

'Fine. Marvellous, actually. I've been away. New York,' she added, her voice as bright as she could manage.

He supported himself on the bookcase with one hand. She guessed that the walk up the stairs had taken it out of him and it had the effect of making him seem quite fragile. Certainly he looked nothing like the vital elder statesman she regularly saw on the television, popping up to discuss the state of the economy, or at some literary party in the society pages of the *Mail*. Heading up the Carlyle family had not been his original destiny, but once he had been handed the role, he seemed to have grown into it. The shallow youth she had met in that summer of 1958 had been replaced by someone far more impressive.

'So how was last night?' she continued. 'Still going strong, that tradition? Clarissa always liked a party. No need to change that just because we're getting on a bit.'

'Your friend came, with Will.'

His words stopped her in her tracks.

'Which friend?'

'The American girl. Amy.'

She felt the cold twist of betrayal.

'What was she doing there?' she asked with as much nonchalance as she could manage.

'She came with Will. I believe they might be together.'

'Really?' she replied. It was suddenly becoming clear why they wanted to see her this evening. They had evidently been up to no good – meddling, she supposed – and were coming to confess and apologise.

There was a long pause that seemed to go on for ever.

'Amy told Clarissa that you're ill,' said Christopher finally.

'She had no right to do that.'

'It was with the best intentions.'

'Really.'

'Are you getting proper care?'

There was sympathy in his voice but she chose to ignore it. She didn't need anyone's charity – least of all his. Perhaps he was not aware that she was worth tens of millions – a fortune she had created herself. She was tempted to tell him.

'There's not a great deal anybody can do, if the truth be told.'

She looked at him intently. Christopher and Edward had always shared a resemblance, though Christopher had always been the poor facsimile of his brother. But the similarities were enough for her to see Edward in his face, and for a second she wanted to reach out and touch him.

'I have to tell you something.'

Georgia knew what was coming before he even uttered a word. She could see it in his eyes. Guilt, sadness, shame. A shame that had been eating away at him for decades.

'Edward did not rape Clarissa,' he said finally.

She sank her top two teeth into her bottom lip and for a moment she could taste blood. She had wanted to hear that admission for over fifty years, but now that it had come, they seemed the saddest and most futile words in the world.

Regret almost suffocated her. She closed her eyes and had to sink down on to the sofa.

'She would never have let him go to jail, you know,' said Christopher quickly. 'She certainly never wanted it to end up the way it did.'

'How generous of her,' growled Georgia. She was not sure she could bear the sight of him any longer.

'She was wrong and she was foolish. We both were.'

'Oh, I could think of a lot stronger words to describe your wife, Christopher. She was evil, although I will say one thing: she was a lot cleverer than I ever gave her credit for. It was really quite a plan, wasn't it, and it all worked out so beautifully for you.'

She looked up and could see that he was crying.

'How much did you know, Christopher? How culpable were you?'

'Enough,' he said, his voice so quiet she could barely hear it. 'I'd been dating Clarissa for a few weeks before my twenty-first. We first met at your party and kept in touch. You could say I had a bit of a schoolboy crush on her. She took me to a hotel in the City after just a couple of weeks and we spent the night together. I don't how experienced she was as a lover, but she blew me away. She was very physical and quite the temptress, and I would have done anything for her, even though I suspected she was a little bit in love with Edward.'

'Did anyone know about your relationship?'

'No. She wanted to keep it a secret. I think she was hedging her bets.'

'So you planned the rape claim together.' She could hear her own voice, cold, unrecognisable, as if she was listening to someone else.

'No.' He spoke with such plainness that she believed him.

'About a week before the party at Stapleford, we had another night in a hotel. She spent most of the time trying to convince me that I should assert my position in the family a bit more. I hadn't been to university and by this point I had already put in three years at the bank. But I wasn't taken seriously, whereas Edward was being groomed for a very senior role as soon as he finished at

Oxford. Clarissa convinced me that it wasn't right, and I believed her. I came away from that night feeling resentment against my brother, and just wishing that he would get out of my life, get out of the bank, where he had immediately overshadowed me.'

He brushed a tear off his papery cheek and continued.

'As you know, Clarissa came to my twenty-first. We slipped off and had sex in the wine cellar. The next thing I knew, we were all in the middle of this drama. She was claiming rape. Edward was adamant that he was innocent.

'I managed to get a couple of minutes alone with her to ask her what the hell was going on, and she told me not to breathe a word about the fact that we had had sex. She was smart and knew the way it was all going to pan out – no police would be involved, but Edward would be taken out of the picture until the scandal died down.'

'So she let you believe that Edward had raped her?'

'I didn't know what to believe. Within a week it had been arranged that Edward was going to Singapore. The Hamiltons agreed not to press charges. After all, the last thing they wanted was for word to get out that Clarissa was a rape victim. She would never have found anyone to marry her.'

'When did she tell you the truth?'

'A few weeks after Edward left for the Far East. When she admitted that she had staged the rape, I was angry, confused. Clarissa was adamant that she had done it for my benefit, although I suspect she was also furious that Edward had asked you to marry him. But I couldn't deny that the situation had worked out in my favour. I was suddenly the golden boy, the favoured son, and Edward was the proverbial black sheep.'

'Until he died.'

They stood there in silence.

'She wept for two days when she heard the news.'

'I've wept for a lifetime,' said Georgia coldly.

'We were both devastated, but what could we do? We had lied and covered up the truth, and we just had to carry on with it.'

'I've asked myself many times whether the pair of you sleep well at night.'

'I do not.'

Georgia sank her head into her hands and tried to rein in the emotions that were desperate to get out.

'We can't change the past, Georgia. I wish we could. I wish we could bring my brother back. I wish you'd had the chance to grow old with him.'

Her eyes were closed to hold back the tears, but she heard footsteps coming towards her and she felt him put something on the arm of the sofa.

'I don't expect you to ever forgive us, but I think you deserve to know the truth. Your friend Amy was right about that.'

'What's this?' asked Georgia, looking at the set of keys he had placed next to her.

'I think he would have wanted you to have this,' he said, then turned and walked out of the flat.

She held the keys in the palm of her hand until the cold metal turned warm. Then she got her coat, pulled it on and took the stairs slowly, one at a time, until she was out on the street. Christopher was gone, but at the kerb sat a cherry-red Aston Martin that she instantly recognised.

Her breathing felt shallow and her hands trembled.

She walked over and touched the paintwork, and for a second she was back on Putney Bridge in her dripping wet dress. She kicked off her shoes and bent down slowly, carefully to pick them up, every joint and muscle in her body reminding her that this was now the twenty-first century, not 1958. Although it was a cold winter's day, the roof of the convertible was down. As she put the shoes on the passenger seat, she noticed a parcel propped up in the back. Frowning, she touched the brown paper and traced her finger around the edges of the large rectangle.

She had no idea if she was meant to open it, but it was too tempting to leave it there.

She pushed one finger into the paper, then used both hands to strip the packaging away. Inside was a painting, and it took her a moment to realise that it was one of her mother's *Ribbons* series. At the time it had been seen as a difficult composition, but looking at it now, it was like a decent Jackson Pollock rip-off. Her mother was quite the visionary.

It took a minute for the significance of the painting to sink in. The series of pictures had been bought by a rich collector, and the money had not only kept them off the breadline for several months, but had allowed Georgia to have her dance. They had never known the identity of the collector. Once the money had been banked, it hadn't mattered. Now, as she realised what Edward had done for her, the tears finally began to flow.

She went round to the driver's seat, climbed in and gripped the wheel. When she closed her eyes, she could almost feel him.

She started to smile. She would be back with him soon, and she knew he would be waiting. Wiping her eyes, she pushed the key into the ignition and started the engine. It gave a quiet, satisfied growl, as if it was happy for her to be behind the wheel. Oh, she had loved him. She had loved him with all her heart. And he had loved her too. Suddenly she wanted to tell someone about it, and looking at her watch, she realised that Sally and Gianni's lunch would not yet be over. And as she motored down the street, the wind whipping in her hair, she was suddenly young again, and he was by her side. And at that moment, she was happy.

GUIDE TO
MODERN MANHATTAN

'LET ME SHOW YOU 'ROUND...'

Before I sat down to write this book I took a four-day trip to Manhattan, just like Amy and Georgia. I'd been to New York many times before, but never in the run-up to Christmas and, to my delight, it was everything I hoped it would be – the cold hint of snow in the air, the streets bustling with excited shoppers and, as ever in New York, there was movie-set glamour on every street corner.

Here is a guide to an assortment of the places we visited, some of which made it into the *The Proposal*, others which I know and love from previous trips to this dazzling city . . .

Serendipity 3

I love this *Alice in Wonderland*-style café so much that I have its menu pinned up on my kitchen wall at home. But it always seems that everybody else in New York wants to drop in for their famous Frozen Hot Chocolate too, so book ahead for lunch even if you just want to try the dessert. Get in the mood by watching the lovely Kate Beckinsale and John Cusack film, *Serendipity*.

225 East 60th Street, NY

Taim

This tiny Israeli take-away is a West Village local's favourite and you might even see famous fans like Gwyneth Paltrow there too. It's a scrum to get served but the ginger and mint lemonade and amazing falafel with melt-in-your-mouth hummus make it well worth it.

222 Waverly Place, NY

Grand Central Station

New York's most famous railway hub. Surround yourself with the buzzing commuter crowd, marvel at the beautiful Beaux-Arts building and soak up the real Manhattan. The Grand Central Oyster bar is great too for station food but not as we know it (be sure to try the cheesecake).

87 East 42nd Street, NY

FAO Schwarz

A brilliant toy shop near Central Park South that featured in the recent *Smurfs* movie. A must for the young or young at heart.

767 5th Avenue (at 58th Street), NY

Prune

I was tipped off about this shabby-chic Lower East favourite by a cool American friend who said the Saturday morning brunch queues are worth the wait. My Dutch pancakes were sweet, thick and delicious. Even better is the Bloody Mary menu – I went for the Virgin Green Lake (with a wasabi and beef jerky swizzle stick) but there's another dozen to choose from.

54 East 1st Street, NY

Plaza Athénée

I wanted Georgia and Amy to stay somewhere in New York that represents pure old-school glamour, and this Upper East Side institution fitted the bill perfectly. Quiet, discreet and elegant (it was Princess Diana's preferred New York hotel, and still attracts the stars), its location on a quiet side street that's a stone's throw away from everything is just perfect.

37 East 64th Street, NY

Bleecker Street

This is one of my favourite spots to shop in the whole city. It's got an eclectic range of shops, from Murray's Cheese Store with its bright yellow frontage and strong scent that wafts down the street, to the famous Magnolia Bakery, and with everything from Coach to James Perse in between. Molly's Cupcakes is another great place for a sweet treat, especially for the 'swing-chairs' at the counter.

Murray's Cheese Shop – 254 Bleecker Street, NY

Magnolia Bakery – 401 Bleecker Street, NY

Molly's Cupcakes – 228 Bleeker Street, NY

Trump Wollman Skating Rink

A must for any winter visit to New York. It's particularly romantic at night and is open from October to April.

Central Park South (59th Street) and 6th Avenue, NY

21 Club

One of Manhattan's most iconic restaurants. Choose a banquette table in the downstairs bar and quiz the waiter about the model aircraft hanging from the roof and the speakeasy history of the place (the wine vaults are fascinating). George Clooney favours table 8 and Humphrey Bogart sat at table 30 on his first date with Lauren Bacall.

21 West 52nd Street, NY

Joe's Pizza

Christina Aguilera recommended this to *Jaunt*, a travel magazine I set up a few years ago. Since then, every time I go to New York I make the pilgrimage to Carmine Street for a slice or two. The chewiest, tastiest pizza on the planet.

7 Carmine Street, NY

Katz Delicatessen

That scene in *When Harry Met Sally*. You know the one. It was filmed here – and the salt beef sandwiches might send you into raptures of your own.

205 East Houston Street, NY

The Loeb Boathouse Central Park

One for a summer rather than winter New York experience. A great spot for lunch overlooking the lake, where you can hire out a rowboat afterwards.

East 72nd Street and Park Drive North, NY

The Guggenheim

It's a toss-up between which is my favourite New York museum – the elegant Frick with its Old Masters collection or the stunning Guggenheim, if only for the incredible spiral Frank Lloyd-Wright design of the building.

1071 5th Avenue, NY

Lady Mendl's Tea Salon

Set in the dining room of one of New York's most romantic and elegant hotels – The Inn at Irving Place – afternoon tea at Lady Mendl's Tea Salon is like stepping into an Edith Wharton novel. Channel your inner debutante and go.

Lady Mendl's at The Inn at Irving Place – 56 Irving Place, NY

Liberty Helicopter Tours

A helicopter ride! Around the city! Incredible views you'll remember for a lifetime.

Downtown heliport – 6 East River Piers, NY

ACKNOWLEDGEMENTS

Thanks, as usual, to the wonderful team at Headline, particularly my editor Sherise Hobbs who was passionate about *The Proposal* from the moment I told her about it. Continued thanks to my family and friends who are always there to help and support me, and who never complained when I disappeared to meet not one, but two book deadlines this year.

The idea for *The Proposal* began when I went to see a wonderful exhibition at Kensington Palace called 'The Last Debutantes' in 2010. As I left the Palace I was convinced that the 1958 Season would make a fascinating backdrop for a novel and I began researching the era in between writing my usual summer books.

Thanks to all those 1958ers who spoke to me about their memories of the time – you really made it come alive. I am also grateful to the staff at the British Library who assisted with all the archive publications from 1958 which provided such detail. Thank you also to Cynthia and Carmela Corbett and the staff of the Plaza Athénée.

Delving into the life and times of the last debutantes was one of the most fascinating and enjoyable things I have done in my novel-writing career. If you are interested in knowing more I can recommend Fiona MacCarthy's *Last Curtsey* and David Kynaston's *Modernity Britain* which are both excellent insights into 1958 and the dying days of the Debs.